PLATFORM
AND PULPIT

THE PLATFORM SPELLBINDER

(*Portrait by* BERTHA NEWCOMBE, 1893)

PLATFORM AND PULPIT

BERNARD SHAW

EDITED WITH AN INTRODUCTION BY

DAN H. LAURENCE

HILL AND WANG

New York

This book is the second in a series of volumes of the most significant of
Bernard Shaw's previously uncollected writings edited by Dan H. Laurence.
The first volume was *How to Become a Musical Critic*.

CONTENTS

INTRODUCTION

At the meeting of the British Association for the Advancement of Science, at Bath on 7 September 1888, "the dovecots were much fluttered," reported the leader-writer of *The Star*, "by the appearance of a strange and rather startling figure . . . [who] calmly denounced as robbers some of the men the world is accustomed to regard as the ornaments of society, the patterns of morality, and the pillars of the church. This was Mr George Bernard Shaw. The whole thing was done, not with the savagery of a wild and illiterate controversialist, but with the light touch, the deadly playfulness, and the rapier thrusts of a cultivated and thoughtful man. . . . To the propagation of his ideas, he gives up willingly time, labour, the opportunities of self-advancement. To such men we can forgive much; their enthusiasm and their self-devotion are more important than their opinions."

For several years before this date, however, Londoners gradually had grown accustomed to hear—and even to respect—the opinions of the youthful orator who, in the words of a Socialist co-worker, stood before them, "a tall, lean, icy man, white faced, with a hard, clear, fleshless voice, restless grey-blue eyes, neatly-parted fair hair, big feet, and a reddish untamed beard." His interests seemed limitless; he bounded to his feet to express strong convictions on virtually any subject, whether on the nationalisation of accumulated wealth or on Browning as a scientific poet. So unusual was it for him not to contribute his tuppence worth to a discussion that, on the one occasion in 1888 when he failed to speak at a meeting, he considered the fact sufficiently noteworthy to be recorded in his diary.

For years he lectured every Sunday, without fee, to groups of any political or religious persuasion, anywhere within a radius of fifty or sixty miles from London, more frequently than not paying his travel expenses out of pocket. At the start he had had difficulty drawing audiences, noting early in 1885 that he was to have lectured at St John's Coffee House, Hoxton, "but found no audience there in consequence of W. Morris being round the corner lecturing." Soon, however, a mere announcement of his name was sufficient to ensure a capacity audience, many of those in attendance being young women drawn to what an interviewer defined as "a blend of bland and blond Mephistopheles with meek and mild curate," and quite obviously suffering from Prossy's Complaint. By 1886 his jealous lover, the tempestuous Jenny Patterson, was writing in agony: "Perhaps Miss Black will also follow you to Croydon? . . . Tell [her] not to poach on my preserves. Dont encourage the poor foolish creature. Tell her to sit at the feet of some other lecturer if it's information she seeks." Later, Beatrice Webb recalled that virtually every "advanced" female of the day "worshipped at the Shavian Shrine"—and as Annie Besant evidenced, not all of them were young!

It was not his romantic charm alone, however, which attracted attention to Shaw. Even his political opponents admitted that he was the best platform logician in London. His moderation was another asset, for though he was fiercely uncompromising, he eschewed violence; well-mannered, he gave his audiences strong doctrine, but never personal abuse. He was a "man of the people to the tips of his boots," reported the *Labour World*, and respected as "the most original and most inspiring of men . . . irrepressibly brilliant."

But Shaw's suave, self-assured manner on the platform had not come naturally; it had been assiduously cultivated. As one of his characters says in *Geneva*: "Public oratory is a fine art. Like other fine arts, it cannot be practised effectively without a laboriously acquired technique." Shaw learned to speak, he later confessed, "as men learn to skate or to cycle—by doggedly making a fool of myself until I got used to it." His "first assault on an audience" occurred at a meeting of the Zetetical Society, which had been founded in 1878 to "furnish opportunities for the unrestricted discussion of Social, Political, and Philosophical subjects," and to which Shaw's friend James Lecky had "dragged" him on 28 October 1880. "I had an air of impudence," Shaw noted in *Sixteen Self Sketches*, "but was really an arrant coward, nervous and self-conscious to a heartbreaking degree. Yet I could not hold my tongue. I started up and said something in the debate, and then, feeling that I had made a fool of myself . . . I vowed I would join the Society; go every week; speak in every debate; and become a speaker or perish in the attempt. I carried out this resolution." He suffered agonies, he remembered, that no one suspected. "I could not use notes: when I looked at the paper in my hand I could not collect myself enough to decipher a word. And of the four or five points that were my pretext for this ghastly practice I invariably forgot the best."

Eventually the nervousness diminished; soon Shaw eagerly was preparing a full-fledged oration to deliver before the Zetetical membership. "The title which I should prefer," he informed the Society's secretary J. M. Fells in August 1881, "is 'On what is called The Sacredness of Human Life, and its bearing on the question of Capital Punishment.'" He laboured over the draft for more than six months, the completed paper finally being ready for inspection in November. A week before Shaw was to make his début as a lecturer, however, he informed Fells that "I have overtaxed the patience of the Almighty, and he has smitten me"; he outlined numerous physical disorders with which he suddenly had been afflicted, ranging from sore throat to "the first hollow cough of phthisis," but it is probable that much of this was psychosomatic, for he added that he would "cheerfully die" rather than "face the task of remodelling and enlarging my paper, which I find to be unpresentable and idiotic at present." Presentable or not, the paper was delivered by the novice on 8 February 1882 at the South Place Chapel—and was enthusiastically received.

Exhilarated by his initial success, Shaw haunted London meeting places, analysing the techniques of the speakers, and taking advantage of every opportunity to participate in the discussions; in rapid succession he joined the Dialectical Society, the Woolwich Radical Club, the Bedford Debating Society, the Browning Society, the Fabian Society. Chairmen grew accustomed to receive a scrawled note, handed up from an irrepressible young man in the audience, informing them that "Mr George Bernard Shaw would like to ask a question." To improve his technique and to develop vocal resonance he studied elocution; to confound his opponents he spent long hours in the British Museum reading treatises on political economy, municipal reform, and theology, developing a habit of filing notes on small cards which he studied en route to a lecture engagement or meeting. Self-confidence and imperturbability became his hallmark; except for an occasional formal paper he eschewed written lectures, outlines, or notes on the platform, preferring the freedom of extemporaneity. When urged to do so, he might draft a syllabus of his lecture for a prospectus, but, to the bewilderment of the readers of the prospectus, he invariably departed from the syllabus. "What is the use," he would ask, "of saying a thing twice over?"

Unlike many of his fellow speakers Shaw did not depend for his success on mere oratory; he was not concerned with rabble-rousing or spell-binding. "My real successes," he noted, "have been when Ive carried a division without getting a round of applause." An orator, he told an interviewer in 1936, "begins in a rambling fashion, goes on till he makes a point that hits home, makes another point, and spends the rest of his speech repeating and repeating those points, hammering at them, until the audience is in a frenzy of enthusiasm. But that is letting your audience dictate to you, instead of [you] dictating to them—which they dont like, but I do." He was not averse, though, to theatrics or a bit of chicanery to gain his effects. He understood and appreciated "the provocations and interruptions of debate, which give experts such effective opportunities for retort that they are courted rather than resented"; on more than one occasion he "deliberately prompted interruptions to score off the interrupter." He could also, he boasted, "play cat and mouse with any opponent," a fact soon discovered, to their dismay, by Wells, Belloc, Chesterton, and other formidable opponents.

Of all his speaking activities, Shaw much preferred open-air lecturing, and was frequently to be found expostulating beneath the Reformer's Tree in Hyde Park. He lectured at street corners in virtually every London neighbourhood, in parks and public squares, at the gates of the East India docks; on numerous occasions he took round the hat for "the cause." Out of doors, he said, "you invariably have a willing audience, because the man who has had enough simply passes on." An audience in a lecture room, after an hour or so, becomes uneasy and is anxious for the speaker to conclude. But in the open air Shaw more than once held his audience for as long as four hours at a stretch.

He was, of course, a controversialist, who claimed that he never spoke "without giving grave offence to a very large number of people. . . . After all, my business is to say what other persons do not say—what they leave out." Accused of being "a half-truth merchant," whose arguments were clumsily unbalanced, he countered that "truths, like other things, have two sides; and most people can only see one side at a time. I have often had to turn the other side of a familiar truth to the spectators." His speeches coruscated with wit, but he denied vehemently that he lacked seriousness; "I am only a leg-puller," he insisted, "in so far as I pull crooked legs straight." But many of his auditors, outraged by the political, religious, and social views he espoused, were able to ingest these opinions only by the self-delusion that Shaw was indulging in levity. Thus was created a paradox of the public simultaneously decrying Shaw for playing a "Joey" rôle and seeking desperately to set a jester's cap upon his head.

So affable was Shaw, however, in responding to his critics that even the most hostile audiences were at times disarmed. In 1892, when he made his first lecture appearance at Oxford, a body of Magdalen College undergraduates, irked by the invasion of their precincts by a "radical," locked the doors on Shaw as he spoke, wrecked the adjoining chamber with "a vigorous bombardment of coals, buckets of water and asafoetida," and destroyed the speaker's hat and umbrella. Although they had hoped to force the invader to depart by the window, down a rope made of two dampened blankets which the students had thoughtfully provided, Shaw managed to effect an escape down a back staircase— though not before having a bucketful of water tossed at him (fortunately, the wielder of the bucket suffered from "infirmity of aim"). Imagine the surprise to the students when Shaw next day wrote (via the pages of the *Pall Mall Gazette*) to thank them for their "enthusiastic welcome" and for the generosity of "the thoughtful and self-sacrificing" scholars who "voluntarily suffered exclusion from the room in order that they might secure the door on the outside and so retain my audience screwbound to the last syllable of the vote of thanks." The chastened Magdalen men presented Shaw with a new hat—and invited him to come and lecture again!

Ironically, although Shaw's popularity as a speaker proliferated through the years, his opinions and advice more often than not went unheeded. His classicist friend Gilbert Murray charged him with "the damnable vice of preferring rhetoric to truth"; fellow-socialist C. E. M. Joad, recalling that Shaw's voice, the first time he heard him speak, "was so fresh, so easy, so bland, so confidential, as if it wanted you to share its confidence, its intonation convey[ing] so persuasive a suggestion of there being no deception, of Shaw having, as it were, nothing whatever up his oratorical sleeve," was obliged to admit that, although he had been swept off his feet, "I cannot remember what Shaw said."

Shaw himself was aware of this dilemma—but he ascribed the lack of effect on listeners to a flaw in his audience rather than in himself. "I, who have preached and pamphleteered like any Encyclopedist," he wrote in the preface to *Major Barbara*, "have to confess that my methods are no use, and would be no use if I were Voltaire, Rousseau, Bentham, Mill, Dickens, Carlyle, Ruskin, George, Butler, and Morris all rolled into one, with Euripides, More, Molière, Shakespear, Beaumarchais, Swift, Goethe, Ibsen, Tolstoy, Moses and the prophets all thrown in (as indeed in some sort I actually am, standing as I do on all their shoulders)." But though his efforts might be considered abortive, though he had spent the best part of his life "inciting the English to act sensibly without for a moment gaining their confidence," he refused to permit disillusion to detract him from the path he had set for Don Juan: "As long as I can conceive something better than myself I cannot be easy unless I am striving to bring it into existence or clearing the way for it." By the turn of the century (when he was forty-four) he had lectured more than a thousand times; before he died he nearly doubled the figure. In his sixties he still stumped the provinces at elections, providing "chin music for Socialist candidates," and he continued to lure the public, by his presence on the programme, to subscribe to Fabian lecture series in the King's Hall each spring and autumn. In his seventies he orated at Fabian and I.L.P. summer schools.

INTRODUCTION

But in 1933 he bade farewell to the lecture platform—a spectacular farewell, before an audience of several thousand, from the stage of New York's Metropolitan Opera House. "I regard the platform as obsolete," he told an interviewer; "the microphone's the thing. It is foolish to talk to a few hundreds when you can talk to millions." And talk to millions he did, harnessing the B.B.C. to his use. He considered the difference between the platform and the microphone incalculable. Audiences could listen to a speaker in complete comfort, and the instant he ceased to interest them, they could "switch him off." The speaker could address his audience "intimately and cosily," and "use delicate *nuances* of expression that would never 'get across' in a public hall." The speaker did not have to face the risks of "interruptions, missiles, stink bombs, patriotic songs, suffragettes, or having the platform rushed by a lynching mob"; he was neither contradicted nor questioned. And the auditor was protected from "imposture, carelessness, thoughtlessness, insincere phrasemaking, drunkenness, and humbug" by "a detective of magical efficiency," the microphone. Shoddy might "pass on the platform with hypnotized audiences," he concluded, "but at the fireside under the microphone it would just drop dead."

Shaw approached the microphone without an atom of apparent self-consciousness; he addressed his audience in a fatherly manner, expounding his views with all the air of a teacher instructing an impressionable child. His language was simple, his comments candid and uncomplicated. And through his wireless addresses he reached not just Britain but the world, gaining universal popularity. He became G. B. S.—World Statesman, often pontificating rather than polemicising, but still striving at ninety as he had at thirty to inculcate in his fellow men a need to recognise intellect as the greatest of the passions: "a genuine artist," as his friend the Reverend Stewart D. Headlam described him, "an *idealist* with romantic notions of life and conduct, and evidently most sincerely impressed with an awful sense of *duty*."

DAN H. LAURENCE

New York, *June* 1961

EDITOR'S NOTE

Bernard Shaw's custom of speaking extemporaneously resulted, not infrequently, in the publication of corrupt reports of his utterances. "My flesh sometimes creeps," he bemoaned in a letter to the *Pall Mall Gazette* in 1891, "at the things I am represented to have said, especially when the report is based (as it sometimes is) on an attempt to take me down verbatim by the sort of stenographer who can write a hundred and sixty words a minute for three minutes, and then, within a quarter of an hour, falls to a hundred and forty, to a hundred, to eighty, to an agonized and desperate sixty, and finally to utter ruin and confusion." Fortunately, Shaw was called upon to place his imprimatur on the texts of many of the speeches reprinted in the present volume, but in those instances where he was not invited to perform this service, the editor has had to make some arbitrary decisions in order to give meaning to faulty texts. Alterations in grammar, spelling, and punctuation have, where necessary, been freely made; more significant textual emendations are indicated by insertion within square brackets.

As this volume is one in a series intended to complement the Standard Edition of Shaw's works, Shaw's idiosyncratic dicta have been observed in all matters of spelling and punctuation within his texts, as well as in matters of general style and design.

The editor makes grateful acknowledgment to the following for assistance in the preparation of this book: the British Broadcasting Corporation, Mr Ivo L. Currall, Mr Allan M. Laing, Mr William Rodgers of the Fabian Society, Mrs Georgina Musters, Mr Samuel Boone (Head, Photographic Services, University of North Carolina), Mr Edward Hingers, Mr Richard Hughes, Cecil Houses Inc., and the staff of the British Museum Newspaper Library, Colindale. He is especially indebted to Miss Dorothy E. Collins, Executrix of the Estate of G. K. Chesterton, for her generosity in authorising publication of the verbatim report of Chesterton's speeches in the debate of 1911.

D. H. L.

PROPRIETORS AND SLAVES

(Lecture delivered before the members of the Liberal and Social
Union, at the rooms of the Society of British Artists,
London, 26 February 1885. *The Christian Socialist, April*
1885; reprinted in *Liberty* (Boston), 23 *May* 1885)

I am here this evening in an invidious position. The Liberal
and Social Union, a body of ladies and gentlemen of more than
ordinary culture, have done me the honor of inviting me to
address them on the subject of Socialism from the point of view
of a Socialist. From that point of view, unhappily, I must regard
the Liberal and Social Union, in spite of its hospitality, and the
human race generally, as cannibals of the most dangerous description, whose power must be completely neutralized before
they will cease to retard the evolution of the social instincts of the
race by perpetually preying upon oneanother. The very deep and
sincere admiration which we all entertain in this century for ourselves cannot but make this Socialistic conclusion unpalatable;
but it is so well supported by history that I should be trifling
with the audience were I to pretend that their generosity of disposition, cultivated intellects, exalted ideals, and genuine indignation at the rapacity of their fellows has ever prevented them
from purchasing the necessaries of life at prices which obviously
entail abject poverty on the producers of these necessaries, or
from drawing dividends year after year from mines and railways
which they have never even seen, much less worked upon. I have
myself disgracefully consumed in idleness so much of the wealth
produced by peasants from the soil they tilled, that they have
been left far poorer than I, who did nothing for them. Yet I
have never been reproached for this. On the contrary, I should
have been far more highly esteemed and courted had I been able
to plunder three or four thousand peasants instead of one or two.
However, I made the most of my limited opportunities, and have
little doubt that those whom I address now have done the same.
We thus meet on equal terms, and can proceed to discuss our

1

subject quietly and cautiously, as becomes people who all dwell in the same glass house.

Mankind, in order to live, must have access to the earth and the fulness thereof. Hence, if the earth be owned by a private person, he can cause his fellow creatures to die by refusing them access to the land. This power makes them his slaves. He has only to say, "I will grant you access to the land on condition that you do for me whatever I choose to dictate," and they must, on pain of death, accept that hard condition. It is known to us all that the land of England today, excepting the barren highroads and a few patches of common which have accidentally not been stolen, is owned by private persons. The rest of the community are therefore the slaves of these private persons, or of the capitalists to whom they have sublet their powers in order that they may ultimately resume them in a more effective stage of development. We are, then, divided into two great sections: proprietors and slaves. Now, slaves are always separated into classes according to the nature of their services. Your shepherd need be little better off than your sheep. Allow him a hut, a coarse garment, and the wherewithal to keep alive himself, his wife, and a rising generation of shepherds and shepherds' wives, and all your purposes will be served as effectually as if you treated him like a prince. Therefore you do not treat him like a prince, and you do treat him like a shepherd. But you need a physician as well as a shepherd, and him you cannot have on these easy terms: your life and that of your wife and children depend on his skill, in order to acquire which he must practise for years on your other slaves in a hospital, and have at his disposal museums, libraries, dissecting rooms, paupers alive and dead, and oral instruction from experts in his profession.

And this is not enough. As he is to be your intimate associate, the repository of some of your most private affairs, and the confidential adviser of your wife, he must be no rebellious, rough, and uncultured slave, but a pampered, softly-nurtured retainer, with lowlier serfs alloted to do menial work for him, and a degree of comfort and consideration which you yourself may perhaps be unable always to attain. You cannot have him more cheaply; and so, though you complain of the expense, you pay the price.

But you get him as cheaply as possible, caring nothing for his needs, but only for your own. This is proved by your treatment of your shepherd's doctor. To him you deny the social consideration you allow to your own medical adviser, because, as you do not associate with him, his lack of social polish does not inconvenience you. All you need from him is that he will keep your shepherds in working order, and for this professional ability alone suffices. Hence, your shepherd's doctor is a much less expensive slave than the general practitioner who attends *you*. But you naturally select the best doctor for yourself, and leave the worst to your shepherds. This enables you to claim that under your admirable system doctors are rewarded in proportion to their merits. By this you mean that the best doctors waste their superior skill in preserving the lives of idlers whose existence is an evil, whilst the worst doctors are busy killing useful and industrious men. Thus the reward of the best man is the privilege of ministering to the worst.

Between the shepherd and the physician come many grades of slaves. There is the workman, the foreman, the clerk, the manager, and the secretary. Each of these grades has its lawyer, its doctor, and its divine. Then there is the soldier—sometimes a cheap article who has but to obey orders, charge with the bayonet at men with whom he has no quarrel, shoot and be shot at, and give three cheers when titled persons inspect his buttons; sometimes a comparatively expensive gentleman, versed in trigonometry and tactics, and yet not above levying executions on slaves in default with their tribute. With all these varieties of servitude, the slave section gets minutely stratified into classes. Ignorant of the causes that have produced the stratification, each stratum despises or envies the others. The doctor despises the shepherd because he is ignorant and uncleanly; the shepherd mistrusts the doctor because he is the friend of his tyrant. The difference in comfort between the extreme strata is immense. The unskilled laborer is allowed 2s. 6d.—thirty pence—a day. The eminent barrister is allowed fifty guineas, or 12,600 pence a day. The barrister does not get fifty guineas every day; but neither does the unskilled laborer get half a crown every day. When both are in work—when the proprietors need their services—

3

the barrister gets 420 times as much as the unskilled laborer, in spite of the fact that the proprietors have denied to the laborer the education and comforts they have allowed to the barrister in his nonage. It is sometimes alleged that differences such as these are due to differences in the sobriety or ability of the individuals. If sobriety be indeed the cause, then, if the barrister drink one bottle of wine a day, as many eminent barristers do, the unskilled laborer must drink 420 bottles of wine a day before the barrister can be considered 420 times as sober. Nor is it probable that any man has 420 times, or even four times, the ability of another.

When the external conditions are equalized, the man who can double the average achievement is looked upon with wonder. The argument that thrift is at the bottom of it all is far sounder. We estimate a man's thrift by the amount of money he possesses. The barrister has 420 times as much money as the unskilled laborer. Hence, we argue that the barrister is 420 times as thrifty as the laborer. If we accept this short method of computing thrift, the conclusion is logical, if not eminently satisfactory to the laborer; but this sort of thrift is evidently not a virtue which the laborer can cultivate or not as he pleases. Neither sobriety, nor thrift, nor any ordinary quality can induce the proprietors to raise the laborer to the class of their most favored slaves. Should he gain promotion by absolute genius, he will still be at a disadvantage at many points with the most commonplace members of the class to which he is elevated. In either class he will still be a slave, receiving out of the full exchange value of his services just what is sufficient to maintain him and enable [him] to reproduce himself with such culture and habits as may be necessary to make him an efficient servant and, if his services bring him into personal contact with his employers, an agreeable associate. All the rest he must surrender as rent or interest to his masters.

I fear that I must, for lack of time, venture to assume that my hearers already know how this system is made automatic by the action of competition. I am aware that such an assumption exposes me to the risk of being misunderstood; for it would be affectation on my part to pretend that any company of English ladies and gentlemen can be depended upon for even a rudimentary knowledge of economics and sociology. Bad as we are, I believe that, if we all understood how we are living, and what we are doing daily, we should make a revolution before the end of the week. But as we do not know, and as many of us, foreseeing unpleasant revelations, do not want to know, I can only assure you that I am in perfect concord with standard economists when I state that competition is the force that makes our industrial system self-acting. It produces the effects which I have described without the conscious contrivance or interference of either master on the one hand, or slave on the other. It may be described as a seesaw, or lever of the first order, having the fulcrum between the power and the weight. The power is the labor force of the slaves; the weight is the body of proprietors who have to be raised above the level of the slaves and maintained there. Hence, the more numerous the slaves are, the lower they sink, and the higher they raise the proprietors. Conversely, if the slaves decrease in number they rise a little and the proprietors sink. Hence, the Malthusians urge the workers to reduce their numbers as much as possible. Unfortunately, when the masters find their end descending too low, they allow the weaker members of their own body to slip down to the other end of the lever, into the slave class, until the former preponderance is re-established.

Socialists insist that people should stand on the firm earth, and not on a seesaw, much less on a lever which is always at see and never at saw. They seek to disable the lever. Now, the way to disable a lever is to remove the fulcrum. What is the fulcrum of this lever of competition? Clearly it is private property in the raw material and machinery indispensable to subsistence. The slave submits to the master solely because the master has the power to withhold from him the means of subsistence if he rebels. The master of the land says, after St Paul, "If a man will not work for me, neither shall he live." Deprive him of this power of condemning his fellow man to death, and the fellow man will snap his fingers at him, and quote St Paul more accurately in his turn. To deprive the proprietor of this power, you must deprive him of his private property in the land and capital of the nation, which is just what the Socialist proposes. This is why the masters raise so loud an alarm when an attack on private property is proposed. Unfortunately for themselves, they have set the example of disregarding it. The so-called right of private property is a convention that every man should enjoy the product of his own labor, either to consume it or exchange it for the equivalent product of his fellow laborer. But the landlord and capitalist enjoy the product of the labor of others, which they consume to the value of many millions sterling every year without even a pretense of producing an equivalent. They daily violate the right to which they appeal when the Socialist attacks them. Nor is their inconsistency so obvious as might be expected. If you violate a workman's right daily for centuries, and daily respect the landlord's right, the workman's right will at last be forgotten, whilst the landlord's right will appear more sacred as successive years add to its antiquity.

In this way the most illogical distinctions come to be accepted as natural and inevitable. One man enters a farmhouse secretly, helps himself to a share of the farm produce, and leaves without giving the farmer an equivalent. We call him a burglar, and send him to penal servitude. Another man does precisely the same thing openly, has the impudence even to send a note to say when he is coming, and repeats his foray twice a year, breaking forcibly into the premises if his demand is not complied with. We call him a landlord, respect him, and, if his freebooting extends over a large district, make him deputy-lieutenant of the country or send him to Parliament, to make laws to license his predatory habits. We need not even contrast two different men. Let us take the case of a railway shareholder, who lives idly on his dividends, having purchased the power of making the railway officials work for him. This man robs every unfortunate railway porter daily of a share of the value of his work, without incurring the least punishment or even disapprobation. Yet if he were to do the same thing in another way, if he were to attack a railway porter in a lonely street and rifle his pockets, he would render himself liable to imprisonment and disgrace. And it is not at all improbable that, at his trial, the fact of his being a holder of railway shares would be brought forward as affording a strong presumption of his honesty and respectability.

6

Of the mental confusion caused by the toleration of these anomalies, and the failure to recognize them as such, we shall very possibly have some examples before we separate this evening; but we need not depend on our own efforts for assurances that if the upper classes consume luxuries they pay for them; that a tradesman will not give a landlord a coat or a leg of mutton for nothing, any more than he will give it to a laborer; that landlords should be satisfied with fair rents (as if privately appropriated rent could be fair under any circumstances), or that capitalists should content themselves with reasonable interest (as if interest could possibly be a reasonable charge); that men will not do their best unless they have the incentive of knowing that the more they produce, the more they will be robbed of; that railways are constructed by buying pieces of paper in the Stock Exchange, and could not be constructed in any other way; that the money spent in drink annually would suffice to raise the East-end dock laborers to affluence; that Robinson Crusoe was a capitalist farmer and shipowner; that people should not indulge in wild talk about revolutions; that if we divided up all the money in the country we should only have £30 apiece (which, by the bye, is rather a dangerous fact to obtrude on a man who has less than £30); and above all, that if we did away with landlordism and capitalism today, we should have all our social inequalities and evils back again in six months—that is to say, that if we remove the cause, the effects will still continue. This hotch-potch of error and nonsensically-advanced truth can be, and has repeatedly been, disentangled and refuted, but to no purpose as regards the men who utter it; for a man who does not understand his own proposition cannot understand a refutation of it.

And the landlords and capitalists have no longer any skilled apologists. Political economy in the days of McCulloch and John Stuart Mill said what it could for them; but Mill finally dropped them, and his successor Cairnes let out the truth at last that rich idlers are an unmitigated nuisance in a community. The more enlightened idlers are themselves growing ashamed. They do something (which usually has to be undone by somebody else) and plead that they are working. Gentlemen laboriously get

7

called to the bar, and, as briefless barristers, feel that they can read Cairnes with equanimity. Ladies educate themselves, learn to paint or play the violoncello, and feel that *their* lives, at least, have not been wasted. Both ladies and gentlemen will give alms, get up concerts and bazaars, join societies for mutual improvement and admiration. They are not asked to do any of these things, yet they do them. They *are* asked to work as hard for the workers as the workers work for them; and that they will not do. Many of them have got to the point of being willing to sacrifice almost anything for the poor, except the power and practice of robbing them. Nevertheless, that is what they must sacrifice now, if they would avert another failure of human society. Such failures, though not absolutely irretrievable, are very tedious. The human race has hitherto never succeeded in establishing a permanent social state. They tried on a large scale in Egypt; but the experiment, after progressing hopefully for centuries, collapsed. They tried again in Greece with some valuable results, but with the same end. Then Rome tried her hand, and made a tremendous mess of it. Now we are trying and, so far, are doing worse even than the Romans. Every reformer has his pet reason for the decay of these civilizations; and I will not assert that luxury and slavery rotted away the foundations of them all. But I may at least claim that luxury and slavery did not prove so beneficial that we need apprehend much danger from ridding ourselves of them.

The main difficulty of the Socialist is not, however, in convincing people that the present condition of society is a bad one. Intelligent members of the proprietary classes admit that when the life of the masses is described to them. The lower classes know it by experience without being told. It is even possible to obtain general assent to the proposition that the millennium is incompatible with private property. But the mass of the people—particularly those who are not in absolutely wretched circumstances—are loth to move, and afraid of the unknown that lies at the other side of change. They admit that they are ill, but when the Socialist prescribes exercise—violent exercise sometimes—they peevishly demand a remedy of the patent medicine description. "Give us something definite," they say; "what is it that you are driving at?" "Abolish private property in land, and prevent the employment of the means of production as capital," replies the Socialist. "That is definite enough, is it not?" "But how are you going to do it?" persists the other. At this the Socialist loses his temper. "*I* am not going to do it," he retorts. "*We* are going to do it; and the ways and means must be settled by us in council when we have made up our minds on what we have to do. If you choose to sit down and let other men decide on a plan, you will probably find, when it is put into practice, that your interests have been overlooked—and serve you right too. If you have no ideas on the subject, that only proves that you have never read the works of the men whose schemes you were sneering down as Utopian the day before yesterday." The Socialist then recommends Engels and other German authors to his assailant, who probably does not know German. So he falls back on the sacredness of private property, and declares that, after all, a man has a right to do what he likes with his own.

This alleged right of a man to do what he likes with his own is the private property principle which the Socialist attacks. It is already obsolete except in the case of land and the means of production. Property in other things is subject to the condition that it shall not be used to injure or oppress. A landlord, for example, if he wishes to turn his arable land into pasture, or his pasture into a deer forest, is permitted to drive hardworking husbandmen or shepherds off his property into overcrowded towns, or, for the matter of that, into the sea, with impunity, because he claims a right to do what he likes with his own. But the landlord owns other things besides land. He owns guns and sticks. If he were to take the stick and give one of the husbandmen or shepherds a thrashing with it, the plea that the stick was his own and that he had a right to use it as he pleased would not save him from punishment. Still less do we allow him to present his gun at a tenant, and, by threatening him with death, compel him to give up what he has gained from the soil by his labor. Yet what he may not do with a gun, he may do, and does, with a writ of ejectment. Such a power is subversive of property in the only sense in which property is a sane institution. But the landlord, by studiously confusing private property outside and independent of the law and the commonweal, with the public right of every man to possess and enjoy what he produces, succeeds in persuading careless reasoners that to attack private property is to attack the commonweal. He says in effect, "If you abolish my right to wear another man's coat, what becomes of my right to wear my own? The right to wear coats is sacred; and if you violate it, society will be impossible."

One can understand a landlord using this argument, but it is not so easy to understand the many silly people who are not landlords, but tenants, and who yet repeat it in defence of their despoilers' power to plunder them. The inability to comprehend economic problems indicated by such suicidal utterances on the part of the slave class is a serious matter. The utterances are very common; hence it may be inferred that the inability is very general. For this reason the abolition of private property, the equitable distribution of labor and of the products of labor among the community, and the nationalization of rent will have to be accomplished by an enlightened minority. They will have to overcome the active resistance of the proprietors and the inertia of the masses. If this be once done, the masses will acquiesce, and the proprietors will no longer exist as a class.

But the proprietors may fight. Lord Bramwell explicitly declares that they will fight. They scare many persons from Socialism by threatening to compel Socialists to shed their blood. Unfortunately, they are accustoming the public to bloodshed. Revolting as it is at first, there is nothing to which men so rapidly grow habituated; they even develop a taste for it. When we have had a little more practice in fighting for our bondholders abroad, we will think little of fighting against them at home, should occasion arise. Civil war is horrible; but we have supped full of horrors in our city slums, and an open, well-ventilated battlefield, with wounded men instead of rickety children and starving women, would be an absolute improvement. The proportion of corpses would be about the same, and the suffering would be less prolonged, whilst excitement and hope would take the place of dulness and despair.

These humane considerations constantly tempt the poor to violence, and weaken the influence of those who would restrain them until the steps to follow the battle have been thoroughly debated. It is still harder to stay those who would hasten a revolution by intimidation. We know the cause of dynamite explosions, but not their effects. We know, for example, that if we raise the temperature of water to 212 deg. Fahrenheit, it will boil; and we know just as certainly that, if we destroy the liberty of the press and the right of public meeting, dynamite will explode. Russia and Austria first discovered this fact; and we, in a truly scientific spirit, have verified it experimentally in Ireland. Now, if Socialism be not made respectable and formidable by the support of *our* class—if it be left entirely to the poor, then the proprietors will attempt to suppress it by such measures as they have already taken in Austria and Ireland. Dynamite will follow. Terror will follow dynamite. Cruelty will follow terror. More dynamite will follow cruelty. Both sides will thus drive one-another from atrocity to atrocity solely because we, the middle class, instead of interfering on behalf of justice, sit quaking and complying with ignorant and cowardly journalists who devote the first half of an article to calling the dynamitards "dastardly wretches," and the second half to clamoring for more dynamite in the shape of further restriction of our liberty and further license to our oppressors.

If, on the other hand, the middle class will educate themselves to understand this question, they will be able to fortify whatever is just in Socialism, and to crush whatever is dangerous in it. No English government dare enact a Coercion Law or declare a Minor State of Siege against the Radical party. The result is that the Radical party never makes us shake in our shoes as the dynamitards do. I trust, then, that the middle class will raise the Socialists above the danger of Coercion, Minor Siege, and consequent dynamite, by joining them in large numbers. When a Revolution approaches, those who are within the Revolutionary party can do something to avert bloodshed: those who hold aloof can only provoke it. A party informed at all points by men of gentle habits and trained reasoning powers may achieve a complete Revolution without a single act of violence. A mob of desperate sufferers abandoned to the leadership of exasperated sentimentalists and fanatic theorists may, at a vast cost of bloodshed and misery, succeed in removing no single evil, except perhaps the existence of the human race.

ACTING, BY ONE WHO DOES NOT BELIEVE IN IT

(Paper read at a meeting of the Reverend Stewart D. Headlam's Church and Stage Guild, London, 5 February 1889. Shaw himself drafted the report of the meeting (reproduced below) for publication in *The Church Reformer, March* 1889)

At the meeting of the Guild on the afternoon of 5 February, Mr Bernard Shaw read a paper entitled "Acting, by one who does not believe in it; or the place of the Stage in the Fools' Paradise of Art." After a characteristic prelude on the Guild work generally, Mr Shaw began to work up to his point, thus :

One of the questions I come here to ask is: "Would the Church and Stage Guild be satisfied if it could bring the whole nation, including the Bishop of London and his Puritanic following, into the same frame of mind with the theatre-loving folk? If so, then certainly it does not take itself so seriously as I take it; for my own feeling is that the attitude of the Puritan towards the actor is to be preferred to that of the "first-nighter" by just as much as superstitious horror is easier to bear than contempt.

This lively opening was followed by a number of instances all tending to convict critics—whom Mr Shaw set up as typical theatre tolerators—of habitual disdain for actors. Dr Johnson's Punch epigram about Garrick was cited; and Mr William Archer and M. [Jules] Lemaître were quoted to shew that Dr Johnson's feeling is still general among those who have taken the trouble to form any definite opinion of actors as men. Then Mr Shaw continued:

The ground of this contempt is obvious. The dramatic critic believes in acting, and regards the man on the stage as an actor. In English, acting means shamming. The critic, then, despises the stage as a sham, and the actor as a wretched impostor, disguised in the toga of Cæsar, and spouting the words of

Shakespear—a creature with the trappings and the language of a hero, but with the will of a vain mummer—a fellow that fights without courage, dares without danger, is eloquent without ideas, commands without power, suffers without self-denial, loves without passion, and comes between the author and the stalls much as a plaster of colored earths and oil comes between Raphael and the Cook's tourist.

Now, even if the actor admitted that he is no more than this, which no actor does, he could retort with terrible effect on his literary censor. "Granted," he might say, "that I am incapable of doing the deeds I play at, pray do you practise what you write about? If it takes no real courage to fight a duel on the stage, does it take any more to write the scene in which that duel occurs, or to criticize my fencing? If I have not the will of Cæsar, had Shakespear, or have you? Is the inventor of the sham scene, or the actor, or the delighted spectator the most futile and ridiculous from your point of view? Are the real virtues and the real trials of the actor at all different from those of the men who condemn him without being intelligent enough to see that they must plead guilty themselves to every count of their indictment?" The reason that this retort is not actually made is that it satisfies neither the enthusiastic actor, who generally does suppose that he only needs opportunity to become all that he pretends to be on the stage, nor even the cynical actor, who at least knows that, in proportion to the opportunities, competent actors of Cæsars are much scarcer than real Cæsars, the inevitable conclusion being that, for any given man whatsoever, it is much easier to be Cæsar than to act Cæsar. And, indeed, if we consider how the achievements for which we honor Cæsar are really the achievements of many thousands typified in one; if we could subtract from his reputation the fame of the things he never did, and of those which fell out quite otherwise than he intended them; if we make due allowance, in calculating his stature, for the height of the wave of fortune on whose crest he came to his throne, then, considering on the other hand how absolutely individual and unaided is the task of the great actor, we begin to perceive why no actor has any consciousness of paradox when he hears it claimed that the first Napoleon was a commonplace person in comparison with Talma. I might go on to make some amends to the critic by pointing out that he may with some color claim to be the rarest of all species in his highest development, but such a process would be endless and idle. I have said enough to bear the trite moral that the contempt of one for another, whether it be the contempt of the historian for the statesman, the critic for the actor, or the virtuous person for the vicious, is as a hood to the eyes and a wired lawn to the feet of the seeker for justice.

But there is a contempt that is harder to escape than any of these—the contempt of a man for himself. The most terrible doubt that can come into the mind of a man is a doubt as to the utility of his profession. No class of men—not even doctors—can be more subject to that sort of doubt than artists. All art is play; and all play is make-believe. How, then, be an artist without being a rogue and a vagabond? Make a few thousand a year and the thing is done, as far as the opinion of others is concerned. But self-opinion, what of that? Must the novelist know himself a liar, the sculptor an image-man, the actor an illusion, a simulacrum, a glittering sword that will not cut, a burnished hydrant that will not extinguish anything? The eternal cry of the artist's soul is for salvation in this matter: the claim which he most vehemently urges is the claim for the reality of what he plays at. When Mr Archer, in a methodical, cold-blooded way, asked Signor Salvini whether his stage tears came unbidden; whether his voice broke of its own accord; whether he deliberately simulated affections without physically experiencing them; whether, to put it shortly, he was anything more than an elaboration of the doll which says "mamma," and shuts its eyes when it is placed in a horizontal position, the great actor replied, with the roar of a wounded lion: "If you do not weep in the agony of grief; if you do not blush with shame, glow with love, tremble with terror; if your eyes do not become bloodshot with rage; if you yourself do not intimately experience whatever befits the diverse characters and passions you represent, you can never thoroughly transfuse into the hearts of your audience the sentiment of the situation." No protest could be more passionate than this. The greatest actor of the day proclaims with all his force that he is no actor at all; that there is no such thing as acting; that he is no sham, no puppet, no simulacrum, but in real earnest all that he pretends to be; that Othello, Hamlet, and Samson are not merely aped by him, but live and suffer in his person; that he throws himself into them because in them he realizes himself as he never could realize himself in the prosaic parts that are played off the stage, such as those of the stock-broker, the lawyer, the painter, or the dust contractor.

M. Coquelin, on the other hand, renounces his professional reality in the temper in which Diderot renounced the prospect of a hereafter. He shakes his head at the tragedian, and says: "No, my friend: you are not Samson, not Othello, not Hamlet: you are Salvini." It is in vain for the tragedian to accept the statement and declare that Othello is Salvini simply because Salvini is Othello; the comedian has too good a digestion to confuse himself with metaphysics. When Mr Archer interviews him, he replies to the question about the sincerity of the break in his voice by then and there breaking it in a heartrending manner as if it were a walnut. And in this action we have the clue to the citadel of Coquelin's self-respect, which he has maintained in spite of his confession that he is a sham—that is, an actor. He has to depend for his salvation on the pride of the craftsman in his skill, the delight of doing a very difficult thing consummately. That M. Coquelin adds to this the moral satisfaction of believing that the thing he does is beneficial to his fellows we need not doubt: therein alone could consist his superiority to the skilful burglar; but for my part, though I cannot but relish the humorous side of M. Coquelin's theory that Mascarille is nothing but a cleverly worked marionet, I am not imposed on by it for a moment. For if it were sound, what a contemptibly shiftless and limited auto-maton he would be! Salvini's reason for not impersonating Mascarille is clear: Mascarille is not Salvini; and therefore Salvini cannot be Mascarille. But what is Coquelin's reason for not acting Othello or Hamlet? On his own theory there can be none except that he is an inefficient puppet. I will not insult you by pleading what have been called "physical limitations," and con-cluding that M. Coquelin is debarred from heroic characters by the upward turn of the tip of his nose. M. Coquelin's presence and voice are far more imposing than those of many actors who have made their mark in tragedy. Avoiding odious comparisons with contemporary players, I would refer you to the photographs of Charles Kean and Ronconi, and to the ample testimony accessible concerning them; and then ask whether you can doubt that M. Coquelin is at least as well fitted for heroic parts by his face, his figure, his voice, and his stage acquirements as either of these tragedians. If M. Coquelin is really an actor, he ought to be able to pass from Mascarille to Hamlet with no more difficulty than Artemus Ward's wax figures passed from the sacred parts they played in New England to the murderers whom they represented in the Wild West.

The truth is, of course, that M. Coquelin is less an actor than any other comedian on the stage. So far from being a mere mask with no individuality, to be put on by Shakespear, Molière, or any other author, he is one of the few points in the human mass at which individuality is concentrated, fixed, gripped in one exceptionally gifted man, who is, consequently, what we call a personality, a man pre-eminently himself, impossible to disguise, the very last man who could under any circumstances be an actor. Yet this is just what makes him the stage-player *par excellence*. We go to see him because we know he will always be Coquelin, because every new part he plays will be some new side of Coquelin or some new light on a familiar side of him, because his best part will be that which shews all sides of him and realizes him wholly to us and to himself. If no such part exists in dramatic literature, then the want of it is the great sorrow and unfulfilment of his life. If he finds such a part, he seizes on it as oxygen seizes on certain metallic bases. In it he becomes for the first time completely real: he has achieved the aspiration of the hero of Ibsen's fantastic play and become himself at last. This is not acting: it is the final escape from acting, the ineffable release from the conventional mask which must be resumed as the artist passes behind the wing, washes off the paint, and goes down into the false lights and simulated interests and passions of the street.

At this point there was a general suspicion that Mr Shaw was going to evaporate in a neat paradox of the stage being the real world, and off-the-stage the unreal one, thus turning inside out Shakespear's fancy about all the world being a stage. But he went on to shew that kindred self "realizations" were being constantly sought and sometimes achieved in ordinary life. He cited the case of a woman making a very bad wife whilst her husband was poor, and becoming a very good one when he grew rich and supplied her with the means of self-realization. Then, harking back to the stage, he went on:

Let us take another instance. A man has a strong sense of mischievous humor, and a certain mercurial vivacity and agility which make rapid and riotous movement essential to his complete satisfaction. His sense of the ludicrous feeds on his veneration and eats it up. Nevertheless, he is a goodnatured man and possibly a timid one. When he sees a cripple painfully traversing the streets, he is sorry for him, but cannot resist laughing at the notion of knocking his crutches from under him and flying, pursued by a policeman, only to lie down unexpectedly in his pursuer's path, and upset him, too, in the mud. But he does not do these things, because the cripple would be hurt, and the policeman would make him pay too dearly for his jest. In order to give the fullest expression to the craving of his whimsical side for action and exhibition, he must find a scene where these restraining conditions do not exist. He finds it on the stage or in the circus ring as a clown. This instance is an extremely improbable one, because although to a schoolboy of twelve a career of mischievous trickery without moral responsibility or ulterior risk may seem the fullest self-realization, to the adult man, with his passions and ambitions, it appeals very feebly and intermittently. As far as can be gathered at present, there has never been but one genuine clown—Grimaldi. I myself have never seen one who was not an obvious sham; and I observe that, though everybody agrees that a good harlequinade would be delightful, an actual harlequinade is seldom witnessed except by novices. Still, we all have a clown in us somewhere; and Garrick's Petruchio, Lemaître's Macaire, and Mr Irving's Jingle and Jeremy Diddler may be regarded as the outcome of the impulse felt by these actors to realize for a moment the clown in themselves. This, of course, is a realization of only a side of themselves; but there are very few parts in drama which will hold an entire man or woman.

The ordinary actor realizes himself for the most part off the stage in his private character; and only the unrealized residue, which may be the unworthiest part of him, finds its expression on the boards. Sometimes it is a part of him which he would be quite content to leave unrealized if he could afford to drop his profession. The walking gentleman in us does not crave for realization; but if the manager is already provided with a Macbeth, we must place the walking gentlemen at his service or else starve. On our way up to Macbeth, we must perforce allow many sides of us to be turned to the footlights which we would fain hide. Embryologists tell us that we have been many strange things in our time. Had you and I been arrested in the early stages of our career, and exhibited, as some of our fellow creatures have been, in bottles of spirits of wine, we must have figured as mere ascidians, or a little later as rudimentary fishes, or reptiles, or birds; for we passed through all these stages on our way to our present vertebrate dignity; and we have still not merely a bone or two and certain muscles and even organs quite irrelevant to our humanity, but we have even some tastes and habits which seem referable rather to our winged or finned stage than to our sober citizenship. And beyond a doubt, each of us has not only the bird and fish in him, but also—and how much more strongly!—the savage, the barbarian, the hunter and slayer, the warrior, the murderer, the thief, the coward, and the fanatic. How often must the actor, to serve a purpose not his own, but imposed on him by public, author, and manager on pain of starvation, night after night realize in his part the murderer and the coward in him until such realization becomes a mere trick of simulation, and his pleasure in acting becomes a combination of the mere craftsman's pleasure in the cleverness with which he does it, the frail mortal's delight in applause, and the economic man's appreciation of a large salary and a steady engagement!

This was practically the end of Mr Shaw's exposition of acting as metaphysical self-realization rather than shamming. The rest of his paper was evidently intended to stimulate the critics present to a fierce discussion. After incidentally remarking that "next to the plot of a melodrama, the silliest convention in it is the villain," and asking why "a plot must be substituted for a story, and actors and actresses for human beings," he hit out with the dogma that "dramatic criticism is the quintessence of art criticism, which is itself the essence of human folly and ignorance," and proceeded to give an amusing autobiographical sketch, at the outset of which he indulged in a pointed fling at the unreality of "acted" Church services.

When I was a boy, I was taken to church, to the theatre, to the concert room, and to the public picture gallery. Church proved so unpleasant that I have never gone since, except once when my friend the Warden induced me to go to hear a Bishop, who struck me as excellent material for a dramatic critic. In the theatre, the concert room, and the picture gallery, however, I was happier than anywhere else indoors, and out of mischief.

Then came an account of his eagerly reading books about art, and a description of the "critics' conventions," with which his mind got packed.

I was capable of looking at a picture then, and, if it displeased me, immediately considering whether the figures formed a pyramid, so that, if they did not, I could prove the picture defective because the composition was wrong. And if I saw a picture of a man foreshortened at me in such a way that I could see nothing but the soles of his feet and his eyes looking out between his toes, I marveled at it and almost revered the painter, though veneration was at no time one of my strong points. I did not read dramatic or literary criticism much, and therefore I never explained the failure of a play on the ground that the fourth act was longer than the third, or ascribed the superiority of Great Expectations to Dombey and Son to the effect produced on Dickens by the contemplation of Mr Wilkie Collins's plots; but I said things quite as idiotic, and I can only thank my stars that my sense of what was real in works of art somehow did survive my burst of interest in irrelevant critical conventions and the pretensions of this or that technical method to be absolute.

Then came the explanation of the mysterious phrase, "Fool's Paradise of Art," in the title of the paper.

But the main thing was that this cloud of silly illusions which I supposed to be Art was still my refuge from real life, my asylum from the squalor and snobbery outside, from the bewilderment of a world in which, as in church, everybody was pretending to enjoy what he disliked, and praising one course of conduct whilst pursuing another; above all, from the irksomeness of the struggle for bread and butter. When at last I made a plunge into London, I soon found out that the artistic people were the shirkers of the community. They ran away from their political duties to portfolios of etchings; from their social duties to essays on the delicacies of their culture; and from their religious duties to the theatre. They were doing exactly what I had done myself, in short—keeping up a Fool's Paradise in order to save themselves the trouble of making the real world any better. Naturally, they hated reality; and this involved some awkward consequences for them. For since the climaxes of Art are brought about by the successful effort of some powerful individuality or idea to realize itself in an act of some kind, whether picture, book, or stage impersonation, these artistic skulkers had to be continually dodging great works of art, or else devising ways of discussing and enjoying their accidental methods, conditions, and qualities so as to ward off their essential purpose and meaning. And they, or rather we, did this so effectually that I might have remained in my Fool's Paradise of Art with the other fools to this day, had I not, to preserve myself from the dry rot of idleness, attempted to realize myself in works of Art.

These works of art were Mr Shaw's novels, which he described as "bad sermons, which failed because I, thanks to skulking in picture galleries, was a nonentity; and the realization of a nonentity in a novel is not interesting." He gave up novel-writing, and pursued the Real by way of the incessant lecturing on Socialism which distinguishes his present phase of self-realization. "As it happens," he remarked, "I have an incorrigible propensity for preaching. In conversation this did not make me so unpopular as might have been expected; for I have some unconscious and unintentional infirmity of expression which often leads people to doubt whether I am serious in my sermons." Socialist propaganda brought Mr Shaw into contact with Mr Stewart Headlam:

He, not being a dramatic critic, saw what none of the dramatic critics could see, that the world behind the footlights was a real world, peopled with men and women instead of with despicable puppets. He proclaimed the solidarity of the stage with the stalls by founding the Church and Stage Guild. The critics stared, laughed, and promptly set up a convention that the Guild was a ludicrous combination of parson and ballet. Mr Headlam affected them just on one point. He disclosed to them the fact that the ballet is the richest mine of idiotic conventions that exists: it is practically dying of them. The critics are now eagerly learning the jargon of these conventions, in order that their minds, hitherto a blank on the subject of dancing, may be filled with a basketful of irrelevancies to it.

As to any chance of reforming these gentlemen, or obtaining help from them in reforming the drama, I am inclined to think it would be less trouble to undertake the work without them. They never learn anything, never discuss anything, never believe anything, never doubt that they are heading the march that is really leaving them almost out of sight. They cannot tell you anything about a play or an actor that is of the smallest consequence, though they will tell you a dozen things that are quite beside the point. They can write as good a notice of a perfectly hollow play as it is worth; but confront them with a great piece of acting and they will astonish you by the ingenuity with which they will evade the main point, and, like cuttlefish, conceal their bonelessness in a cloud of ink. Salvini startles them by his Othello; and the town rings with their opinions as to the exact length to which a man should go in pretending to cut his throat. Not long ago, the true relation of the actor to the dramatist was thrust before them by a French playwright, who, having to write plays expressly for Madame Sarah Bernhardt, could not help seeing that his task was to provide her with a vehicle for the expression of herself and not with a mask and domino. Under these circumstances, what did this much admired dramatist do? He deliberately took that part of Madame Bernhardt's nature which she shares with any tigress, and he exploited that to the uttermost farthingsworth. Finding that it paid, he did it again. The critics had not a word to say, except to protest against their nerves being shaken by the exhibition on the stage of implements of torture and of the bowstring at full stretch. This was what they called "realism," save the mark. But after two years of Theodora and La Tosca, they began to complain that their actress was vulgarized. Sarah was *encanaillée*. Having at last discovered a fact, the next thing was to find a wrong and ridiculous reason for it. But the true reason was so obvious that even the coincidence that Madame Bernhardt had grown a little older and stouter did not suffice to take its place. Some of the better critics did see plainly enough that somehow M. Sardou had been playing it rather low down. But why did they not see that in time? Why did they make much of this abominable Theodora on its first night, instead of at once protesting against it as a vile degradation of the actress, of the stage, of the drama, and of the playgoing public? Simply because the whole affair was not real enough to be worth troubling about. After all, the play was a sham, the woman a puppet: why should you expect a cultivated man to make a fuss about these things, and incidentally to make himself ridiculous? Besides, such considerations disturb the Fool's Paradise. It is a deliberate planting of the Tree of the Knowledge of Good and Evil there—a part of that infernal conspiracy to make art didactic which the great writers of the past fell into because they were not up to modern "form."

I do not propose to bring further evidence against the critics now: they will perhaps supply it themselves in the course of the discussion. I have said enough to make myself thoroughly misunderstood; and I will conclude by restating the views upon which I base my respect for the actor and the stage, and my despair of the critics. 1. That acting, in the common use of the word, is self-falsification, forgery, and fraud. 2. That the true goal of the stage-player is self-realization, expression, and exhibition. 3. That the drama can only progress by making higher and higher demands on the players' powers of self-development and realization. 4. That the critic who rejects this view lapses into a vicious contempt for the player, and, having no valid standard, is compelled to coin conventions which will not circulate anywhere outside his own circle of accomplices. These are the points on which I invite you to enlighten me by a frank discussion.

But the discussion, after all, did not get beyond a volley of questions and fragmentary remarks from Mr William Archer, Mr Oscar Wilde, Mr Edward Rose, Mr Hubert Bland, Mr Belfort Bax, Mr A. R. Dryhurst, the Rev. T. Hancock, the Rev. Stewart Headlam, Miss May Morris, and Mrs Bland (E. Nesbit).

WHAT SOCIALISM WILL BE LIKE

(Lecture delivered before the Hammersmith Socialist Society at William Morris's Kelmscott House, Hammersmith, 12 July 1896. *The Labour Leader*, 19 *December* 1896)

My lecture will be very short. It consists of three words—*I dont know*. Having delivered it, by way of opening a discussion, I will proceed to make a few remarks. The first thing that strikes one in discussing the matter with a Socialist—if you have a critical habit of mind, as I have, professionally—is the superstitious resemblance of the notion your ordinary Socialist has of what Socialism will be like to the good old idea of what heaven will be like! If you suggest that under Socialism anybody will pay rent or receive wages your ideal Socialist jumps on you. If I venture to suggest that such questions as who shall be allowed to live on Richmond Hill, under Socialism, will have to be settled much as it is today, by seeing who will pay most to live there, such an eminent and enlightened Socialist as Mr Hyndman immediately loses his temper, and retorts that that is a disgusting middle-class idea! If Mr Hyndman agreed with Dr Merlino, who boldly suggested that an application of scientific landscape gardening would make all London beautiful, I could understand that feeling.

I am afraid we get a great many converts because Socialism is supposed to favor the idea that people will then have got at the back of their work—a sort of kingdom of heaven on earth, when something will cease from troubling. The other day, at a meeting of the Fabian Society—of the very able executive of which I happen to be a member—when we proposed that the society should present to the International Congress some sort of affirmation of our views on Socialism, one Socialist—a most self-sacrificing and stalwart worker for the cause—was driven almost to frenzy by the very plain statement that, instead of Socialism proposing to abolish the wage system, the only object of Socialism was to secure that everybody should be paid wages —absolutely steady wages, in the employment of the community —wages regulated by the general convenience and moral sense of the community. Under Socialism we shall require policemen. Possibly their duties will not be exactly the same as now, but then, probably, everybody will ride a bicycle, and will anybody tell me that we shall not want some representative of the community to look after citizens in the street? Having got your policeman, then, how are you going to pay him the "entire product" of his labor? Whatever you pay him will be wages, so our sole object will be to proceed steadily to pay everybody wages.

We shall proceed to make the shopkeeper a municipal official, to sell goods at a price to be determined in the interests of the whole community—generally with regard to the cost of production, although it might be desirable to put a high price on gin, for example, and a very low price on some other commodity. Our municipal shopkeeper will have a definite status and a pension to look forward to when he retires. Many people look forward to Socialism as a system where everybody will get what they want without having to pay for it. One cannot do that now (except when the shopkeeper is not looking), but our present system of society does it under the names of Rent and Interest, by means of which an idle rich man gets his goods for nothing. But under Socialism we want our shops or stores having customers with not a farthing to spend without having earned it by their own labor. But there would be modifications of this. We have already found out that it is bad public economy to have a toll-keeper for roads and bridges, and the cost of these is now defrayed out of the rates. So when we have a good Socialist system well in work, and people have lost the habit of imagining that anybody was going to live for nothing, the towns would make the same arrangement about bread. We would come to the conclusion that it would save a lot of trouble and bookkeeping to turn into the stores an ascertained required amount of bread, and let everybody take as much as they wanted, and they would pay for it out of their rates. Of course, you would have a certain number of individuals who under no system of society could be induced to work at all, and you would lose a little bread in that way, but you would save the policeman's labor and the community would in the end gain more than it lost.

But it would damp my ardor for Socialism very considerably if I thought that everything would be done by the County Council. There is no reason to believe we shall ever sanction any law which would prevent a man working for himself, or from hiring another man to work for him for wages if he chooses. Suppose London were Socialized tomorrow: then, of course, the County Council would be equipped entirely with Socialists. The public want newspapers, and we will suppose the County Council ran them. I imagine they would be bad newspapers, but that would not matter—they would be all the more popular. But a certain section of the public would like good literature and independent criticism. But if the County Council produced a newspaper which told the truth boldly, every councillor would lose his seat in a week. So all such undertakings would have to be carried on by individuals. Do you suppose that at my age I would go and earn my livelihood in the municipal shop or in any "honest" way? I would not do it. I earn my livelihood by my pen, mostly in writing criticisms which people— especially those criticized—for the most part do not like. Am I to understand that any Socialist contemplates that when someone had got a little money or credit in an honest way—say enough to start a newspaper—some Socialist authority would say: "No; that would be private capitalism: we will not allow you"? If so, I would start a revolution against Socialism the very next day. The man who wanted to employ me might be foolish —or grasping—but since Socialism would have guaranteed me a comfortable livelihood, a private individual could only secure me by offering at least as good terms as the community.

So there could be no wage slavery practised. If the private individual were able to give a man better terms than the community it could not be by monopoly of land and capital. It would be that he had beaten the public authority in supplying the public need with some new invention, want, or organization which the public were willing to pay him for. Under such circumstances I fail to see any reason for interference. On the contrary, nothing more fatal to human progress than such interference can be imagined. The public bodies under Socialism could watch the results of private enterprize. To the enterprizing man who had invented something—say the bicycle, the typewriter, or the electric light—and made a success of it, the State would step in and say: "Very kind of you to shew us. We will take on that business." Then the private enterprizer would have to turn and invent something else. Under the present system we pay the successful private enterprizer too well, and thus rob him of incentive to renewed ingenuity! In point of fact, however, a great deal of so-called private enterprize is in no sense such. For example, owing to increase of population a village grows to a town. Thirty miles distant another village does the same. It is desirable, in the interests of the community, that a railway should be made between the two places. Will anyone say that the making of such a railway involves "enterprize" or "initiative"? But under the present system, instead of its being done on the public incentive, we leave it to a number of individuals who want to get dividends. So under Socialism "private enterprize and initiative" would necessarily be limited to something which really was new. No man would have a chance of getting outside the public routine unless he had found out a new public want and was willing to take on himself the risk of working it out.

What we really want done is to have all the large industries of the country—about which there is no "enterprize"—organized by the public authorities, and also, of course, to have all rent of land and capital—all the economic rents (which have the effect of putting unearned money into private pockets)—put into the hands of the State. No one now supposes that £17,000,000 should every year go into the pockets of half-a-dozen private gentlemen in London as "rent." We are agreed that every farthing of that should go to the London public authorities, in so far as it arises from a monopoly of situation. Suppose a man wanted to go into business for himself under Socialism. Since no man would have discovered a new method of making land, he

26

would have to pay, for the land he occupied, its full economic rent to the community. If he hadnt capital himself I presume he would borrow from the State, and would pay interest for it. And by the "State" I mean the nearest authority representing the people.

Now, suppose a man found out something so much wanted—which the State could not supply and the public were willing to pay for—that he became thunderingly rich. Suppose another man—say, a dentist—did the same. Suppose this dentist were exceedingly clever. It would be all very well to say to him: "You shall be the town dentist, and we will pay you good wages." He would say: "No, thank you; I don't need my labor organized by the community. I will pay you rent for the premises I wish to occupy, and put up a brass plate. Here we are—free citizens—I will charge what I like!" If the carrying out of our views leads to increased prosperity, every member of the community would have more to spend on their teeth, and they would bid against each other for the services of this extraordinarily clever dentist.

Then you have your artist. I grant that if he painted very great pictures he would not make much money. But suppose he painted popular pictures, like Gustave Doré, for example. It was found possible to put them all into one room, erect a turnstile at the door, and charge a shilling for leave to pass it. I do not see how, under Socialism, the community could interfere with that! I see no Socialist ground of public policy for doing so, although under such circumstances a man might become very rich. A man painting a picture is not the same thing as a man making a loaf of bread. The man who buys the loaf consumes it, but the man who pays to consume a shillingsworth of the picture leaves it intact, and the sight of the picture is something which can be continually sold, and it becomes, not less, but more valuable. Tis true the average man does not go to look at a picture because he likes it, but because many other men have gone to see it.

Again, take four musicians who play string quartets. By constant practice together they at last acquire extraordinary skill in playing chamber music very beautifully. Everybody wants to hear them, and people are quite willing to pay to hear them. What is to prevent them, under Socialism, agreeing with an organizer and putting up a turnstile like the artist? And, bear in mind, chamber music cannot be properly played and appreciated in a big building like St James's Hall. If you have not heard a string quartet played in a small room you have never heard chamber music played and heard at all properly. Now we, as good Socialists, having the community's good at heart, let in, say, fifty persons and exclude the remainder. How are we to ascertain who the people are who should hear it? Our musicians would put the fifty seats up to auction, and it is appalling to imagine how much they might fetch! The organizing agent would probably get much more than he would pay the instrumentalists—although he would pay more than the London County Council bandmen get.

Then take the drama. I do not know whether, under Socialism, people will still want to hear Shakespear. I doubt it—I hope somebody more up to date will turn up. So let us suppose you had a small body of persons who had extraordinary skill in producing Ibsen's dramas. A gentleman [Charles Charrington] who has produced A Doll's House in every quarter of the globe tells me that the most successful performance he had ever given took place in an ordinary house. It is impossible to present Ibsen properly in a big theatre. Well, suppose this gentleman organized exceedingly fine performances of A Doll's House under Socialism, and said: "I will not have them produced in your big theatres, because it is not possible to produce them with proper effect there. So I will produce the play in my own house, and put the seats up to auction." Well, I reckon that under Socialism I should be in a position to give ten guineas for a ticket—and I would give it straight away! And so, again, our extraordinarily clever producer of Ibsen would get enormously rich. Not to multiply examples, I see no reason why any man should be interfered with in the spontaneous pursuit of his plans, and so it might be possible for certain individuals to be considerably richer than others.

Tis true, Socialism looks with suspicion on inequality of wealth, but that does not contradict the equality Socialism aims at. And it is impossible to form any Socialist system whatever without assuming equality of condition. There might be, as

28

under the feudal system, various strata—men in one grade being superior to those in another; but within the particular grade and rank it is impossible to proceed on any basis save equality— that is to say, equality before the law and equal political rights. There is one mechanical inequality to which we Socialists have a great objection—that is, a large inequality of purchasing power. For instance, tomorrow morning a certain number of young persons will begin to work for the first time, being just grown up. It is the interest of the community that the work they start on should be that which is most needed for the wellbeing of the community. But owing to the unequal distribution of wealth what happens is that numbers of these new workers will start working for rich men, as flunkeys or building barges and yachts, for instance—things the community is not in want of. So it must always be a matter of public policy to prevent any large class of men becoming enormously richer than their fellows. To prevent this you have nothing to do but go at them with a progressive income tax. An income tax is an exceedingly Socialistic institution. In fact, that is one of the objections of the upper class to it. But I do not think any such danger would arise. By the very terms of the case such instances as I have mentioned would be exceptional. A painter would only be able to get people to pay to look at his pictures on condition that they are very exceptional. So would the quartet party. From my knowledge of the general musical amateur I should say it would generally be better for him to listen to anybody but himself. And in regard to dramatic companies, I am not sure you would not have private theatricals under Socialism in every second house. But you may depend upon it the professional actor would have to be very good indeed. So would the great surgeon-dentist. Exceptional skill only would avail.

Nevertheless, I think it would be not only not dangerous, but very desirable, to have a few persons with a little extra money to spend. They could not spend it on themselves. A man with a gigantic fortune, let him try his utmost, cannot live more expensively than the richest *class* of the community. If a millionaire wants to buy a loaf of bread he doesnt go into a baker's shop and find special loaves made with gilt tops. He buys the same kind of bread you and I buy—perhaps he buys a bit better suit of clothes than mine! Under Socialism there would be a general level of prosperity, and everybody would be able to buy good bread and good clothes. So, beyond the point of general prosperity your enormously rich man would be forced to have a hobby of some kind. Take our friend William Morris, for instance. He is now doing a very useful thing, recklessly spending large sums of money in collecting specimens of the finest printed books in Europe. Our comrade is an artist. He is buying these old books because they are worth looking at. Here he is, spending his superfluity of income on something no government could do. No doubt, Morris's collection will some time find itself in public hands, and will be enjoyed by the community. Of course, we Socialists are given to talk art, but how many of us who speak with enthusiastic admiration of Morris have even spent half-a-crown on art in our lives!

Questions elicited the following further opinions from the lecturer:

Under Socialism every single trade would have a tight trades-union looking after the interests of that particular trade.

With regard to exceptional ability—the artist, for example. Of course, we all look forward to the time when he will exercise his abilities without the motive of extra gain. At the same time I dont think we are quite right in telling people authoritatively that he will do that. Such a man may be *forced* to get all he can, as being the only way of settling who wants to hear him most! Further, the artist is apt to be a very selfish person, because it is necessary for him to sacrifice himself to the cultivation of his art, and so he becomes reckless of the interests of other people. And there is a large class of artists whom you will never get unless you pamper them excessively.

Would I communize beer and spirits as well as bread? Everybody eats bread, and, roughly, about the same quantity. If you communize it no man could object that he had to pay for it out of the rates and didnt eat it, but the moment you touch beer you are asking the teetotaler to pay for what other people drink. Similarly, if you communize the theatre you will have the religious people claiming the communization of chapels. And remember, you can have a municipal brewery without communizing beer. And I hope it is quite certain that we shall never have Socialism until every man is a sufficiently well-educated Socialist —that is, until he realizes that he ought not to thrust his tastes on other people. On the other hand, if a teetotaler were to say, "I refuse to allow you to communize beer, even on a basis which gives me an equivalent advantage," I dont think his objection should be tolerated.

I am asked if I would object to characterize my lecture as an Individualist Anarchist view of Socialism. I have never admitted there is any contradiction between Individualism and Socialism. I object to the present system because it gives no scope for individuality. I will call it, if you like, an Individualist Socialist lecture.

THE DYNAMITARDS OF SCIENCE

(Speech delivered before the Annual Meeting of the London Anti-Vivisection Society, London, in the St Martin's Town Hall, 30 May 1900. *Monthly Record and Animals' Guardian,* *June* 1900; reprinted as a pamphlet by the Society, 1900)

MOTION.—"*That this meeting regards vivisection as cruel, immoral, and dishonoring to humanity, and calls on Parliament to prohibit the practice.*"

I am seconding this resolution at the very great advantage of not being a doctor or a scientific man myself. Like all of you I have been much moved by the speech which Dr [Walter R.] Hadwen has just delivered; but every time he harrowed my feelings, I consoled myself with the reflection that he was a doctor and was probably wrong. [*Laughter.*] For my part, I must confess to you at once that I do not believe that any experiment can be tried in this world which may not be of some use to somebody or other, or which may not lead to some discovery. I have never objected to experiments on the ground that they are useless. I do not see how it is possible for any course of experiment performed not to lead to increase of knowledge in some direction or another. I grant that if you study the history of experiment, you will hardly ever find that the experimenter discovers the thing he intended to discover. You will find, for example, that at the beginning of modern science men were not trying to lay the foundation of modern science: they were trying to find the Philosopher's Stone. They did not find it; but they found something else. Therefore, even if I were qualified professionally to do so, I do not think I should take my stand here tonight on the uselessness of vivisection. Nothing can be proved to be useless.

Let me give you an illustration or two. Some years ago an exceedingly interesting experiment was unintentionally tried by our fleet. Two of our great battleships, the Camperdown and the Victoria, attempted to cut a certain evolution rather too finely, with the result that the Camperdown ran down the Victoria, the Victoria capsized, and hundreds of lives were lost. Well, that was an exceedingly interesting experiment. [*Laughter.*] It is admitted that a great deal was learned from it. I think I am right in saying that, until that experiment was tried, hardly any commander of a battleship believed that he could ram another battleship without sinking himself as well as his adversary; but by that experiment it was proved that the thing might safely be done. [*Laughter.*] Within the last few days we have had another experiment. We took one of our old warships, the Belleisle, and we set the Majestic, one of our new battleships, to fire upon her and try how soon she could sink her. You have read all about it in the newspapers. Well, there was one imperfect thing about that experiment on the Belleisle. The men in that ship were made of what is called non-flammable wood. [*Laughter.*] It appears to me that this vitiated the experiment. Looking at the matter from the purely knowledge-seeking point of view, it seems to me that we should have put flammable live men on that ship instead of non-flammable effigies. [*Laughter*]. Undoubtedly it would have been most instructive. One or two of them would certainly have survived the experiment and been able to tell the Admiralty a number of things which would have been of great use to us in our next naval war. [*Laughter.*]

I think you see the point I am driving at. You do not settle whether an experiment is justified or not by merely shewing that it is of some use. If that were the only thing to be considered we should kill our soldiers and sailors in time of peace simply to find out what our new guns and explosives could do; for I am sure that in the present state of public enthusiasm about military matters, a great many Britons would say that the science of war is of very much more importance to our national welfare than the science of medicine. Yet the doctors seem to think utility a sufficient justification of vivisectional experiments which do not always stop at animals, and, let me add, logically, should not stop at animals; for surely, if a doctor believes that vivisectional experiments on animals are justified by what they teach him, then, since he knows that these experiments must necessarily be less instructive than experiments on human beings, he must be a coward if he does not sacrifice one or two comparatively value-less human beings in order to find out a little more accurately what he is trying to discover. You see, you cannot bring a question of this kind to a utilitarian test at all. If you once begin that particular line of argument you will find yourself landed in horrors of which you have no conception.

Let me give you an example of this, which will explain to you how I arrived at my opinion on the subject of vivisection, and why the scientific arguments convinced me at once that it is a thing we have to set our faces against. As you know, in this country we not only ill-use animals—and doctors, by the way, are not the only people who ill-use animals—["*Hear, hear*"]—but to a very much greater and more nationally disastrous extent we ill-use men and women. ["*Hear, hear.*"] When I began my public activity I addressed myself to this question of the ill-usage of men and women. My friend, Mr Herbert Burrows, whom I am glad to see here tonight, also addressed himself to that; and we have both been now for a number of years studying the methods by which a nation can get rid of that great evil of the ill-usage of men and women. Well, Mr Burrows and I have been constantly opposed by a certain very interesting and logical class of social reformers. I remember, at a place not very far from here, delivering one of a series of lectures to persuade this particular class of reformers that their methods were not the right methods.

I think I am right in saying that, at the last lecture of that series, which Mr Burrows delivered, one gentleman had brought with him to the lecture his particular method of social reform in his pocket. Well, nothing happened on that occasion, except that Mr Burrows probably argumentatively silenced the gentleman. [*Mr Burrows—shaking his head—"No, no."*] Of course not: they were proof against argument. [*Laughter.*] But that gentleman went a few days afterwards—I think you will remember the occurrence—for a walk in Greenwich Park; and when he was within a short distance of the Observatory, his method of social reform in his pocket exploded and blew him to pieces. [*Laughter.*] His method of social reform was dynamite.

Now I venture to say that if the catastrophe I have described to you had left that gentleman in a position to argue with you, you would have had to be very careful what ground you took, or he would have got the better of you with his argument, because you will observe that the logic of utility is on the side of dynamite. [*Laughter.*] In the first place, there is the argument that our civilization produces more misery, more death, disease, and destruction in the course of one year than all the dynamitards in the world have ever produced since explosives were invented. The dynamitard argues, "Supposing I blow a Cabinet Minister to pieces, it will cause him little suffering. I employ so high an explosive that it is practically a humane process. Dynamite does not require an anesthetic because its operation does not involve any pain. [*Applause.*] On the other hand, it will call attention to social problems in the only promptly effective way; for nothing is ever done until a startling catastrophe wakens up the people to the need of social reform. It was the cholera that forced us to adopt sanitation. It was the Crimean War that forced us to reform the Civil Service. Dynamite is a remedy of the same order: why not use it?" You will find it very hard to get over that line of argument if you sanction it when you want your diseases cured. If you are prepared to allow a few animals to be tormented by vivisectors on the ground that, as a result, you are going to relieve the great mass of physical suffering among mankind, then you are logically bound to believe that the dynamitard is right to blow up his Cabinet Minister.

I do not know when it was that Mr Herbert Burrows first joined the Anti-Vivisection movement; but I am sure that when he first came across it, he had, after that old experience of ours, no more difficulty in making up his mind about it than I had. Give me such a book as Mr Stephen Paget's,[1] and I have only to read the preface to understand that the vivisector is the dynamitard of science. ["*Hear, hear.*"] The arguments are the same; the character of the acts advocated is essentially the same; the justification is the same. And they are all open to the same objection, that they advocate a practice which makes life entirely horrible. ["*Hear, hear.*"] Once allow irresponsible persons an absolute right to spread torture and death all around them, if only they will promise you the millennium, and you will be landed in dynamite in Politics, just as you are already landed in vivisection in Science. The question is one of human character: you have got to make up your minds whether you will live your life honorably or not.

If a man comes to me and says, "My children are starving; I myself am in a miserable condition, and I cannot bear to see my wife hungry and looking on her starving children: can you recommend me a method of putting an end to it?"—there are various methods which I might recommend. I might recommend him to rob the first rich citizen he met in the street. No doubt, if the operation were carefully performed, and the police were not there, it might be successful [*laughter*]; and the result would be that the man might buy food, and go home, and feed his wife and children, and be able to say to himself, "That rich man will never miss those few shillings: the money he did not need ha; enabled me to buy food for my wife and family, and make them v ell, and I have only done my duty as a father and a husband." Can anything be more conclusive? Yet we all know that we must draw our line of conduct higher than that. We must apply the test of character, and ask ourselves not merely, "What will happen if I do this particular thing?" but "What sort of a man shall I be if I do it?" And we must apply the Kantian test, and ask, "What will happen if everybody takes to doing such things?" Apply these tests to vivisection and you will see that no man whose life is worth living will have anything to do with it. Like our Chairman,

[1] *Experiments on Animals* (London, 1900).

35

I make no pretense to criticize vivisectional experiments on the ground of their technical failure or success. I dogmatically postulate humaneness as a condition of worthy personal character.

I have only one other thing to say. I have just received a little volume which I would commend to your attention: namely, the Report of this Society. It is a little red book and has a number of very interesting photographs in it. These are the photographs of many distinguished men who have borne their testimony against vivisection. If you are any judge of human faces you will admit that most of these give a deal of weight to our movement. ["*Hear, hear.*"] Now, I would suggest to Mr [Sidney] Trist that in making our next year's Report, instead of having an unbroken row of portraits of Anti-Vivisectors, he should intersperse them with portraits of vivisectors so that the public could have an opportunity of comparing the faces of the men, as an index of their character. If Mr Trist can manage that, perhaps the Report of next year will be even a stronger argument in our favor than the Report of this year.

THE COURT THEATRE

(Reply to a toast by the Earl of Lytton, at a dinner honoring the managers of the Court Theatre, held in the Criterion Restaurant, London, 7 July 1907. Published in the souvenir brochure of the proceedings, *Complimentary Dinner to Mr. J. E. Vedrenne and Mr. H. Granville Barker*, 1907)

A good deal has been said here tonight as to how much our guests of the evening owe to me. My lord, ladies and gentlemen, I assure you they owe me nothing. They are perfectly solvent. The success, such as it is, has been a perfectly genuine one. There are plenty of managements who will make a brilliant show of success if you give them a sufficiently large subsidy to spend. Vedrenne and Barker have had no subsidy. They have paid me my fees to the uttermost farthing, and they have had nothing else to pay or repay me. This does not mean that the highest theatrical art is independent of public support, moral and financial. The Court Theatre has had to cut its coat according to its cloth, and it has never really had cloth enough. But it has paid its way and made a living wage for its workers, and it has produced an effect on dramatic art and public taste in this country which is out of all proportion to the mere physical and financial bulk of its achievements.

I am glad to have the honor of speaking here for the Court Theatre authors, because if they had to answer for themselves they would be prevented from doing themselves justice by their modesty. Modesty, fortunately, is not in my line; and if it were, I should follow the precept offered by Felix Drinkwater to Captain Brassbound, and be modest on my own account, not on theirs. As a matter of fact, I am overrated as an author: most great men are. We have, I think, proved that there is in this country plenty of dramatic faculty—faculty of the highest order too—only waiting for its opportunity; and it is the supreme merit of our guests this evening that they have provided that opportunity. You may say that genius does not wait for its opportunity: it creates it. But that is not true of any particular opportunity when there are alternatives open. Men of genius will not become the slaves of the ordinary fashionable theatres when they have the alternative of writing novels. The genius of Dickens, who at first wanted to write for the theatre, was lost to it because there was no theatre available in which his art could have breathed. I have myself tried hard to tempt Mr Wells, Mr Kipling, Mr Conrad, and Mr Maurice Hewlett to leave their safe and dignified position as masters of the art of fiction, and struggle with new difficulties and a new *technique*—though the technical difficulties are absurdly exaggerated—for the sake of redeeming the British drama from banality. But it was too much to ask. They all knew the story of the manager who, after receiving favorably a suggestion of a play by Stevenson, drew back in disgust on learning that the author in question was not what he called "*the* Stephenson," meaning the librettist of a well-known light opera, but one Robert Louis Stevenson, of whom he had never heard.

If Mr Maurice Hewlett was persuaded at last to make an experiment at the Court Theatre, it was because he knew that

Vedrenne and Barker would know his worth and respect his commanding position in literature. Without that no alliance between literature and the theatre is possible; for it is hard enough to make one reputation and conquer one eminence without having to set to again as a stranger and a beginner on the stage. If Mr Galsworthy, after winning his spurs as one of the finest of the younger novelists, brought to the stage in The Silver Box that penetrating social criticism, and that charm of wonderfully fastidious and restrained art which makes me blush for the comparative blatancy of my own plays, it is because there was at last a stage for him to bring them to, and that stage was the Court stage, the creation of Vedrenne and Barker.

Barker, by the way, was not, like Vedrenne, wholly disinterested in the matter, for he, too, is a Court author, and he, too, produces work whose delicacy and subtlety require exquisite handling. It is Vedrenne's just boast that he has produced Barker. The same thing is true of all the Court authors, more or less. Mr St John Hankin, the Mephistopheles of the new comedy, would have been suspected by an old-fashioned manager—and suspected very justly—of laughing at him. Mr Vernon Harcourt and Mr Housman, whose charm is so much a charm of touch, would not have had much more chance than Mr Henry James has had on the long-run system. Literary charm is like the bloom on fine wall-fruit: the least roughness of handling knocks it off; and in our ordinary theatres literary plays are handled much as American trunks are handled at the boat trains. Mr Gilbert Murray has not merely translated Euripides—many fools have done that, and only knocked another nail into the coffin of a dead language—he has reincarnated Euripides and made him a living poet in our midst. But Vedrenne and Barker made a Court author of him when no other managers dared touch him.

The difficulties of the enterprize have been labors of love, except in one unfortunately very trying respect. There has been no sort of satisfaction in the unremitting struggle with the London press, which from first to last has done what in it lay to crush the enterprize. I know this uncompromising statement will surprise some of you, because in every newspaper you see praises of Vedrenne and Barker, ecstasies over the Court Theatre acting, paragraphs about the most frequently played Court author, and so forth. That has become the fashion, and the indiscriminate way in which it is done shews that it is done as a matter of fashion rather than of real appreciation. But if you turn back from this new convention to the points at which newspaper notices really help or hinder management—to the first-night notices of the first productions—you will see what I mean. There you will find a chronicle of failure, a sulky protest against this new and troublesome sort of entertainment that calls for knowledge and thought instead of for the usual *clichés*.

Take, for example, the fate of Mr [John] Masefield. Mr Masefield's Campden Wonder is the greatest work of its kind that has been produced in an English theatre within the recollection—I had almost said within the reading—of any living critic. It has that great literary magic of a ceaseless music of speech—of haunting repetitions that play upon the tragic themes and burn them into the imagination. Its subject is one of those perfect simplicities that only a master of drama thinks of. Greater hate hath no man than this, that he lay down his life to kill his enemy: that is the theme of the Campden Wonder; and a wonder it is—of literary and dramatic art. And what had the press to say? They fell on it with howls of mere Philistine discomfort, and persuaded the public that it was a dull and disgusting failure. They complained of its horror, as if Mr Masefield had not known how to make that horror bearable, salutary, even fascinating by the enchantments of his art—as if it was not their business to face horror on the tragic stage as much as it is a soldier's business to face danger in the field. They ran away shamelessly, whining for happy endings and the like, blind and deaf to the splendid art of the thing, complaining that Mr Masefield had upset their digestion, and the like.

And what they did brutally to the Campden Wonder they did more or less to every other play. As we rehearsed our scenes and rejoiced in the growing interest and expectancy of our actors as they took the play in, we knew that no matter how enthusiastic our audience on the first night would be, no matter how triumphant the success of our actors, the next day—always a day of reaction at the best of times—would bring down on them all a damp cloud of grudging, petulant, ill-conditioned disparagement, suggesting to them that what they had been working so hard at was not a play at all, but a rather ridiculous experiment which was no credit to anybody connected with it. The mischief done was very considerable in the cases of new authors; and the discouragement to our actors must have had its effect, bravely as they concealed it.

Now, we were all—we authors—very much indebted to our actors, and felt proportionately disgusted at the way in which they were assured that they were wasting their time on us. I should like to make my personal acknowledgments to all of them, but that is a duty reserved for a later speaker; so I will only give, as an instance, the fact that my own play, John Bull's Other Island, failed as completely in America without Mr Louis Calvert as Broadbent as it succeeded here, where it was carried on his massive shoulders. The success was his, not mine: I only provided the accessories. Well, you will say, but did not the press acknowledge this? is not the play always spoken of as a masterpiece? is not Mr Calvert's Broadbent as famous as Quin's Falstaff? Yes, it is—*now*. But turn back to the first-night notices, and you will learn that the masterpiece is not a play at all, and that Mr Calvert only did the best he could with an impossible part. It was not until Man and Superman followed that the wonderful qualities of John Bull were contrasted with the emptiness and dulness of its successor. It was not until Major Barbara came that the extinction of all the brilliancy that blazed through Man and Superman was announced. And not until The Doctor's Dilemma had been declared my Waterloo was it mentioned that Major Barbara had been my Austerlitz.

Now, I want to make a suggestion to the press. I dont ask them to give up abusing me, or declaring that my plays are not plays and my characters not human beings. Not for worlds would I deprive them of the inexhaustible pleasure these paradoxes seem to give them. But I do ask them, for the sake of the actors and of Vedrenne and Barker's enterprize, to reverse the order of their attacks and their caresses. In the future, instead of abusing the new play and praising the one before, let them abuse the one before and praise the new one. Instead of saying that The

Doctor's Dilemma shews a sad falling-off from the superb achievement of Major Barbara, let them say that The Doctor's Dilemma is indeed a welcome and delightful change from the diseased trash which they had to endure last year from this most unequal author. That will satisfy their feelings just as much as the other plan, and will be really helpful to us. It is not the revivals that we want written up: the revivals can take care of themselves. Praise comes too late to help plays that have already helped themselves. If the press wishes to befriend us, let it befriend us in need, instead of throwing stones at us whilst we are struggling in the waves and pressing life-belts on us when we have swum to shore.

LITERATURE AND ART

(Lecture delivered from the pulpit of the Reverend R. J. Campbell's City Temple, London, 8 October 1908. *The Christian Commonwealth*, 14 October 1908)

I make no distinction between literature and art. Literature is one of the forms of art and all art is one. The old idea that art is rather a wicked thing still survives, and there are congregations who would consider that the discussion of art among serious-minded people is a form of wickedness only second to that of putting me into the pulpit to expound it. A few years ago I wrote a play called Major Barbara, and one of the things I am proudest of in connection with that play is that I induced certain prominent members of the Salvation Army to come to the theatre, for the first time in their lives, to see that play; and they liked it. At that time I tried to persuade the Salvation Army to make use of the very remarkable quantity of artistic talent that they have in their ranks, and which they use in the way of singing certain kinds of songs which are dramatically effective at their meetings. I tried to induce them deliberately to go in for theatrical entertainments, and I offered them the second act of my play—the conversion by a member of the Salvation Army of a sinner—as a sample of what might be done. I was met very sympathetically by the more genuine and religious people in the Army, but I suspect they were hampered by some people whose support they could not afford to dispense with, and who had rather curious ideas on the subject of art, and did not like the idea of anything being enacted by the Salvation Army unless it was literally true. They seemed to have the idea that to invent a story or write a drama was to tell a lie—it was to pretend that something had happened that had never taken place.

Now I want to face the question, How far is art guilty of the sin of lying? How far can art substantiate its claim to be the method of inspired revelation? Because art, and particularly the art of literature, does pretend in this country especially, and more or less throughout Christendom, to be the method of inspired revelation. It is believed by the great mass of Christian people in this country that when God wished to reveal Himself to the people He did not write an opera or compose a symphony or paint a picture. He wrote a book—in fact, a number of books—which are connected together in the volume called the Bible. From that point of view, the Bible is a work of art, of very remarkable character, of very fine art. Now, how far can that claim be substantiated?—how far is the art of literature in particular the method of inspired revelation? That brings us back to the difficulty of the Salvation Army; because if the test which was proposed to be applied to Major Barbara be applied to the Bible—accuracy of information as to whether certain things actually happened—if you make that the test of divinely inspired truth, the Bible would fall down at once; it would be impossible to substantiate it. I am going to suggest to you that that is really not the sense in which inspired revelation, or anything else that is art, is true.

If asked "Is the Post Office Directory true?" you would all say "Yes." If, again, you were asked, "Is the Sermon on the Mount true?" you might answer "Yes" or "No," according to your convictions. But the second question, although asked in the same terms, is completely different from the first; the two things are not on the same plane. Take another example. Suppose when Mr Campbell leaves the City Temple this evening one man asks him, "What is the shortest way to Aldersgate Street Station?" and, before he has had time to answer, another man says, "What shall I do to be saved?" Both men are asking "the way," and yet the answers must be very different. The first question is simply a request for accurate information; the second is really a request for revelation. You can get accurate information from almost anybody, but for revelation you have to go to the inspired speaker, writer, composer, painter. In trying to bring home to you the difference between the work of the great artist and the man who merely conveys information, I shall bore you a little, but I presume you are—I was going to say accustomed to that, but this is the only religious congregation in London that is not accustomed to it. [Shaw then proceeded to read out of that day's Times a number of unconnected items of accurate information, parenthetically explaining that although he was reading them with an intelligent air, most of them he did not understand.] When you have a mass of disconnected facts flung at you haphazard, you can get nothing out of them—neither religion, nor politics, nor economics.

If you stand on Holborn Viaduct and take a snapshot of the things that are occurring, you have an exact, superficial record, but you know nothing of Holborn Viaduct in any spiritual or truthful sense. If, on the other hand, another man, instead of saying, "There are men and women walking up and down the street," says, "I see a ladder stretched from earth to heaven, with angels ascending and descending," you would not only find that man much more interesting than the other, but I suggest that there would be genuine truth at the bottom of what he said, that there was something to be got out of it, that possibly he was a man able to make a revelation to you. When a man writes a drama or a book or preaches a sermon or employs any other method of art, what he really does is to take the events of life out of the accidental, irrelevant, chaotic way in which they happen, and to rearrange them in such a way as to reveal their essential and spiritual relations to oneanother. Leaving out all that is irrelevant, he has to connect the significant facts by chains of reasoning, and also to make, as it were, bridges of feeling between them by a sort of ladder, get the whole thing in a connected form into your head, and give you a spiritual, political, social, or religious consciousness. Literally, then, the work of the artist is to create mind. Mr Campbell, for instance, has not merely to save your soul; that would be a very simple thing if you have a soul; his real difficulty is to create your soul; and he can only do that by placing before you the picture of the world and the significance of it, so that you become, not merely a person possessed of accurate information, but in the largest sense a human being, which means to a certain extent a poet, a person susceptible to art.

Now, some artists will say to me, with disgust, "Why, you are declaring that art should be didactic!" I do declare that; I say that all art at the fountainhead is didactic, and that nothing can produce art except the necessity of being didactic. I say, not in the spirit of vulgar abuse, but in the solemnest Scriptural use of the terms, that the man who believes in art for art's sake is a fool; that is to say, a man in a state of damnation. It is possible for a man to be a fool, and yet to be an accurate observer, even to be an artist of considerable power. Thackeray, for instance, was a more accurate observer than Dickens, but he was inferior to him in his power of judgment. You almost always agree with Dickens—who was a great man and a great artist—in his judgments, but you continually find Thackeray perversely admiring the wrong things—he had not shaken his soul free from a false, social standard. Again, if you compare the neo-Darwinians with a writer like Samuel Butler, you see that men may be admirable naturalists, as far as the observation and classification of phenomena go, but absolutely deplorable philosophers. Charles Darwin was not a Darwinian in the sense that some of his followers, notably Weismann, are; they have taken all the knowledge Darwin provided and added to it, and deduced from it a fatalistic conception of the universe. They have made it a soulless accident, and tried to convince us that all that has happened in the world would have happened just the same if there had not been such a thing as consciousness.

Now, Samuel Butler was a great artist, and also keenly interested in science, and his philosophy was a very different one from that of present-day Darwinians. It requires a tremendous, and even heartbreaking, effort to produce a work of art, and no consideration of mere money-making will induce a man to make it. As a matter of fact, the inducement does not exist, because the man who produces a really new and original work of art always gets far more kicks than hapence. The odd thing is that when, for the first time, a new work of art comes into the world people do not look at it with indifference, but they are moved to the most furious and violent indignation. That has been the history of nearly all the great works of art that have made a new epoch. They have cost a tremendous effort; and the point I want to make is that nothing will nerve a man to make that effort except the necessity of being didactic; that is to say, in the words of the Bible [Jer. xx. 9], unless the word is in his heart as a burning fire shut up in his bones, and he is weary with forbearing—nothing short of that will induce a man to make the tremendous effort of creating a new art and bringing it into the world.

And great artists, in order to get a hearing, have to fascinate their hearers; they have to provide a garment of almost supernatural beauty for the message they have to deliver. Therefore, when a man has a message to deliver in literature, with great effort and toil he masters words until he can turn them into music. He becomes a master of rhetoric that affects you like music. You cannot read it as you do the paragraphs in The Times that contain mere accurate information; it acts on your senses and imagination in some strange way that, although you do not altogether understand the content of it, yet you feel that it is a great ringing message to you, a penetrating message that goes home. It startles you, and you take an extraordinary delight in it. The great musician who has a new message must somehow or other find new methods and combinations of sound. When Beethoven has written his symphonies and discovered new charms in sound, and, after the usual struggle with the recalcitrants against the message, people have begun to appreciate the new beautiful music, then there comes a succession of musicians who are not really artists in the sense of being creators, but are only confectioners. Thus, after Bach and Beethoven comes Schubert, who writes symphonies and songs that are a pure delight, but they are made of sugar from beginning to end; and there are people who prefer confectionery to the bread of life— for a time. The works of the great masters are the only things that really last. After the confectioner, who deals in derivatives, not originals, comes the popularizer; and we have to recognize that the average man cannot always take the message direct from the great mind. If you want to win people away from the older and narrower forms of what used to be called religion, which I call irreligion, you not only want the great spiritual seers and the German Higher Critics, you want an intermediary, such as Matthew Arnold. On religious subjects I never could read Arnold, but other people find him helpful. Let me mention a little personal thing which I beg you to keep an absolute secret. There came a time, as you know, in the career of Mrs Annie Besant when, from having been attached to a comparatively materialistic school of scientific thought, she became a theosophist. It so happened that Mrs Besant and I were working together in the Socialist movement for some years before that happened, and Mrs Besant was converted by Madame Blavatsky. Now, the curious thing is that what she learned from Madame Blavatsky I had been telling her for several years, and Mrs Besant never believed me and did believe Madame Blavatsky. When I said it she did not think I was serious, or she thought it was one of those curious twists in my mind which are perhaps due to the fact of my being an Irishman.

An enormous number of people who had the Bible preached at them in their youth were quite unable to get out of the book any of the truths that are in it. Many of them had to give up the Bible and learn those truths in other quarters, from literature and art of the secular kind—although no art is really secular in the sense of being contrasted with religion—they had to learn them from some source which they imagined was entirely unconnected with religion, and even hostile to it; and it was not until they had learned from an outside source that they came back to the Bible and discovered the truths that had been there all the time.

Take, for instance, the portrait of Christ in art. In the old Netherland school, in the pictures of Van Eyck He is represented as what He was, a working man; but in course of time He loses His simplicity, and people insist on His being depicted as a modern gentleman, dressed in beautiful robes.

If art can reveal the truth, art can also lie. An artist can be not only divinely inspired, but diabolically inspired, and one of the

46

greatest dangers of the present age is the use made of art to propagate lies instead of truth. In fact, the men who are using art to propagate truth are engaged in a constant struggle with the men who are using art to propagate falsehood. Napoleon was, in his way, a great artist, and he deliberately impressed the imagination of the French people, and indeed of the world, through artistic means for ends which finally became entirely corrupt. At the present moment a great deal of literary and rhetorical art is being employed for the purpose of driving this country into war with Germany—one of the most damnable crimes that could possibly be imagined. The moral is that you have got to be carefully on your guard against all this. There is a great deal of literature that is corrupt. The Bible is not a thing that is past and gone; new Bibles are being produced every day, true and false. There are people who will swallow as inspired revelation any sort of stuff that, so to speak, has the word Mesopotamia in it. And that is the just punishment of the people who taught us for so many years that our proper attitude towards the Bible was to shut our eyes and open our mouths. They thrust the Bible down our throats—unfortunately it does not do you any good when you take it in that way—but they entirely forgot that they created a precedent or formed a habit which induced other people to thrust their nostrums down our throats.

One word as to the incidental cruelty of art in perverting people's senses. One horror that affrights the eye in this country is the horrible contrast between a shining white collar and the color of human flesh. It could only have grown up among people who have become so little cultivated in art that they have lost their sense of color lines altogether. It is the sort of thing that a man like Velasquez could not endure. The only man who really looks well in black and white is a negro. By the study and love of art my eyes have become so cultivated that the spectacle of myself in a looking-glass or in a shop window in a shiny white collar would give me greater pain than does the utter contempt of the English public when it passes me by without one.

Be on your guard against the idolatry of art—the spirit which says, "This is the absolute, inspired truth, and we will burn anybody who questions it." That is at the bottom of the idolatry of the Bible which would like to burn people who do not believe that the story of the Garden of Eden is a record of literal fact, which in my childhood led to the practice of exhibiting in shop windows little Testaments with bullet wounds in them, and inscriptions pointing out that soldiers who had gone into battle with those Testaments in their pockets had been miraculously saved. That is as gross an act of idolatry as ever disgraced a South Sea Islander. Another example of idolatry in art is the picture of Christ given in Dean Farrar's Life of Christ, as compared with that given by Mr Campbell.

I admit to you that Mr Campbell has made me believe in Christ. I assure you that—it is, of course, my personal idiosyncrasy—the effect of Dean Farrar's Life of Christ on me was to make it quite impossible for me to believe in Christ at all; it would be too discouraging, too intolerable to believe in that particular Christ. In the case of many other people Dean Farrar's book has been the means of making them believe in Christ, making Christ real to them. I was the wrong sort of person for that treatment, and as a matter of fact I had for a long time ceased to regard Christ as a person who was true in the sense [in which] that term is used; I regarded Him as a work of fiction. I said, If you read the Epistles you see that they are historical documents, but if you read the Gospels you see that they are fiction, works of art. As I have pointed out to you, it does not follow that because a thing is not literally true it is false in any moral sense; on the contrary, it may be all the higher revelation on that very account. But I had ceased to believe that there was any reality at the back of it at all.

Now, Mr Campbell put before me a credible Christ; he recreated Christ for me, he reconstructed the environment, he made me see the Jesus of history in a way that I had not done before. He picked out the significant facts in the way I have described and placed before me something credible. What was more, he placed before me something that was interesting. What was more, he placed before me something which I desired to believe in, which on the whole I was quite content to believe in. I said, Here at last is really something which an educated man living in the twentieth century can believe, and here also is a

SOCIALISM AND MEDICINE

Person whose ideas are worth examining; here is a Person, by the way, a great many of whose ideas are coming to the front again after having been completely submerged for centuries in a great flood of something that called itself Christianity, but which was frank irreligion, frank commercialism. Dean Farrar had the power of drawing and making real a certain figure which responded to the needs of some people; on the other hand, a different type of artist is able to put another figure before you, and able immediately to make you believe where other people have entirely failed. There you have two Christs, very strongly contrasted; and yet it is conceivable that the most harmonious co-operation may exist between the people who believe in the Christ as conceived by Dean Farrar and the people who believe in Christ as Mr Campbell represents Him. To me they are different conceptions, but I do not say that either is untrue; each of them is a revelation of a particular type of mind and character. It is my belief, to which nobody else is committed, that because Mr Campbell among you has thrown off the priest and has become the inspired artist, that that is the reason he has come to share the privileges of the artist, to inspire love, and to escape the odium of the priest.

SOCIALISM AND MEDICINE

(Paper read before the Medico-Legal Society, London, 16 February 1909. *Transactions of the Medico-Legal Society 1908–1909*)

Since I have no professional qualifications of any kind, I should just like to say a word as to what emboldens me to address the Society on this particular subject.

I was born in the year 1856. That does not seem—if I may judge from the expression of your faces—to convey very much to you; but if you will remember that Darwin's Origin of Species was published in 1859 you will understand that I belong to a generation which, I think, began life by hoping more from Science than perhaps any generation ever hoped before, and, possibly, will ever hope again. I give the date in order to get out of the minds of any of you who may entertain such an idea that I am in any way hostile to science. Science will always be extraordinarily interesting and hopeful to me. At the present moment we are passing through a phase of disillusion. Science has not lived up to the hopes we formed of it in the 1860s; but those hopes left a mark on my temperament that I shall never get rid of till I die. Therefore I have, more or less, all my life concerned myself with science, because throughout my lifetime science has been very largely going wrong on social questions. I may say that almost all my life it has been my good fortune to number amongst my best friends members of the medical profession. During rather more than half my life I could not afford to pay doctor's fees at all; during the other part of my life I could afford to pay them better than most people; but it never made the slightest difference in the way of medical attendance to me. I have always had the very best private medical attendance and advice, and the fact that I hardly ever took it has not created the slightest coolness between the profession and myself.

Now, the doctor of the present day has been practically driven into the position of a private tradesman; and the first thing I want you to take note of is that the medical profession has never really accepted that position except insofar as it was forced to accept it. Theoretically it has never accepted it at all. But the facts have been too strong for the theory. Nowadays almost all the old pretensions and delicacies are dropped. A doctor gives you an opinion and you ask him what you owe him as boldly as you say "How much?" to a shopkeeper; but I can remember the time when you did not do that—when the pretense still remained that the doctor's fee was an honorarium. You paid it rather furtively, and he received it with an air of surprise and gratification as a *present* which he by no means demanded or expected. You will find some of the older medical men still have that manner: the younger men simply take their money and make no sort of pretense about it.

Nevertheless, trade in medical advice has never been formally recognized, and never will be; for you must realize that, whereas competition in ordinary trade and business is founded on an elaborate theoretic demonstration of its benefits, there has never been anyone from Adam Smith to our own time who has attempted such a demonstration with regard to the medical profession. The idea of a doctor being a tradesman with a pecuniary interest in your being ill is abhorrent to every thoughtful person. You find that advertizing in the ordinary way is a thing forbidden; you find that, when a professional man has become so successful that he wants to "weed out" his poorer patients and keep his richer ones, he resorts to the College of Physicians to raise his prices; but the College makes him relinquish forever the power of recovering his fees in the County Court, which is what the ordinary trading physician has to do very largely at the present time.

Now, you must thoroughly understand, when I call the ordinary private practitioner a tradesman, I am not reproaching him in any way. If I were anybody else it would not be necessary for me to make that statement; but the folly that seems to attack all my press colleagues when they report any public utterance or mine also infects my audiences, and leads, too often, to the assumption that everything I mention I mention in a disparaging way. I am certain if I made a remark about Westminster Abbey tomorrow to the effect that it is a remarkable building, we should see newspaper paragraphs next day headed "Bernard Shaw sneers at Westminster Abbey." I assure you I am speaking of this—as I do of all subjects—in an entirely dispassionate way. The doctor is a tradesman; and I want to point out that he has no alternative to being a tradesman. There being no exhaustive State organization of his profession, naturally the doctor is forced by circumstances—however repugnant to his feelings it may be—to go into the commerce of healing and to become a professional "medicine man"—a professional healer—the grossest of impostors, a man who sells cures, because that is what the public go to him for. He has to resort to the County Court to recover his fees; and he has no standard fees of any kind. The great mass of the medical profession have to get what they can—and be very glad to get it; and at the other end of the scale you find that even for operations of great importance there is no fixed fee. The operator gets what he can when he operates on the millionaire— he bleeds him, not only physically, but to the utmost of his ability in the metaphorical sense of the word.

51

One result of this compulsory commercial competition in the medical profession is that it has made the doctor most appallingly and humiliatingly poor. I do not suppose many gentlemen listening to me in this room are what may be called abjectly poor; but the average doctor of the present time is an abjectly poor man.

I will give you a little history which I have given in public before to non-professional audiences, and that is the history of one of my numerous uncles. I had many uncles: in fact, I can illustrate almost the entire history of the nineteenth century from the personal adventures of my uncles. Now, this uncle [Walter Gurly] was an Irish doctor—then a higher class creature than an English doctor! He was a man of property—Irish property; but as his father lived to be a very old man he had to take to a profession, and he took to the medical profession. He qualified as M.R.C.S., and for some portion of his life, being an adventurous person, he preferred to go about the world in ships and to act as surgeon to a Transatlantic steamship company. Towards middle life he married, and thereupon came to England and bought a practice. When I was a young man in Dublin several of my intimate friends were doctors; and they were rash enough to talk shop with freedom before me. Among other things, they used to discuss their fees; and it always came to the same thing—none of them would take less than a guinea; none would tolerate a man that took less than a guinea, or consider him a gentleman, or a man that they ought to go into consultation with. Of course, they had to make concessions in a poor country like Ireland: they would give you four visits for the guinea; but they would not go beyond that: they would not take five shillings for one visit. My uncle had these ideas when he bought his practice. It was one of those nice practices where your patients live mostly in country houses, with parks, carriages, and horses. My uncle had a horse and trap, and maintained his position of an Irish gentleman, and had a great contempt for poor doctors. One rival came and settled in the district—a disgraceful person who took half-crown fees: my uncle's contempt for him was beyond expression. He would not meet him in consultation, and considered that such a person should be wiped off the face of the earth. This was at Leyton, known to you now as a part of London which is covered all over with small houses lived in by men some of whom are fortunate enough to be laborers earning a guinea or eighteen shillings a week, but mainly by clerks with fifteen shillings a week and a family, and appearances to keep up. Their little houses are built on the parks and country estates to which my uncle used to pay his visits.

The change occurred before he had been more than three or four years in practice. I saw the whole process going on, and after it had completed itself I used occasionally to go down and stay with my uncle. My uncle's clothes at that time had become very shabby, and the horse and trap had been sold. I slept in the next room to him and occasionally heard the night bell; and this is the sort of thing I used to hear: "Who is that?" "Who did you say?" "What road?" "Oh; have you got the money?"—"Rattle it at the tube then." You know, ladies and gentlemen, if you were a doctor practising at Leyton you would not think that funny. It may appear to you to be one of my jokes, but it is—like most of my jokes—an exceedingly serious matter. I took occasion after one of these experiences to say to my uncle: "You used to be very indignant with So-and-so because he took a half-crown fee; would you take a half-crown fee?" "Yes," he said, "and be very glad to get it." I said, "What is the smallest fee you would take now?" He replied, "The Royal Mint has not yet coined so small a coin but that I would take it."

Now, the problem of the medical profession is not really at the present time a problem of gentlemen in Harley-street who are either rich or pretend to be rich. It is the problem of people like my uncle. Remember that four out of five of the adult male population of this country are laborers working for weekly wages. In London they have the benefit of the very best medical advice: they get the Harley-street advice: they go to the hospital and get operated upon by the most skilful surgeons. But they also form clubs and offer a practitioner like my uncle the post of club doctor. I do not know if any gentleman here has any club practice. If he takes one and cannot afford an assistant, one of the things that will happen to him is that he will give up ever taking off his clothes! The night bell of such a practice never stops. One loses the habit of going to bed under such circumstances.

The man who has to endure this poverty and slavery is a man who has probably in the early part of his life done a great deal of gratuitous work, and to the end of his life will continue to do so. He has to suffer all the effects of competition like a tradesman; but a great deal more is expected from him than from a tradesman. Nobody expects a baker to allow any hungry person to come into his shop and take a loaf without paying for it; but doctors must not allow anybody to perish for want of medical assistance if they are in a position to render it, whether they get paid or not. They always have to give a good deal of gratuitous advice. Furthermore, when their actual work stops through illness or anything else, their earning stops. If you compare them with the man of business or with the ordinary tradesman, you will find the tradesman or man of business has a great advantage in this way. When the tradesman leaves his shop, business does not stop: he leaves a shopman there to do his work. A man of business can go to his club and to public meetings, and spend a great deal of time in telling other people how busy he is; and in the meantime the whole machinery of his business is being worked by shopmen, porters, clerks, and so on. Now, none of you gentlemen here can leave a message to say, "I have gone out to Hurlingham,"—or something of the kind—"my butler will attend to you." Directly you stop working your earning powers and your income stop.

You have appearances also to keep up, which means that you have to incur heavy expenses solely to gratify the vanity of your patients. Just as people insist on their servants wearing a particular livery, so they insist on their doctor wearing a particular sort of hat and coat. He has to have a carriage and horses; and even if he is not married he has to have a house when two rooms would be amply sufficient; and he has to keep a staff of servants to clean that house. So much so that a physician in practice in, say, Kensington, will tell you that his living wage is about £1000 a year: that is to say, he cannot begin to save, or to insure his life (the practical test), until he has turned the point of spending £1000 a year. All this is expected by the patients. Without it he would lose his practice. Now you see why it is that even doctors who are in a tolerable practice are, many of them, much poorer than they appear to be, and why the great mass of doctors have to be described as miserably poor men.

And now I have brought you face to face with the attitude of Socialism towards the doctor. The attitude of Socialism towards the poor man is always that the poor man is necessarily a bad and dangerous man. The attitude of the man who is not a Socialist is that poverty is a very good thing; that it develops character, and in other particulars has a beneficial effect. He shews the poor every sign of sympathy except becoming poor himself: that step he never takes! But the really sensible man—whether a Socialist or not—always regards poverty as a bad thing and a poor man as a dangerous man. If you are going to have doctors you had better have doctors well off, just as if you are going to have a landlord you had better have a rich landlord. Taking all the round of professions and occupations, you will find that every man is the worse for being poor, and the doctor is a specially dangerous man when poor.

For the doctor's poverty, like the layman's, drives him necessarily into doing things which he would not do if he were independent. He is—like most men—as honest as he can afford to be. But he cannot afford to be scientifically honest. Ordinary commonplace honesty is a cheap thing. The honesty that prevents your stealing my umbrella does not cost you much. But scientific honesty is a monstrously expensive thing. I remember once discussing with a well-known bacteriologist [Sir Almroth Wright] the cost of the really scientific carrying out of certain apparently simple operations. We took the ordinary half-crown operation—vaccination. We calculated what it would cost a private practitioner to carry out a vaccination scientifically in a thoroughly honest way, and we came to the conclusion that the cost would be about £2000. I do not put that down as an absolutely trustworthy figure, but all of you who know anything about the cost of a laboratory properly equipped for vaccine-therapy, and the time and skilled labor needed for determining the patient's opsonic index, will not be surprised by the figure. My uncle simplified and cheapened his practice enormously by allowing himself to be convinced by clinical observation that there is no such thing as infection, and that all the latest methods in therapeutics are fads; and many a doctor today agrees with him because he cannot afford more expensive scientific views.

The truth is that the carrying out of all the various hygienic measures which doctors know to be necessary would be so expensive that the slightest attempt to enforce them on patients, or to let patients know that the absence of them was dangerous, would cost a man his practice and his livelihood. If you take the great mass of patients that doctors have at the present time, what they want is not really medicine or operations, but *money*. They want better food and better clothes, and more frequent changes of them. They want well-ventilated and well-drained houses. But what is the use of prescribing these things to unfortunate people who can hardly keep body and soul together? If a doctor goes to an ordinary patient and says, "Well, my friend, you have to go to Egypt, or to St Moritz, or to have your house put in order to the tune of two or three hundred pounds; or you have to take such-and-such a diet"—which will involve spending more on the patient in one day than is available for the whole week for the entire family—if he orders things like that, the patient will get another doctor. The patient, not being able to afford scientific treatment, demands cheap cures; so, as the doctor has no other means of livelihood than pleasing the patient, he prescribes cheap cures, and thereby becomes a swindler.

I am speaking in a cold scientific way: we must look at these things in that way. The moment you go to the real problem that the doctor has to tackle (that is, the problem of keeping his patient in health), you see at once the truth of what I have to say. You find that not only does the ordinary patient demand cheap cures, but he has the greatest objection to sanitary legislation of any kind. He knows too well what will happen if he reports his landlord to the local authority. I served for six years on a public health committee in London, and I know something about medical officers of health and private practitioners, and the significant contrasts between them. On one occasion we got a fit of doing our duty. There was a certain street which was in an abominably insanitary condition. We had had the power for years to come down on the landlords and force them to put the houses in proper order and, if necessary, do it ourselves and make them pay. At last we used it, and made every landlord in that street put his houses into good sanitary repair. The result was, the landlords turned out every family into the street and got in a better class of tenant, leaving the unfortunate evicted ones to wander about the streets for days. They would not move on. The police were sent to shove them about; and what with shoving them about and telling them they must go, and their making up their minds to the inevitable, we at last got rid of them, but not till there had been a public scandal and one old man had died. That is what happens when you attempt to carry out genuine hygiene.

You will understand that the neighbors all took up the outcry against the cruel sanitary authorities; and if any doctor who attended on them had made the slightest hint about the drainage, or said anything that seemed to lead to sending in the sanitary inspectors, that doctor would never have got another case amongst them. So you see that our very Public Health Acts force quackery on poor doctors. The doctor, depending on his patient for his livelihood, is dependent on the patient's ignorance, and finally has to flatter all his delusions and give him the bottle, and let him believe when he gets well that the bottle cured him. What else can he do? He is rather like the sort of person you get when you engage a servant from one of those big charitable institutions that train servants. These servants are trained in a magnificent building (it has to be a magnificent building or people will not subscribe to it), and the girl is taught how to work in a kitchen with most elaborate ranges and all sorts of scientific appliances, and then everything is taken upstairs in lifts and distributed, and so on. Then she is sent out as a servant in a lodging-house, where there are no scientific appliances. She has to begin to learn how to cook in a back kitchen, how to drag everything up and down stairs herself, and how to go without kettles and saucepans, and make the most miserable shifts, and after some time she unlearns what she learned before.

That is what happens to a doctor. He gets his training at the hospital, a completely equipped building beautifully built with no right angles but rounded corners for sweeping the dust out of, with windows that open entirely to the outer air; and then, after all that (exactly like the servant), he is suddenly pitched into a poor district and has to go through life in surgically dirty clothes and do his work in surgically dirty rooms with surgically dirty people who cannot afford the necessities of science; and he gets a sort of skill at it. He has to adapt himself to these conditions, and it is perfectly wonderful the sort of results he manages to get out of it. He becomes—on an unscientific basis—a competent man of his own sort; and when you see what he does and how he pulls people through, you really begin to think he is more admirable than the men at the top of the profession who can order and prescribe what they like regardless of the cost. Not that these men at the top of their profession have not also a great deal to struggle with in the way of ignorance and superstition in their patients. I have often wondered why some of the most eminent members of the profession are so fond of sending their patients away to the ends of the earth. It cannot be altogether generosity towards their brethren in St Moritz and Egypt. My belief is that they get so sick of their patients that they say, "After all, I am full of practice: I can replace more patients than I can lose. I cannot stand these people any more: I must send them away."

Now I want for a moment to contrast the general practitioner, as I have been painting him, with the medical officer of health. I am not going now to speak of the sort of medical officer of health you sometimes meet with in the country—a man who gives for a very mean payment a portion of his time, and makes the rest of his living by private practice. He has been found out now, and we are going to get rid of him and combine our small local authorities together so that they can get the entire time of a first-rate man for the whole district. It was my good fortune when I was on a local authority to have Dr [John Frederick] Sykes to manage things in my particular parish [St Pancras]; and a very hard time he had in dealing with my fellow vestrymen, or borough councillors as they became. He used such troublesome words as streptococcus; and though they would not have paid him so much if they had always known what he was talking about, they suspected that the streptococcus was no better than it ought to be. He had a great deal of trouble; nevertheless his position was a most independent and responsible one compared to that of a private practitioner. For example, he was judged altogether by the vital statistics of his district. Dr Sykes's income did not get larger when the district got sick. The private practitioners' did. They revelled in an epidemic.

I remember going through one smallpox epidemic. Vaccination raged: you could see the private practitioners getting new ties and new hats. When the death-rate went up they always looked better off and happier. That was not the case with the medical officer of health: he looked more worried: it was a bad time for him. From time to time the question of his salary came before the borough council. There was always a fight, because you could not get the ordinary borough councillor to understand why several hundred a year should be paid to a doctor who gave no bottles. But there was only one point upon which it could be argued, and that was the vital statistics of the district. Then Dr Sykes was independent of those borough councillors: they had no power to dismiss him. If a jerry builder wanted to evade the by-laws and to get rid of a doctor who was determined to carry them out (I may mention that this only happens when the builders on the Council are housing speculators: the builder who builds to order supports the by-laws, as they make additional work and profit for him) they had no power to discharge him. The Local Government Board had the final say in the matter; and if an attempt was made to damage him with the Local Government Board, the Local Government Board had only to ask: "Do the figures shew that he is neglecting his duty? If he is not, why do you want to get rid of him?" So, unless some unheard-of breach of duty was revealed, his position was secure. I take it the medical officer of health is in an ideal position—the Socialist position—the position that one wants Socialism to place all doctors in.

Now I come to the question of the organization of the medical profession. A doctor at the present time is expected to do everything connected with his profession. Now, we do not apply that to the other professions. The judge sentences a man to be hanged, but he is not expected to be the hangman. If he were a doctor he would be expected to be the hangman. A bishop is not expected to blow the organ; if he were a doctor he would be expected to blow the organ. A field-marshal is not expected to play the drum, but if he were a doctor he would be expected to fight a battle one day and the next take a job from the drummer boy. You have men of extraordinary dexterity as operators, whose whole time should be reserved for the most difficult cases; and you find these men poulticing whitlows and doing trumpery dressings that should be done by the nurse. You find them prescribing for ladies who have the same reason for asking for tonics (with a good deal of ether in them) as the charwoman has for asking for gin.

I daresay this sometimes makes men resourceful. You may have noticed how resourceful some country doctors are—how they are equal at a moment's notice to almost any occasion. In town you can call in a specialist; consequently the London general practitioner is apt to be rather timid. But in the country a doctor may have to tackle an operation which he has never done, and perhaps never seen done before; and if he does not do it to perfection, at any rate the patient does not know it. But the end of all this rough and ready resourcefulness is that the best men get their time shockingly wasted.

I take it doctors are very like other men. I know that I hurt the feelings of a great many doctors by saying so, but you must allow me to take it for granted—certainly as long as the present system of qualification exists—that all doctors are not equally able. There is a main body of average practitioners, a minority of first-class men, and another minority of well-intentioned murderers. I remember once asking the late explorer Stanley, who had some experience of men in Africa and elsewhere, what percentage of men are any good. "Six per cent.," he replied without hesitation. I said, "You are pretty pat with it"; and he said, "Yes, you get a lot of fellows who are all right when they are led; but men who can be left to lead—six per cent. and no more."[1]

___

[1] In Stanley's Autobiography, published after the delivery of this address, he gives "one in six" (more than 16½ per cent.) as the proportion of educable men to rank and file. But in conversation with me, and with special reference to African exploration and the proportion of men who could be trusted with unaided leadership, his reply was as given above.—G. B. S.

Now, I do not think the vagabond adventurers on whom explorers have to rely for manning their expeditions are typical of the men working at home in the professions. I should think the percentage of leaders in the medical profession would be higher than in the exploring profession; but I think ten per cent. would be high enough. Taking the profession as a whole, it must present a classification of men corresponding fairly to the classification of cases into those which an ordinary practitioner can handle, those in which he requires the counsel and supervision of a superior man, and those which can only be handled by a specialist who handles nothing else. Consequently, in order to get the maximum of hygienic influence and the greatest economy in using the skill of the profession, you want to get it organized so that different grades shall do different work and that the time of the best men shall not be wasted on mere routine. Such organization is impossible while private practice is the rule: it can only be done if the profession is organized publicly by the State.

Now for a word on the economics and psychology of private practice. Medical practice will never be put on a scientific basis as long as the private practitioner is in his present position of being at the mercy of the patient through being employed by the patient and paid by the patient and liable to be sacked by the patient. There is no use in giving the patient advice that the patient does not believe in. If you will go back in the literary history of this country as far as the Pickwick Papers you will gather a good deal of Mr Pickwick's notions of hygiene. You will find that he believed that all healthy and decent people should sleep in four-poster beds with curtains drawn closely round to exclude the night air. I think it is possible that at the time when Mr Pickwick was supposed to have lived there may have been one or two doctors who did know that the air inside the curtains of a four-poster bed was not good to breathe; but if any doctor at that time had said as much he would have lost his practice. If Mr Pickwick had been told to sleep near an open window or take a cold bath every morning, he would probably have given the doctor who told him so to the police as a lunatic. You must remember [that] even as late as the year 1840, when the unfortunate

Boddington, of Sutton Coldfield, wrote a pamphlet declaring that the proper way to treat pulmonary consumption was the open air way, he was practically ruined. He was driven out of practice as a dangerous crank who made his profession ridiculous. And so he did: the public thought his views ridiculous. If anybody had said to Mr Pickwick that to take a glass of brandy and water whenever he felt cold was not the best way to keep himself warm and in good health, he would have lost Mr Pickwick's confidence forever.

At the present time a doctor's danger lies in the opposite direction. He sometimes finds his patients in the habit of getting up at six o'clock and walking on the dewy grass with bare feet. He does not dare say that this is overdoing it, or that taking cold baths is a rheumatic practice, or that perhaps a glass of port wine a day is no worse than two bottles of ginger ale. The patients who do these things are really just as ignorant as Mr Pickwick. They may be right—I do not know whether they are—but they are acting without any more scientific authority. The walking on the wet grass and the vegetarianism, and so on (I am a vegetarian as you know) is all just as wildly unscientific as the old plan of keeping out the night air; and, I suggest, one of the things you want to release the doctor from is that abject dependence on his patient which at present forces him to flatter every fashionable fad and practise every fashionable quackery.

Mind: not for a moment do I suggest that the doctor should have any power to coerce the patient even for his own good. British liberty includes the right to prefer Christian Science to medical advice, and woe betide you if you attack that liberty. But the doctor must be equally free to tell the patient that he is a fool pursuing a delusion if that is the doctor's real opinion. Otherwise the doctors will presently find themselves forced to pretend that they are Christian Scientists. Public opinion will be the final arbiter in any case; but it is important to give every doctor an interest in educating the public scientifically, whereas now the doctor has the very greatest interest in preventing the patient knowing anything at all. You even write your prescriptions in Latin. Education only leads to the doctor being found out; and this is really hard on the doctor, because what the patient really finds out is his own ignorance and that of the generation that corrupted the doctor in olden times.

Until the doctor is independent of his patients he can never be independent of fashion. I should like a scientific man to take up the psychology of fashion. A fashion is nothing but an induced epidemic. Your Bond-street tradesmen are able to take their patients (if I may use that expression) and compel them to buy things they do not want; to replace clothes that are not worn out; to exchange pretty and comfortable articles for ugly and uncomfortable ones because of fashion. So is it with the doctor in private practice. In my own recollection there have been many changes of fashion in medicines and operations. I can remember the time when everybody was given mercury, and then the time when mercury was put out of countenance by salicylic acid. Still more extraordinary is the fashion in operations. It is very curious, but people get a craze for operations. You have people who insist on your cutting out their vermiform appendices, or their tonsils, or their uvulas. Even the most serious and terrifying operations are in demand. I do not wish to be extravagant, but I cannot believe that all the ovariotomies that were performed after Spencer Wells found out how to do it successfully were necessary. Of course, in the surgical and medical professions, as in all others, there are men who will do anything by which they can make money with impunity; but all surgeons are not recklessly selfish, and I have known of ladies and gentlemen who had heard and read so much about operations that they felt that they could not live without them. Such people are a tremendous temptation to poor doctors.

Next in importance to the need of curing the doctor's poverty comes the need for curing him of his delusion that statistics are a matter of common sense and not of special training. Statistics in the hands of an amateur are much more dangerous than drugs. Let me take an imaginary case. Supposing, for instance, some eminent medical man managed to convince the public, and the whole profession too, that every child needs a pint of brandy per month, but that care must be taken to administer the doses only when the child's digestion is in perfect order and its teeth sound. I have no hesitation in saying that presently there would be an overwhelming body of evidence to prove that the brandy treatment was the real secret of health in children. There would soon be a demand to give the children a gallon of brandy, and the brandy would be increased until the good that accrued from the child's teeth and digestion being attended to would be outweighed; but until that point the improvement would be attributed to the brandy instead of to the real cause. It is extremely difficult to get people to understand the gigantic difference between attention and neglect. It hardly matters what you prescribe for people if it will only have the effect of getting them to attend to some point of health that they have not attended to before.

When I began my public health career there were certain things we made people do to their houses at great expense; and they would complain: "Why is it that this particular thing you force us to do is perfectly different from the thing you forced us to do a few years ago? You actually prosecute us today for having a contrivance in our houses which you compelled us to put in a few years ago." We had not an answer ready for that. One day on the Health Committee a question came up with regard to a mica valve not being in order, and a builder said: "Ought we to prosecute a man for that? A mica valve never is in order, and never can be." However, the committee said that under the by-law the man must be prosecuted. I said I thought if mica valves did not work we should give up compelling people to put them in, and I thought the committee very stupid; but now I think they were very wise, because the mica valve necessitated the plumber being sent for. It is perfectly possible that the particular type of sanitary appliance we were then enforcing increased the death-rate by, say, five per cent. But if the incidental attention it involved at the same time reduced the death-rate by, say, fifteen per cent., there was a net gain of ten per cent. It is not until you have entirely substituted attention for neglect that the evidence you get for the effect of your particular specific or appliance on the death-rate is worth twopence. Apart from its indirect effect, it may be doing more harm than good.

Then there is the prophylactic illusion. I can prove to you on overwhelming statistical evidence that two of the surest ways of preventing deaths from zymotic diseases are the wearing of a tall hat and familiarity with Wagner's music. I will undertake to shew that in the case of people who do not wear tall hats, or do not know Wagner's music, deaths are much more frequent. The trick is very simple. You make a law enforcing some prophylactic—vaccination, or anything else. Every householder is compelled to obey that law because the police can get at him and make him suffer. The one person you cannot get at is the tramp, whose habits make him horribly subject to disease. Consequently, you have only to contrast the mortality among the householders and the vagabonds to make out a tremendous case in favor of any prophylactic you can impose on the householders.

Supposing a hundred years ago somebody put forward a theory that the real source of typhus fever lies in the top joint of the little finger, and that if everybody had that cut off typhus fever would disappear. Had that been carried out, the theory would seem proved beyond doubt at the present time to a large number of medical men and the general public, because there is no denying that typhus has disappeared. It is shown that cancer and madness are enormously on the increase. I am not very alarmed, because a great many things are called cancer which were not called cancer before; and we are putting up the standard of sanity —though in my opinion it is not high enough yet. Well, on the one hand you have the believer in vaccination saying that the disappearance of smallpox is due to vaccination; and on the other hand you have the disbeliever saying that the increase of cancer and madness is due to vaccination. There are bushels of statistics to prove both contentions to the complete conviction of people who dont understand the art of the statistician.

You find, too, a constant danger of people making mistakes because they exaggerate the prevalence of disease. Take hydrophobia. The people who are most impressed by the Pasteur Institute believe that every person bitten by a mad dog must die of hydrophobia unless saved by cautery or inoculation. If that were true the Pasteur Institute would be the most wonderful place on the earth. In my youth hydrophobia was much discussed in medical circles in Dublin because one eminent physician contended that the cases were simply cases of tetanus from the lacerated wound caused by the bite. That was before the days of the bacillus. I heard some of these discussions, and at none of them was it assumed that the percentage of cases of hydrophobia following the bite of a mad dog was higher than two or three. No doubt this was guesswork, but it had the effect later on of making me doubt whether the Pasteur Institute was not killing people instead of curing them. I do not say that my doubts were justified, but nothing will remove them but a demonstration—if such a thing be possible—that the deaths at the Institute, rare as they are, are rarer than they certainly were before Pasteur was born. As to the hackneyed nonsense talked about the former prevalence of disfigurement from smallpox, it was repeated by Jenner himself before regular vaccination began. He attributed it to inoculation, and he describes smallpox epidemics of so mild a character that the persons attacked did not go to bed or even stay in the house. Again I say, you cannot be too suspicious of amateur statistics.

The last thing I want to say to you is this: You must have the medical profession socialized because medical men are finding themselves more and more driven to claim powers over the liberty of the ordinary man which could not possibly be entrusted to any private body whatever. If you are going to have compulsory hygiene (and remember every day you are making strides in that direction) the compulsion must be democratic and not professional. We are going to get rid of vaccination: we have done with that. But the discarding of vaccination does not mean going back to the *status quo ante*, but the institution of more scientific methods of immunization. We shall still impose on the citizen measures which have not been imposed on him before, many of which he will resent, and will hear fiercely criticized and denounced. Now, if we are going to do these things, and going to compel people on the scale on which you are going to compel them, then there must be democratic control. It would be intolerable tyranny unless it were controlled by the people.

Take the case of the Peculiar People. When I was a young man the Peculiars were never convicted, and for this reason—the case was always the same—that when the doctor was examined and the lawyer defending the prisoner came to the question "Do you swear that if the case had had medical treatment the patient would have survived?" the doctor always—as a man of honor—said he could not give any such evidence. How could he? Perhaps it was a diphtheria case, and perhaps several of his own patients had died of diphtheria. If he had sworn such a thing the logical course would have been to have prosecuted him for the murder of his own patients. The standard of intelligence (I will not say of honor) in the medical profession has since fallen so low that doctors now swear in the box that if they had been called in the child would have survived, and the unfortunate Peculiar is sent to prison. I do not know how doctors can bring themselves to do it; for however strong the presumption may be that a little scientific attendance would have saved the case, the doctor who swears it takes upon himself the attributes of God Almighty. Nevertheless, it is very hard for him to let the child be slaughtered (as he believes) with impunity because its father prefers the advice of St James to that of a properly qualified medical man.

More and more we are being driven to treat the whole community as we treat the Peculiars: that is to say, there is coming to be a sharp opposition between the authority of the parent and the authority of the doctor; and we are coming more and more to the point of giving the doctor the power of deciding what is to be done with the child, and denying that power to the parent. It is a startling change, and one that will be fought energetically. But we are going step by step in that direction. We are sending the child to school in spite of the parent, and having the child weighed and measured and its teeth seen to at school in spite of the parent. We are feeding 55,000 school children in London without consulting their parents as to the healthiness of the diet, and we shall soon be clothing them on the same terms. It is impossible to leave the powers over our bodies and souls which all this involves in the hands of private practitioners with private pecuniary interests and private class prejudices, not to mention private scientific partisanships. You must make up your mind to it that the inevitable result must be socialization of the medical profession.

What will happen to the surviving private practitioner when you have the doctor in the responsible, and dignified, and independent position of a public servant instead of a private tradesman I do not know. I daresay there will still be private practitioners: there is nothing in Socialism to suggest that there will not be; but both doctor and patient will have what Socialism will provide for everybody: that is, a refuge from private enterprize if they desire it. If a doctor finds his dependence on the caprice and ignorance of patients intolerable, he will always under Socialism be able to get an independent position in the public service. With that alternative available he could not be compelled to commit the humiliating concessions and the treacheries to science that are now forced on him. Having the alternative of public service he will be in as independent a position as if he were a public servant; and on the other hand the patient, having the alternative of calling in a public doctor whose sole interest is to get him well as soon as possible, will be as well off with the private doctor as he would be with the public doctor.

DISCUSSION

Sir T. CLIFFORD ALLBUTT, K.C.B.—I was requested to speak tonight but I had no very clear idea of the line which would be taken, and I have not therefore prepared anything. But our profession was to be socialized. This revolution—or transformation —was to be applied with considerable scarification to ourselves; and yet, after all, Mr Shaw has behaved with much reticence and propriety, and I really think it would not pain Mr Shaw much to say that we—most of us—agree with very much that he has said. We all have our own trademarks; he has the trademark of socialism. The names of these things do not much matter; it is really the things themselves we are concerned about.

I suppose I have been asked to speak tonight because, last October, I addressed a large body of medical men in Manchester on the organization of the medical profession, and I think we have that very bright future before us as part of the organized body of society. What is the next thing to do? Why, to be healthy and to be happy. I entirely agree that in time, when these transformations take place, it will be much more honorable for our profession than must be the case in such practices as the large out-patient practice of a hospital; still more so among those very heavy labors of medical men in the poorest parts of our towns. Mr Shaw has said under those circumstances a man must do the best he can; but, after all, it is mixed up a great deal with what we might call magic. Is it not something handed down from the magical that we sent these people home with their bottles of medicine? No doubt they derive a great deal of comfort from those bottles of medicine. But it is quite obvious to us all that that must be a very transitory state of things.

In a certain district, after a very conscientious physician had worked in the guardians' hospital for years, and was going to retire, I said to the guardians, "This is an opportunity to bring this hospital in line with modern scientific medicine. By means of a medical school we can attach this to a great modern medical machine." I found it was rather like hitting a feather bed—not making much impression. But presently one of them said, "The fact is, the guardians do not want a particularly skilled or able medical man, because he will be wanting to be doing this and that, and it is very expensive; we would much rather go on—and we intend to go—in our own simple humdrum way, and to select the humblest man we can hear of, and carry things on as before." Although we may speak under different flags and give our opinions different colors, I think we shall all agree that Mr Bernard Shaw, when he takes up his sword, certainly slashes down to the quick, and I think we must admit at that quick there is a great deal of truth to be found, and expressed with a great deal of gentleness towards our own profession.

I think there is a great deal of difference between competition in trade and competition in a profession. If a man says, "I sell a better soap than my neighbor," the ordinary person can find out readily whether it is better or not. But when it comes to advertizing that "I, Jones, am a better man than Edwards or Wilkinson," that is a very different kind of competition, and I think we cannot put the two things together, because in the case of a doctor the public cannot find out, perhaps, whether they are in the hands of a skilful or an unskilful man.

Then about that reveling in epidemics—I do not attach much weight to the expression, but I think one ought to say this. I knew of one exceedingly able doctor in one of the Yorkshire dales who had a practice worth £1200 to £1400 a year; he had to contend with an epidemic of typhoid fever, and he set himself day and night to deal with the matter, and it broke his sleep and health. He did succeed in twenty years in eradicating that disease, and the result was he broke himself down and reduced his practice to £700 a year, at which figure his widow had to sell it. Now that is the kind of reveling in epidemics which I think is very common in our profession. I do say that the medical men of this country are actually cutting down their own incomes by their self-devoted attempts to put an end to the very epidemics which, it may be said, they have lived upon. I think that it is good that we have been led to realize tonight that, under whatever flag it may be, the position is a very unsatisfactory one, and that it does want some such entire transformation as that which Mr Shaw has sketched out for us.

Sir VICTOR HORSLEY.—We are all very indebted to Mr Shaw for his speech tonight. We had hoped to hear a speech on the nationalization of the medical profession. We did hear part of a speech on that subject. Anyone who listened to Mr Shaw must have felt he was anticipating the report of the Poor Law Commission which we shall have in our hands tomorrow. We are, as Mr Shaw says, face to face with the greatest social problem that the profession has had to meet. I am not going to follow Mr Shaw in his discussion on the conduct of medical men, or into his not very fully informed account of hydrophobia, etc. We have to consider what has been laid before us as a brilliant exhibition of the necessity of the reconstruction of our profession. It amounts to this—that from one point of view we are not organized as a profession, or we were not organized as a profession five or six years ago. Mr Shaw dates his existence from 1856, I mine from 1857, and the medical profession from 1858, and so on. But, ladies and gentlemen, what is the idea of organizing the profession? It is to ensure that every practitioner should make a living wage. I have no shame in being called a tradesman. I sell my knowledge, and in that respect I am a tradesman. I hope I am an honorable tradesman, and that honorable conduct stamps me as a professional man. Well, the British Medical Association is trying to organize the medical profession, in the sense that a man should obtain what he deserves. The interests of the medical profession are the interests of the public. Mr Shaw has told us of nationalizing of the profession, and a bringing into higher relief these associated interests. To put the medical man into a more honorable position is to ensure better treatment of the public. All we have to do is to see that the members of the profession are not going to lose by this transformation. We have the right to work, and we also have the right to be properly paid for that work.

I will not detain you further. I hope you agree that we owe Mr Shaw a debt of thanks for putting before us this nationalization of our profession in such a brilliant manner.

Dr F. J. Smith.—I feel as a member of this Society that no subject so interesting to the profession and to the public has ever come before it, and therefore we owe a debt of gratitude to Mr Bernard Shaw for his presence with us here tonight, and for the very evident interest the public, when informed of our movements, takes in the profession. I feel in two minds about Mr Bernard Shaw. One feels he has his serious aspect, and then he pokes his funny stick at us and then we feel a little hit on the raw. I am not sure that it is not good for us.

As to the socialization of the medical profession, I can certainly agree with Mr Bernard Shaw that socialism is coming. When I entered the hospitals there were sixty or seventy fellow students. Out of that number I believe I should be right in saying not more than two or three are at the present moment entirely supporting themselves by their public appointments. It is true that another ten or twelve are half or part timers. If we take the last few years we shall find instead of two out of sixty it is more a matter of about fifteen out of about forty who are entirely supporting themselves by their public work done at the public expense. Socialism in medicine (if by that term we are to mean that the medical man becomes the official servant of the public) is coming rapidly. But then it may be we have God before us in this matter or it may be we have Mammon. It is said we cannot serve them both; but I feel we may be going from one to the other when we substitute for our private patients—as our masters—a body of men steeped to the lips in ignorance of everything that hygiene means. We alone stand forth as the high priests of hygiene. Mr Bernard Shaw has told us of Dr Sykes's experience. That experience is by no means confined to Dr Sykes; it is even more rampant now (because there are more of them) than it was in Dr Sykes's day. We must be careful to mind we do not step from the frying-pan into the fire. We must try to make the public believe we are entirely disinterested in trying to educate them up to our standard of belief.

Dr LAWSON DODD.—I have no right—as a general practitioner—to address this meeting this evening, and I shall not take up more than a few moments in supporting the contentions that Mr Shaw has put forward, and which have been backed up so eloquently by Sir T. Clifford Allbutt.

I would just draw attention to two factors in the medical profession; the first is the start in life the medical student has when he changes his atmosphere after leaving the hospital. The particular weapons that he must use in catering for a large practice must be such things as social amenities, motor cars, capacity to play games and join various religious organizations; and he often ultimately gains success on account of the possession of some of these quite unimportant factors.

My second point is, there is nothing more true than what Mr Shaw has emphasized, namely, the unsatisfactory and demoralizing influence of competition in the profession. Whatever else it may do it tends to split up the profession, and break up that sense of brotherhood which should be the underlying principle of all professions, and especially the medical profession. I think the abolition of competition, and the placing of the profession on a co-operative footing, where a free interchange could take place, would do more than anything else to do away with that.

Then the profession is being faced by another form of competition, namely, the great public medical services. You have, to a large extent, already nationalized your profession. "Part of the host have crossed the flood, and part are crossing now." You have a very keen competition between the public medical service and the private, unorganized medical services. You have springing up what may be called preventive treatment, and school doctors, and so on. You cannot stem the tide, and I think the only way of escape is the way mentioned tonight. On those lines only will you be able to avoid the competition between practitioners which is degrading, and the competition between the private and public practitioner.

Mr BERNARD SHAW.—There is very little for me to reply to. I was very much gratified by the speech of Sir Clifford Allbutt; but I was not surprised to find that he and I are practically on the same platform. In any little public controversy I may have had on medical questions I think it must have been obvious to the cleverest of you, since I have generally acquitted myself pretty well, that I have very good prompting from within. The reason I write so admirably on medical subjects is that I always consult a highly qualified medical man first! I myself belong to a profession that is made up of quacks. In literature there is no qualification expected: anyone who can buy threepennyworth of stationery is free to turn author, and doctor the souls of the public in the literary way as best he can. But it is a profession for the honor of which I am very jealous; and I do not think there is any great disagreement possible between the professions. All men who really feel the public function of their profession, and all men who have what I may call the scientific point of honor, attach enormous importance to intellectual integrity. I believe it is impossible for them to come to any real disagreement on a question like the organization of the professions.

Sir Victor Horsley said something about the Report of the Poor Law Commission which will be published tomorrow. I know nearly as much about that Report [as], and perhaps more than, many here. I did not refer to it by name; but I tried to place you tonight at the point of view of that Report. You will find in the Majority and the Minority Reports (and you will find the Minority Report[1] much the abler document) both parties on the Commission agreeing that there will be a great increase of the public medical service; and I hope those who have heard us tonight will be prepared to rejoice at that.

Then there is one thing I cannot resist saying with regard to what Sir Victor Horsley said. He said you are now at last

[1] The Minority Report of the Poor Law Commission was drafted by Beatrice and Sidney Webb, and published by the Fabian Society.

organized to get a living wage: that is to say, that in 1901 you reached the point the carpenters and bricklayers reached in 1801. But that is not enough: you want a handsome, secure, and dignified position; and you should have that guaranteed not by the mere chance of private practice, the chance being all the greater when public health is low, and all the less when it is high. You should have it guaranteed by the State, and depend for your promotion on public health and not on private illness.

Then as to reveling in epidemics. It was smallpox I referred to and re-vaccination. I do not at all doubt the case cited by Sir Clifford Allbutt; but was it not in the last degree disgraceful to society at large that his friend, in doing a great public good by doing away with disease, should have lost so heavily by it? What a warning to us all to cultivate disease instead of extirpating it! Surely that is a conclusive illustration of the need for bringing the doctor's private interest into harmony with the health of the community.

THE IDEAL OF CITIZENSHIP

(Address delivered at the Progressive League Demonstration in the City Temple, London, 11 October 1909. Published as an appendix to the "popular edition" of the Reverend R. J. Campbell's *The New Theology*, London, 1909)

I suppose I have addressed as many hopeful progressive leagues as any man in London. I have sampled them nearly all for the last thirty years, but I think this is the first time I have addressed one in the City Temple. I have been looking at this remarkable meeting for some time, and it brings up in my mind, by mere force of contrast, the meeting which I think was most unlike this of any I have ever attended in London. It was in a small and very shabby room in the neighborhood of Tottenham Court Road. I do not suppose there were more than twenty enthusiasts present; but they were very determined enthusiasts— so much so that they declined to elect a chairman, because that meant authority, and they were going to destroy authority. They were a very mild set of men, and therefore they called themselves

Anarchists, as almost all very mild men do. The difficulty about them was that they were really not very dangerous men, except one. There was one man—a young man—there, a pioneer, a fragile and mild creature; and he really was dangerous, for he had provided himself with a dynamite bomb, on which he was sitting during the entire time I was addressing that meeting—a fact of which I was not aware at the time, or perhaps I should not have addressed them with so much self-possession as I did. Well, taking him as being the only dangerous man there, who was he dangerous to? Two days afterwards he took his bomb to Greenwich Park and blew himself into fragments with it— unintentionally. That is a thing that many progressive leagues do, though they may not blow themselves to pieces in such a very decisive way. It's almost a pity they dont. You see, not being really dangerous men, and not finding an effective way of quarreling with the world, they very often quarrel with themselves and oneanother.

What interests me about this meeting is that I have some hopes that you are dangerous people. Mr Campbell has described you as religious people. Well, if you are really religious people, you are really dangerous people; for, after the experience that I have had of various forward movements, I have discovered that the only people who are dangerous are the religious people. I have been in movements which, as you know, in some ways have been very highly intellectualized. They have been able to give very convincing demonstrations, for instance, to the working men of this country that whenever they produce a pound somebody robs them of ten shillings. There was a time about the middle of the last century when many able men—Karl Marx was one—really did believe that if you could only bring that intellectual demonstration and the fact of that robbery home to the working men of Europe they would combine together and rise up against that robbery and put an end to it. I dont know that I hadnt some hopes in that direction myself at that time, when perhaps I was more intellectually active than I have been of late years; but I discovered by experience that no man has the slightest objection to being robbed of ten shillings out of a pound if the remaining ten shillings will make him reasonably comfortable.

I find on reflection that, although I myself have probably made more money for newspaper proprietors than they always thought it necessary to hand over to me, that fact does not make me uncomfortable, doesnt even put me on bad terms with the proprietors of newspapers. The mere money question does not really move me. I always feel that a certain type of commercial man ought to have a great deal of money—a great deal more money than I have, in fact—because he seems to enjoy that and nothing else, whereas my difficulty in life has been that money is more or less a nuisance to me. I want to get a state of communism in which there shall not be any money. I never could understand why people of any business faculty should not be able to average a day's consumption without a pocket full of coppers and having to make all sorts of ridiculous calculations. However, I dont want to go too far ahead even for this audience. I want to come back to my theme of the hopefulness of the religious character of this League. And, remember, congregations believing themselves to be religious are no new thing. I want to go back even more than the thirty years during which I have been addressing progressive leagues. I want to go back to my own childhood.

Also, finding myself in the City Temple, I want to yield to an irresistible temptation to tell a profane story; and it will not only be a very profane story, but it will be a true story, and it will have a certain illustrative value. Now, try to imagine me, a very small boy, with my ears very wide open, in what Mr Gilbert K. Chesterton calls my "narrow, Puritan home." Well, on the occasion which I am going to recall, there were in that narrow, Puritan home three gentlemen who were having what they believed to be a very heated discussion about religion. One was my father, another my maternal uncle, and the third a visitor of ours. The subject of the dispute was the raising of Lazarus. Only one of the parties took what would then, I think, have been called the Christian view. I shall call it the evangelical view, a less compromising term. That view was that the raising of Lazarus occurred exactly as it is described in the Gospels. I shouldnt object to call that the Christian view if it had not involved the opinion, very popular amongst religious people at that time, that the reason why you admired Jesus and followed Jesus was that He was able to raise people from the dead. Perhaps the reason why some of them always spoke very respectfully of Him was a sort of feeling in their mind that a man who could raise people from the dead might possibly on sufficient provocation reverse the operation. However, one of the parties took this view. Another, the visitor, took the absolutely skeptical view: he said that such a thing had never happened—that such stories were told of all great teachers of mankind—that it was more probable that a storyteller was a liar than that a man could be raised from the dead. But the third person, my maternal uncle, took another view: he said that the miracle was what would be called in these days a put-up job, by which he meant that Jesus had made a confederate of Lazarus—had made it worth his while, or had asked him for friendship's sake, to pretend he was dead and at the proper moment to pretend to come to life.

Now, imagine me as a little child listening to this discussion! I listened with very great interest; and I confess to you that the view which recommended itself most to me was that of my maternal uncle. I think, on reflection, you will admit that that was the natural and healthy side for a growing boy to take, because my maternal uncle's view appealed to the sense of humor, which is a very good thing and a very human thing; whereas the other two views—one appealing to our mere credulity and the other to mere skepticism—really did not appeal to anything at all that had any genuine religious value. I therefore contend that I was right in taking what was, at any rate, the most amusing point of view. I think you will see that there was a certain promise of salvation in the fact that at that time one of the most popular writers on Bible subjects was Mark Twain, and Mark Twain mostly made fun of them.[1]

But now I want to come to the deeper significance of this scene. The one thing that never occurred to these three men who were urgently disputing was that they were disputing about a thing of no importance whatever. They believed they were disputing about a thing of supreme importance. The evangelical

[1] Shaw is presumably referring to *The Innocents Abroad*, published in 1869, when he was thirteen. A slightly revised version of the second half of the book, under the title *The New Pilgrim's Progress* was issued in London, 1872.

really believed that if he let the miracle of the raising of Lazarus go he was letting Christianity and religion go. The skeptic believed that to disprove the story of the raising of Lazarus was to make a clean sweep of the Bible from one end to the other, and of the whole fabric of religion. Supposing any person had come into that room and said: "Gentlemen, why are you wasting so many words about this? Suppose you take out of the Gospels the story of the raising of Lazarus, what worse are the Gospels, and what worse is Christianity? Supposing even that you add to them another half-a-dozen raisings from the dead, how much stronger is the position, how much happier is anybody for it?" As a matter of fact, I think such a sensible person would have admitted that my maternal uncle had the best of the situation, as he did squeeze a sort of pitiful laugh out of the controversy, which was the most that was to be got out of it. Yet that really was the tone of religious controversy at that time; and it almost always shewed us the barrenness on the side of religion very much more than it did on the side of skepticism.

If you come to the sort of religious controversies that are started nowadays—and started very largely by Mr Campbell— you will find that they are of a very much more enlightened kind, that the beliefs from which they start are different. For instance, a man spoke to me lately of the early Christians and of the Founder of Christianity. "Well," I said, "I am not exactly an expert on these matters, but you appear to be speaking of Jesus as the Founder of Christianity and of the apostles as early Christians. If I am correctly informed by an authority for whom I have very great respect—and he is the preacher at the City Temple—Jesus was not an early Christian. He was a late Christian: His enemies might almost be inclined to sneer at Him as a decadent Christian." Now, if you get men thoroughly to realize that Jesus did not come at the beginning of a movement which never did begin except in the sense, perhaps, that the world itself began somewhere; if you get people suddenly to shift their point of view so decidedly as to see Him as the summit and climax of a movement, and then begin to ask why it changed after His death, you then have something worth disputing about; you see men with their minds moved instead of their tempers;

you begin to count these men as religious men. And it is the fact that such a change has really taken place that gives me some sort of hope that something may come of your Progressive League.

After all, to come now to the secular part of the matter, you are at a very hopeful moment in the political history of our country. If there were to be a general election tomorrow there would be this astonishing thing about that general election, that for the first time within the recollection of most active men here the election would be about something that we really care for. It is no doubt true that this startling political novelty cannot be attributed to any very deep change of heart on the part of our rulers. I am afraid that it is altogether due to the fact that a few years ago Mr [Joseph] Chamberlain violently upset a very respectable apple-cart called Free Trade, and, by suddenly starting a campaign of Tariff Reform, made his opponents aware that he would keep beating them at the polls unless they found something real to differ from him about at last. And the particular thing they found to differ from him about was the means of raising the revenue. He persuaded the country that it could be raised from the foreigner by Tariff Reform. It became clear to the party that opposed him that, unless they could raise a good surplus somewhere else, they would be beaten by Tariff Reform. And, accordingly, they began to make the sort of speeches that I have been making for the last thirty years. Nobody ever paid much public attention to me, but a great deal of attention is being paid to the Cabinet Ministers who are now taking a leaf out of my book. You see that it sometimes happens, when men are led by quite interested motives and irreligious motives into religious movements, that they presently begin to get some religion out of the movement. It is quite possible that a Cabinet Minister who was never in the City Temple in his life, but who on a wet night found himself outside when he had forgotten his umbrella, and the place open, might come in with no other object in life except to get out of the rain. But that would not save him from Mr Campbell's net, and from going out a very different Cabinet Minister from what he was when he came in. I have great hopes, therefore, that the numbers of these politicians who are being led by the quite irrelevant circumstances I have described into the progressive arena may possibly find some salvation in your movement.

I must, in conclusion, say that what Mr Campbell said to you tonight—that your business was to permeate other people—is a very wise saying. I belong to a society called the Fabian Society. In many ways it is a feeble and ridiculous society, but it owes a great deal of the work it has been able to do to not making certain initial mistakes. Other Socialist bodies usually proposed to enlist everybody except the capitalists in their own ranks. Their program was—"We will explain our good intentions and our sound economic basis to the whole world; the whole world will then join us at a subscription of a penny a week; then, the whole of society belonging to our society, *we* shall become society, and we shall proceed to take the government of the country into our hands, and we shall inaugurate the millennium." But what disabled them was that the world wouldnt come in; and whilst the world remained outside they treated the world more or less as the outsiders, whereas it was really they themselves that were the outsiders.

The Fabian Society set its face against that from the beginning. The Fabian Society said that its sound should go out into all lands, but it did not say that everybody else's sound should come into its own little penny trumpet. The Fabian was a man who was never urged to join the Fabian Society: in fact, when he first tried to do it he usually found some difficulty; but, once he was in it, then what he was told to do was to join every other society on the face of the earth he could possibly get into and make his influence felt there. Now, that is what you have got to do. If you once begin to run your Progressive League in a spirit of hostility to all other leagues whatever, and assume that all the people outside your League are heathens—although you will probably be entirely right in that belief—the assumption will not be a good assumption for you, so you had better not make it. What you have to do is to place before the man who will not take an ideal from you in religious terms—and it is not everybody that can—a simple ideal of citizenship. First you must make it clear that he is not to be a poor man. You must always be down on poor men: you must learn to dislike poverty, because if you dont do that the poor will not listen to you.

I tell you, ladies and gentlemen, that the most popular lecture I ever delivered in London was one I delivered at the request of the superior persons at Toynbee Hall who step condescendingly down from the universities to improve the poor. They told me they had a very poor audience—one of the poorest they could get in Whitechapel—and they asked me would I address it; and, when I said yes, they said, "What subject shall we put down?" I said, "Put down this as the subject: 'That the poor are useless, dangerous, and ought to be abolished.'" I had my poor audience; and they were delighted: they cheered me to the echo: that was what they wanted to have said. They did not want to be poor.

What you must say to the ordinary citizen is this: "My friend, there are certain things that you ought to do for your country; and there are certain things you ought to demand from your country; and one is as important as the other. You must not submit to poverty either on your own part or anybody else's. But you must not go about the world thinking or talking of money as if you yourself, *by* yourself, could make it. It must never come into your mind that any of what is produced in the world has got to belong to you because it could not have been made without your brains and your organizing faculty and your invention and your talent. What every man has to keep before him is this: In the first place his country's claim on him, which is to benefit by his life's work, which he must do for his country to the very best of his ability. You have got in the very short space of life which is yours, and which is your only chance, to give the world everything you possibly can. Remember that there are debts to pay which are debts of honor. There is the debt you owe for your education and your nurture when you were young; and I hope the day will soon come when every person in this country will have a very large debt of that kind. You ought to pay that debt; you ought to pay for the sustenance of yourself in your prime; and you ought to provide for your own old age; and I say that the man who does not feel obliged not only to pay these debts, but to put in something over, so that he dies with his country in his debt, instead of dying in his country's debt—I say that man is not worth talking to.

In return you must demand from your country a handsome, dignified, and sufficient subsistence. Every worker has a right to that, and there must be no question of the nature of the work done. If anything, the men who do the more disagreeable kinds of work should be compensated for their disadvantage.

The duty and the demand I have just put before you have always been the tradition of honorable men in all professions. It is there, waiting to be appealed to; but for a whole century past we have been appealing to the other—the commercial instinct to try and make money for yourself, which has always meant taking away from other people as much as you can. If you will only appeal from that base instinct to the straightforward and honorable instinct, you will find that hundreds of thousands of people round you who have no idea that they are Socialists or anything of that kind have that instinct, and that all they want you to do is to shew that the thing is possible. Very largely, I think, it will be your business to shew that it is possible; but I hope you will also be able to shew them that the pursuit of it makes people extremely jolly and extremely happy. Let your pioneers take a leaf out of the book of the Salvation Army. Dont go about with long faces sympathizing with the poor and with ills. Take poverty and illness in extremely bad part; and when you meet a man whose wife is ill or who is poor, and all that sort of thing, dont say to him that it is the will of God, which is a horrible blasphemy. Tell him in solemn Scriptural language that it is a damnable thing, and that you have come to try and put a stop to it because *you* are the will of God. And then you will have put the man you are talking to on the high road to understand that his will is the will of God too.

SMOKE AND GENIUS

(Speech delivered before the Annual Meeting of the Coal Smoke Abatement Society, London, 13 June 1911. Published in the Society's annual transactions, 1910–11; reprinted in *Smokeless Air*, Winter 1950)

I propose the following resolution: "That this meeting, recognizing the harmful effects of coal smoke on life and property, pledges itself to support the efforts of the Coal Smoke Abatement Society in diminishing the evil." I would like to make a few remarks on the nature of genius. You might say that genius has nothing to do with smoke abatement and that it is not what you have come to listen to. But I know little about smoke, which is a common thing, and everything about genius. I am in that line myself. [*Laughter.*]

A man of genius is not a man who sees more than other men do. On the contrary, it is very often found that he is absent-minded and observes much less than other people. If you met a man of genius in Whitehall and asked him what had passed up that thoroughfare while he has been there you would probably find that he would be reduced to a condition of stuttering imbecility, but if you asked the nearest policeman, who might or might not be a man of genius, he would tell you a number of useful facts. This being so, what good is a man of genius? where does he come in? Why is it the public have such an exaggerated respect for him—after he is dead? The reason is that the man of genius understands the importance of the few things he sees. William Blake, whose genius is perhaps more beyond dispute than that of any other Englishman, saw a quite common thing, and wrote of it in language which you would probably describe as monstrously exaggerated. He writes, in his Songs of Innocence, of a linnet in a cage which "puts all Heaven in a rage." An ordinary man would never have thought of that. The ordinary man only sees a linnet in a cage, and looks on Blake's lines as one of those absurd things which men of genius say. I rub this in because I myself am always being accused of exaggeration.

To the ordinary inefficient mind there is one thing which can be seen over and over again without any importance being attached to it, and that is a smoking chimney. No importance used to be attached to it until there came along a man of genius who began bombarding the local authorities with spirited draw-ings representing smoking chimneys—and occasionally there were details on them as to how long they had been smoking. The artist was evidently representing something. Some members of the local authorities apparently concluded these sketches were intended for their portfolios, and began to collect them. But it began to be apparent that the man who did these drawings believed that it was extremely important for England that smoke should be put an end to. The man was Sir William Richmond. That was the beginning of the movement, and the extent to which it will progress will depend upon the number of men of genius in the community. If any of you present will send a cheque for five guineas to the treasurer he will to that extent prove that he is a man of genius. There is no use in expecting an ordinary person to do anything. The affairs of the world must be directed by men of genius. The few people who see these things will have to become centres of propaganda, and will have to back the movement up in every way they can. They must wake up the common man to things which he has hitherto taken as a matter of course.

Some time back Sir Almroth Wright delivered a scientific address in London containing a great deal of valuable matter. The Press took no notice of that valuable matter; but Sir Almroth having casually let fall a remark that he was rather skeptical of the value of washing, we read everywhere, "Distinguished physician says we should not wash ourselves." [*Laughter.*] I sympathize with Sir Almroth Wright, because we are fellow countrymen. One has to be an Irishman to understand the antipathy and instinctive dislike that every Irishman has to washing. Anyone going to Ireland will understand the feeling. [*Laughter.*] The fact of the matter is that washing is not a natural function. Sir Almroth Wright has often remarked that some of his patients remove a considerable portion of that skin which nature intended should ward off germs, and he has suggested that we should be careful to preserve that outer layer. But in a soft climate such as Ireland's it is very disagreeable to put cold water on the skin; and as for hot water, one has only to look at people who take hot baths to see that they are the only people who look incurably dirty. Personally, I do not think I have really washed myself—except as regards the visible portion of my body like my face and hands—since the time when somebody else did it for me. It is true I have got into the habit of taking a cold bath; but that is not washing. I do it as a stimulant, and I often think I had better

84

have taken to whisky. [*Laughter.*] When I first came to London one of the first things I noticed was that everybody wore gloves. Where I come from only a few wear them occasionally as a tribute to their superiority. But before I had been here many days I discovered that I must do so now. According to any decent standard everyone ought to be cleaner than they are.

The real secret of healthy cleanliness is to have a clean atmosphere and clean clothes, and until you get rid of smoke you can never have a clean atmosphere. [*Applause.*] A clean atmosphere would probably prolong our lives and enable us to save money. We talk about the saving in coal by preventing smoke; but there would also be an enormous saving in soap. There is no doubt about the saving; in fact, if it were possible for a commercial company to realize that particular profit for themselves the whole place would be flooded with prospectuses of new joint-stock companies for coal smoke abatement. Unfortunately, it is not realizable as a commercial asset. All we can do is to rely on individuals and on public opinion. We should cut all those persons who have smoky chimneys. We should refuse their invitations to dinner, alleging as the reason: "I have seen black smoke proceeding from your kitchen chimney." Coal smoke is not like original sin, a thing we are obliged to put up with.

It was said once that dust could not be done away with on our public roads. I myself have driven a motor-car amid the execrations of the populace. Now dust is almost abolished. If every motorist will now make it a point of honor to drive at a reckless speed in order to stir up any dust there is remaining, and will also make a point of driving rapidly through a pool whenever he sees a Bishop near, these two pests, dust and mud, will soon become things of the past. And, with a similar object in view, I suggest that those who want to get rid of coal smoke should make a practice of carrying about a bag of soot and throwing it over people's collars and shirt fronts, in order to convince them of the evils of smoke. [*Laughter and applause.*]

SHAW VS CHESTERTON

(A debate between Shaw and G. K. Chesterton in the Memorial
Hall, London, 30 November 1911. *The Christian Commonwealth*, 6 and 13 *December* 1911)

SHAW

I assert that a Democrat who is not also a Socialist is no
gentleman. I say it in the most insulting personal sense of the
term. I have to define the three terms and their alternatives—the
alternative to a gentleman, which is a cad; the alternative to a
Socialist, for which I dont know the exact name; and the alternative to a Democrat, which is an idolator.

By Socialism I mean the state of society which proceeds from
one fixed and immutable condition—that the entire income of
the country shall be divided exactly equally between every
person in the country, young or old, without regard to their
industry or character, or anything but that they are live human
beings. By Socialism I do not mean Collectivism. Collectivism
is a necessary condition of Socialism, but so is it of any intelligent
ordering of society. My definition of Socialism is the definition
of the man in the street; the Socialist is the man who wants to
divide up. All the wealth of any country must be divided up
between its inhabitants every day on one principle or another.
What distinguishes the Socialist is that he says you must divide
up equally. If you divide the wealth of any people according to
a moral or intelligent system, whatever it be, you are thereby
just as much committed to Collectivism as a Socialist. Collectivism without Socialism might be a system of tyranny, of slavery
so infernal that I can conceive only one thing worse—the existing state of things.

There is no such thing as a panacea or plan by which you can
set society on a nice satisfactory basis and then it will march
spontaneously and automatically forward doing justice. People
hold that if you only started fair, if you had what some Liberals
call equality of opportunity, things would spontaneously go on
happily. That is impossible. If anybody could discover a plan by
which society could be re-started today, and ever after we might

live like South Sea Islanders, I would resist that as I would resist plague, pestilence, and famine. I believe in the necessity for a daily output of virtue. Salvation is a continuous operation, like breathing. If you stop breathing for five minutes you are dead; if you stop saving yourself for ten minutes you are damned. Social questions will never be settled once for all, but will have to be continually settled.

What are the two systems before us? There is the medieval system, and between that and Socialism I contend there is nothing really practical at all. About the end of the eighteenth century a number of fantastic visionaries put forward one of the most extraordinarily extravagant and impracticable ideas ever put before the world—the idea that every person should be paid according to his talents or character. English Liberals called it payment by results. All that is utter nonsense, and the people who are talking as if it could be done are simply trying to distract attention from the injustices and absurdities of our present system. What is really keeping society together is the old medieval system of stratified equality. Practically every laborer in the same district is getting the same pay, every mechanic and artisan the same pay, but when you get above that level the fees of the professional man are calculated in the first instance with reference to the state of life proper to a man doing that kind of work. You have got today the actual practice of equality, class within class. In the army you pay your privates the same, although you have every possible diversity of character among them; you pay all your sergeants the same, your majors, your colonels. Among your generals you may have a Napoleon or a Cæsar, or the sort of gentlemen who distinguished themselves in the Boer War. No matter, if their rank is the same they get the same pay. Can you conceive any one of these men after a battle asking for an extra five shillings on the ground that he had been five minutes longer under fire? Your first instinct would be, what a cad that man is!

Now you begin to see why I say that the man who wants more is no gentleman. I do not blame the man who believes in idolatry and hierarchy, who says men will not obey or respect oneanother unless you set certain men apart, for inequality of payment is one means of setting them apart. But you cannot say that if you are a Democrat. If you say to your fellow men, I grant you political equality, and religious equality, but I wont grant you cash equality, you can have no respectable motive for the denial. Practically you are like the officer who demands five shillings more because he is five minutes longer under fire. I have said nothing about the enormous and overwhelming practical arguments in favour of equality; I have not pointed out to you that without equality your politics must be what they are at present, a mass of corruption and imposture; that your churches must be what they are, professional conspiracies against the human race; because I should feel that I put Mr Chesterton in the position of defending the present system, which I know he does not approve. I have put it on the personal and national point of honor because I believe on my soul it is on that that the whole question will finally turn.

CHESTERTON

I approach this question with all the more diffidence and difficulty because of the extraordinarily brilliant and interesting address Mr Shaw has delivered upon a totally different subject. The subject we are supposed to be discussing is an algebraical formula consisting of three unknown quantities—Democrat, Gentleman, and Socialist. I dont know whether I am a gentleman, I am sure I am a Democrat and that Mr Shaw is not a Democrat. I cannot remember a single word he has ever written or spoken shewing belief in Democracy; certainly he has uttered none such this evening. I dont know what is the social rank of a person like myself who presumes to be a gentleman, and not a Socialist, compared with the social rank of the gentleman who is a Socialist, and not a Democrat, like Mr Shaw. The opposite of a gentleman is not a cad, any more than the opposite of a sailor is a pirate. Nor is it true that everyone who is not a Democrat is an idolator. He may really believe that mankind is better governed by a special class of men or by one man. A Democrat means a person who believes that the direct action of citizens upon the State is the best method of government. What "a Socialist" means in the mind of Mr Shaw I have great difficulty in discovering from his remarks. I always use the word in a definite sense. A Socialist

88

believes that the monstrous division of modern property can only be cured by the Government, the State, coming in and coercively claiming all the property and paying it back in wages to the citizens.

Mr Shaw said Socialism means the absolutely equal payment of all human beings without respect to class, sex, or age. Does he mean that a new-born babe shall be at once in receipt, I cannot say enjoyment, of the income which would be right and proper to a grown, working human being? [*Mr Shaw:* "*Yes.*"] Well, it is barely possible a community might solemnly vote incomes of £500 a year to new-born infants, but the alternative is much more probable, that wages would be cut down to the level of those of the babe.

While there are thousands of good arguments for Socialism, there is no argument which has any reference to Democracy. Democracy is a distinct idea from Socialism. It is not true that the assumption by the State of all the powers of economic action would produce a self-governing State. Supposing we all had wooden legs and were living together in a hospital, and there was a rule that we should take the wooden legs every night into the cloakroom and get a ticket for them. We should avoid a great many definite evils; one man could not steal another's wooden leg, or pawn his wooden leg, or make a corner in wooden legs. But if you want a society in which people shall govern themselves, you have not advanced a single step by collecting and redistributing all the wooden legs. All you have done is to ensure yourself against certain kinds of evil which have nothing to do with democracy. You may think this is a monstrous and fantastic example. I and a large number of people think that depriving an ordinary man of the direct and absolute sense of personal property is exactly like cutting off his leg and giving him a wooden one.

The railwaymen's strike was not a revolt in favor of Socialism, but against a State Board of Conciliation—the very institution by which you propose to cure all their ills! Many of the workmen told the Commission they would prefer to go before the masters than argue with the Board. The strikers were in revolt against Socialism. Why do you suppose socialistic boards or committees will be different? "Under Socialism they will be able to elect their members of Parliament." They are able to do it now. "Under Socialism they will be able to check and criticize committees appointed." They are able to do it now. Why dont they? The strikers came out in the name of the institution of property. The ordinary poor man in this or any other country believes profoundly in the rights of property. They have only one very small property left; years and years of Protestant enlightened progress have taken away from them every other kind of property. They still have some possession of their own bodies. And to the capitalist who, using the Socialist arguments, says this will be bad for the community, trade will be stopped, food will be held up, much suffering will follow, they answer, as Naboth answered to that great ancient Socialist, King Ahab, who was also strongly opposed to peasant proprietorship, and who, for the good of the State, desired that he, who was the government, should absorb the little vineyard, "The Lord forbid that I should give the inheritance of my fathers unto thee."

SHAW

Mr Chesterton says I have defined nothing, and he cannot make out what I am driving at. I defined Socialism as that state of society in which the income of a country would be divided exactly equally amongst all the people of that country, without reference to age, sex, or character. Mr Chesterton did make out the baby part of it. There are several babies who at the moment of birth came into £40,000 or £50,000 a year. My modest request is that the baby should come into its dividend of the country's wealth. Mr Chesterton thinks a baby does not require so much as a man. The baby requires a great deal more. The grown man is able to produce; the baby is not able to produce anything. Mr Chesterton said that wages would be cut down to the level of the baby. There is no objection to that if you give the baby the proper wage. I am not only in favor of the old-age pension, but also of the life pension and of the baby pension. Coming to the objection that cutting off a man's absolute and direct sense of property is a calamity, I take it that it is one of the conditions of life for everybody that there are certain things they call their own, not in the economic sense of real property. I propose a certain distribution of property so that everybody shall have some. For practical purposes it must be measured by income. [*Mr Chesterton:* "*No.*"] I say the State should distribute money, which gives a man command of the things he likes, in equal proportions—what do you say? [*Mr Chesterton:* "*I dont mind.*"] That is trifling with the question; you must mind. I wish I could persuade Mr Chesterton that I really am a serious man dealing with a serious question. Since Mr Chesterton does mean apparently that everybody is to have their share, what is the share to be? Are you to have more or less than I? Is any man to have more than another? If so, why? Is any man to have less than another? If so, why? I say every one should have enough so far as the resources go.

Mr Chesterton says the railway strikers were out against Socialism. My impression is that they were to some extent against their leaders and members of Parliament because they were not Socialistic enough; that is, so far as the strike had any political significance. But were not the men really out for recognition of their unions for better wages? They were out for a nearer practical approach to equality. Mr Chesterton sees in it an argument against democracy. He says, What difference will Socialism make? They are able to elect members of Parliament now. Has Mr Chesterton ever taken part in an election? In how many was the man you had to support the man whom you would have freely chosen? You cannot select your own member of Parliament, because you have not got equality of income. You cannot select your own wife for the same reason. As to the definition of a gentleman, he is a man who will not be bought; who demands from his country a dignified existence in return for the best service he can give; who also in a larger sense always feels the force of the old explanation, "Inasmuch as you have done it to the least of these you have done it to me." Any injury to any part of the community is a wound to his own honor.

When men are stranded and living on short rations, the ordinary man feels instinctively, I must take my share and no more than my share in this emergency. The gentleman has that feeling all through his life. As for the cad, he is the man who cannot see why he should do anything unless he is paid, and doesnt mind being paid at other people's expense. And it is because our system has put the political government, moral education, and religious education into the hands of cads that I am a Socialist.

CHESTERTON

It is for exactly the same reasons that I am not a Socialist. I cannot understand why so dexterous and brilliant a debater as Mr Shaw should have wasted so much time in attacking the present system of industrial England. Who except a devil from hell ever defended it? I detest it as much as he does. I object to his solution not because it is a violent change, but because it will be, so far as I can see, so devilishly like it. The existing system is proletarian. Large masses of men depend upon wages doled out to them by somebody else. The whole Socialist theory is proletarian. I do not care whether the man who deals out the money is called Lord So-and-so, and is the employer and head of the great soap works, or whether he is still called Lord So-and-so (as he probably will be) and called the Social Administrator in the name of the State of the same soap works. You cannot draw the line across things and say, You shall have your garden hose, but not your garden; your ploughshare, but not your field; your fishing rod, but not your stream; because man is so made that his sense of property is actually stronger for such things as fields or gardens or water than for such comparatively unnecessary things as garden hose or rakes or fishing rods. The proposition I put in the place of the one Mr Shaw ought to have maintained is, that if you want self-government apart from good government you must have a generally distributed property. You must create the largest possible number of owners. I pause for one moment on the baby. Mr Shaw said that the baby should receive wages. Does Mr Shaw mean that every infant is to be detached from the labor and responsibility of his parents? If so, the whole human race will violently disagree.

SHAW

Mr Chesterton says a babe should be dependent on its mother. As if I had been suggesting that it should not be! He must know that, as now, the income must be given to its mother and guardians, and spent for it. When we come to the question of absolute property it really does seem to amount to this: Mr Chesterton wants a distribution of property, and the only difference between him and the Socialist is that the Socialist says there shall be equal distribution. If you agree with me that it should be in equal proportions you are a Socialist. If you do not agree, in heaven's name, I ask you for the last time, Will you tell me in what proportion you want it distributed?

CHESTERTON

Mr Shaw has favored me with another definition of Socialism —equality in the possession of property. This is not the normal definition of the term. That the State should be in possession of the means of production, distribution, and exchange was always called Socialism when I was a Socialist. And the answer to that proposal is, first, that this method has in the course of the greater part of human civilization been abolished; and, secondly, it is no good telling me that there cannot be a peasant proprietary civilization. There is and has been over the greater part of Europe and Asia. I think that existence preferable to the beautiful existence described by Mr Shaw in cities, and it is perfectly certain that the vast majority of the white men of the world who are living that kind of life are happier than the majority of the people within a few miles of this hall.

THE CRIME OF POVERTY

(Speech delivered at the War Against Poverty Demonstration, under the joint auspices of the Independent Labour Party and the Fabian Society, in the Albert Hall, London, 11 October 1912. *The Labour Leader*, 17 October 1912)

I have received many letters during the last few days from gentlemen who, seeing that I was advertized to take part in a meeting for the abolition of poverty, suggested that I might make a modest beginning in the form of pecuniary accommodation to themselves privately. But all these gentlemen made the mistake of representing themselves as being miserably poor. I am present at this meeting because there is nothing in the world I hate more than a poor man. I should be a Conservative if I had sympathy for the poor.

It happened that when I was a small child my nurse used to take me out for exercise in the open air. She did not exercise me in the open air; she took me to visit her friends. Her friends were mostly poor people. I thought them most horrible people. I simply detested them, and I still detest them. I think such people ought not to exist.

I am perfectly determined not to be poor if I can help it. I dont want to be rich. I would be content with, say, four or five thousand pounds a year. But I am not content to have four or five thousand a year and to be surrounded by dirty, ignorant people who have only a pound a week.

I am not content to have a nice house myself. I want everybody else to have a nice house; I have got to look at those houses. The only reason why I like my drawing room to be nice is that I have to look at it. I dont eat it. For the same reason I want other people's houses to look nice—on the outside, at any rate. If I thought your houses were beautiful inside, you might have the opportunity to enjoy the inestimable favor of hearing my brilliant conversation, which is celebrated throughout Europe.

I want to cure poverty as an abominable disease and as a very horrible crime. I never had any sort of enthusiasm for the ordinary movements for the suppression of crime. If a man is by disposition a murderer you cannot make him a philanthropist. You cannot turn a real, genuine, congenital thief into an honest man. He may be a very pleasant man—I have known many charming thieves—but you cannot change him fundamentally. We are always clamoring to do the impossible.

You can, however, take a dirty man and you can clean him. You can take an ignorant man and you can teach him. You can take a poor man and you can give him money. Then he wont be a poor man any longer.

Therefore, in standing on this platform I claim to be standing upon the only practical platform that exists in England. All the other parties are setting out to do something which cannot be done. That is how the governing classes occupy themselves. They imagine it will keep the people quiet.

Our method of proceeding by demanding a minimum is really the method by which all civilizations have advanced. The law imposes upon everyone in this hall a minimum of clothes. I am sorry the law does not go further and impose a minimum as to the quality of the clothes. I strongly object to the quality of clothes worn in London today. It is foolish to say that everyone should be dressed if you do not say that they shall be well dressed.

In the same way we must insist on a minimum of honesty. We allow a man to be a large shareholder, but we prevent him from being a pickpocket. We insist on that minimum of honesty even for millionaires. But a pickpocket is nowhere nearly so harmful to the community as the poor man. The poor man breeds disease and casts a blight over the people. The first thing to do, therefore, is to insist upon a minimum of money in everyone's pockets.

We have gone so far in this direction as to give a man five shillings a week when he is seventy years of age. I defy you to give one reason for giving a man of seventy five shillings a week, which is not a far better reason for giving a man of twentyseven £500 a year. The thing can be done. There is no difficulty in producing a higher standard of life. You are stupid enough to waste your opportunities. With the exception of a few ladies and gentlemen, everyone who is working is producing more than he consumes. Roughly, he is producing twice as much. What should we, if we were reasonable beings (which I know you are not), expect to follow as a consequence of that extraordinary fact? Would you not expect this country to be getting richer and richer from one generation to another? Would you not expect the children to be healthier and heavier, the men and women stronger and more beautiful? Would you not expect its slums to be disappearing by magic, its disease to be passing away, the necessity for working long hours to be ceasing? Would you not be expecting this earth to be fulfilling its real destiny, to be transforming itself into the Kingdom of Heaven?

What are we actually doing with this enormous surplus of wealth? We are throwing it into the pockets of people who use it, not for the improvement of the country, but for its degradation. When are you going to stop it?

Some enthusiasts tonight have asked, "When are you going to turn out the Government?" They know very well that we have not the heart nor the power to turn out even the people who interrupt us in this audience. Turn out the Government? We have not the strength in the House of Commons to turn anybody out; it is as much as we can do to keep ourselves in.

The task before us is to turn out a whole epoch of civilization, to turn out a generation which has become entirely corrupt by worn-out traditions and prejudices, to inaugurate and bring in a new epoch. It can only be done by the spreading of a great conception among the people, of a higher conception of life. You, who are here, are a picked and chosen few. I wish you would go amongst those who think they are money-making, and who are really grinding each other down, and break their windows. Other movements besides the Suffrage movement need to be militant. We want a conviction of sin and of salvation, a wave of intense shame at existing conditions which shall make them intolerable to those who imagine that they profit by it.

The hammer of public opinion is needed and, I repeat, a genuine conviction of sin. The greatest curse of poverty is that it destroys the will power of the poor until they become the most ardent supporters of their own poverty. We have to talk to these people, and, if possible, talk sense.

I am not sure that the interrupters tonight have not set us a good example. I suggest that you go to other political meetings, and when someone says, "Bulgaria," or "Ireland," or "Land Reform," you say, "What about Poverty?" Such action will begin by you being turned out. I hope it will end in a bad epoch being turned out.

PROPERTY OR SLAVERY?

(Speech in a debate with Hilaire Belloc, Queen's Hall, London, 28 January 1913. *The Book of Public Speaking*, Vol. 5, ed. Arthur Charles Fox-Davies, London, 1913)

The greatest man who came forward in the nineteenth century to champion Socialism left us this watchword: "Call no man master." I want to make my own attitude on that subject perfectly clear. At a very early age I was solemnly dedicated to be a servant when I was baptized. I am exceedingly proud of that, and I intend to remain all my life a servant. I think, and I speak not as a pious man, that the finest thing that can be said of anyone at the end of his career is, "Well done, thou good and faithful servant." We are all born to service, and any man who shrinks from his share of that service is a thief or a beggar. I do not think that we ought to aim at being a community of thieves or beggars. The method of putting service on to somebody else is the method of private property, which I am here to condemn root and branch. Organization is essential to the higher life of society and to the religious possibilities of life. Mr Belloc occasionally speaks as if he admires a peasant, but although it is open to him to become a peasant he does not do so. [*Laughter.*] Mr Belloc abhors slavery, and so do I. We both want to do away with it. Mr Belloc says, "Distribute private property." I say, "Abolish private property."

I am not in the position of challenger on this occasion, and, therefore, I am not bound to put forth any alternative scheme, but I do so because while doctors differ patients die; and if I do not lay down a scheme people may take Mr Belloc's for want of a better. Mr Belloc's scheme is to take real property, the land of the country, for instance, which is at the root of the affair, and parcel it out among the inhabitants under the impression that they will live happily ever afterwards. This has already been tried and has broken down. It has produced all the evils of our existing industrial organization. If all the world were parceled out into a beautiful mosaic of fertile fields large enough to be managed by a single pair like Adam and Eve, then, no doubt, if every man and woman were a born farmer and farmer's wife, if we limit the population and we exclude the Chinese [*laughter*], then we shall abolish slavery and we shall abolish starvation. But unfortunately the earth is not made in that way, nor in any way resembling it. Some parts of the world are enormously fertile, in others the climate is so cold and inhospitable that only a few explorers go there and come back and say they have been there [*laughter*], and some more sensible explorers come back and say they have been there, although they have not been there. [*Laughter.*] The result of the inequalities in the productiveness of the earth is that if you give every man three acres the man who owns the less productive soil will speedily become the slave of the man who owns the soil that is the more productive.

Then with regard to the inequality among men themselves. It so happens that the peculiar faculty of exploiting property is extremely unequally diffused among men. It is an unamiable quality which results from a few sordid qualities, and the absence of a number of valuable qualities, and happily for the human race the majority of men have not got it. In stories you will read of a Jew who came penniless to a village in Russia, and at the end of two years owned the entire village. Let me tell you a secret: those men are not always Jews. [*Laughter.*] A Jew cannot live in the North of Ireland. [*Laughter.*] If Mr Belloc were to exterminate the entire Jewish race, and he sometimes expresses himself in language which leads me to believe that it would not be altogether an uncongenial exploit, he would still find plenty of persons who were not Jews, but who have this peculiar faculty of exploiting property, a faculty which demands the sort of low cunning in betting on horses or playing cards. If one puts money first and honor second it is easy to get rich even now, although it is difficult to get rich when one puts honor, religion, and the welfare of the community first.

The great Robert Owen, not by his virtue but by the faculty of organizing industry, made a fortune and became the absolute master of a number of workmen. He made a series of experiments in the education of those workmen's children which have served as models to many of our educational institutions. People say what a great man Robert Owen was, but I object to Robert Owen having that power over the children, just as I object to the power that Robert Owen's competitors had to slave-drive those children.

I will mention Mr [Edward] Cadbury, because I know that is a name that annoys Mr Belloc. Mr Cadbury has organized the cocoa industry, and in consequence of that has become the absolute lord and master of the Cocoa Press, thereby obtaining control of a large part of the livelihood of Mr Gilbert Chesterton,

Mr Belloc's friend and my own.[1] I think that large and flourishing intellectual property, Mr Gilbert Chesterton [*laughter*], ought perhaps to be under the control of the community, that it ought perhaps to be under the control of the Church. [*Laughter.*] I can understand that it ought to be, at any hazard, under the control of the high conscience and public spirit of Mr Gilbert Chesterton himself, but I cannot conceive for one moment that it ought to be under the control of Mr Cadbury, and yet Mr Cadbury stands conspicuous as a philanthropist among the whole mass of employers of labor, most of whom have no other motive apparently than to aggrandize themselves at the expense of other people.

Why was it that the Church lost its hold in the Middle Ages? It was because it was corrupted by private property. Why was it that the Church had practically gone, and that the Press arose to protect the people? What has become of the Press? What has bought up the Press? Private property. The Church bought justice, corrupted kings, corrupted juries, and corrupted judges, and all that private property began with what Mr Belloc has advocated—a distribution of land among the people. One hundred years ago every man in America could get a property for the asking. Now there is no greater hell of slavery on the face of the earth than the United States of America. All that has grown, not from the historical sources of conquest, but from private property. I believe in Socialism, and if Mr Belloc thinks there is anything impracticable in Socialism let him tell me what it is.

ETHICAL PRINCIPLES OF SOCIAL RECONSTRUCTION

(Paper read before the Aristotelian Society, London, 23 April 1917. *Proceedings of the Aristotelian Society 1916–1917*. Also in *The New York American*, 1 and 8 *July* 1917)

The ethical principles imposed on us by the war are simple enough. War throws us back on the crude ethic of immediate

[1] Cadbury was Director of The Daily News Ltd. Chesterton contributed a weekly article to *The Daily News* from 1901 to 1913.

self-preservation. Every contrivance, however diabolical, which saves British and destroys German lives is right, and every contrary wor_ _nd deed is wrong. It overrides all higher ethics, from the ten commandments to Herbert Spencer's principles. Liberty has become a public danger, and homicide a science and a virtue: we pray that friendly Americans may be drowned; and we deliberately produce artificial famine, earthquake, and thunderbolt, on a scale which makes the most appalling natural catastrophe seem insignificant in comparison. And we take our part, directly or by consent and contribution, with a sense of ethical approval so heightened that manifest fools are seen in all directions almost bursting with their own importance, which nobody ventures to challenge, whilst philosophers are intimidated, or, if they resist the process, suppressed by force. All this is as inevitable as an act of trespass may be to a man pursued by a bull, or an appearance in the street with nothing but a nightdress on, if even that, to a woman escaping from a burning house. There is not much interest in discussing whether, being inevitable, it is also right. The inevitable is practically outside ethics; and the inevitabilities of war drag us back from the forward side of good and evil, to which Nietzsche invited us, to the side we thought, until war broke out, we had long left behind us.

It is important to note that our sense of moral superiority to the cruder ethic thus violently forced on us does not enable us to evade its consequences. We had arrived at the conclusion that, as William Morris put it, "no man is good enough to be another man's master," and that if we give irresponsible power over us to any man he will abuse it. At the beginning of the war, finding ourselves obliged to give such power, we tried to hide the gravity of the breach of the principle involved by an absurd idolatry of the persons we had to trust. During the first months of the war our generals and admirals were Cæsars and Nelsons; and the members of the Government were Solons, Solomons, and Marcus Aureliuses; whilst those who ventured to criticize them were pro-German traitors. Nonetheless, all these gentlemen abused their power and their irresponsibility, and most of them have had to be superseded. Whilst the higher ethic of peace remains in abeyance, and the crude ethic of war in full activity, not a single consequence of the violation of the higher ethic is spared us. We are saving our skins at the cost of our souls, very prudently, because if we pawn our souls to the god of war we may redeem them some day; but if we lose our skins there is an end of us, souls and all. Thus, though we must accept the bargain, we cannot escape paying the price. The reason people feel so much more virtuous during the war than they ever pretended to be before it, is that it has debased the ethical currency to such an extent that the man who had not sixpennorth of virtue to bless himself with can now flourish a character worth twenty sovereigns of gilt lead.

The ethical situation is, however, not so simple as this, because our ethics of peace were very far from being the ethics of Immanuel Kant or Plato. When we say to Germany, "Thou shalt starve ere we starve," and she says the same to us, we are both only saying what we said to our own countrymen and neighbors in the false peace of commercialism. To many a man this war has brought salvation from the most callous selfishness and the most hoggish quarrelsomeness. The war between the patriotic German and the patriotic Briton is an ennobling activity compared to the war between the kitchen and the drawing room, the farmer and the laborer, the employer and the trade unionist, the landlord and the tenant, the usurer and the borrower, not to mention the competitive war which each man wages with his fellows in all these hostile camps. The ethics of our trenches are higher than the ethics of our markets. A man may pass through a barrage with less damage to his character than through a squabble with a nagging wife. Many domestic and commercial experiences leave blacker and far more permanent marks on the soul than thrusting a bayonet through an enemy in a trench fight. We, therefore, have the complication that the retrogressive transition to the primitive morality of war may involve a progressive transition from a narrow and detestable private morality to a comparatively broad and elevated public morality.

We must also take into account the ethical illusions of the war. The primitive ethic of war, that they shall take who have the power, and they shall keep who can, is so revolting to highly civilized men that they can reconcile themselves to it only by setting up an elaborate fiction that they are acting in shocked self-defence against an unprovoked and wicked attack, and that, in defending themselves, they are defending liberty, humanity, justice, and all the other virtues, their enemies being, consequently, human fiends devoted wholly to the triumph of evil. This is manifest nonsense; but those who believe it sincerely may be cultivating their character at the expense of their intellect, just as those who look the truth in the face, and yet hack their way through, may be cultivating their intellect at the expense of their character. Those of us who believe that our intellect is a very important part of our character, and that stupidity and ignorance are more disastrous than roguery, will derive only a very doubtful and troubled consolation from the fact that both Germans and Englishmen believe that they are fighting for something more than the balance of power; for if sacrifice for an ideal is good for man, hatred of the enemy and assumption of moral superiority is very bad for him. Still, the thing exists and has to be taken into account. It may make the combatants fight more fiercely, but it precludes all terms of peace except those imposed by force; for none of the belligerents will agree to a stalemate on a footing of moral equality.

Now, it is not conceivable that a treaty concluding a war should have any higher ethic than war itself. All the belligerents will take what plunder they can. None of them are pacifist States; they are all steeped in blood; and most of them are empires holding down subject nationalities ruthlessly with all the circumstances of cruelty and oppression which attend such holdings-down. They have all kept treaties when it was [in] their interest to do so and broken them when it was [in] their interest to break them. All have been guilty of frightful cruelties; and those who are not fighting for a European hegemony are fighting openly to wrest territories from oneanother. Germany will stay in Lille and Antwerp if she can; France will take Alsace-Lorraine if she can; Austria will keep Serbia and Bosnia if she can; Russia will get Constantinople if she can; Rumania will take Transylvania if she can; Italy will hold the Trentino if she can; and we shall keep the German colonies if we can. In addition to territory they will, if they can, bleed their enemies white in indemnities;

and if they have to abandon territory they will devastate it so as to reduce to the utmost its value to the conqueror. And, according to the ethic of war, they will be quite right in doing so, and would be guilty of a political crime if they sacrificed the smallest fraction of the fruits of victory. What else is war for?

Even Bismarck could not restrain Germany from annexing Alsace-Lorraine in 1871, and today there is no Bismarck to make the attempt. Thus there will be no ethical reconstruction. There will be a division of spoils and shifting of frontiers on the basis of the established militarist ethic. The proceedings will be governed by the example of England and Germany. Our war ethics were perfectly expressed at the beginning of the war by the late Lord Roberts. He founded himself on the "will to conquer" of the British race, claiming its satisfaction as a good in itself; and he held out to the rest of the world as its highest interest that it should be governed, as one-fifth of the human race is already governed, by men educated in the public schools of England, meaning thereby Eton, Harrow, Winchester, and Rugby. The Germans, though they may not have phrased this creed quite so bluntly, have adopted it as they have adopted so many other of our institutions, and opposed Pan-Germanism to our Pan-Anglicanism. There is a great deal to be said for both, but not relevantly to the present symposium, which pursues newer ethics, or reconstruction in the light of newer ethics. Suffice it to say here that neither England nor Germany will change her ethics if she vanquishes the other, and that there is no likelihood of France and Italy rising above the moral level of England and Germany. As to Russia, it has cost her a revolution to catch up with her Allies in political evolution. She could not, if she would, be more magnanimous.

But all this presupposes that the fighting will produce a decision. It is not yet clear that this will be the result. Hitherto there has been no lack of victories, but these have been reduced to absurdity by the fact that among the most conspicuous have been victories of the Ottoman empire over the British. The Turks drove us into the sea from Gallipoli, and compelled us to surrender Kut at discretion. Yet we are now in Baghdad, leaving nothing for the Turks but a glorious page of their history. The Germans have a whole volume of victories to their credit. They have captured famous fortresses, and great seaports, and capital cities, and they have driven the British army, the French army, and the Russian army before them in the nearest approach to headlong rout that modern warfare admits of. Yet they have obtained no decision. All the belligerents, except perhaps Rumania, have plenty to boast of. The French have completely regained the military prestige they lost in 1871; and our improvization of an army on the modern scale, even before we resorted to compulsory service, shews that the new conditions have found us as formidable as we were when we fought Louis XIV and Napoleon. The honors of Verdun and of the Somme are with France and England. The exploits of Russia in Galicia and her rush almost to Cracow are as romantic as the rush of the Black Prince to Crécy. Italy is in Cortina. Belgium is aureoled with ruinous glory. Heros and victories and deathless pages of history are six a penny in Europe now, but there is no sign of a decision, and the cost of the operations is so prodigious that the belligerents begin to fear that a decision too long deferred, even if favorable, may be more disastrous than a present capitulation on any sort of reasonable terms.

Therefore, it may happen that the war will end either in a stalemate or in a decision manifestly not worth its cost. In that case there will be at least an attempt at a genuine ethical reconstruction. We shall admit that President Wilson is a great philosopher-statesman, and that Lord Roberts was a barbarous romantic schoolboy; and the Germans will agree, substituting Von Bernhardi for Roberts.

The principle of reconstruction is clear enough: we must renounce the Will to Conquer, and assert the rights of civilized communities to be governed according to their own lights and not according to those of English public schoolmen, Prussian Junkers, or any other persons claiming to represent a super-civilization. But this may not produce much change; for our lights are very largely snobbish lights, and the rule of the Junker, whether British or Prussian, is, in fact, very largely government according to our present lights. The Will to Conquer has dominated the European situation, not because of its rarity and elevation, but because of its vulgarity. The war may make us drop it as we drop a coin that burns our fingers, but that is not renunciation and conversion: the boy who drops the hot penny is as keen about money as he was before. How is the penny to be kept hot? Clearly by penalizing war and by police measures making the penalty judicial and certain. Yet, as the nations can be policed only by a supernational authority, the renunciation of the Will to Conquer involves the renunciation of sovereign nationality and the subordination of nationality to a supernational power.

Half-a-dozen supernational schemes have already been put forward. Those which have been carefully thought out provide for a supernational legislature as well as a supernational tribunal backed by a supernational militia to enforce the laws of the legislature and the decisions of the tribunal. I take for granted a knowledge of these schemes, and proceed to point out their psychological superficiality. They assume either that the supernational authority will at once represent the whole human race, thus fulfilling the dream of Anacharsis Cloots and Tennyson, or at least that because Russia and Japan are among the eight great Powers they must necessarily combine with the western Powers in the new organization. I suggest that such a combination would be wrecked by its psychological heterogeneity, or else, like the old Concert of Europe face to face with the Turk, avert the wreck only by paralysis. Really stable supernational combinations will not be parliaments of man and federations of the world: they will be civilizations, homogeneous in color, in religion, in tradition, in philosophy, and intermarriageable without miscegenation. The war suggests strongly that a combination between the Germans and the English is inevitable, because they abuse oneanother in exactly the same terms, and hate oneanother in the same way. They understand the French, the Poles, the Italians, the Hungarians, and the Irish very imperfectly, but they understand oneanother like brothers; and they are regarded by the other nations as the chief dangers to the liberty and peace of the world. They have largely peopled the United States of America. In spite of their misunderstandings of the French,

Irish, and Poles, they are accustomed to them and have an admiration for them which is sometimes affectionate and often ridiculous. They can live with them and work with them comfortably; for they share the same religion and irreligion, the same Feudalism and Liberalism and Democracy. They wear the same sort of clothes, eat the same sort of food, and intermarry without the least sense of miscegenation.

Thus, from Warsaw to San Francisco you have a clear unit of civilization; and if Germany, as is probable, has after the war to choose between alliances in the east and in the west, and, choosing the west, consolidates friendly relations with the United States, neither England nor France can prudently stand out of the combination, their accession to which would integrate the Netherlands and Scandinavia almost automatically. Russia would look eastward, for the tradition of Peter and Catherine would fall with the tradition of Frederick the Great and Lord Roberts, and Russia would form an Asiatic unit. The Latin republics of South America would look to Spain and the south of Europe. Roughly, what will happen is that the nations, unable now to stand alone against the empires, will group themselves into alliances. The alliances which are too heterogeneous will fall to pieces as our present alliance must when the fear of Germany is dispelled; but the Powers will regroup themselves until, psychologically, homogeneous groups occur and produce stability. Every group thus stabilized will act as a nucleus, and enlarge itself until its possibilities are exhausted, at which point it will be a practicable supernational organization, and a unit of what may be called pretersupernational organization.

It is evident that one of the important factors in what I call psychological homogeneity is ethical homogeneity. Any combination between communities with different ideas of right and wrong can hold only for some specific purpose on the merits of which both happen to agree; and the most obvious of these is war, which all the civilized Powers consider wrong. After the present experience this conviction seems likely to be strengthened. Consequently, though supernationalism will be limited by general psychological homogeneity, it may be possible to induce the supernational groups to make pretersupernational compacts to maintain the peace of the world. Let us suppose, for example, that what may roughly be called a Lutheran group be formed in Northern Europe and North America, a Catholic Latin group in Southern Europe and South America, a Byzantine group in Russia and Russian Asia, and some groupings, at present incalculable, of Mahometanism in central Asia and of the yellow peoples further east. War between sections of such magnitude would be so calamitous that such notions as pan-Lutheranism, pan-Catholicism, pan-Byzantinism, pan-Mahometanism, and so forth would be ridiculous: the only Pans left would be the Peter Pans, the boys who never grow up; and in relation to the maturity of the new social structure the Peter Pans would be seen in their just proportions, and not, as at present, admired as people with exceptionally big ideas, noble aspirations, and burning patriotisms.

In all this, however, it has been assumed that the nations now divided against oneanother are unanimous within themselves. This, as we know, is very far indeed from being true. Wars have always been to some extent a device of the propertied classes to confuse the issue between themselves and the proletariat, and to stave off revolution; and the present war is by no means an exception. To say that monarchs resort to war to divert popular indignation from the throne is a commonplace, formulated long ago by Catherine the Second. What has not been as generally noticed is that revolutionary governments do the same; for their inexperience, with that of their upstart officials, produces so much popular dissatisfaction that their downfall is inevitable unless they can, by engaging the country in a very dangerous war, make it afraid to venture on another internal change. Those who speak of the revolution in Russia as if it must be the end of all trouble for us in that country need to be reminded of this.

The tendency of revolution to produce war in this way depends for its force on the extent of the change effected by the revolution. If the class which gains the ascendancy has been politically trained before the revolution, the tendency will not exist; for instance, in the revolution which banished the Stuarts and placed William of Orange on the throne of England there was no substitution of an untrained for a trained class in the government: there was in that respect no change at all and, consequently, no increase in belligerence. But in the French revolution the power fell into the hands of the middle class and the nobility. The middle class had no experience of government, and the nobility, which had been reduced a century earlier by Richelieu to a mere retinue of courtiers, knew nothing either of business or political administration: consequently the revolution was followed by twentyfive years of war for the sake of war. Taking these as the two extreme cases recorded for us by history, we may infer that a revolution in Germany, where democracy is more real because more scientific than in the great avowed democracies, would be much less likely to produce reckless belligerence than in Russia, where not even the Tsardom and the bureaucracy had mastered enough of the art of popular government to avert a revolution in the middle of a war.

This brings us to the question of political homogeneity, which is as indispensable to a supernational combination as any other factor. As long as it remains true that in a western federal democracy, where the President has no legal power to pledge the federated states to any foreign enterprize, his word is nevertheless as good security as minted gold, whereas in an eastern autocracy, where the autocrat can legally pledge the life and conduct of every soul in his dominions, his word affords no security that any provincial governor or general will not act in flat defiance of it according to his own tastes or the whims of his mistress, so long will it be impossible for states of the western democratic type to form stable combinations with states of the eastern autocratic type.

We must, therefore, postulate for supernationalism a certain political stability in the constituent nations which is unattainable without a considerable development of internal organization, sufficient at least to make it possible for the nation to enter into engagements which shall not be subject to the caprice or failing powers of monarchs or other individuals, or to private interests of any kind, whether they be the family interests of the reigning family and its courtiers, or the commercial interests of private adventurers. It is difficult to see how these can be got rid of except by getting rid of monarchs and courtiers altogether, and reorganizing the industry of the country as a public concern: that is to say, by adopting republicanism and socialism. And as republican and socialistic institutions can have no stability in the presence of inequalities of income, which continually tend to upset them, and have historically always finally succeeded in upsetting them, we may take it that equality of income, involving the complete dissociation of labor with income, and consequently a system of compulsory labor for the community, will be the ultimate goal of internal reform as far as our present vision reaches.

In short, then, ethical reconstruction will take the form of a substitution of the ethics of communism for the ethics of commercialism, and of the ethics of democracy for those of feudalism. Nothing short of these changes will involve any ethical change at all except in the backward direction of crudity and barbarism. I am, of course, aware that the nature of the reconstruction may be entirely unforeseen, and that its ethics may be at present quite unthinkable. But we have no reason to suppose that war, which is nothing, after all, but an intensification of the fear of death, will enlarge our minds. An urgent possibility of death may induce a man to make his will after neglecting that duty for many years, but it does not alter the provisions of the will nor increase the sum he has to bequeath. In the same way a war may stimulate or frighten us into carrying out a number of reforms which we have merely dreamt of or written papers about before, but it cannot increase our intellectual capital. Everyone who has been face to face with death knows that it has the power, by the intensity of its reality, to reduce many of what we believed to be our gravest concerns and most important convictions to the idlest vanities and the shallowest affectations. It also, by the extraordinary efforts we find ourselves able to make to escape from it, reveals reserves of power in ourselves which we had never before discovered.

Now, what the presence of death can do, war can do. Matters that seemed of vital importance in politics three years ago seem silly now, and national efforts that would have seemed crazily impossible in 1913 have proved as easy as the Daylight Saving

Act. Therefore, we shall be able to consider many measures after the war that were not practical politics before it. Yet we shall not have new ethics, nor new politics, nor new economics, nor indeed any new synthesis or dogma. What will happen is that we shall no longer say of any important social reform that it is impossible because it would cost twenty million pounds. And we shall not say that the British people would never stand this or that sacrifice of their personal convenience, much less their lives, to social principles. That is a considerable advance in our executive effectiveness, and enlarges widely the possibilities of applying the principles we have already thought out. Therefore, we cannot say that the war will make no difference. It will not, however, make a new heaven and a new earth; for these mean a new philosophy, and the war will certainly not produce that. We shall be fortunate if we recover without excessive effort the ground it has already lost us by throwing us back to the primitive ethic of the battlefield.

MODERN RELIGION

(Lecture delivered under the auspices of the Hampstead Ethical Institute, in the Hampstead Conservatoire, London, 13 November 1919. *The New Commonwealth*, Supplement, 2 *January* 1920)

You are the citizens and subjects of an enormous empire which contains several hundred millions of people. The first thing that any empire or any political organization requires is Religion, and it must be a religion which can be accepted by all the persons within that political organization. That may be a simple thing when the political organization is a small one, and consists of people who have all been brought up in the same way, and attended the same place of worship, and had the same teaching, but when it is a political organization which extends over the whole of the earth, which embraces very different climates, very different religions in the sense of organized religions, very different creeds, and so on, then the matter becomes very different. The official religion of the British Empire would appear to be the religion of the Church of England, an institutional religion, but the difficulty is that the Church of England is supposed to be a Christian religion, yet in the Empire only eleven per cent. of the inhabitants are Christians, and a great many of that eleven are a very queer sort of Christian. For instance, a large number of them do not even profess to believe in the Christian religion in the institutional sense, do not attend any place of worship, do not read religious books, do not listen to sermons—some come and listen to me for preference. Is there any likelihood of the principles of the Church of England becoming universally credible? Is there any likelihood of their recommending themselves to the enormous majority who have not yet adopted Christianity, and do not shew any sign of intending to do so? You have the privilege of living at the same time as one of the most distinguished churchmen the Church of England has ever produced. I myself can remember Dean Stanley and Mandell Creighton, the Bishop of London; and they—especially Mandell Creighton—were men of quite extraordinary ability. But at the present time you have a churchman among you who, I think, for intellectual force, for courage and character, for penetration, will probably be remembered quite as long as Mandell Creighton, and I think will possibly take a higher intellectual rank. I mean the Dean of St Paul's [William Ralph Inge]. Now, the Dean of St Paul's tells us with reference to those tenets which every postulate for the post of minister or clergyman of the Church of England is required unfeignedly to embrace—that is to say, there are two Creeds, there are the Thirtynine Articles, and there is the matter of accepting the Bible as being a perfectly literally true document containing a correct scientific account of the origin of species and the creation—the Dean of St Paul's tells you that if the bishops were to refuse to ordain any postulant for the clergy who could not unfeignedly and in his plain sense accept that Creed, those Thirtynine Articles and that doctrine about the Scriptures, the clergy would consist exclusively of fools, of liars, and of bigots. Those are his words, they are not mine, and this is deliberately told you by the ablest churchman you have, in a position—that of Dean of St Paul's—which is technically perhaps not quite so high as that of the Archbishop of Canterbury, but really carries with it equal authority, especially when the person who holds it is perhaps rather a cleverer man than the Archbishop of Canterbury. Now, under those circumstances, not only would it appear that there is no chance of whatever genuine religion you are going to make the foundation of your empire being the Church of England, it would appear to me that if that is true there will very soon be no Church of England at all in the old-fashioned sense of the word. You may anticipate that the Church will broaden, that it will relax its tests and so on. You have no historical warrant for believing anything of the kind. Everything you know of the history of these great institutional churches in the past will tend to convince you that as the Church is more and more attacked, challenged, instead of liberalizing itself, it will do exactly the other thing, it will draw its lines tighter. It will say, Sooner than give up our old doctrines we will recruit exclusively from the fools, the liars, and the bigots. You know, for instance, that the Roman Catholic Church in the nineteenth century, when it also had to sustain a tremendous attack from modern thought, instead of relaxing its doctrine immediately added to it dogmas which the Middle Ages never dreamed of, and would probably never have tolerated; it drew its lines very much tighter. And when there was a Modernist movement in that Church it excommunicated and threw out those Modernists, with an affirmation of doctrine which even the fools, liars, and bigots, if I may quote the Dean again, would not venture to impose on the Church of England.

Consequently, I think you must thoroughly make up your minds not merely that, whatever the great modern religion is which is going to be a practical religion for the empire, it will not be the Roman Catholic Church or the Church of England, but it will not be a church at all. You will find that human nature divides itself in a particular way. You meet a kind of man whose religion consists in adhering to a church, who requires a church, and requires to be led by a priest; who adopts the creed and articles of a church; he attends the services of the church, and that is his religion. Very often it does not go any further than that, but still, there is the thing for him. To him religion means adhesion to a church and observance of a ritual, and the placing of authority in spiritual matters in the hands of a special class. Now, over against the natural-born churchman there are men of another type, and these men are always really mystics. They do not believe in priests; they very often hate them, and they hate churches. They are deeply religious persons, and instead of priests they have prophets, and these prophets come, if I may say so, practically at the call of God. These men believe in the direct communion of their own spirit with whatever spirit it is that rules the universe. They believe that the inspiration of that spirit may come to anybody, and that he may become a prophet. In the strict sense you may almost say that these people are genuine protestants; I could say so without any qualification only, unfortunately, we have got what many members of the Church of England do not call it, an Anglican Catholic Church. They call it a Protestant Church. If in my native land you called it a Protestant Church, an Anglo or an Irish Catholic Church, I dont know what would happen to you. The thing would not be tolerated for a moment. I, as a born and baptized Irish Protestant, have always maintained that a Protestant Church is a contradiction in terms: that the genuine Protestant knows no Church and knows no priest; practically he believes in the direct communion between himself and the spirit that rules the universe, and the man he follows is a prophet and not an ordained priest, not a man who claims an apostolic succession because a long succession of hands have been laid on heads, and so on; claims practically that apostolic succession is a direct inspiration, which may come to him and which may come to anybody. Now, that distinction between the churchman, between the person the Dean of St Paul's calls the institutionalist, and the genuine out-and-out Protestant mystic, will always cause a certain division, therefore any religion that is going to unite men will have to be a religion which both of these people can accept. It must have room for mystics, prophets, and for priests, and it must be a religion of such a character as will prevent the priests from stoning the prophets, as they always do. Some of you who have had a perfectly conventional religious education, that is to say an entirely unintelligent one, have been very likely left to draw conclusions

for which there is no warrant. For instance, in reading the Bible
—you have heard it read in churches, and you have perhaps
had it imparted to you by an ordained clergyman—you have
derived an impression that the prophets of whom you read were
only a sort of old-fashioned clergy. You are entirely wrong in
that; they were prophets who were stoned by the old-fashioned
clergy. If you read them carefully you will see that they are continually complaining of the persecution which came from the
Church of their day. You must keep that distinction in mind.
And we have to consider this point, as to whether it is possible
to get any sort of common ground where you can get a religion
for your empire.

Now, some of you who are thoroughly modern, educated,
and intellectual persons may say: Why do you want a religion
for your empire at all? Why not be pragmatic? as the modern
phrase goes. These religious people are continually pursuing
ideals of rightness and truth. Well, you may say, in the modern
pragmatic way, anything that works is right; anything people
believe is true. That is what constitutes truth, and that is what
constitutes right. I do not deny that if you wish to be an accomplished man or woman of the world, and get on nicely, easily,
and sensibly in it you had better be acquainted with this peculiar
view. In the ordinary intercourse of society it has its uses. But it
is not any use when you come to governing a great state. There
it is no use saying that the thing that works is right, because
things that you know to be abominably wrong, and that you
cannot pretend to be made right by any sort of working, can
nevertheless be made to work politically if only you will put
sufficient brute force into making them work. Let me take two
particularly atrocious examples of bad and tyrannical government in the modern world. Take, for instance, the government
of Russia by the Tsars. This I can only describe by saying that
if you take as true the very stupidest, the most mendacious, the
most outrageous and prejudiced account that you can find in
our more reactionary papers today of the régime of Lenin and
Trotzsky in Russia, you may assume quite safely that the present
state of things in Russia is practically heaven compared to what
it was under the Tsar, and the fact that we nevertheless made an

alliance with that power is a thing that ought to make you very carefully consider whether there may not be some sort of divine retribution in the heavy price we had to pay for making that alliance, and making it with our eyes open.

The other instance of atrociously bad government which has lasted for three or four centuries, I need hardly tell you, is the case of my own country, Ireland. Nevertheless, it worked. The Tsar's government worked perfectly; not without a certain amount of friction, because it was made to work by the simple process of getting rid of any person who was opposed to it, putting him in prison, killing him, or otherwise persuading him to be quiet. You will see, therefore, that to suppose a country can be governed pragmatically, that any country can justify its government because it can say it works, is entirely out of the question. Six months of that would knock the pragmatism out of the most inveterate agnostic, the most inveterate shirker of fundamental moral questions you can find anywhere. In the same way, there is no use in saying that anything the people can be induced to believe to be true is true. That is not so at all, because, just exactly as the most tyrannical state can make a government work, in the same way you will find that that same government, by means of a State Church, or by means of an institution like the Holy Inquisition, the Holy Office, as it was called, can also get anything believed. If you kill all the people that dont believe it, or at any rate silence them; get hold of the education of the children; take them from their earliest years and tell them it is true, and it is very wicked to doubt it, and very unpleasant things will happen in the next world if they doubt it, you can immediately create such a body of belief as will pragmatically justify the most monstrous creed you can possibly put before the human mind.

Accordingly, when you come to governing a country, there is no use in talking pragmatism. You have to come back to your old Platonic ideals. You will have to use your reason as best you can, to make up your mind there are certain things that are right and certain things that are true. You may always have at the back of your mind the fact that you may be mistaken, but you cannot sit down and do nothing because you are not sure what you have to do. In governing a country you have to arrive at the best conclusion you can, the conclusion that certain institutions are in harmony with what we call the Platonic ideal of right and truth, and trust your instinct more or less to guide you, and also, of course, trust history and experience; except that if you are a politician in this country you will never know anything about history, and your experience is mostly that of trying to cheat other people. Nevertheless, insofar as our laws and creeds can be dictated by persons who have had rather a better preparation for public life than that—gentlemen like the Dean of St Paul's, although he has certainly had the most frightful antecedents anybody can imagine; no one ever came out with [such] intellectual distinction in the face of such dreadful disadvantages —I must interrupt myself to say that in justice. He is the son of the Head of an Oxford College and a Doctor of Divinity. His mother was the daughter of an Archdeacon, and, in spite of that, he went deliberately, with his eyes open, and married a lady who was the granddaughter of a bishop and the daughter of an arch-deacon. He has been an Eton schoolboy and Eton master. He has taken every possible scholarship that could be got at the University, and how it is he has come out of that with any mind whatever I do not know. It only shews what a splendid mind it is that he was able to stand all that. As I say, if you take men of that type, and get them to dictate your creeds and your laws, you will find that they will have to fall back for public purposes on the good old Platonic ideals. They will have to believe in absolute ideas with regard to right and truth, absolute at least for the time. They will have to make an elaborate series of laws in order to maintain what they call right government, and in order to hold up the truth to people.

I rather think that the religion of the future will dictate our laws, particularly our industrial laws—because remember that in the future law will not be the very simple thing it has been in the past, a mere matter of preventing ordinary robbery (I do not mean the robbery from which this country really suffers, which is the robbery of the poor by the rich, but what the policeman recognizes and charges you with as robbery and murder). All that is very simple, but we now know that in the future governments will have to do a great deal more of what they are already doing on a scale which fifty years ago would have seemed perfectly Utopian; that is to say, they will have to interfere in the regulation of industry, will have to dictate the rate of wages, or rather, as a matter of fact, there will not be wages at all. What governments in future will have to recognize as one of their first duties is the very thing they do not interfere with at all, and that is, the distribution of the national income among the people of the country. And when you come to that you will see that the religion of the future will be very largely a Marxist religion. That will mean nothing probably to a good many people here because there will be persons who are not Socialists and have not read Marx, and persons who are Socialists and have only pretended to read Marx but never really have. Therefore I had better explain exactly what I mean. What I mean is that one of the things Marx impressed on the world, and he did it to a certain extent by exaggerating it, was that the economic constitution of society was practically at the bottom of everything in society. That was put forward not only by Marx and by Engels, of course, but also by an English historian, Buckle. In his History of Civilization you will see the importance he gives to the economic basis, and if one might caricature Marx's position we may suppose him saying something of this kind. Some of the gentlemen in the Natural History Museum at South Kensington will tell you: If you bring me a single bone of an extinct antediluvian monster, I will reconstruct the entire monster from that bone; which, of course, is an easy thing to do, as nobody can possibly contradict him when he has reconstructed it. Marx may be imagined as saying in the same way: If you will bring me from any period of history, if you can dig it up, the tool a man worked with, or dig up some evidence of the conditions under which he worked, whether a cottage industry, factory industry, or what not, from that alone I will reconstruct the entire politics, religion, and philosophy of that stage of civilization, whatever it was. That, of course, is an exaggeration. Nevertheless, it is enormously important, and it must be recognized in the future by any religious nexus that we may spread, it must be acknowledged that you have to begin with economics. One may illustrate that in a very simple way. Here am I addressing you on a very important subject, a very lofty subject. I am accordingly stretching my intellect as far as I possibly can to rise to the occasion. I have in action all the highest part of me, we will say, all the best bits of my brain for your benefit. Supposing you keep me here for a long time—I know you wont do that, it is extremely likely I would keep you here even when you wanted to go away—nevertheless, supposing you said, We really cannot stand this fellow with his airs and intellect and philosophy, and all this sort of thing; talking about his superiors, like the Dean of St Paul's and persons of that kind, and daring to criticize. We will take the conceit out of this man; we will see how long his philosophy and lofty ideas, his notions of history, conceptions of the future, will last. You would have nothing to do but to keep me on this platform and take care I did not get anything to eat or drink. You would find that as the hours passed away, in spite of all my efforts to keep on a high level, the whole question of religion would gradually fade into the background of my mind, and the question of getting a drink, and getting something to eat, would steadily grow, and at last you might really bring me to a point at which I would be prepared simply to spring on the chubbiest and nicest-looking persons in this audience, and practically eat them in order to save my life. You must remember humanity is like that. The first thing you have got to do if people are to have any religious, intellectual, or artistic life, is to feed them. Until you have done that they cannot begin to have any sort of spiritual or intellectual life. You must attend to that first.

Therefore I take it the religion of the future, the religion—whatever it is that is to unite all the races of the empire, and to reconcile them all to one common law—will be, I may put it shortly, a thoroughly Marxist religion, in the sense that it will see that the economic question comes first.

Having said that, I want just to say a word as to how far that religion will be a tolerant religion. There is a great deal of nonsense talked in this country about toleration, and the reason of it is this, that since our national Church, the Church of England, began as a heresy—it broke off as you know from the Roman Catholic Church, therefore it began as a heresy—it was persecuted as a heresy, it had to fight under the imputation of being heretical, and the result was it had to fight for toleration and, consequently, it has become a tradition in this country that toleration is an indispensable thing, that you must always tolerate—not that you ever do it as far as you can help it, but nevertheless we have all rather persuaded ourselves that we are tolerant. I do not think any person who has ever candidly examined his own mind would really for one moment suppose he was going to be tolerant. Take, for instance, the question how far do we tolerate the Indian religions? We do tolerate them up to a certain extent; I am not sure we are justified in doing so; but is any person here prepared to tolerate the institution of Suttee? the institution by which a woman is encouraged, when her husband dies, to burn herself on his funeral pyre? We have put that down by simple persecution. Indians tell you that if India became entirely self-governing and independent tomorrow, probably there would be a return to Suttee by a large class of Indians. The moment you are brought face to face with anything of that kind you perceive you are not tolerant. In the same way, there are institutions in this country that I am not prepared to tolerate. I am not at all tolerant with regard to children, for instance. In the matter of toleration you have to draw a very distinct line between the religions, the beliefs and creeds which you will allow to be preached to persons who have grown up, who are able to choose and judge, and the religions which you allow to be fed into those children when they are very young and impressionable, when they may have something stamped on them for life which they may never be able to get rid of, and [are] quite unable to resist. If you asked me whether, if I had the power, I would tolerate teaching such a thing to a child as Calvinism, which is the religion of the north of my own country, the good old Ulster of the Calvinists, I would reply that nothing would induce me to tolerate it for a moment. I would not hear of it for one instant. Let the child, if you like, when it grows up to years of discretion, even before it ceases to be going to an educational institution—there does come a time when I would say, it is now necessary for the child to learn, as a matter of history and understanding its neighbors, that there is such a horrible belief in the world as Calvinism, such an unspeakably wicked thing, at least as I think, and he must learn also that some people think it an exceedingly nice thing, that the Ulster and a great many Scotch people apparently enjoy it. But as to letting a religion of that kind—or indeed I am not sure that I am in favor of any institutional religion—get access to children when they are very young, I am rather inclined to think children would have to be finally protected against everything but what I have called the modern religion, particulars of which I will come to presently, that is to say the general ideas of right and truth which will govern the politics of the whole empire; undoubtedly the young children must be governed according to them, but when it comes to tolerating the teaching of religion, I think it is our first duty to protect children against that particular thing, and I should protect them if I had one of these particular creeds myself —and I daresay I have a lot of them sticking to me—I should be quite willing to have children protected against that [creed] just as much as anybody else's.

I want you to think the thing out and remember that although there is a case for toleration it does not exist in the case of young children, only in the case of people who are competent to judge, and of course you must practise the widest toleration, because the probability is that the most advanced, the most hopeful direction in which your religion and intellect, your artistic doctrine or philosophy, is pushing forward and improving itself is precisely the direction which will hold you and make you think it is blasphemy. For that reason it is very desirable that you should not persecute movements in that way; you should only persecute in the case of things which are entirely abhorrent to your nature, and when you come to do that I am not at all sure you should not do it thoroughly. For instance, to go back for a moment to the case of India, although there is such a tremendous lot to be said for our method of tolerating religion in India we have had no excuse for staying in India at all. As long as we are persecuting it, passionately and vigorously saying, Your Eastern institutions are abominable, we are going to root them out with fire and sword, the probability is we are making India think, we are teaching India something. It seems to me if the Indians could only come over here and have a good persecuting go at a lot of our stupidities and idolatries they might improve us a good deal and in that way there may be something to be said for the domination of one civilization by another; that is to say, the more bigoted and persecuting it is the more cause there is to suppose it is doing something, but the moment you get a broad, tolerant, liberal relation between the two every excuse for your intervention has gone; as long as you pretend you are in India on a great mission from God, that you are missionaries, you may have been right or wrong, at any rate it is a creditable motive. Now that you tolerate, now that you have said, Yes, we all have the same God; it is all perfectly right, we will allow them to practise their religions in that way, where does it lead you? The Indian says, All right, what are you here for? We have to admit we are here looking after money, because we get money out of you, and we get berths for our sons in the Indian Service, and so on. All your excuse is gone and finally under the influence of that you will have to clear out.

That is the advantage of liberal toleration, that it leads to your clearing out, which is exactly what you ought to do, and some of these days will have to do; but remember when the clearing comes about, when you have practically in India what we call a self-determining territory, when you have Egypt and Ireland with practically all their national individual aspirations satisfied, by that time the days of separate nations will have gone; by that time there will have to be bonds, the Empire will probably be a more real thing than it has ever been before. There will still be a Commonwealth, a common interest, bonds of all sorts, therefore there will still remain the necessity for a common religion, a common thing that binds them together in a common ideal of what is right and true.

Now, all this of course is a mere preliminary to my lecture. Some of you thought probably it was just going to be over; you little knew your man. Can we see any convergence towards a common faith, a common belief, on the part of modern men, especially those modern men who have practically discarded the creeds? People who go to Church and who are institutionalists by instinct, [who] like to go to a service, who are Churchmen yet do not believe the literal inspiration of the Scriptures, [who] do not believe the Thirty-nine Articles, [who] find it impossible, for instance, unreservedly and unfeignedly to believe one Article which affirms transubstantiation and the next Article which flatly denies it. That is your idea of an English compromise, it is a very British compromise. Nevertheless, there are many people who are sufficiently consecutive in their ideas to find certain difficulties. I suppose none of you has ever read the Articles. I have read them. They are so extremely short that it is very difficult to forget one completely before you go on to the other, and yet you find places in them where unless you can perform that feat it is not easy to see how you can accept the whole thing. But out of the welter that has ensued on the scrapping of the old creeds, out of this break-up which is indicated by the Dean's statement that practically if you believe what your grandfather and grandmother believed you are either a fool or a bigot or a liar, that is to say if you say you believe them you are a liar and if you do believe them you are either a bigot or a fool—is there anything coming out of this and is there anything coming out of science? When I was a young man—I was born in the year 1856 —when my mind was being formed, as they say, I had very great hopes of science, and the people at that time had extra-ordinary hopes of science, because science came to us as a deliverer from the old evangelicalism which had become entirely intolerable.

There are, of course, people of the old evangelical type about, but I do not think there are any of them here because I am not the sort of preacher they run after. But I can remember when it was quite a general belief that you had a God who was a personal God, of whom they had a perfectly distinct image. He was an elderly gentleman, he had a white beard—I am an elderly gentle-man and I have got a white beard, but I am not a bit like him. Nevertheless, there is a gentleman friend of mine, and a socialist, who is exactly like him, and that is my friend Mr H. M. Hynd-man. Those of you who know him will recognize what the God who was believed in in my youth was like. If you have not had the privilege of meeting Mr Hyndman you had better seek it. If you get Blake's illustrations to Job you will find a picture of the old gentleman there. You may remember how this was focused by the tremendous sensation which was made by Ibsen; the first play with which he practically stormed Europe was the play Brand. The one thing one always remembers is that Brand, the hero, meets a young man and they discuss a little theology and Brand says, "Your God is an old man, I have no use for him." That really, I think, was the first time it suddenly flashed on Europe that, after all, supposing God were to be conceived as a young man? I remember when I was young I had it pushed into me that everything that was pious was old; even when I read the Pilgrim's Progress, which I did when a very small child, when I came to the second part, even Mr Valiant-for-Truth I conceived as an old man, at any rate a grown-up person. I remember my surprise afterwards when, arriving at years of discretion to discover by carefully reading the introduction in verse which a child always skips, that Bunyan had conceived Valiant-for-Truth as being a young man in all the glory of youth. But in those days the ruler of the universe was an elderly gentleman, and you had to be very careful about that elderly gentleman because the one thing he was watching to do at every turn was to strike you dead. You used to be told if you were not very careful—there was always one phrase used—if you said anything that implied the slightest doubt about that old gentleman you were told that you would come home on a shutter. I had when young a vision of the blasphemer, the atheist, the infidel, always being brought home on a shutter—they were never brought home in an ambulance, a hearse, or any other way, but always on a shutter.

I can remember, too, when I was a young man I was at a bachelor party and they began to dispute about religion. There was a pious party there and there was a young man who evidently was a bit of a secularist, and they began disputing about Charles Bradlaugh, who was the great atheist preacher of that day. It was alleged he had on one occasion in public taken out his watch and challenged this God, this old elderly gentleman, if he really existed and if he were the truth to strike him dead within five minutes. Well, you have no idea of the bitterness of the controversy. The pious people, of course, alleged it as being the most frightful and horrible defiance of God that could be conceived, but the secularist, instead of taking the line you would expect, passionately denied that Bradlaugh had done anything of the kind. He said Bradlaugh was too good a man. I said, "Look here; after all, if people do believe this crude thing, that the world is regulated by a very touchy deity who strikes people dead, is not that a very practical way of testing it?" And with that I took my watch out of my pocket. You have no idea of the effect it produced. Both the secularist party and the pious party went into transports of terror. Our host had to appeal to me as his guest, and as a gentleman, not to think of such a thing. Of course, it being my duty as a guest, I put my watch back and said, "After all, the thought has come into my head; the challenge may not have been put into words, but it has been suggested." They were exceedingly uncomfortable for the next five minutes. You, ladies and gentlemen, laugh at this, but in those days it was impossible for people to laugh at it; they were too frightened. Even the skeptical people felt extremely uncomfortable. When that is what is called religion, then you have got such a horrible oppression, the whole thing is such a nightmare, that if anybody will come and offer any kind of argument by which you can convince yourself you can get rid of it, you will jump at it without being very critical.

The argument that people found most difficult to get over was the argument from design. You know the old argument—if a savage took up a watch and saw the way it was arranged, even he would say it was not a casual or accidental growth, that it was a thing designed by a designer. Thus, in the middle of the century, evolution had been entirely forgotten. Evolution was first introduced about the year 1780, and until 1830 it was very much in men's minds; it was very much discussed. But in 1830 discussion about it had been exhausted, and it was almost forgotten. Then Charles Darwin, a grandson of one of the old evolutionists, Erasmus Darwin, suddenly made a discovery, with Alfred Russel Wallace, not of evolution, but [of] a particular method which simulated evolution, which was called natural selection. You are all probably familiar with Darwinian Natural Selection, but the point that affects our argument tonight is this, that Darwin was able to shew that case after case of what appeared to be the most exquisite adaptation of means to ends, the most perfect evidences of design, apparently unquestionable cases of a thing having been made and designed for a particular purpose, was nothing of the kind, that simply the pressure of environment had produced the appearance. To put it roughly: supposing there was a hole in a wall and somebody found a cannon ball near it which exactly fitted, people used to say that was the very clearest evidence that some intelligent person made that hole in the wall to fit the cannon. Darwin showed it was entirely wrong; the cannon ball knocked the hole in the wall, and nobody meant the hole to be there at all. That is what natural selection means as opposed to the old evolution, and there came, as you know, a fierce controversy between Samuel Butler, whose life some of you have been reading, and Darwin. People are rather puzzled at the extraordinary ferocity of the quarrel. I have very often told the story, though it is not told in the biography, of Butler saying to me in the courtyard of the British Museum, in a dogged kind of way, "My grandfather quarreled with Darwin's grandfather; my father quarreled with Darwin's father; I quarreled with Darwin, and my only regret in not having a son is that he cannot quarrel with Darwin's son." Many people reading the biography cannot understand why Butler was so extraordinarily bitter, but the reason was that he was one of the first men to perceive the full significance and meaning of this Natural Selection of Darwin's which was taken up by the scientific world and then by the whole world, and embraced with the most extraordinary enthusiasm as being a new revelation of the beginning of all science, and was applied to everything, so that people declared that the whole mass of evolution had been a matter of natural selection. Butler said, "This doctrine banishes mind from the universe. It presents you with a universe which no man with any capacity for real thought dares face for a moment. It takes all design, all conscience, all thought, out of it, and the whole thing becomes a senseless accident and nothing else. My mind refuses to entertain that." And then Butler set himself to work out what genuine evolution was, and although all through his life Butler was very much slighted, and everyone thought Darwin was one of the greatest men of science that ever existed, now we are all coming round to Butler's view.

But why was it people jumped at Darwin in that way? As a rule, people are not fond of science; they are not much given to studying it. The reason simply was that Darwin destroyed the old evangelicalism, the conception of the continually interfering elderly gentleman with the white beard, who was constantly sending people home on a shutter. He took that weight off the human mind, and people were so enormously relieved to get rid of it that they emptied the baby out with the bath; they practically threw aside everything, and they had a curious notion that since the old evangelical views had been taught in connection with morality, they had not only got rid of the mistakes and crudities and superstitions of the old evangelicalism, but they believed they had got rid of religion and right and wrong altogether, and we entered on a period of pragmatism and materialism which has lasted for fifty years, and which has ended in one of the most appalling wars the world has ever seen; you can trace that war exactly to these purely materialistic ideas. We are very fond of blaming the Germans for this; let us not forget it was an Englishman, Darwin, who had banished mind from the universe; we have occasionally said the Germans are only imitators of us; that they steal our inventions and ideas. I am afraid in this case it is right, they did steal scientific materialist ideas and work on them, but in that particular it is not for us to throw stones. England is undoubtedly the place those ideas came from in the first instance. Such a thing cannot last; it is too entirely against all our poetic instincts. One knows practically as Butler knew that we cannot empty the universe out like that and make the whole thing to be a series of accidents. We know there is intention and purpose in the universe, because there is intention and purpose in us. People have said, Where is this purpose, this intention? I say, It is here; it is in me; I feel it; I directly experience it, and so do you, and you need not try and look as if you didnt. It is like a man saying, Where is the soul? I always say to a materialist of that kind, Can you tell me the difference between a live body and a dead one? Can you find out the life? What has happened? Here is a man struck by a shell; what has happneed? He is made of exactly the same chemicals as before, the same silica, the same carbon; you can find no difference whatever; but somehow he ceases to live, and he is going to tumble to bits. What kept him that strange fantastic shape for so many years? What keeps me in this definite shape? Why do I not crumble into my constituent chemicals? None of these material people can tell me that. It was that continual question. When people began to get frightfully bored by being told everything was sodium and carbon and all that, they said, We are not interested in sodium and carbon except when we want it on the dinner table; cant you talk of something more interesting? And the more interesting thing was life, the most intensely interesting thing on earth, and one began to see that right along the whole line of evolution.

You begin with the amœba; why did it split itself in two? It is not an intelligent thing for anybody to do. You cannot pretend there is any particular accident in that. You cannot see any case that natural selection makes. But somehow the amœba does it. It finds that perhaps two are better than one, but at any rate it does split itself in two, and from that you have a continual pushing forward to a higher and higher organization; the differentiation of sex; the introduction of backbone; the invention of eyes; the invention of systems of digestion; you have a continual steady growth, evolution of life, going on. There is some force you cannot explain, and this particular force is always organizing, organizing, organizing, and among other things it organizes the physical eye, in order that the mechanism can see dangers and avoid them, see its food and go for it, see the edge of the cliff and avoid falling over it. And it not only evolves that particular eye, but it evolves what Shakespear called the mind's eye as well. You are not only striving in some particular way to get more and more power, to get organs and limbs with which you can mould the universe to your liking, you are also continually striving to know, to become more conscious, to see what it is all driving at. And there you have the genuine thing, you have some particular force. The Chairman quoted my expression, and called it the Life Force. Bergson the French philosopher has called it the vital impulse, the *élan vital*. You have many names for it, but at any rate here is a particular thing that is working this miracle of life, that has produced this evolution and is going on producing it, and it is by looking back over the long evolution, and seeing that in spite of all vagaries and errant wanderings one way or another, that still the line as it goes up and up, seems to be always driving at more power and more knowledge, you begin to get a sort of idea; this force is trying to get more power for itself; in making limbs and organs for us, it is making these limbs and organs for itself, and it must be always more or less trying to get more perfect limbs and organs.

If it goes on and on one can perceive that if it is practically given a free hand as it were, if the obstacles are not too many for it, it will eventually produce something which to our apprehension would be almost infinitely powerful and would be infinitely conscious; that is to say, it would be omnipotent and omniscient. And you get a sort of idea that God, as it were, is in the making, that here is this force driving us. You always have the humbling thought when you are told by your teachers, God made you; you look in the looking-glass, and say, Well, why did he make me? Was that the best he could do? And when you do not look at yourself but look at somebody else, the impression is tremendous. You really do see that somehow or other, assuming that all the organisms that have been made are visible, are sensible to us, we cannot be satisfied that we are the last word. It really would be too awful to think there is nothing more to come but us. Nevertheless, we may hope if only we give everybody the best possible chance in life, this evolution of life may go on, and after some time, if we begin to worship life, if instead of merely worshiping mammon, in the old scriptural phrase, and wanting to make money, if we begin to try to get a community in which life is given every possible chance, and in which the development of life is the one thing that is everybody's religion, that life is the thing, then co-operation with this power becomes your religion, you begin to feel your hands are hands of God, as it were; that he has no other hands to work with; [that] your mind is the mind of God; that he made your mind in order to work with. Then you not only get an enormous addition in courage, self-respect, dignity, and purpose; get turned aside from all sorts of vile and base things, but you get a religion which may be accepted practically by almost all the Churches, as they purge themselves more or less of their superstition. Because, as I pointed out, instead of purging themselves of their superstition, their method is usually to defend themselves against attack by thickening the crust of superstition. In that they kill themselves. But new churches are formed, and in spite of all their efforts even the existing churches become more liberal.

But supposing I talk in terms of this religion which I have haltingly tried to explain to you, what is the great advantage it gives to me personally? It is this. I never have the slightest difficulty in talking to a religious man of any creed whatever; in fact, I get on perfectly well with Roman Catholics and dignitaries of the Church of England if they are really religious. I do not pretend to get on with people who have no religious sense whatever. I should bore them. But if I come across religious people, Indian, or Irish, or Mahometan, or anybody else, we can meet on this common ground. You find that this thing is in everybody, the hope of this thing. The moment you clear up people's minds, and make them conscious of this, that moment you discover that the roots of this religion are in every person, and you may get a common bond all over the empire.

This religion you will see growing up all through your literature, not only in Butler and Bergson, and even in my own works, but you find it coming in all directions, distinctly in the novels and poetry of Thomas Hardy, [and] everywhere in Mr Wells. Mr Wells goes on at a tremendous rate. You never know what will come. He suddenly rushes out and says, Hurrah! I have suddenly discovered something no one has discovered before. I have discovered God. He discovers the things that were discovered the first two centuries after Christ. There has also been a tremendous discovery of Christ himself. In the days of the old gentleman with the white beard who sent people home on shutters, Christ himself was almost as great a caricature of what we have on record of the real Christ as the elderly gentleman was of the real spirit of the universe, the Life Force. There has been a sort of rediscovery of Christ. People suddenly begin to discover that their religion is a universal religion, and they also begin to discover that there have been other Christs, and that there are Christs even at the present time; that that spirit which was in Christ you will find among Buddhists, among all sorts of persons,

persons whom the evangelicals used to call heathen and idola-
trous, and used to give large subscriptions to convert them. Then
they used to give large subscriptions to convert the Jews. The
whole missionary idea of the old evangelicals was entirely wrong,
and furthermore, if they had only read their gospels, they would
have seen it was wrong on the authority of Christ himself. Christ
never attempted to establish a church; he was there in the middle
of Jews and Pharisees; he never asked any Jew to become a
Christian. He did not mean to establish a church. He meant
practically he was one of the prophets. What he was dealing
with was mysticism. He wanted the Jews to accept something
in addition to whatever creed or institution they believed in;
to accept his universal religion. He wanted the Gentile also to
accept it; the circumcized and the uncircumcized alike; and when
he found people wanted to go and act as missionaries, to go somewhere else and try to tear up by the roots some man's religion
and substitute his own, Christ told them quite plainly, Do not
do that; if you go and try to pull up what you think are the tares
you will pull up the wheat as well. Of course, we never used to
listen to that. We sent missionaries; we plucked up as we thought
the tares in their religion, and the result was the missionary's
convert has become a byword throughout the world as a person
with no religion at all. It turned out that the wheat had come up
with the tares.

RUSKIN'S POLITICS

(Lecture delivered at the Ruskin Centenary Exhibition, held at
the Royal Academy of Arts, London, 21 November 1919.
Issued as a book by the Ruskin Centenary Council,
London, 1921)

There have been very few men, I think, in whom our manifold
nature has been more marked than in Ruskin. If you go round
this exhibition, you will find several portraits exhibited as portraits of Ruskin, but it is surprising what a number of other
people they are portraits of. Somewhere behind me on that wall
there is a bronze dish, and on that bronze a portrait of Ruskin
in profile. That is one of the most remarkable portraits in the

exhibition, because whatever its merits may be as a portrait of Ruskin—and probably some of you will have said on seeing it, "That is not very like the Ruskin we are familiar with"—it is not at all a bad portrait of Mozart. Almost all the genuine portraits of Mozart are profiles. No doubt some of you have been taken in by the usual music-shop portrait of a handsome young nobleman who was a contemporary of Mozart. But in the genuine Mozart portraits there is a peculiar salience about the profile; you will see in them that Mozart's upper lip came out with a certain vivacity in it peculiar to the man, which spoils his beauty as compared with the portrait of the nobleman, but nevertheless gives you the great musician, who at the end of his life subordinated his music to his social enthusiasms and wrote his last opera nominally on the subject of freemasonry, but really on that social upheaval which was then preparing the French Revolution and has been developing ever since. Now look over there to my left, and you will see a portrait of Ruskin by Herkomer. But it is more like John Stuart Mill. If you look at some of the photographs that were taken in the Lake country, when Ruskin was an elderly man, those of you who enjoyed the acquaintance of Grant Allen will be struck by the fact that they are very good portraits of Grant Allen: you feel that if Grant had lived a little longer, he would have been exactly like that.

Thus the portraits give you by their resemblances the evolution of the artist into the prophet. He begins as a painter, a lover of music, a poet and rhetorician, and presently becomes an economist and sociologist, finally developing sociology and economics into a religion, as all economics and sociology that are worth anything do finally develop. You follow him from Mozart to Mill, picking up on the way the man of science, Grant Allen, also a little in the sociological line, but very much interested in science and material things, and material forms and shapes, just as Ruskin is in Modern Painters. Finally, you have the portraits made by Mr Severn of Ruskin in his latest time, when Ruskin was hardly a human being at all, when almost the nearest resemblance that occurs to you is his resemblance to God as depicted in Blake's Book of Job. You get, in short, to an almost divine condition.

I daresay you have already had lectures on all the phases of Ruskin represented in those portraits; and now it has come to my turn to deal with Ruskin as a politician. I think Ruskin was more misunderstood as a politician than in any other department of his activity. People complained that he was unintelligible. I do not think he was unintelligible. If you read his political utterances, the one thing that you cannot say of them is that they were unintelligible. You would imagine that no human being could ever have been under the slightest delusion as to what Ruskin meant and was driving at. But what really puzzled his readers—and incidentally saved his life, because he certainly would have been hanged if they had grasped what he was driving at, and believed that he believed it—was that he was incredible. You see, he appealed to the educated, cultivated, and discontented. It is true that he addressed himself to the working classes generally; and you can find among the working classes, just as Mr Charles Rowley has found in the Ancoats quarter of Manchester, a certain proportion of workingmen who have intellectual tastes and artistic interests. But in all classes his disciples were the few who were at war with commercial civilization. I have met in my lifetime some extremely revolutionary characters; and quite a large number of them, when I have asked, "Who put you on to this revolutionary line? Was it Karl Marx?" have answered, "No, it was Ruskin." Generally the Ruskinite is the most thoroughgoing of the opponents of our existing state of society.

Now, the reason why the educated and cultured classes in this country found Ruskin incredible was that they could not bring themselves to believe that he meant what he was saying, and indeed shouting. He was even shouting in such terms that if I were to describe it merely as abusive I should underdo the description. Think of the way in which his readers were brought up! They were educated at our public schools and universities; they moved in a society which fitted in with those public schools and universities; they had been brought up from their earliest childhood as, above everything, respectable people; taught that what respectable people did was the right and proper thing to do, was good form and also high culture; that such people were the salt of the earth; that everything that existed in the way of artistic culture depended on their cultured and leisured existence. When you have people saturated from their childhood with views of that kind, and they are suddenly confronted with a violently contrary view, they are unable to take it in. For instance, to put it quite simply, they knew that there were the Ten Commandments, and that the Ten Commandments were all right; and they argued from this that as respectable people were all right in everything they did they must be living according to the Ten Commandments. Therefore, their consciences were entirely untroubled.

I have here a volume of Ruskin which I took up this morning, intending to read it, but had not time. I opened it at random, and happened on a page on which Ruskin gave the Ten Commandments according to which in his conception our polite and cultured society really lives. This is the only passage I shall read today, though I feel, of course, the temptation that every lecturer on Ruskin feels to get out of his job by reading, because anything he reads is likely to be better than anything he can say of his own. Ruskin says:

> Generally the ten commandments are now: Thou shalt have any other god but me. Thou shalt worship every bestial imagination on earth and under it. Thou shalt take the name of the Lord in vain to mock the poor; for the Lord will hold him guiltless who rebukes and gives not; thou shalt remember the sabbath day to keep it profane; thou shalt dishonor thy father and thy mother; thou shalt kill, and kill by the million, with all thy might and mind and wealth spent in machinery for multifold killing; thou shalt look on every woman to lust after her; thou shalt steal, and steal from morning till evening; the evil from the good, and the rich from the poor; thou shalt live by continual lying in millionfold sheets of lies; and covet thy neighbor's house, and country, and wealth and fame, and everything that is his. And finally, by word of the Devil, in short summary, through Adam Smith, a new commandment give I unto you: that ye hate oneanother.

If anybody is going to tell me, here or elsewhere, that this is unintelligible, I do not know what to think of that person's brains. Nothing could well be clearer. But, as I have said, and repeat, it was profoundly incredible to those to whom it was addressed.

Ruskin's political message to the cultured society of his day, the class to which he himself belonged, began and ended in this simple judgment: "You are a parcel of thieves." That is what it came to. He never went away from that, and he enforced it with a very extraordinary power of invective. Ruskin was a master of invective. Compare him, for instance, with Cobbett. Cobbett had immense literary style, and when he hated a thing, he hated it very thoroughly indeed. Think of Cobbett's writing about the funding system—think of his writing about the spoliation of the Church by Henry VIII—think of his writing about the barrenness of Surrey, which cultured society likes so much and which Cobbett loathed as a barren place—think of what he said about "barbarous, bestial Malthus"—think of Cobbett at the height of his vituperation. Then go on to Karl Marx. Karl Marx was a Jew who had, like Jeremiah, a great power of invective. Think of the suppression of the Paris Commune of 1871, and then of that terrific screed that Marx wrote, exposing the Empire, denouncing the Versaillese generals, execrating the whole order of things which destroyed the Commune so remorselessly. There you have a masterpiece of invective, a thing which, although it was not reproduced in any of the newspapers, or popular literary issues of the day, nevertheless did leave such an effect that when, thirty years after, a proposal was made in the French Chamber to put Galliffet into a public position of some credit, the governing classes having forgotten that a word had ever been said against him, suddenly that terrible denunciation of Marx rose up against him and struck him absolutely out of public life. Yet when you read these invectives of Marx and Cobbett, and read Ruskin's invectives afterwards, somehow or other you feel that Ruskin beats them hollow. Perhaps the reason was that they hated their enemy so thoroughly. Ruskin does it without hatred, and therefore he does it with a magnificent thoroughness. You may say that his strength in invective is as the strength of ten because his heart is pure. And the only consequence of his denunciation of society was that people said, "Well, he cant possibly be talking about us, the respectable people"; and so they did not take any notice of it.

I must now go on to Ruskin's specific contribution to economics and sociology, because that, as you know, today means a contribution to politics. In Ruskin's own time this was not so clear. People did not understand then that your base in politics must be an economic base and a sociological base. We all know it today, and know it to our cost; and will know it to our still greater cost unless we find a way out, which, it seems, lies not very far from Ruskin's way. Ruskin took up the treatises of our classic political economy, the books by which our Manchester Capitalism sought to justify its existence. In this he did what Karl Marx had done before; and, like Marx, he did it in a way which I do not like exactly to describe as a corrupt way, because you cannot think of corruption in connection with Ruskin: nevertheless, he did not take it up as a man with a disinterested academic enthusiasm for abstract political economy. I think we must admit that, like Marx, he took it up because he was clever enough to see that it was a very good stick to beat the Capitalist dog with.

Marx took up the theory of value which had been begun by Adam Smith, and developed by Malthus, and, seeing that he could turn it against Capitalism, tried to re-establish it on a basis of his own. Thus we got his celebrated theory of value, which is now a celebrated blunder. What Ruskin did was this. He held up to us the definition of value given by the economists, and said: "These gentlemen define value as value in exchange. Therefore," he said, "a thing that you cannot exchange has no value: a thing that you can exchange has value. Very well. When on my way to Venice I go through Paris, I can buy there for two francs fifty an obscene lithograph, produced by the French to sell to English tourists. When I reach Venice, I go to the Scuola di San Rocco and look at the ceiling painted there by Tintoretto, because it is one of the treasures of the world. But that ceiling cannot be sold in the market. It has no exchange value. Therefore, according to John Stuart Mill, the obscene lithograph has a higher value than the ceiling, which in fact has no value at all. After that, I have no further use for your political economy. If that is the way you begin, I hesitate to go on to the end; for I know where your journey must land you—in hell. You may be under the impression that after all hell is a thing you can think of later on; but you are mistaken: you are already at your destination: the condition in which you are living is virtually hell." Then he gave his version of your Ten Commandments. If you had said to him, "We may be in hell; but we feel extremely comfortable," Ruskin, being a genuinely religious man, would have replied, "That simply shews that you are damned to the uttermost depths of damnation, because not only are you in hell, but you like being in hell."

Ruskin got no farther than that in political economy. It was really a pregnant contribution, but he did not go on. Having knocked the spurious law of value into a cocked hat, he did not go on to discover a scientific law of value; and he took no interest in and never reached that other very revolutionary law, the law of economic rent. I see no sign in his writings that he ever discovered it.

When Karl Marx (let me make this contrast) demonstrated that, in his phrase, the workingman was being exploited by the Capitalist—and Karl Marx took a great deal of trouble to establish what he called the rate of surplus value: that is to say, the rate at which the Capitalist was robbing the workingman—he made a pretense of doing the thing mathematically. He was not a mathematician, but he had a weakness for posing as a mathematician and using algebraic symbols. He tried to determine the quantitative aspect of exploitation. That sort of thing did not interest Ruskin. Ruskin said to the Capitalist, "You are either a thief or an honest man. I have discovered that you are a thief. It does not matter to me whether you are a fifty per cent. thief or a seventy per cent. thief. That may be interesting to men of business who are interested in figures. I am not. Sufficient to me that you are a thief. Having found out that you are a thief, I can now tell you what your taste in art will be. And as I do not like a thievish taste in art I suggest you should become an honest man." And I daresay the Capitalists who read it said: "Aha! that serves Jones right!" I doubt if they ever applied it to themselves.

Though Ruskin was certainly not a completely equipped

economist, I put him, nevertheless, with Jevons as one of the great economists, because he knocked the first great hole in classic economics by shewing that its value basis was an inhuman and unreal basis, and could not without ruin to civilization be accepted as a basis for society at all. Then Jevons came along and exploded the classic value theory from the abstract scientific side. Marx also never grasped the law of rent, never understood one bit of it any more than Ruskin did. Nevertheless, Marx did establish Marxism, a thing of which you hear a good deal, and which is therefore worth defining. Marxism does not mean this or that particular theory: it does mean that the economic question is fundamental in politics and sociology. No doubt some of Marx's disciples—after the way of disciples—have pushed that view a little hard.

You know that some of the curators of the Natural History Museum at South Kensington are eminent naturalists and paleontologists. In my youth—I do not know whether they do it still—their favorite swank was to say, "If you will bring us the smallest bone of any extinct monster, from that small bone we can reconstruct the whole monster." I remember in my youth being impressed by that—not so much by the wonderful thing they said they could do, as by their cleverness in discovering how safe it was to say they could do it: for when they had reconstructed the monster, who could come along and prove that it was not a bit like the original? Nobody could produce a live monster from his back garden and compare the two.

In the same way Marx said, in effect, "If you will bring me the tool or machine with which a man worked, I will deduce from it with infallible certainty his politics, his religion, his philosophy, and his view of history and morals." That, of course, like the South Kensington offer, was a great swank. Nevertheless, it epitomizes an important truth, and makes you feel the dramatic power with which Marx brought into economics and politics his view of the fundamental importance of economics. Our own historian, Buckle, had taken very much the same line; but I think I can give you a simpler illustration of the importance of the economic basis, and why it was that Ruskin, beginning as an artist with an interest in art—exactly as I did myself, by the way —was inevitably driven back to economics, and to the conviction that your art would never come right whilst your economics were wrong.

The illustration I will give you is this. Here am I addressing you, a cultivated audience. I wish to keep before you the most elevated view of all the questions Ruskin dealt with. I am straining all my mental faculties and drawing on all my knowledge. Now suppose you were to chain me to this table and invite me to go on and on. What would happen? Well, after some hours a change would take place in the relative importance of the things presenting themselves to my mind. At first, I should be thinking of Ruskin, and attending to my business here as a lecturer on Ruskin. But at last my attention would shift from the audience in front of me to that corner of the room behind me, because that is where the refreshment room is. I should, in fact, be thinking of nothing but my next meal. I should finally reach a point at which, though I am a vegetarian, I should be looking at the chubbiest person in the audience, and wishing I could eat that chubby person.

That is the real soundness of Marxism and of Ruskin's change of ground from art to economics. You may aim at making a man cultured and religious, but you must feed him first; and you must feed him to the point at which he is reasonably happy, because if you feed him only to the point at which you can make a bare drudge of him and not make him happy, then in his need for a certain degree of happiness he will go and buy artificial happiness at the public-house and other places. Workingmen do that at the present day: indeed we all do it to a certain extent, because all our lives are made more or less unhappy by our economic slavery, whether we are slaves or masters. Economics are fundamental in politics: you must begin with the feeding of the individual. Unless you build on that, all your superstructure will be rotten.

There you have the condition postulated by Marx and every sensible man. That is why Ruskin, when he was twenty, gave you Modern Painters, and at thirty, The Stones of Venice, also about art, but very largely about the happiness of workingmen who made the art; for the beauty of Venice is a reflection of the happiness of the men who made Venice. When he was forty he wrote Unto this Last, and there took you very far away from art and very close to politics. At fifty he gave us the Inaugural Lectures, and, finally, Fors Clavigera, in which you find his most tremendous invectives against modern society.

Now, since Ruskin's contemporaries neglected him politically because they found the plain meaning of his words incredible, I put the question whether in the course of time there has developed any living political activity on behalf of which you might enlist Ruskin if he were living at the present time. It goes without saying, of course, that he was a Communist. He was quite clear as to that. But now comes the question, What was his attitude towards Democracy? Well, it was another example of the law that no really great man is ever a democrat in the vulgar sense, by which I mean that sense in which Democracy is identified with our modern electoral system and our system of voting. Ruskin never gave one moment's quarter to all that. He set no store by it whatever, any more than his famous contemporary, Charles Dickens—in his own particular department the most gifted English writer since Shakespear, and resembling Ruskin in being dominated by a social conscience. Dickens was supposed to be an extremely popular person, always on the side of the people against the ruling class, whereas Ruskin might, as a comparatively rich university man, have been expected to be on the other side. Yet Dickens gives no more quarter to Democracy than Ruskin. He begins by unmasking mere superficial abuses like the Court of Chancery and imprisonment for debt, imagining them to be fundamental abuses. Then, suddenly discovering that it is the whole framework of society that is wrong, he writes Hard Times, and after that becomes a prophet as well as a storyteller. You must not imagine that prophets are a dead race, who died with Habakkuk and Joel. The prophets are always with us. We have some of them in this room at the present time.[1] But Dickens the prophet is never Dickens the Democrat. Take any book of his in which he plays his peculiar

[1] Shaw here indicated the presence in the audience of Dr William Ralph Inge, the Dean of St Paul's.

trick of putting before you some shameful social abuse, and then asking what is to be done about it! Does he in any single instance say: "You workingmen who have the majority of votes: what are you going to do about it?" He never does. He always appeals to the aristocracy. He says: "Your Majesty, my lords and gentlemen, right honorables and wrong honorables of every degree: what have you to say to this?" When he introduces a workingman, he may make that workingman complain bitterly that society is all wrong; but when the plutocrats turn round on that man and say to him, "Oh, you think yourself very clever. What would you do? You complain about everything. What would you do to set things right?" he makes the workingman say, "It is not for the like of me to say. It is the business of people who have the power and the knowledge to understand these things, and take it on themselves to right them." That is the attitude of Dickens, and the attitude of Ruskin, and that really is my attitude as well. The people at large are occupied with their own special jobs, and the reconstruction of society is a very special job indeed. To tell the people to make their own laws is to mock them just as I should mock you if I said, "Gentlemen: you are the people: write your own plays." The people are the judges of the laws and of plays, but they can never be the makers of them.

Thus Ruskin, like Dickens, understood that the reconstruction of society must be the work of an energetic and conscientious minority. Both of them knew that the government of a country is always the work of a minority, energetic, possibly conscientious, possibly the reverse, too often a merely predatory minority which produces an illusion of conscientiousness by setting up a convention that what they want for their own advantage is for the good of society. They pay very clever people to prove it, and the clever people argue themselves into believing it. The Manchester or anti-Ruskin school had plenty of sincere and able apologists. If you read Austin's lectures on jurisprudence, for instance, you will find a more complete acknowledgment of the horrors inevitable under Capitalism than in most Socialist writers, because Austin had convinced himself that they are the price of liberty and of progress. But then nobody in his day conceived Socialism as a practical alternative:

indeed, it was not then practicable. Austin's argument, or rather his choice of evils, is no longer forced on us, so we need not concern ourselves about it except as a demonstration that Ruskin's skepticism as to government by the people as distinguished from government of the people for the people is shared by his most extreme and logical opponents as well as by his kindred spirits.

Is there, then, any existing political system in operation in Europe at this moment which combines Communism with a belief in government by an energetic and enlightened minority, and whose leaders openly say, "There is no use talking about Democracy. If reforms are to wait until a majority of the people are converted to an intelligent belief in them, no reforms will ever be made at all. If we, whose intentions are honest, wait for such an impossible conversion, the only result of our sitting down and doing nothing will be that another energetic majority, whose intentions are evil, will seize the lead and govern in our stead. Democracy in that sense would be merely an excuse to enable us to go on talking, without ever being called upon to take the responsibility of doing anything. Moreover, our opponents would kill us"?

Can you point to any political body in Europe which is now taking that line? Let me lead you to it gently.

In Germany, Socialism has been represented by the Social-Democrats, and they had a great apparent democratic success in the way of getting members into Parliament, and becoming the largest group there, besides founding many newspapers, and figuring as an established institution in the country. Their theoretic spokesman is Kautsky. Some years before the war there was a certain Internationalist Socialist Congress. As usual there was some controversy between the French and the Germans, the French being led by Jaurès, who was then happily still alive. The Germans claimed superior authority in the Socialist movement because they were so much more largely and systematically organized. They cited their numerous branches, their newspapers, their millions of votes, and their representation in Parliament, in which, by the way, they had a self-denying ordinance that none of them should take office until the Capitalist system was overthrown. This saved them much trouble. They had only to sit and criticize their opponents; and they criticized them very eloquently and very thoroughly. When the German leader, Bebel, had detailed all those advantages and thrown them at the head of the French, he said, "What have you French Socialists to shew in the way of Socialist organization comparable to that?" Jaurès simply said: "Ah, if we had all that in France, *something would happen.*" Which shut up the German party.

You see, it had been driven in on Jaurès, himself a great talker, that mere talking is no use. It comes to no more than the talking about Christianity which has been going on for nineteen hundred years, during which official Christianity has been incessantly trying to find excuses for disregarding the teaching of Christ. I remember when I was busy as an unpaid and quite sincere Socialist agitator in this country—there were twelve years of my life during which I delivered a long public address on Socialism certainly three times a fortnight—one of the things that puzzled me at first was that I met with so little opposition. I found that I was almost like a clergyman talking pious platitudes. Nobody objected. Nothing happened. I apparently carried my audiences enthusiastically with me. Nevertheless, Capitalism went on just the same. I began to understand that the leaders of Socialism, the men with the requisite brains and political comprehension, must not wait as Kautsky would have them wait on the plea that you must do nothing until you have converted the people, and can win a bloodless victory through the ballot-box. The people seldom know what they want, and never know how to get it.

As against Kautsky, Europe has in the field a very interesting statesman named Nicholas Lenin. He says, "As long as you talk like that, you will not do anything, and dont really mean to do anything. In this world things are done by men who have convictions, who believe those convictions to be right, and who are prepared with all the strength they have or can rally to them to impose appropriate institutions on the vast majority who are themselves as incapable of making the institutions as of inventing the telescope or calculating the distance of the nearest fixed star."

Do not forget that this attitude of Lenin is the attitude not only of all the prophets, but of, say, Mr Winston Churchill and Mr Arthur Balfour. All our military and governing people who have practical experience of State affairs know that the people, for good or evil, must, whether they will or no, be finally governed by people capable of governing, and that the people themselves know this instinctively, and mistrust all democratic doctrinaires. If you like to call Bolshevism a combination of the Tory oligarchism of Ruskin and Mr Winston Churchill with the Tory Communism of Ruskin alone, you may. So it comes to this, that when we look for a party which could logically claim Ruskin today as one of its prophets, we find it in the Bolshevist party. [*Laughter.*] You laugh at this. You feel it to be absurd. But I have given you a demonstration, and I want you now to pick a hole in the demonstration if you can. You got out of the difficulty in Ruskin's own time by saying that he was a Tory. He said so himself. But then you did not quite grasp the fact that all Socialists are Tories in that sense. The Tory is a man who believes that those who are qualified by nature and training for public work, and who are naturally a minority, have to govern the mass of the people. That is Toryism. That is also Bolshevism. The Russian masses elected a National Assembly: Lenin and the Bolshevists ruthlessly shoved it out of the way, and indeed shot it out of the way as far as it refused to be shoved.

Some of you, in view of the shooting, repudiate Bolshevism as a bloodstained tyranny, and revolt against the connection of Ruskin's name with it. But if you are never going to follow any prophet in whose name governments have been guilty of killing those who resist them, you will have to repudiate your country, your religion, and your humanity. Let us be humble. There is no use in throwing these terms at oneanother. You cannot repudiate religion because it has been connected with the atrocities of the wars of religion. You cannot, for instance, ask any Roman Catholic to repudiate his Church because of the things that were done in the Inquisition, or any Protestant to admit that Luther must stand or fall by the acts of the soldiers of Gustavus Adolphus. All you can do is to deplore the atrocities. Lenin said the other day, "Yes: there have been atrocities; and they have not all been inevitable." I wish every other statesman in Europe had the same candor. Look at all that has been done, not only by Bolshevists, but by anti-Bolshevists, by ourselves, and by all the belligerents! There is only one thing that it becomes us to say, and that is, "God forgive us all."

FOUNDATION ORATION

(Delivered before the Union Society of University College, London, 18 March 1920. A verbatim report was issued by the Society as a pamphlet, 1920. When shewn a copy in 1929, Shaw claimed to have been unaware of the existence of this text, and made some conjectural corrections "to make sense of the most absurd passages." These corrections have been incorporated in the text below)

I am rather alarmed by the elaborate provision here of a desk and of a light, and so on, which I hold to be improper to the delivery of an oration. [*Laughter.*] I have very often been asked to deliver a lecture, or to deliver an address, but I do not think I have ever before been asked in set terms to deliver an impassioned oration—[*laughter*]—which I suppose, as a matter of honor, should be entirely unpremeditated, and which really on my part is only premeditated in the sense that anything that is uttered by an elderly gentleman, who has been in the world for over sixtythree years, must more or less have been meditated on in some way or other. But, quite honorably, I am playing the game here tonight. I have brought no notes; I have made no particular preparation. I believe I gave a title, which I have forgotten—[*laughter*]—but I will in the circumstances do the best I can. My main object is to avoid one of those set addresses. You know that in Universities where they have what they call a Rector, they ask some distinguished person every year or some other period to deliver what they call a Rectorial address. He writes it out very carefully for publication, and it usually has in it all the marks—the too-familiar marks—of discourses which have been written out very carefully for publication.

Now, I should say that one of the first things that a student at a University has got to feel, if he has any business at the University at all, is that intellect is a passion, that intellect is really the noblest of the passions, and that it is the most enjoyable of the passions, and the most lasting of them. I take it that every student in this University, with the ideals that he holds up to himself, has thought almost at any time, if he were listening to music, if he were dancing—jazzing, I believe, is the term which is used— [*laughter*]—if he were even making love—[*laughter*]—he still would feel that it would be a more delightful thing, that he would be better employed, that he would be happier, that he would be more passionate, if I may put it that way, if he could withdraw into the nearest grove and meditate, let us say, on the properties of numbers. [*Laughter.*] When I say that I am by no means joking. I am saying a thing which has needed saying almost throughout my lifetime.

I do not know whether this country ever was very faithful or devoted to matters of the intellect, but it certainly has turned its back on them, and betrayed them very largely, as I say, during my experience. It has come to this, that the word "passion" has come to be reserved almost exclusively in use for quite trivial sensuous enjoyments. There are certain words which have dropped out of use. For instance, when I was young—I was born really in the seventeenth century—[*laughter*]—I am speaking quite seriously. The explanation of that is that I am an Irishman —[*laughter*]—and I was born in the year 1856, and that meant being born in the seventeenth century, with a strong dash of the sixteenth. [*Laughter.*] My father lived in the sort of house that Samuel Pepys used to live in. It had the same kind of sanitation. It had the same kind of furniture. Almost the only thing that was at all modern was that there was gas, and it would have been better if there hadnt been gas. [*Laughter.*] For the rest it was seventeenth century. I have used a pair of snuffers. I remember what they were for. I remember the sort of candle you used the snuffers for. I understand the saying of Charles V. It is a dark saying to almost all of you. You may remember that there was a discussion in the presence of Charles V as to what was the highest test of a man's courage, the discussion taking place among soldiers, amongst men with the experience which many of you have recently acquired. Charles V, who had had this experience, said that the really brave man was the man who would snuff a candle with his fingers. I have repeatedly seen my own countrymen do it. I never had the courage to do it myself. On that test I fail.

However, I am merely illustrating the fact that I can go back to the eighteenth and seventeenth centuries, where men did not use the word "passion" in the vulgar and trivial way in which it [now] is used. One very common word and thing to be sought for was the word "sublimity." In talking of Art and Science, they were always talking of sublime achievements, and you were supposed to aim at sublimity. Now all that has gone out. In my time, as I say, I find myself very largely abused, and even accused of having very serious deficiencies in my own person, because I, on the whole, have found it necessary, if I were to interest myself, or attempt to interest other people, that I should aim at certain qualities of thought instead of certain commonplace qualities of sensation. I believe, myself, that the important person on whom the fortunes of the world are going to turn is the thinker. The thinker will have to be a real thinker.

There is a sort of person who has grown up in my time who is going to be rather severely sat upon and got rid of. He was a person of extraordinarily romantic disposition. He was a person of absolutely boundless credulity. He could swallow anything, provided it were absurdly improbable, and he always called himself a man of science. [*Laughter.*] And to some extent he used to pervade University College very largely, and some of his traditions may still exist there; but you will have, I think, in the future to turn your backs on science in that popular sense which it got in the nineteenth century, which was very like the popular sense that passion got in the nineteenth century. Science became very largely a matter of the collection of facts—a study of facts. The great man of science in those days was the naturalist, pure and simple, the collector. He always came a long way after the highest kind of man of science, who really was the man who knew, as it were, by instinct. When some great fact of the Universe is discovered, what usually happens is that some person comes along with great scientific capacity, and announces it as a thing that is perfectly obvious to himself, and which he observes, and then years after—nobody takes any particular notice of it, or takes the thing in—you have to have a certain number of very excellent workers, who are merely what I call naturalists, and they have to collect a large number of facts, and when they have collected a very large number of facts to prove the statement which was made by the seer, if I may call him so, then they generally take the credit of discovery to themselves, and assume it could not have been arrived at in any other way.

To take a familiar example, Leonardo da Vinci, who was a painter, engineer, and a number of other scientific things of that kind (for painting is a scientific thing). He mentioned as a thing quite obvious to himself that the earth was one of the moons of the sun. Well, nobody, as I think, took any particular notice of that. A gentleman named Galileo came afterwards, and after a great many interesting observations and experiments, he managed to get the credit of having proved this discovery. And the man of science—I do not know exactly how to distinguish, because I am conscious I have begun to use the term in a rather disparaging sense—but the man of science believes that science, the body of knowledge called science, consists of things which have been proved. One of the things that you must understand is that you can prove anything. [*Laughter.*] There is nothing so absurd that you cannot prove. But there is another thing. If you will only take trouble enough to prove things you will make this discovery, that proving a thing will not establish it, either with you or anybody else, for this reason, that when you have proved a thing up to the hilt by every law of logic, by every operation of the human mind, by every observation of the laws of evidence and conditions of proof you can possibly imagine, you will not have established the thing. You will have established a certain alternative. You will have to say to yourself, "Either this thing is true, or what I have achieved is a *reductio ad absurdum.* That is to say, the conclusion is so entirely unacceptable to me, that I prefer to say my logical process has either been wrong or else, if you prove to me my process was right, and that I omitted nothing and overlooked nothing, I shall have to set to work to overthrow the whole scheme of logic and all the laws of evidence, and to scrap them, rather than accept this thing that I have proved."

You must, if you are speaking to genuinely scientific people, have that continually before you. You will never be able to get on absolutely certain and sure ground. You will find in your scientific work, so far as it is really work of discovery and work of the establishment and proof of facts of nature—you will discover you will be always employed in trying to prove things that, for some very curious reason that you cannot understand, you want to prove; and if you dont want to prove them you will never believe them, no matter how much you prove them. You are led by science into a sort of mystical region. For the moment there are certain things that will occur to you. In the course of your studies you will give up certain beliefs, probably, which were instilled into you perhaps by your nurses or your parents. You will probably give them up on what you suppose to be reasonable grounds, but if you are really vigilant in the scientific way, you will discover that the reasons for which you discarded those beliefs have been staring you in the face all your life, and that you made no fresh discovery, only a redirection of the attention. You will realize you are in a world where you are surrounded by a mass of the most extraordinarily interesting and suggestive and revealing phenomena, and yet you cannot see any of them, except the ones to which your attention has been directed, possibly by some force within yourself, possibly by your attention [being called to it] by other people. But until your attention has been called, you are like a blind man as regards all those things to which your attention has not been directed. That gives an extraordinary interest to the world, because you know there are thousands of things for you to discover.

A hackneyed illustration of this is the fact that when you come to understand the constitution of the human eye, or when you have come to accept the explanations of the human eye which are given to you by physiologists at this date—[*laughter*]—you learn that when you look at an object, you co-ordinate the images in your two eyes so that they exactly register one over the other to make a single image of the thing you were looking at, but at the moment you see that single image you necessarily have on your eyes a double image of all the other objects you are not looking at. And yet, instead of your vision being hopelessly confused by this crowd of double images, you know very well that until, by a simple experiment, and by a little practice in watching this experiment, your attention is directed to this, you are not aware of them. It is the same thing intellectually, and one of the advantages of working with a number of other people, being in a University or in a University College, is that you are in the middle of a number of people, all of whose attentions have been directed to various objects, and that in the course of discussion with them, they will probably make you aware of a great many things you have not been made aware of before. And you will find that the effect of these things on you is sometimes to give you an ardent desire to believe in them, and you will very likely do a very great deal of scientific work with the object of proving that they are true, and if the effect is contrary, you will probably put in a certain amount of work in proving they are not true. Your proof or disproof will not amount to very much. Your scientific belief, you will find, will amount to a matter of attention.

I recall a summer evening many years ago, when a very young man, standing on the pier at Broadstairs at midnight. [*Laughter.*] There was a beautiful moon. Not being a romantic person— [*laughter*]—I was enjoying the air and the landscape, but I was not sentimental, and I was alone—[*laughter*]—except for the presence of a gentleman, whom I did not know then, who was a member of the Royal [Astronomical] Society, and who, I think, was a hundred and two years of age. [*Laughter.*] But this gentleman [Henry Perigal], seeing me looking at the moon for a long time, stepped up to me, and said to me very politely, "You are looking at the moon very attentively, sir." I said, "Yes, it is a fine night." [*Laughter.*] He said, "May I ask how far off you would say the moon was?" Well, I looked at the moon, and I said perfectly sincerely and frankly—I have no scientific professions; I gave an honest answer—I said, "I should think about forty miles." [*Laughter.*] I will confess I had expected to shock this gentleman a little, and I perceived I had interested him in quite a notable way. "That," he said, "is a very interesting answer. May I ask how you have arrived at that figure?" [*Laughter.*] I said, "I am judging by the look of the thing." "Ah!" he said; "well, you are

149

a very good judge, because (he said) the exact distance, leaving out fractions of miles, is thirty-seven miles." [*Laughter.*]

Well then, I began to perceive that, whereas I had not altogether been innocent of an intention to get a slight rise out of the old gentleman, the old gentleman had, as a matter of fact, got a rise out of me. I said, "I have no doubt you are quite right, but I think it is somewhat less than the usual calculation," and he said, "That is so." Then he gave me a very elaborate and, to me, entirely convincing—because I did not understand it—[*laughter*]—demonstration. The only thing I can remember now about it, and it is possible some mathematician or astronomer in the audience may understand it—the only thing I can remember of what he said was, if astronomers, instead of using the method of parallax and calculating the distance of a star in that way, would trace the actual orbit of the star by using a geometric chuck on a lathe, they would arrive at correct conclusions. [*Laughter.*] I am shortening the explanation very considerably. [*Laughter.*] I have a slight knowledge of what a lathe is, but not the slightest of what a geometric chuck is. The only association one has of a chuck is perhaps with the pier at midnight, and the moon, and so on, but it is not a geometric chuck. [*Laughter.*] That gentleman, at intervals until he died, which I think occurred about ten years later—[*laughter*]—used to send me elaborate documents, which I read with great interest, and this demonstration that the astronomers were all wrong seemed to me to be just as convincing as the demonstrations by the astronomers themselves, which I occasionally come across, that they are all right.

I have ever since, as indeed you will see from the story, entirely refused to conceive this conception of an enormous number of billions of miles. I always talked to my friend Sir Robert Ball on one basis. I was intensely interested in astronomy. I said to him, "I will give you one hundred and fifty miles, and you will have to get everything into that, but there is no use in talking of inconceivable things, millions of space and all that." [*Laughter.*] That belief has become so fashionable now that there are a number of people who will not believe anything unless it contains billions of millions in space or billions of millions of microbes in a drop of water.

But I, being ahead of public opinion, as I usually am—
[*laughter*]—I am going back to small numbers, and you will find
that science will go back to small numbers, and you will find that
the things that will be gradually established, and survive as
scientific facts, are the things that occur to persons like myself,
first mainly in the form of jokes. The ordinary man of science is
very often a person with no sense of humor. [*Laughter.*] Remember, Galileo had no sense of humor. If he had had a sense of
humor, when Leonardo da Vinci made that remark about the
earth being a moon of the sun Galileo would have laughed,
thought it an immense joke, and never would have investigated
the affair.[1] Very likely it was because he had no sense of humor
he went on with it, and did a lot of work which I do not value in
the least, because it proved what Leonardo da Vinci had found
out, and what I suppose almost every sensible man had found
out at the time. But incidentally, and on the way to prove that
particular fact, he had found out a good many other things as
well, and that is another point which I should like to make. Do
not be too particular about working towards some very important
end. The great thing is to work in some particular direction,
because your most valuable discoveries are very likely to be by-
crops, very often amusing reflections that you make by the way.
You never know the particular seed in your own mind that will
germinate. The thing you set out to do may elude you altogether,
but as long as you are going for it you are going somewhere,
doing something, and you never know what may turn up.

I think what is going to establish brainwork on its old high
basis is that it will go very largely in the direction pioneered, let
us say, by Mrs [Mary Baker] Eddy. [*A member of the audience:
"Tut, tut!"*] I heard a gentleman in the distance clicking his
tongue at Mrs Eddy. [*Laughter.*] I purposely mentioned her
because there are many students here who are interested in
medicine and biology, and curiously enough you will find, when
you come to deal with medicine, that your generation will arrive
at the conclusion that no person, no doctor in practice, for example—for there is a general impression that doctors in practice

[1] "A bad shot. Leonardo's 'remark' was in reversed writing in his private
notebook."—G. B. S. (1929).

are scientific men—[*laughter*]—I think you will find that in medicine in your time there will be a controversy which has already begun, and it will be divided into doctors who are on the side of Mrs Eddy, and doctors who are on the other side. The doctors wont say they are on the side of Mrs Eddy. [*Laughter.*] They will mention some authority who enjoys a greater vogue in the scientific world. Nevertheless, you will find that there will be two schools; there will be a school of persons who will regard the human body, the living organism, as presenting to them a purely chemical problem, and a purely mechanical problem; and, on the other hand, you will have people who will regard the human body as presenting to them a vital problem, and, indeed, one may say an almost inscrutable vital problem, a finally inscrutable vital problem. On the one hand, you will have the surgeon, who believes he can mend a broken arm. There are many such surgeons. You can see by the way they speak and write that they really believe that. On the other hand, you will have a surgeon, and if you ask him to mend your broken arm— I have had to ask a surgeon to do that—he will tell you, "I cannot mend it, but I can put the two broken ends of the bone together, so as to give you every opportunity of mending it yourself. I do not know how you are going to mend it, nor does anybody else; but, still, as a matter of experience, if you are not too old, and I put the bones together and you attend to your vital business, you can mend that arm." There you have the whole difference between the two schools. You must look out for the people who know perfectly well that the patient has got to cure himself of the disease, for disease and accident and everything else would have wiped out the human race long ago if people had not this peculiar vital power of working that particular miracle.

Of course, it is a return to the old medical school, who used to call themselves vitalists. Their opponents, the mechanical and chemical school which has been outraging and slaughtering the human race for the last fifty years—[*laughter*]—have been promising innumerable cures and advances, and all you have to do is to shake the papers of the Registrar-General in their face, and to say they have done nothing of the kind. You will find that they more and more will be losing their grip, and you will find more and more that the old vitalist school will be coming back, but coming back with the old vitalism so described that when it is reintroduced at last on a higher plane by, let us say, Scott Haldane,[1] you will find nothing will exasperate him more than to tell him he is a vitalist. When I venture as a writer to couple him with all the modern believers, the genuine biologists, the men who are pursuing this great problem of life, and couple him, for instance, with Bergson, the author of a great treatise on creative evolution, Scott Haldane, instead of being extremely obliged, instead of saying at last he finds himself appreciated, I understand is rather horrified. And you will find this, that all the people you meet in life who have had the misfortune to have what you call a secondary education, are full of superstition, because there are a number of things which they have learned for dishonest purposes. For instance, they have taken in knowledge and pursued it, not for the sake of knowledge or wisdom, but for the sake of passing examinations. [*Applause.*] That, ladies and gentlemen, is an unnatural practice—[*applause*]—and, like [all] unnatural practices, it has a curious, inexplicable, and unaccounted power of destroying the mental organism, just as unnatural practices will destroy the physical organism. One does not know why. There is only one object, I think, which is more to be deprecated than acquiring knowledge for the purpose of passing examinations. There is perhaps a worse thing you can do, and that is to acquire knowledge for the purpose of making money by handing on that knowledge to other people. [*Applause.*]

In a genuine University there should be no teachers—[*laughter*] —and when in a University you fortunately do find men who are inspiring and from whom you can learn something, you will always find those men will not present themselves to you as teachers, but as fellow learners. Consequently, those of you who come to an educational institution, the way to select the teachers who will be of some use to you is to say to them, "Can you teach me this or that or the other?" If they say, "Yes," say, "Thank you; good morning." [*Laughter.*] If they tell you

---

[1] J. S. Haldane, a scientist who conducted extensive researches into mining and industrial diseases caused by poor ventilation. Author of *Mechanism, Life and Personality* (1913).

modestly they can tell you very little about it, but can perhaps put you in the way of learning something, then stick to them.

I suppose I ought to come from the more general and abstract, and I should like to say a word this evening about the kind of brainwork which has got to be done in the world. The world is populated by people who, for the most part, ought not to exist. [*Laughter.*] You have a large working class, and I myself have been interested all my life in Labor questions. I have studied Labor questions. I have studied the life of the working class because it is the life of the country, the life of four out of every five men in the country. I understand the working class, and they understand me. When they ask me to lecture on their conditions in general, I shew immediately my sympathy with them and their aspirations by taking as my proposition that the working classes are useless, dangerous, and ought to be abolished. [*Laughter.*] I point out to them that, though the workingman does compare favorably with many other sorts of people, still he is a detestable person and ought not to exist. You come to the middle class, the class I was going to say to which we belong, but let us say to which our grandchildren, if they are improvident, may sink. [*Laughter.*] Let us take the upper classes generally, and assume we belong to them. They also are a failure. They are not good-looking. [*Laughter.*] They assume to themselves a great deal of what is rather invidiously called brainwork. A large number of them are good enough to undertake in one department or another the government of the country, and the general result is a proposition which I put before you as being unassailable and undeniable.

Taking the human race as it exists at present, it is an absolutely undeniable fact that they are entirely incapable of dealing with the problems of civilization, the social and political problems, which are raised by multiplication of their numbers and their association together under what they call civilized conditions. You find what you call scientific discovery, and what perhaps ought to be called more strictly mechanical discovery; you find that, although we have managed to improve methods of production to such an extent that I remember the President of the

Iron and Steel industry a good many years ago stated that a lace-making machine could do the work of fourteen thousand persons —by this time, I have no doubt, it could do the work of fifteen million persons, or something like it—instead of having more leisure, instead of an enormous improvement of the wellbeing of the human race, you have a blacker poverty, a worse state of things, and a more degraded and miserable life than, as far as one can make out from history, we have ever had before. All the clever things we do are turned against us, because we are unable to do the political part of the work that they involve. You find, when the outcome is an enormous multiplication of wealth, instead of spreading that over the entire population so that every man could now rescue an hour from toil, and perhaps devote it to thought or science, or, at any rate, to a more or less graceful leisure, what have we done? We have, by the greatest care and elaboration of political institutions and legal institutions directed to that end, left the toil of the masses of the people unrelieved, and turned all the accession of wealth right on top of an unfortunate class of whom we make entirely useless idlers, and enable them, not only to be idle themselves, but to take into their employment as parasites upon them—they being parasites—a large number of people who might be engaged in beneficial work. [*Applause.*]

That is the root difficulty, and we have done it really because we have been unable to do anything else. There we are brought up against what is the real central biological problem: how are we going to get rid of our silly selves, and replace ourselves by people who are sensible enough, who—to take the mere problem of building your towns—will make the great increase in the wealth of England result in having all the towns of England much more healthy and pleasanter places to live in, instead of deliberately using it in order to produce two sets of towns—in one town the people being extremely miserable because they have nothing to do, and in the other extremely miserable because they have too much to do, and because the place is so horrible one really wonders [why] it is not wiped out with fire from heaven. I wish we had more fire from heaven, and yet I sometimes congratulate myself we have not. You may congratulate yourselves that this particular affair is not in my hands, because there are a great many towns, the direct result of England's wealth and not her poverty, and without the slightest hesitation, under my régime—[*laughter*]—they would share the fate of Sodom and Gomorrah. If I had that power, and were able to look down on any nation like this nation, in which there was a single child hungry because it could not get food, I would bring my thunderbolts into very prompt operation.

Now the opening is for brainwork. The great opening for brainwork is really remedying this kind of thing, and the way you will have to do it is this. Brainwork is now subject to an enormous division of labor. There was a time—I can go back to it in my Irish seventeenth century—when you spoke of the professions as the Army, the Navy, the Church, and the Stage—[*laughter*]—and you sometimes remembered the Law and Medicine; but now Science is dividing itself up into a tremendous number of different professions. There is specialization in all directions, and what you have to realize is that the moment you create a new specialization, a new branch of science, you have also created a political problem. You have created the problem of the relation of that profession to the government of the country, and the scientific work of that branch will never get a chance until a proper place is found for it, a proper share of the wealth of the country is alloted to it, and a proper discipline devised by the nation for the professors and practitioners of that branch of science. It is no use going on as we are at present. We like going on as we are at present because we are a nation of congenital, and almost incorrigible, anarchists. We say Democracy is the characteristic form of the day, and you ask what does Democracy mean? You quote Lincoln's statement, "Government of the people for the people by the people." You talk to me of government by the people. I laugh at you. You might as well talk of the British drama written for the people by the people. [*Laughter.*]

Gentlemen, government is just as highly skilled a thing as the writing of plays. The man in the street can no more make his own laws and devise his own constitution than he can write his own plays. I am sorry to say he does try to write his own plays to an extent that would surprise you. I very much doubt whether there is a single man or woman in this audience who has not a play in five acts and in blank verse somewhere hidden away among his papers. A large number have been sent to me for advice. [*Laughter.*] Just exactly as the carpenter and the mason, and the miner and the railwaymen, have found that anarchism is no use, have found that the commercial machine would destroy them unless they elaborated a constitution for themselves—unless over and above learning to lay bricks and drive railway trains, they established a relation between themselves and society, devised a political or a social form like the trade union, they could not even survive, and their trade could not survive—it is equally true that all you scientific gentlemen, and you professional gentlemen and ladies, will find that one of the tasks and most important parts of your brainwork will be relating your profession, finding its place in society, and devising a certain code of honor and law regulating your social activities in order that they may not be corrupted, and wasted in the way they are very largely at the present time.

Let me expatiate just a little on this. I was going to say Lord Randolph Churchill—that shews how very old I am—[*laughter*] —I mean Mr Winston Churchill, but the difference is not so great as you might suppose. Mr Winston Churchill said the other day the Labor party could not govern. He was quite right. No party at present existing can govern. Nobody teaches them to govern. You are taught very many interesting things in this College. Has anybody ever taught you to govern? Do any of you know what a Prime Minister is? If you were asked, probably you would say a man like Mr Lloyd George; and, if asked what Mr Lloyd George was, you would say Prime Minister. [*Laughter.*] But you are not taught to govern. Now, what it is that Mr Winston Churchill has had evidently in his mind—God knows why—is that his people and his class can govern. The reason is that in a certain way they can, because they have got a ready-made machine, a thing which has grown up historically, largely by deliberate contrivance, by actually writing down and agreeing to certain instructions, bills of rights, juries, and so on, largely by an unwritten constitution, but, at any rate, a certain machine of government has grown up, and it goes crashing its way on.

One of its latest achievements has been the slaughter of some-where about thirteen millions of men in Europe quite un-necessarily, the slaughter mostly of young men at frightful loss to the whole body; among us of some nine hundred thousand young men, the loss to us of a large number, which I cannot give you, of young German men, every one of whom was a loss to us just exactly as the loss of every one of our young men was a loss to Germany—that is the result of your political machine as it is at present. That is the sort of thing it is doing. That is the sort of thing it will inevitably do again, in spite of the perfectly sincere declarations of the people who are working it that they had rather, on the whole, it did not occur again; but, still, they are building their fleets and piling up their armaments for the time when it does occur again, and they rather think, on the whole, since America is building a fleet, it will take the form, in the first instance, of a war with America. Therefore, they beg you all not to say a word in public or private that would create the slightest ill-feeling between ourselves and America. The reason Mr Winston Churchill has something to say for himself when he declares Labor cannot govern is that the problem before the workingman, whether a carpenter or biologist or mathematician —the people doing creative work have the same common interest finally in getting the proper political machinery—they have a task which is far harder than the task Mr Churchill has set for himself, and his likes.[1]

Let me illustrate it in this way. If you bring me a motor car, and if you will put the petrol into it—I dont know where—if you will put the oil into it—I dont know where—and if you will do what is called "tuning it up"—I dont know how or why—[*laughter*]—but if you will do these things, and put me into the motor car, I will drive it in excellent style as long as you like in deserts and up mountains, up hill and down dale. I have done it for perhaps a hundred thousand miles. Most of you could do the same thing, or could learn to do it in a fortnight. And in the same way, with our political machine and social constitution as it exists at present. Gentlemen of Mr Winston Churchill's class, of

[1] The transcription at this point is corrupt and garbled, but as Shaw failed to alter it in 1929, it is reproduced as originally published.

no very conspicuous intelligence, finding the machine ready-made, are able, after a little tuition, say, as secretaries to some Cabinet Minister, but occasionally without any preparation at all, to attach themselves to the machine, just as I attached myself to the motor car, and they learn to pull a few wires, and the thing goes. It goes, of course, over the bodies of an immense number of human beings, but the thing works, and goes on after a certain fashion. Mr Winston Churchill is justified in saying, "We do that, but a Labor Government cannot do it." A Labor Government could do the thing in the old fashion.

You have seen, for instance, that a leader of Labor like Mr [John Robert] Clynes or Mr [James Henry] Thomas, when he enters the Cabinet and takes on a department, and begins working the old machine, works it just as well as Mr Winston Churchill and his friends, and sometimes works it conspicuously better because he is rather more, by his training as a worker, in touch with reality. But you see it is no use being able to work the old machine when it is the wrong means of doing the wrong thing. The really terrible task before the Labor party and the worker, in a wide sense, is that they not only have to do the work, but they have to create a new machine. [*Applause.*] Remember, that is a pressing necessity. Everything confirms the belief that we are now at the point which has so often been reached by civilizations before, the point at which the whole thing is going to smash by its own mismanagement, and we shall have to begin all over again. If you get Mr Flinders Petrie[1] here to talk to you about it, he will tell you of the numbers of civilizations which have existed in the past, of which we have the records, which have reached a stage very similar to that which we have reached, and have broken down. You do not as yet know whether we have not actually broken down.

Look at the state of Europe. We are starving Europe, and we do not know if we have really starved it. If we have, we ourselves shall be starved. While watching the tremendous rise in prices, look at our statesmen. They are in a state of appalling puzzlement. On one hand prices are going up, as they inevitably must

[1] Sir William Flinders Petrie, Professor of Egyptology at University College, London, 1892–1933.

in this country if all the supply of food is to be allowed freely to go out to a starving Continent. Prices will go up, and it will be impossible to live. On the one hand you have a call for releasing food to go to starving children of Vienna, East Galicia, and Russia; and on the other hand you have a call for control in this country. People say, "When we had control we could get standard suits of clothes at a reasonable price. Now we have got to pay £20, or go to Mr Mallaby-Deeley." [1] [*Laughter.*] If we get control you may hold back the food, and we may keep it to ourselves; but yet, from the general world point of view, that does not seem to be very fair.

Polish children in East Galicia may say, "You declared you undertook this war to set us free. Are you not going to share your food with us?" I simply say, while you are faced with that problem, you do not know whether you have starved Europe or not, and until you know that, you do not know whether you have starved yourselves or not. If we have starved ourselves, there will soon be an end to science and the passion of thought. If you try an experiment on me, and say, "Go on talking in this remarkable manner that you are so fond of"—[*laughter*]—"and we'll do the eating"—[*laughter*]—you will find, whereas I am now with my most noble faculties ranging over the highest subjects for your edification, in the fullest play, that as I went on and on, and the dinner of which I have just partaken got more thoroughly digested and absorbed and assimilated, that the intellectual quality of my discourse would suffer. I gradually would begin to find that the things of the intellect would begin passing away, and the things of the dinner table would become foremost, and in the long run I should be simply a hungry man, and if you kept it up long enough I might end by an attempt at cannibalism to save my life. [*Laughter.*]

You must give Europe a full meal before Europe can begin to think. Europe has to begin to think, and a great deal of that thinking must be done by people like you. Therefore, you see as your problem that we have smashed up Europe, and, in smashing

[1] After the 1914–18 war Harry Mallaby-Deeley, M.P., bought up surplus government clothing, and Mallaby-Deeley's cheap suits became a music-hall joke. He was made a baronet in 1922.

it up, we have shewn our political constitution is a thing that can be no longer endured. The whole world has to be reorganized, has to be reset. That has to be done by thinkers, and men of science in the very best sense, and has to be done in the interests of humanity. That will be your work. If you here have any other end in view you are wasting your time, and the time of the University. It is to be a part of your work along with the specific work of your science. Dont imagine you can say, "I am not going to bother about politics or sociology; I will allow other people to work in a place called a Cabinet or Parliament, or anything else where they will have no chemistry or mathematics, and I will allow them by mere division of labor to do the thing." It is that sort of thing that has produced the unreal political world in which you live. You will have to take your share in it. You will have to have your professional organization, not merely for greater discovery on your own special lines, but for the political and social organization of your profession, and that is perhaps the particular opening for brainwork which I thought was the one thing which would provide me with enough to say, to justify me in asking you to make the drain on your attention I have done. You have been kind enough to listen to me. I will take no further advantage.

THE NEEDS OF MUSIC IN BRITAIN

(Address delivered before the National Conference of the British Music Society, London, 6 May 1920. *British Music Bulletin, November* 1920)

The branches of the British Music Society and musical people generally throughout the country have before them absolutely unlimited opportunities of gathering together a few persons with very high ideals in music, and elaborating schemes whereby *if* the municipality could be induced to grant them a couple of thousand a year, and *if* Lord Howard de Walden[1] would give them twenty thousand pounds, they could build a handsome concert room or opera house, get the best artists from every part

---

[1] President of the British Music Society.

of the world, and effect an extraordinary elevation of the culture of the neighborhood. The number of such schemes brought before me personally I can hardly count. Lord Howard de Walden probably finds at least a dozen of them every morning on his breakfast table. It is pure waste of time to add to their number. My advice to you is, have nothing to do with them.

We have now to ask ourselves what else the projectors of these schemes can do. We have already discussed what can be done through the municipalities in a public way.[1] This morning we come to what can be done by individuals. I know something about that, because, though I was brought up in a town where there were practically no official or commercial opportunities of hearing music, nevertheless before I was ten years old I was so accustomed to good music that I had to struggle with a strong repugnance to what is called popular music. Strauss's waltzes, which were rampant at that time, positively annoyed me. This familiarity with serious music I owed altogether to a man [George John Vandeleur Lee] who, like most musicians, had no private resources, and made his living by giving lessons in singing and playing the piano. But this did not satisfy him. He walked through the streets of the city, and whenever in passing a house he heard some person scraping a violoncello inside, he knocked at the door and said to the servant, "I want to see the gentleman who is playing the big fiddle." He did the same when he heard a flute, when he heard a violin, when he heard any instrument whatsoever—simply knocked at the door and insisted on seeing the poor terrified amateur, to whom he said, "I am forming an orchestra; you must come and play in it." And being a determined person he usually had his way.

Finally he managed to get together a small orchestra. Remember, he was not one of those men who forget that better is the enemy of good, and that he who waits for perfection waits forever. He did not say, "I cannot begin until I have two flutes, two oboes, two clarionets, two bassoons, four horns, two trumpets,

---

[1] See "Debate on the Municipalization of Music," including the verbatim report of Shaw's address on 5 May 1920, in *British Music Bulletin*, II (July 1920), 146-50.

three trombones, kettle drums, and a good string quartet." He did not consider it vandalism to touch a work of Mozart or Beethoven with anything less than that. Still less did he think about English horns or bass clarionets or a battery of tubas. He took what he could get, conducted from a vocal score or a first-violin part, and filled out with the piano or in any way he could. As to four horns, he never dreamed of such a luxury in his life; he was only too glad to get two, and one of them was generally a military bandsman picked up for the occasion. He just took the materials at hand, and found the singers among his own pupils. He taught them to sing, and organized them as a choir. For instance, he taught my mother to sing. She led the chorus; she sang the principal parts; she copied out the band parts; and, I grieve to say, if there was no money to hire the authentic band parts she composed them herself from the vocal score on general assumptions as to the compass of the instruments.

Well, what has been done once can be done again. If you can get somebody in a town to begin in that way, and go ahead with the means that are available, a great deal can be done; and the children who have the luck to be within earshot, like me, will not grow up as musical barbarians. Of course, it will not be always pleasant, because at every concert that is given the daring conductor will be ruined, and will have to begin his teaching next day in debt; but he will have had some satisfaction out of it, not to mention the advertisement. He may even make the thing pay in the end. This enterprize which educated me musically did finally manage to give big oratorio festivals, and to achieve performances of operas by amateurs; and although the opera-singing was not always of the Covent Garden class, still the singing had an extraordinary quality owing to the fact that all the performers knew the music thoroughly from beginning to end, a thing you have never heard at Covent Garden.

Such things can be done wherever there is an energetic musician with some natural gift for conducting. It is easier now than it was in Dublin sixty years ago because, through the spread of the pianola and the gramophone, you can now find plenty of people who have discovered what serious music is like, and acquired a taste for it. Take the case of our friend Mr Rutland

Boughton. In Glastonbury he has done exactly the sort of thing I am advocating.[1] He is one of those happily constituted men who can never see any reason for not doing anything, and he started with whatever means he had and whatever people he could find. Having no band, he accompanied on the piano. There being no theatre, his partner [Christina Walshe] made a fit-up, painting the decorations on anything that was lying about, and making the dresses out of fabrics of all sorts. The result is that they have given performances which have given me much more pleasure than I used to have when I was a professional critic in London. And the rehearsing, the social atmosphere of the thing, creates no end of interest and fun: in short, the jolliest kind of social life instead of the deadly dulness of country-town life. Need I draw the moral—go thou and do likewise.

BRITISH DEMOCRACY AND EGYPT

(Opening remarks as Chairman of a Public Meeting under the auspices of the Egypt Parliamentary Committee at the Mortimer Halls, London, 12 September 1921. *The Muslim Standard*, 29 *September* 1921; reprinted in *The New York Call*, 14 *October* 1921)

My first duty is to apologize to you because the meeting has begun late. It is altogether my fault; I had to come two hundred miles to this meeting, and I did not time it quite so accurately as I ought to have done. The convenors of the meeting are in no sense responsible for that. However, as chairman, I have the privilege of cutting my own remarks as short as possible. I will ask you to imagine that all the time that you have been waiting since 8:30 has been already consumed by me in a speech. [*Laughter.*]

I may remind you that for forty years past we—that is to say, the British Empire—have occupied Egypt, and we are under an absolutely solemn pledge to evacuate Egypt. ["*Hear, hear*" and

[1] See "Gluck in Glastonbury," in Bernard Shaw, *How to Become a Musical Critic*, ed. Dan H. Laurence (London: Rupert Hart-Davis, 1960; New York: Hill & Wang, 1961).

applause.] When we gave that pledge we did not mention any date, consequently an evacuation on any date practically up to the Judgment Day may be considered as in fulfilment of our pledge. [*Laughter.*]

Well, that being so, we are getting very curious to know, some of us, as to what is going on in Egypt. We receive extremely conflicting accounts. We receive official accounts, we receive popular accounts, and we receive, rather more rarely, accounts from the people who really know. The people never know, the officials never know, but a few people who really take the trouble to find out and who are neither officials nor in the usual sense popular—they do know something about it, and I hope some of those gentlemen will be able to tell you this evening what is going on.

You see, this "empire business" that we are in has become rather a difficult one, because of the introduction of modern Democracy. Now, in the old times, when there was no nonsense about Democracy—[*laughter*]—you could form a government, and if you were to occupy or annex any particular distant place, you could appoint a man to look after that place; it was his business to know something about it and do the very best he could, and he was responsible for it. But now, thanks to the blessed invention of Democracy, it is nobody's business, nobody has any responsibility at all. If you complain to Mr Lloyd George, or any modern minister, about it, he says, "Well, the thing is in the hands of the people; the people settle the whole thing by their vote; whatever goes on is the result of their vote."

You can just imagine what the upshot of that type of thing is. If you want to know anything about Egypt, the only means you have of knowing anything about Egypt, or Ireland, is to read the newspapers; and you know perfectly well that whenever you see anything about Egypt in the newspapers you do not read it; you turn to Charlie Chaplin, you turn to Mr Beckett and "Boy" McCormick,[1] and so on, and you read the things that really interest you. [*Laughter.*]

[1] Joe Beckett beat "Boy" McCormick for the British Heavyweight Boxing Championship at the Royal Opera House, Covent Garden, on 12 September 1921, the very day of Shaw's lecture.

And you must also remember that, the press being the only means of information, under the influence of Democracy the press is undergoing a very remarkable change. When I was a young man newspapers contained news, though they also contained a good deal of political comment. When I began life every self-respecting journalist always started his paper by a dissertation on foreign policy, usually about Lord Palmerston. He knew nothing about foreign policy, he possibly knew less about Lord Palmerston—[*laughter*]—but at any rate he had to keep up a sort of convention of that kind. Then, fortunately, they began to teach the people of this country to read. They did not teach them anything else, and they did not teach them that very well, but they taught them sufficient to read the newspapers. Accordingly, those people who were speculating in newspapers found that it paid to give the people what they wanted, and the people did not want politics.

Lord Northcliffe, you may remember, established a paper called The Daily Mail. He began by making it a very good newspaper, an excellent newspaper—but nobody bought it. [*Laughter.*] He happened to get into his hands, by one of the "accidents of commerce," a paper called The Evening News. It was a supernaturally bad paper, but it did give you a certain kind of news. It gave you little bits of news about an "Accident to a Cyclist at Clapham," police intelligence, news and scraps, and things of that sort. It said nothing about politics. Now, Lord Northcliffe, having accidentally got hold of The Evening News—and, I believe, really wanting to get rid of it as a thing too absurd to keep going—found to his surprise that The Evening News was an enormous success, whereas The Daily Mail was a failure. So he started to run The Daily Mail on the lines of The Evening News; he made The Daily Mail as much like The Evening News as he possibly could and immediately The Daily Mail became a success. [*Laughter.*]

I always feel very sorry for Lord Northcliffe when they blame him for not making The Daily Mail a high-class political journal. He tried to make it so, so far as his own culture and information went, and the public simply would not have it. I venture to prophesy that before many years are out no paper will have any news whatever except about the "Accident to a Cyclist at Clapham," and about the "Actress who Poisoned Herself with Cocaine," and about the "deliriously joyful life lived by the adventurous young gentleman who purchased the cocaine for her," and perhaps some scraps of news concerning less important people—the miserable existence of a creature like Einstein, for instance. [*Loud laughter.*] Intellectual pursuits must be banished from the columns of the press. All this has to be!

So, I think, if we want really to find out something about Egypt—and, as I say, the official sources are somewhat biased, there is a conflict of opinion—the only thing is to do what some of us on this platform are going to do—go out and see for ourselves. [*Loud applause.*]

It is very important, you know, because you must remember that it is no use going to a man who lives in Egypt. He never knows anything about it. [*Laughter.*] To refer once more to Palmerston, Palmerston said a very true thing; he said, "If you want to be thoroughly misled on a subject, go and consult the man who has lived there for twenty years and speaks the language like a native." [*Renewed laughter.*] You really want to have a stranger who knows nothing about it, and you want to get the sort of impression that he gets in the first week, because it is very important in a court of criminal law to have jurymen who have never been in court before, except once or twice in the dock, on charges more or less trivial—[*laughter*]—the reason being that you cannot leave the lives and liberties of people in the hands of lawyers and persons of that type who are seeing these things every day and are accustomed to treat them as though they are of no importance. You must have men who come fresh to it, and although we shall hear tonight Egyptian gentlemen, their sense of what is happening in Egypt must be frightfully dulled because they are living in Egypt. Just as I am not impressed with what is going on in Ireland, because I have lived there, I have taken the standard of it, just as a lobster gets used to being boiled. [*Laughter.*] If you want to know anything about the feeling of the lobster you will have to consult some other kind of crustacean who has never been boiled in his life. [*Renewed laughter.*]

Tonight we are to give a sort of send-off to those gentlemen who have never been boiled, who are going to ascertain what those who have been boiled have received at the hands of the British Government. Some Egyptian friends will address you, and although they will speak to you with the disadvantage I have described, you can allow for that disadvantage, and if they give you an unfavorable account to some extent, you can conclude from the point of view of an Englishman [that] matters are about twice as bad as the speakers point them out to be because, as I say, they are handicapped by having lived out there.

THE MENACE OF THE LEISURED WOMAN

(Summation, from the Chair, of a debate between G. K. Chesterton and Lady Rhondda, held in the Kingsway Hall, London, 27 January 1927. *Time and Tide*, *4 February* 1927)

It has been suggested that I should perform the highly abstract operation called summing-up. I am perfectly willing to sum up to any extent, but both Mr Chesterton and Lady Rhondda absolutely refuse to consent to any such proceedings on my part unless they have a word subsequently to sum me up.

This has not been very much of a debate because, I am very glad to say, both the controversialists have stuck pretty closely to the splendid precept of Robert Owen, "Never argue, repeat your assertions." Insofar as there has been any argument, it has consisted as usual in the two parties attributing to oneanother reciprocal positions which it is evident they do not hold, and which as a matter of fact they could not hold, because no human sane being could possibly hold them. There are certain sentences in a debate which lend themselves to that sort of thing. Mr Chesterton made use of a certain phrase about a home system which taken by itself might lead to the oriental system called the purdah system. Of course, Lady Rhondda knows, and I know, that Mr Chesterton is not a believer in the purdah system, and that if he were a believer in the purdah system he dare not say so because Mrs Chesterton is on the platform.

I notice also in the course of the debate he dropped into the habit which the old Norwegian, Henrik Ibsen, tried so hard to get us away from, the habit of dealing with ideals. He used the expression "the home." Whose home? When Mr Chesterton spoke widely of "the home," not anybody's home, but "the home," then he was able to say that a man when he was in his own home was able to say what he liked and even think what he liked. But once we get into the home, ladies and gentlemen, we hardly dare to think at all. Take one of the great thinkers of the world, Socrates. Where did he think? We know very well that the one place in which he could not call his soul his own would be his own house.

The position that Lady Rhondda takes up on this question of leisure was really summed up long ago in the two lines that "Satan will find some mischief still for idle hands to do." But when you come to deal with this question of leisure you must remember that this capitalist system of ours is not going to be eternal. As Mr Chesterton says, it is crashing already by the weakness of its own fibre. Either in its crash it will bring down civilization and bring all of us down with it, or else it will be got rid of by what Mr Chesterton calls distributivism, a more equal distribution of property. But if you are going to have an equal distribution of property you will have to have equal distribution of labor, and then you will have to have, as a consequence of that, equal distribution of leisure. We will all have a lot of leisure and then we will have to consider what to do with it. It will be a matter for ourselves. Mr Chesterton talks of the glorious position of having nothing to do, but, as he knows, that is not a very comfortable position. What he essentially means is that you are going to be in the glorious position of being able to do what you like. But even that is not quite so glorious, as every tramp knows.

I am afraid when people have about six or seven hours a day in which to do absolutely as they like they will all turn to somebody like myself or Mr Chesterton or Lady Rhondda who has a certain amount of eloquence on the platform and will say: "Will you tell us what we like, and we will go and do it?"

I would like, as this is possible, to tell you one of the things to which I attribute my own greatness. It is a resolution which I formed early in life that I never would allow myself to be persuaded that I was enjoying myself when as a matter of fact I was not enjoying myself. I think that you should rub that both into men and women who are threatened with a very large amount of leisure.

As to the question of children, bringing up a single child is undoubtedly a whole time job. The remedy for that is to have six children. Then it will hardly take any time at all because the children will bring oneanother up. In the course of a long life I have observed large families, and I have seen the eldest child, and perhaps the second child, brought up, in the worst sense of that horrible word. What right has any human being to dare to talk of bringing up a child? You do not bring up a tree or a plant. It brings itself up. You have got to give it a fair chance by tilling the soil. But when it comes to the question of bringing up children, you find, in large families, the two eldest children made intensely miserable, to a very great extent their intellect and character destroyed and their lives very largely spoilt, by bringing up. But with families of six, seven, or eight children, by the time the parents have come to the youngest they are tired of it, and have given up that sort of nonsense. What can they do except look on at them? That is the thing you ought to do. You have got to keep them in order, inculcating a certain amount of order into them, but then if there is a fairly large family let them bring oneanother up. Then you will find that, although bringing up one child is a whole time job, bringing up six or seven takes about half an hour a day.

But you know there are other ideals besides the home which you have to be a little careful of. You speak of women in the words "the mother" or "the wife." You had much better talk of Mrs Smith or Mrs Jones or Sally Robinson or something of that kind, because at any rate Mrs Jones and Mrs Smith are human beings, whereas "the wife" or "the mother" means nothing at all. Let us look this matter carefully in the face. I have known a fair number of women in my time. Some of them produced splendid children and were totally unfitted to have charge of them in any way. Others were born mothers; they had a genius for it. Between them come a certain number of people who, with a little assistance and guidance, can get on fairly well. But I think we must recognize that these ideals of "the wife" and "the mother" do not cover the whole number of female beings you have to deal with, and "the home" does not cover the lot of many human beings.

Many of them have to go to sea, for instance, and do other things of that kind. Some keep lighthouses. I wonder if there is a lighthouse-keeper in this audience. If so, I should like him to give us his ideas of the home and home life. You have to deal with all these questions in practice. Finally, you have to remember that the leisured woman is not only a menace to herself and to everybody else, but that the leisured human being who has got nothing to do at all, who is completely leisured—and that is really what we have been driving at—whether male or female, is a predestined miserable person and an injurious person to everybody around. As a matter of fact, if you even keep a horse for purely ornamental purposes, purely for pleasure, you will find that he will be a very valetudinarian horse. You will always have trouble with him. But if you allow him to tug the garden roller for two hours a day he will become a very different horse and very seldom ill.

In the same way we must look forward to the time when we will all have a bit of work to do every day. We do not want to talk about leisured women. We should talk about the completely idle. We have to make up our minds to destroy the idler. We must make up our minds that we will not have the idler under any circumstances. It ought to be a capital crime to be idle. I daresay that Time and Tide and G. K.'s Weekly are willing enough to teach that lesson, but they have no power to ram it down the throats of people and make them read those papers. Unfortunately, other people have that power. Most of the daily newspapers of London today, although you may not know it, are rammed down your throats. They are shoved into the place where our brains should be. That is one of the things we have got to get rid of. I have a number of other intensely interesting things to say, but I have come to the end of my time, and now I have to let Mr Chesterton have a go at me first, and Lady Rhondda will have the privilege of the last word.

WOMAN—MAN IN PETTICOATS

(Speech delivered before a meeting in behalf of the Cecil Houses
Fund, in the King's Theatre, Hammersmith, 20 May 1927.
New York Times Magazine, 19 *June* 1927; reprinted in the
Cecil Houses (Inc.) Report 1927/8)

I am addressing you in the character of a curious old relic of
the Victorian Age. I am even something more antiquated than
that. Being a countryman of Lady Moyers and of Mr St John
Ervine, I have their permission to make a speech.[1] As a countryman of Mr St John Ervine I go back to the eighteenth century.
He was born in the nineteenth century; but as I, like Lady
Moyers, was born in Dublin, I go back to the eighteenth century,
and I have an earlier as well as a longer outlook than many of
you. Whether you would enjoy it if you had it I do not know.
But, at any rate, I have something to tell you which the younger
members of my audience have probably no adequate conception
of—something which has a great deal to do with the extraordinary neglect on the part of organized society to provide for
women the accommodations and conveniences that are provided
as a matter of course for men.

The Victorian age attempted and, to an extraordinary extent,
did actually succeed in one of the most amazing and grotesque
enterprizes ever undertaken by mankind. The Victorians were
romantic people. Confronted as they were with the real human
animal, male and female, they said, "This is unendurable." The
men looked at oneanother, and did not like each other very much;
and that sort of feeling that you must have something to adore,
something to worship, something to lift you up, gave them the
curious notion that if they took the women and denied that they
were human beings; if they dressed them up in an extraordinary
manner which entirely concealed the fact that they were human
beings; if they set up a morality and a convention that women

---

[1] At this meeting Lady Moyers (the former Lily Pakenham) presided in the
Chair, and Ervine shared the platform as Shaw's fellow speaker. Cecil Houses, a
charitable organisation founded by Ada Chesterton as a memorial to her late
husband Cecil (brother of G. K. Chesterton), provides housing accommodation
for indigent women.

were angels; then they would succeed in making women angels, and have a society in which men found happiness in adoring a large congregation of angels.

This was very nice for the men. Also it was rather flattering to the women. But there were limits. It is all very well to be regarded as an angel up to a certain point; but there come moments at which you are seriously inconvenienced by the fact that you are not an angel; that you very seriously require certain accommodations and conveniences which angels can do without; and that when these are denied to you on the ground that you are an angel, you suffer for it. However, in the Victorian age they did not mind that. They went on dressing up the women as angels and pretending accordingly.

I well remember, when I was a small boy, receiving perhaps a greater shock than I have ever received since. I had been brought up in a world in which woman, the angel, presented to me the appearance of a spreading mountain, a sort of Primrose Hill. On the peak there was perched a small, pinched, upper part, and on top of that a human head. That, to me, at the period of life when one is young and receiving indelible impressions, was a woman. One day, when I was perhaps five years of age, a lady paid us a visit, a very handsome lady who was always in advance of the fashion. Crinolines were going out; and she had discarded hers. I, an innocent unprepared child, walked bang into the room and suddenly saw, for the first time, a woman not shaped like Primrose Hill, but with a narrow skirt which evidently wrapped a pair of human legs. I have never recovered from the shock, and never shall.

After that, there was a certain reaction. Primrose Hill began to be reproduced again in various shapes, with bustles at the back and things of that sort. You see them in the old numbers of Punch, in pictures by Leech and others. But, generally speaking, the reduction of women to vulgar flesh and blood continued to be prevented by a system of dressing not at all like what we now know as dressing a woman. In fact, woman was not dressed in the sense we are familiar with. She was upholstered. She was dressed in upholstering fabrics called reps; and if she was not studded with buttons all over her tempting contours like a sort of super-sofa, she was pinched in and padded out so as to produce as much of that effect as possible. You do not remember that. I do. The last woman who bravely kept up the upholstered appearance to the end was my late friend Marie Corelli. She being gone, I look round the world, and I do not see any woman now who is upholstered.

I lived on to an advanced age, and received another shock. I received a visit at Adelphi-terrace from a foreign princess, a very charming woman bearing the name of one of Napoleon's marshals. She sat down on the sofa, and I talked to her; and as she had a very pretty face I was principally occupied by that. But after we had been conversing—though I do not know that she had much chance in the conversation; so let us say when I had been shewing off for a quarter of an hour—I paused for breath, and in the course of my pausing I happened to look down. To my utter amazement I discovered that her skirt came only to her knees. I had never before seen such a spectacle except on the stage. I thought, "Great Heavens! the princess has forgotten her skirt!"; and I almost lost my presence of mind. Well, now all that is gone; I can stand any amount of ladies with their skirts to their knees without turning a hair.

I am telling you all this with a serious purpose. The dress has changed, but the morality has not. People are still full of the old idea that woman is a special creation. I am bound to say that of late years she has been working extremely hard to eradicate that impression, and make one understand that a woman is really only a man in petticoats, or, if you like, that a man is a woman without petticoats. People sometimes wonder what is the secret of the extraordinary knowledge of women which I shew in my plays. They very often accuse me of having acquired it by living a most abandoned life. But I never acquired it. I have always assumed that a woman is a person exactly like myself, and that is how the trick is done.

But the world has not come to that frame of mind yet. In spite of Mr Kipling's attempt to make you understand that the woman is only the female of the species, there is still an idea that men and women are different creatures, the man having many needs and the woman being only one of them.

When I went into active municipal life, and became a member of the Health Committee of a London Borough Council,[1] the question of providing accommodation for women, which was part of our business, was one which I conceived to be pressingly important. And you can have no idea of the difficulty I had in getting that notion, to a limited extent, into the heads of the gentlemen who were working with me on the Committee. At that time women were not on those public bodies; and women's special needs were therefore not thought of. I well remember one of my earliest experiences on the Health Committee. A doctor rose to call attention to a case in which a woman was concerned. He happened to mention that she had been in his hands because she was expecting her confinement. Now, I notice that you all receive that in perfectly decorous silence; there does not seem to you anything funny about it. But I assure you that on that Health Committee—and it is not much more than twenty years ago—no sooner had the doctor uttered this revelation than the whole Committee burst into a roar of laughter. You see, there was not only the angel conception: there was also the inevitable reaction against it. If anyone betrayed the secret or gave it away, half the world was shocked, and the other half roared with laughter.

There was a noteworthy feature in the pantomimes of my early days. No part of the harlequinade was complete unless one of the scenes shewed an old woman dropping from a top window or climbing over a wall, the joke being that in the course of these gymnastics she thrust her leg from under her skirt, in a white stocking, and allowed the audience to see almost up to her knee, eliciting a shriek of laughter. Propriety was saved by the fact that the old woman was obviously a man dressed up as a woman. You can tell from the old comic pictures of those days that to see even a woman's ankle was considered half a shocking thing and half an obscene joke!

I have taken up the time of the meeting with all this because really, unless you grasp it, unless you understand that this thing remains still with us as a superstition even now, when we think

---

[1] Shaw served on the St Pancras Borough Council as vestryman and councillor from 1897 to 1904.

we have completely freed ourselves of it, you will be bewildered when, in dealing with this question of lodging-houses for women, you come right up against it. It is the real reason why, when on that public body I talked and talked to get proper, common, sanitary accommodation for women, I found it impossible for a long time to get over the opposition to it as an indecency. A lavatory for women was described as an abomination. Exactly the same feeling stands in the way of providing for women what is popularly called a "doss house."

Now, this work ought not to be left to Mrs Chesterton. Not that she is not doing it remarkably well; but it is not her job. It is the job of all of us. It ought to be done by the London County Council. But this is not a reason for saying: "Oh, well, we may leave it to the London County Council." If you do, it will not be done. Before a public body takes up something of this kind, its practicability and the public need for it generally has to be demonstrated by private initiative. If you will help Mrs Chesterton to set up, say, a dozen of these doss houses in London, to do for women what Lord Rowton did for men—and why he never thought of the women I am sure I do not know; but he did not: he left it to you—if you set up a dozen of these houses, and prove that they work well, and that they are wanted, then there will be a very fair chance of inducing the London County Council to take them over and to make more of them, until there is a really adequate supply.

But it is we who must begin; and when the Council takes up the work it will make all the other people who are not here today contribute their share. That is why we are beginning as we are today. You must build another house, and another house; and then in the course of another hundred years or so the London County Council will wake up and do its duty.

Let me end with one or two general moral observations. To qualify herself for this work Mrs Chesterton had to become a waif and an outcast;[1] but it was impossible for her to go on with that long enough: I can quite understand why. If you cast a

[1] Like Jack London, who had disguised himself as a down-and-outer in London's East End and then written of his experiences in *The People of the Abyss* (1903), Ada Chesterton had shared the experiences of London's destitute women and reported her findings in a book, *In Darkest London* (1926).

glance at the people sleeping out on the Thames Embankment and in the Adelphi Arches (I live in the Adelphi, but not in the Arches) or huddling on the Waterloo Bridge steps or the other places where you can get out of the wind, your feeling always is "This thing is a social shame." It is an individual shame to you. It is outrageous that these things should be. You do not lack sympathy. You think it is cruel. Your imagination assumes despair, misery, and so on. Ladies and gentlemen, that is not altogether the case. If you will steel yourselves to investigate; if you will, with a perfectly unbiased mind, look at the homeless people, the people who have got into the way of having no place to live in, and nothing material to think of; if you make a careful study of their faces, and estimate their happiness by their expression; and if you will then turn from them and study, say, an ordinary congregation in a respectable church, or even a number of welldressed people taken at random in the rich parts of the town, you will suddenly begin to doubt very much which are the happier people. The truth of the matter is that one of the things that we have to do is to prevent people finding out what a jolly thing it is to be a destitute and therefore irresponsible person. That is the real danger. That is the reason why you must not only do your best to provide lodging-houses for the women, but also do your best to provide them with the shilling to go to the house. That is also important; because if a woman has not got a shilling she cannot go to Mrs Chesterton's house.

If I were to pretend to be deeply moved by the lot of all these homeless women, I should be a mere hypocrite. I am more than seventy years of age; and so much human suffering has been crowded into those seventy years that I am in the condition of Macbeth in his last Act: "I have supped full with horrors: direness, familiar to my slaughterous thoughts, cannot once start me." Another million of starving children has become as nothing to me. I am acquiring the curious callousness of old age. At first, when I was beginning to get on in years, I used to feel sad when my old friends and even enemies began dropping round me. Nowadays I have got over that: I exult every time another goes down. I am a man of the most extraordinary hardness of heart; and I suggest to you that this is an undesirable condition for an old man to be in. I suggest to you that it is a frightful thought that if you are not careful, if you are not more thoughtful and humane than my generation was, there may be, seventy years hence, another old man looking on at horrible preventable evils with a heart as hard as mine. That is clearly an undesirable thing; and so I will sit down and leave the appeal to younger people who have still some sensibilities left.

A RELIEF FROM THE ROMANTIC FILM

(Speech delivered before a demonstration of *Secrets of Nature* films, in the London Pavilion Theatre, 18 November 1927. *The Illustrated London News*, 3 December 1927)

I have to introduce myself—Bernard Shaw—oh, yes, *the* Bernard Shaw. I must also explain that I am an actual real animal; I am not the latest movietone illusion. I am no part really of the show. I have come here, if I may tell you a secret, because I want to get my knife into certain parts of this audience. I am very fond of the movies. I am what they call in America a "movie fan," and the programs very often are not to my liking. The whole business of entertaining the public, which is a very important and responsible thing, is in the hands of the gentlemen whom we call the exhibitors, the gentlemen who keep all the picture palaces and select the films—except when they are selected for them by somebody else; but, at any rate, they select the things that we have to look at afterwards, and I think you will admit that men who discharge this extraordinarily important function ought to be men of business, men of the world, and men of sense.

Unfortunately, they are nothing of the kind. The pictures, the movies, attract a particular kind of man, not a business man, not a man of the world—really a man of the other world, if I may say so, an incurably romantic person. If you have ever been to what is called a "trade show" and seen all the exhibitors there, instead of saying, "Oh, yes, here are men of the world, here are no ordinary sort of persons," you would stare at them and say, "Where on earth did these people come from?" Their heads are full of the most amazing things. They believe that the public are entirely occupied either with wild adventures of the most extravagant kind, or—and this they believe to be at least nine-tenths of the whole attraction—with something that they call "sex appeal." They are full of sex appeal. You may take the greatest trouble to make the most beautiful films, artistic films, interesting films, of one kind or another, and they say, "Where is the sex appeal?" And if there is not what they call sex appeal, they simply will not believe that the public will go and see it.

Take one of these gentlemen and say to him: "Are you aware that when the Dean of St Paul's preaches there are large crowds go to hear him preach? Are you aware there is a big building in Albemarle-street which is filled with people listening to scientific lectures? Are you aware that there are large halls all over the country which are crowded to hear political speeches?" and he will say, "You need not talk to me about that; it is impossible; where is the sex appeal? Where is the sex appeal about Dean Inge?" And you cannot do anything with them. You bring them and shew them the most interesting films, and unless there is what they call sex appeal they will not be converted. And yet the whole experience of the movies shews that sex appeal is a thing that you may neglect almost altogether.

Who are the two people who in the very beginning of this cinematograph business have proved the most universally attractive? I should say Mr Charles Chaplin and Miss Mary Pickford. In their films there is no sex appeal at all. If you could get a film which would be perfect in sex appeal it would not be any use, for this reason: that if the sex appeal was made on the screen by a lady, no lady would go to see it, and if it were made by a man, no man would go to see it. You will find that Miss Mary Pickford is just as popular, if not more popular, with women as with men, which completely disposes of the idea that the attraction is what you call sex appeal. There is the attraction there of beauty and grace and interest, and so on, but it is not sex appeal.

On the contrary, the one painful part of these films, the part that almost makes us either pass it over with a laugh because we are used to it, or makes us feel slightly indelicate because we are looking at it, is the thing that is always put at the end of the film to satisfy the exhibitors. The film may be dramatic, it may be entertaining, it may be a wonderful sketch of character, as you get from Mary Pickford and Charlie Chaplin, but the exhibitors care nothing about that: you must compel Miss Pickford at the end of the film to exhibit herself being passionately kissed by a gentleman. They say, Where is the sex appeal? You say: Look at the last tableau; Miss Pickford is being kissed by somebody; and they accept that as the secret of the appeal. I find it extremely tantalizing to see another gentleman kissing Miss Pickford. If you will procure me the opportunity of kissing Miss Pickford, then I may enjoy that, but when another gentleman is doing it I simply feel indelicate because I am looking on. If I had any prospect, at my age, of attracting the beautiful ladies on the film, I certainly should not like to press my suit with a very large audience of people looking on at me. The very first thing I should demand is privacy. The whole thing is a mistake. The really interesting films are independent of that, and one hopes that before very long, owing to the general public dissatisfaction and feeling of indelicacy at these final embraces, the final embraces will be cut out, and then what will become of the present film exhibitors? They will say: There is no longer any film with sex appeal.

What I think is of importance in an entertainment of this kind is not so much this or that feature in any particular form, but the whole program put together. I believe my experience is probably that of most people. I go to film shows, and I mostly go to listen to the music, which I must say is extremely good as a rule at cinematograph shows; but I see the program, and if I am bored by the program, then I do not go to the movies again for another fortnight. If I really like the program I may go the next day. If you do not want to bore the public you must give them some sort of variety. What sort of variety do they get from these eternal films of adventure and supposed sex appeal, which, of course, are all very well in their way?

Then there is always what they call "the Gazette." You get a sort of newspaper on the screen; it is sometimes a very dull newspaper, but nevertheless it is popular. People always like a program better for having a little interlude, and the attraction is not only the attraction of the news, because, as I say, that is sometimes rather dull. I myself do not always enjoy seeing a perfectly uninteresting gentleman, whom I never heard of before, laying the foundation-stone of a perfectly uninteresting building which is not yet built. The orchestra has really to set-to with great spirit in order to carry me over that little item.

The thing I want to impress upon you is this: that the interest is very largely the interest of seeing something that really did happen as a relief from the wonderful things that you know never did happen, never will happen, and never can happen. It is all very well to get into dreamland for a moment, but you must keep your feet on the solid ground, and there is nothing so pleasant in the middle of all your romance as to have this moment of interest and realities.

We have entrapped a number of the exhibitors into this building, and we are going to shew them something which we have to be very careful about describing. There are some people who would call them educational or instructional films. That is deadly. That not only chokes off the trade exhibitor, but it chokes off the whole world. Nothing would induce me to go to see an educational film. On the other hand, I do want to see the interesting film, because if I know what is being shewn is something that has real interest and existence, then I like that immensely as a relief for a while from the romantic films. What we are going to shew you is a series of things that actually happen in nature. We are going to give a very moving piece of genuine sex appeal. One of the things that you are going to see on the film today is how, when a flower falls in love, that flower opens its arms and invites embraces, and it is a beautiful thing to see. Miss Pickford could not beat it, if she went in for that kind of thing.

We will shew you several flowers. These are things that actually happen in nature, which you have never seen, probably, occur. We make them occur a little faster than they do in nature. They perhaps take several months in nature, and we will shew you the thing occurring in several seconds. But the thing actually does occur, and when you see it I believe you will agree with me that there is a quite extraordinary degree of beauty and grace and appeal in the thing. We will also shew you some diabolically ugly things. We have a film on the earwig here, and I hope you will look at it; but, at any rate, you will know that it is a real earwig. You will find out what happens to earwigs, and you will find out where they come from. I do not know whether we shall be able to shew you where they go to. If you saw it in an ordinary program with others, you would go away with your mind not only filled with romance, but, as a sort of contrast, you would know a lot about earwigs and you might find earwigs interesting—I do not know whether it is a desirable thing or not to do so, but, at any rate, the thing is interesting, and so we are trying to persuade people not to give programs which consist exclusively of these things, because you can have too much of a good thing. I want them to stop having too much of the other sort of good thing—I nearly said the bad thing, but, of course, I do not mean that.

When you have one thundering big film like Ben Hur, there may not be room for anything else; but when you have the ordinary program of two or three pieces, you will find it more attractive if you have one or two of the kind of numbers which we are going to shew you—something which appeals to that very strong love of nature which exists in the Englishman. He has a love of animals, he has a love of insects and flowers, he has a love of sport, a love of politics, and a love of religion; it is part of his character. Trade exhibitors know nothing of this, as I say, except sex appeal. We want to shew them that it takes all sorts of people to make a world. They have gone on imagining that, because there is a very exceptional and romantic set of people in the world, all the world is peopled with exactly such people. They think the whole British public is like that. I want to impress on them that that is not so, that they are very exceptional in their tastes, that in many ways they are extremely morbid in their tastes and ought to see a doctor; they do not get the program that has two sorts of interest in it, and these exciting moments which they see so much in destroy the excitement by giving us nothing else the whole evening, so that at the end of two hours in a picture palace nothing that we can be shewn can raise any emotion in us; but if a few items of ordinary interest were put in for the sake of relief, then the romantic episodes [would] come out with their full value. They have the effect of contrast; you are not worn out looking at them.

CENSORSHIP AS A POLICE DUTY

(Address delivered before the Special General Conference of the Chief Constables' Association, held at Harrogate, 8 June 1928. Published in the Conference *Reports*, 1928)

When I was an infant about seventy years ago there was a vulgar song current which was supposed to be sung by a police officer. It began, "I'm the man who takes to prison him who steals what isnt his'n." Fifty years elapsed from the vogue of that song, and another became popular. That song began, "If you want to know the time, ask a policeman."

Now, that may seem a trivial opening to a very serious subject, yet the difference between those two songs is very remarkable. The entire conception of police duty has changed in the last fifty years. In the first song the policeman appears simply as a thief-catcher, and the moral for the public is, "When in trouble run away from the policeman." But in the second song you find that this is completely changed, and the moral is, "When you are in trouble or difficulty of any kind, go to a policeman." If you want to know the way to the railway station, go to a policeman. If you have lost your children, go to a policeman and he will find them, if, indeed, he has not already done so.

In the course of my lifetime there has been a tremendous extension of police duty, and that extension has changed the policeman from a rough customer, whose business it was mainly to deal with criminals and crime, into what is now called—and it is very significant that the term was quite unknown when I was young—a welfare worker. It has gone so far that you now have women police, and although, if I were a Chief Constable, nothing would terrify me more than this particular development, yet there is no doubt that it is a development which has to be faced.

You will probably presently have women police everywhere,

and as women, as soon as they get into a place, instinctively begin to manage it—and finally have to be allowed to manage it for the sake of a quiet life—I am by no means sure that in another fifty years, when a distinguished dramatist addresses another Conference of Chief Constables, it may not consist exclusively of ladies.

As far as the changes are merely extensive, they do not affect so very much the rank-and-file policeman, the ordinary constable, because the extension of duties in his case can be met by a simple increase of numbers. Although you are all familiar with the difficulties that arise from the constable who has got more zeal than discretion, and the perhaps more common type of constable who has got more discretion than zeal occasionally, yet, on the whole, you can deal with the increase in the duties of the police, so far as the men under your command are concerned, by simply employing more of them. All I need say on that point is that the public and Parliament do not always take into consideration the need for improvement in the pay of the police all round and in their social status concurrently with the increased importance of their duties.

But when you come to the question of the Chief Constable the changes are very serious to him, because he cannot multiply his own number. His responsibility is increased with every addition to police duties, and he cannot meet that by appointing half-a-dozen Chief Constables. There must be a responsible head. There must be someone to hang when things go wrong.

It is this increase in the responsibility of the Chief Constable that has made an organization of the Chief Constables of the Kingdom inevitable. You might be expected to know, but probably you are not so well aware of it as many outside, that you are, as such an organization, one of the most important organizations in the country.

I am by no means sure that if the House of Lords had invited me to address it on this subject I should have taken the trouble to do it. But when I was invited to address a Conference of Chief Constables I recognized it was about the most important thing I could do, and the most influential assemblage I could address on the subject.

CENSORSHIP AS A POLICE DUTY

I want first to divide the objects of your Association into two wellmarked classes. To begin with, there are certain things that are fairly obvious. You want to get together; you want to achieve something like uniformity in police action throughout the country, because the public, which used to be a comparatively stationary public, has now, through the spread of the motor car, become a movable public—a traveling public. If you go about motoring, as I do, it is very awkward to find yourself in one county under one set of regulations and in another county under another. It does not occur to any noticeable extent; but there are instances where one Chief Constable's practice differs from another, and it is desirable to get together to arrive at some sort of uniformity.

Then you have to impress on the public the necessity not only for a larger number of men to cope with the new duties and the consideration of their pay status and so on, but you have to consider keeping them up to date in the matter of equipment. There are lots of things you want—radio, telephones, motor cars, flying squads, and those sorts of things, and you have to keep pressing the authorities for public money to get those things. And also you often have to press for new powers, and those powers must come from Parliament.

In that respect you are a most influential body, because if I were a member of Parliament and I wanted police legislation on certain subjects I should be very much influenced by the opinion of the organized Chief Constables of the country as to whether my proposals were practicable. Whether I was influenced by it or not, Parliament would be influenced by it.

But there is another side to this. You have not only to seek new powers, you have also to resist the tendency to put powers on you, involving duties which not only you could not discharge, but which practically no human being could discharge. The tendency to run to the policeman whenever we are in trouble obviously has its inconvenient side for the policeman. The public is already, to some extent, in the attitude that you can settle all sorts of difficulties by allowing the police to deal with them.

Accordingly, you have to be on your guard against this often very thoughtless imposition on you of powers and duties which would require divine wisdom to carry out satisfactorily. Let me illustrate the difficulties that arise. You have such duties, for instance, as enforcing hours for the serving of customers in public houses; you have to enforce the rule of the road in traffic; you have to enforce the speed limit with regard to motor driving. All that is perfectly simple to deal with.

You may have in one county a Chief Constable who is a teetotaler and a strong prohibitionist. If you asked him his private opinion of what should be the proper closing hours for the public houses he might say, "In my private opinion the proper closing hours are all the time." In the next county you may have a Chief Constable who believes in free trade for public houses, and who would say, "Why should you come down on a public house more than on any other shop that caters for the public?" Or he may think that the hours are wrong, and that others would be far better suited. But it doesnt matter. These things give no difficulty. The two Chief Constables may be in adjacent counties; but they cannot fix one set of hours for one county and another set for another. They have not to make the law, but to see that law is carried out, no matter what their private opinions may be.

In prosecuting a publican one Chief Constable may prosecute him with great self-satisfaction, and may wish, perhaps, that he could drive him out of the trade altogether. Another may prosecute him sympathetically; his attitude may be: "I think the law is hard on you; but I have to administer it." But the result is the same to the publican.

It is the same when you come to the rule of the road. You drive to the left and overtake on the right. I can conceive that a Chief Constable who had done a little driving on the Continent, as I have, might possibly form a strong opinion that it would be far more sensible to drive to the right. It is surprising how easily you get into the trick, and how hard it is to change over when you get back to England. At any rate, it is desirable that there should be uniformity throughout Europe. But that does not matter. The rule is the rule, and the Chief Constable must enforce it. He knows exactly what he has got to enforce there and so does the motorist.

Then you come to the question of the speed limit. I have been driving for twenty years. I have driven certainly a good deal over 100,000 miles in that time—by the way, I hope nothing I say here will be used against me—and in the course of that twenty years I have never taken a drive on any occasion without breaking the law. Never once. And I have often thought what a dreadful thing it must be to be a Chief Constable and be obliged by your position never to exceed the speed limit. I think of you driving in your Rolls-Royces and always having to keep inside that twenty miles limit.

But in all those twenty years I have only once been prosecuted. I was informed that I had passed through a police control at a speed of twentyseven miles an hour. There was no question. There was no room for argument. The constable and I were perfectly civil to oneanother. He was pleased when he got my name, because he knew he would be in the paper next day. And I was equally pleased, because what came into my head was that it was a mercy he did not catch me half an hour before, when I was driving at fifty. But, you see, the point is that there was the law about the twenty miles, and there was no question about it and no room for opinion.

Suppose, however, I had been charged with driving to the public danger! There you are shifting to a power and duty on the part of the police which is quite a different thing to the definite speed limit. You have gone from the region of fact into the region of opinion, and here is where the Chief Constable finds all his troubles coming. All the scandals and rows and protestations in letters to the papers arise in that part of the police duties in which you are dealing, not with definite laws, but with matters of opinion. And this is very serious in the case of the police, because of a certain peculiarity in their position.

Let me illustrate in this way. Supposing I commit a crime. As the burglar said when they brought his previous convictions against him, "It's a thing that might happen to any man." Well, now, what would happen? I belong to a body called the Authors of England. I am one of the playwrights, journalists, authors. My trade organization is the Society of Authors, Playwrights, and Composers. The day after I commit the crime you would see all about it in the papers. "Bernard Shaw in the Dock," "Bernard Shaw accused of Murder," or burglary, or whatever it might be. If it was a more trivial crime the papers might say "G. B. S."

But mark this. The headline in the papers would not be "The Authors and the Public." They would not say the authors committed a murder, or committed a burglary. Agitators would not form vigilance societies to protect themselves against the authors of England. No one would suggest that I had carefully prearranged the crime with Mr [John] Galsworthy or Mr [George] Moore or Miss Ethel M. Dell. The responsibility would lie with me alone.

But supposing a police constable or a Chief Constable makes any mistake. What do you see next day in the paper? The mistake, or the crime, or whatever it may be, is always stated as having been committed by the police. It is always the "Police and the Public." [*Applause.*]

I find myself up against this whenever I have to say anything in public about some particular trial, as I sometimes do. I find I am taken to assume that what has happened is, not that an individual police officer might have done something under some sort of system that I object to, but that Scotland Yard, the Chief Commissioner, the Home Secretary, and all the Chief Constables of the country had met in a secret apartment and conspired against the public to do whatever I was criticizing.

The Chief Constables are therefore under this peculiar responsibility, that the personal mistake of one may make the whole force unpopular. And the trouble always begins with a mistake, not about a matter of law, but of opinion. For instance, disorderly conduct, the public danger in the matter of driving, obstruction, disgraceful conduct in the parks, indecent exposure.

Disorderly conduct; what constitutes it? What is dangerous driving? I have a tendency to believe that everyone's driving is dangerous except my own. My chauffeur sitting beside me has a tendency to regard my driving as dangerous. When he drives I return the compliment. Obstruction would seem to be a matter of fact, and yet I have come within an ace of going to prison twice on the question of obstruction.

After all, what is obstruction? Someone holds a meeting in a public thoroughfare in a way that obstructs traffic. But, after all, how does it obstruct traffic? If I stand still in the street to listen to a public orator someone else cannot walk through me, therefore I am obstructing. As the late great poet William Morris said, obstruction is a crime which we are committing all our lives. You cannot be in the world without obstructing.

As I have said, I myself have been on the verge of getting into trouble by upholding the right of public meeting in public thoroughfares. Strictly between ourselves, I regret that right as an obvious absurdity, a thing not to be tolerated in a big town. And yet you cannot interfere too much with it, because there are so many bodies in this country, particularly religious bodies, who exist by holding meetings at street corners and by making collections at them, that the moment a Chief Constable intervenes, as he did in the cases in which I was concerned, and tries to stop meetings taking place at some inconvenient corner, he suddenly finds himself overwhelmed by an enormous agitation. All the religious bodies in the country rise up, from the leaders of the Nonconformist bodies to the Archbishop of Canterbury; and I do not know any single case in which the police have not had to withdraw their opposition. And yet there are certain degrees of obstruction which you cannot permit. Obstruction becomes a matter of opinion, and a very difficult one.

I need not say anything about the difficulty of deciding what is disgraceful conduct in the parks, because you have a tremendous row going on about a case of that kind in London at the present moment; so I pass on to indecent exposure. One would think it a perfectly clear case if a man walked about practically without anything on; but nowadays he may plead a sun cure. I remember when the spectacle of a man wearing nothing but running shorts would have been regarded as grossly indecent. Now you see them doing that on all the roads.

I am a respectable, dignified, white-bearded member of society, but only last year I happened to be indulging in a sun cure in Italy. I was not aware of the fact that one or two ladies who happened to be in the neighborhood, also indulging in sun cures, carried Kodaks. When I returned from Italy to London, to my utter amazement I found all the illustrated papers, which means all the papers nowadays, full of pictures of me with nothing whatever on except a bathing slip. I can remember the time when that would have been considered shocking indecent exposure.

Now that sun cures are coming in, you no longer know where you are in this matter. Before you charge me with indecent exposure you will have to go to Parliament and say, "Here is Mr Shaw: how much must he have on? Must he have a hat or not? If you make a law that a person must have a hat, we know how to deal with him. If the law says he must have trousers, it must say how long they are to be. We can then prosecute if he hasnt got them. If there is no such law there is nothing against him but our personal opinion, which is no better than his personal opinion."

If you find a tendency on the part of Parliament—and public departments, which, by the way, are now beginning to lay down a great deal of law that does not come from Parliament—if you find them insisting that you must settle these questions: "You are men of sense; what do you get your salaries for?"—then you will have at many points to put your foot down against opinionative duties and say, "We are Chief Constables, and are willing to take on all reasonable police duties, but we are not prepared to do the work of the Pope, for example. We are not prepared to be Plato and Calvin, and Moses, and the Prophets rolled into one. It is not, finally, our business to define what is right and wrong conduct. That must be settled by the authorities representing the entire nation; and when it is settled, then we will see that the settlement is carried out."

You may wonder why I, who undertook to address you on the question of censorship of plays, have not yet said a word about it. But it has been necessary, before I could get you to see the difficulties of the position, to bring you to this point. Because, of all the impossible opinionative duties that could be put on you, the censorship of plays is the most impossible, and the most odious.

And I am going to advise you to resist the imposition of that duty on you with all your might and main. It will give you a lot of trouble. It will give you no credit, and from time to time will bring upon you discredit and ridicule, as it has many times brought on the Lord Chamberlain. Plays, like political speeches and books, bring you up against those constitutional liberties which you are supposed to preserve. Our main liberties are freedom of speech, freedom of the press, freedom of conscience— that is, freedom to worship in any church in any way we like— and the freedom of the stage, which comes in with the freedom of speech and the freedom of the newspapers.

These freedoms, as we call them, are a curious and entirely illogical exception to the laws which are made for the regulation of our other activities. When an author, for instance, says, "I am claiming my freedom to write as I please," he is making a very strong claim. He is not making a claim to write a book which everyone will recognize as being a decent and proper book. That does not require freedom at all. The author is asserting a right to write something which may horrify you.

Experience has led us to concede that curious claim to a great extent, because the history of the world shews that if you refuse to allow a man to express unusual and even shocking ideas there will never be any progress made. Ideas would never change, and a world where ideas never change means stagnation, decline, and decay. That is why this curious exception is made.

When a Chief Constable reads the newspapers he must occasionally wonder whether the freedom of the press is really a good thing or not, because no one knows better the amount of mischief which they occasionally do by the exercise of their freedom. And, in spite of the freedoms, he has to carry out a law which makes blasphemy an offence, sedition an offence, and obscenity an offence. How is he to judge of what is blasphemous and what is freedom of speech?

Take the case of that very wonderful man, George Fox, the founder of the Quakers. Read his diary—a very wonderful book to read, by the way—I dont say you can read it all through, because his experiences, like those of Wesley, are repeated so much, but still you can read enough to see the sort of thing Fox used to do.

He would go into a town and would hear the church bells

ringing, and, as he says, "the sound struck at his heart." He would go to the church, keep his hat on in the church, and bully the preacher in the church. He used to call it a steeple house. He used to denounce the priest and every form of set prayer and ritual. He used to say that when a man addresses his God he might at least address Him in his own language and not in the language of another man.

All that was pretty blasphemous and disorderly, and George Fox was considerably prosecuted and imprisoned and harried about. And yet, in the end, Fox founded that great religious body which certainly, in point of civil behavior, has the highest character of any body in this kingdom. No Chief Constable at the present moment would dream of prosecuting a Quaker for blasphemy. And yet if a Chief Constable were asked to draw the line between what the Quaker says and between what the straightforward street-corner atheist says, he really would be very puzzled how to do it.

Take sedition. You cannot tolerate a gunpowder plot, for instance, which is an extreme example. But how far are you to let the Communists go? You cannot object to Communism as such, because our Police organization, which is the measure of our civilization, is flat Communism. If I were to say, "I wont pay the Police rate; if I want a policeman I will go and make a private bargain with him," you would ask for a remand to inquire into the state of my mind. But though Communism is not seditious, Communists occasionally talk intolerable sedition. There are just as great fools among Communists as among other bodies.

Then, again, take obscenity. What is obscene? Is polygamy obscene? Are you to tolerate, for instance, the Mormon Missionaries? In the greater part of our Empire polygamy is an institution. You might find yourself in a difficulty, say, with an Indian who preached in the street that a man should have as many wives as he can get dowries with. In British India high-caste men marry dozens of ladies, getting handsome presents from the families, because they confer their own caste and rank on the lady. Several of them have hundreds of wives. That is Kulin polygamy. Mahometans are allowed to have four wives if they are foolish enough to complicate their domestic establishments to that extent. Several Christian sects base their advocacy of polygamy on the Old Testament. It is not easy for a Chief Constable to charge the Bible with obscenity.

Take also the burning question of birth control. That is a thing that is going to come up against you. Does the advocacy of birth control come under the legal heading of obscene libel? Are you to prosecute the man who preaches it at the street corner? Take the question of venereal disease. Everyone in this room can remember when this was an unmentionable subject. For instance, there is a very well-known play by a noted French author[1] which dealt with the question, and, at first, the Censor would not allow it to be produced. Yet the time came during the war when the authorities were very glad to have that play performed from one end of the country to the other. Now you have venereal disease discussed by assemblies of ladies and gentlemen all over the country. What was unmentionable yesterday is a common topic of polite conversation today.

Then take the question of nudity. There is a religious sect which left Russia because its members objected to compulsory military service. One of the religious tenets of that sect was that they should not wear any clothes. That was not indecency. It was an article of religion with them. But the Canadian police had to force them to choose between going into clothes or going into prison.

If there is a subject on earth on which you might think there could be no two opinions among decent people it is the subject of incest. But incest is only marriage within the tables of consanguinity; and those tables differ from time to time, from nation to nation, and from religion to religion.

Take, for instance, the play Hamlet, which many people think the greatest of Shakespear's plays. In it Hamlet reproaches his mother for committing incest in such horrible terms that if the actors make it real I always feel very uncomfortable while it is being performed. But what Chief Constables dare prosecute Sir Johnston Forbes-Robertson for playing Hamlet?

But the legal point I want to impress on you is that Hamlet,

---

[1] Eugène Brieux's *Damaged Goods*.

when reproaching his mother for committing incest with his uncle, calling him incestuous, murderous, damned, remorseless, and so forth, is now out of date. What is called incest in Hamlet is not incest now. The incest in Hamlet is that Hamlet's mother married her deceased husband's brother. That was incest within your recollection. Now it is perfectly legal.

Here is another example. There is a play called The Cenci, by Shelley, and one of the most popular operas in the world is Die Walküre, by Richard Wagner. Both works are about incest from beginning to end. In the opera, twin brother and sister discover oneanother, fall in love, and throughout the whole opera their union is regarded sympathetically. It is actually discussed by the gods in the second act, and the principal god is on their side. It is only the god's wife who is against it and who demands punishment for the offenders. As to the spectators, their sympathy is called for on the side of the brother and sister.

Some of you may be very bold men, but there is no man here who is bold enough to stop a performance of Wagner's opera. It is impossible. The thing has got established by virtue of its own importance as a work of art. In the same way, for many years The Cenci was forbidden, yet now it is licensed and has been performed by the great actress Miss Sybil Thorndike, and no one is a penny the worse. You have to tolerate these two famous works; but what would you do if you had to deal with them as new works by unknown writers?

This brings us at last to the question of censorship of plays. Let us begin with the practical difficulties. I sometimes hear of a Chief Constable nowadays having to read a play. If that goes on and you have to read all the plays that are written, I venture to say that in a very short time every one of you will resign his honorable and dignified position and will say, "In future I am going to live by sweeping a crossing. It is better than reading all the plays written in this country." It is wildly impossible. The Lord Chamberlain employs a reader of plays to do it. But even if you read the plays, what would you know about their effect on the stage?

I remember the old days when music halls were very different from what they are now, and when most music-hall songs were indecent songs. If you read those old songs you will find nothing indecent in them. I remember a case, I believe in Manchester, of a very popular young music-hall singer, the daughter of an even more popular lady in the same profession, who was prosecuted because of a certain song she sang. Her counsel had no difficulty in the matter before the magistrates. He simply took the song and read the words, which were perfectly innocent. They were silly, perhaps, but what harm was there in them? The magistrate was about to dismiss the case when the lady in question burst into tears and began to protest. She said, "He is spoiling my song; it is not the words, but the way I sing them." That gave away the whole show.

I remember one well-known comedian in a play which I had to criticize at a time when I got my living by criticizing plays instead of by writing them and being criticized. This comedian had to say to another lady on the stage, "Might I speak to you, miss?" Well, who could possibly object to such a line? Yet as spoken on the stage it became exceedingly indecent and offensive. You can read the play, but you cannot control the gesture made, and do not know what the play will be like when it comes to the performance.

Again, you may come to a passage which appears to be revoltingly blasphemous. That occurred in a play of mine. I wrote a play which, if it had not been put in dramatic form, might have been a religious tract, The Shewing-up of Blanco Posnet. The Lord Chamberlain handed it to his reader, Mr [George Alexander] Redford. He was a little puzzled by the play. It had a passage in it, "He is a mean one; he is a sly one." Mr Redford could not make out to whom the speaker was referring. I presume he asked someone in the office who was meant by the "mean one; the sly one." The reply must have been, "I am afraid he is alluding to God Almighty, because immediately afterwards, when someone asks who it is, he points upwards."

What could Mr Redford do? He could not allow God Almighty to be described on the stage as "a mean one; a sly one." He issued a license conditionally on all references to God Almighty being cut out. The result was curious. I could not allow the play to be performed with these lines cut out, because without them it became a senseless, rowdy, blasphemous, coarse play—a horrible play, a thing I could not have my name connected with.

But you can imagine Mr Redford's astonishment when, on the first Sunday after the play was published, no less than three sermons were preached on the subject of the play. The clergy were delighted with it, and it has been the subject of several sermons since. When Lord Sandhurst became Lord Chamberlain he withdrew the ban, and the play is now licensed. Yet, if you had been in the position of Mr Redford you would have found it very hard, on coming to that passage, to see that the dramatic effect was no more blasphemous than the reproaches addressed by Job to his Maker in the Bible are blasphemous. The truth is, Mr Redford and the Lord Chamberlain were confronted with a task which, in itself, was impossible. You cannot tell whether or not a play will do harm until you have seen it performed.

All the argument for stopping the play to prevent the evil is equivalent to the argument for handcuffing me before I get back to my hotel, on the ground that if you do not I might punch someone's head on the way. You have got to allow the dog his first bite. The moment they come to you and talk about reading plays and prohibiting them, you should say, "No, let them perform it first, and if there is an offence we can deal with it then. We cannot come in beforehand. The thing has been tried out and it is of no use. Not only have the most scandalous plays got through, but edifying plays like Mr Shaw's The Shewing-up of Blanco Posnet have been stopped." And think of the number of people who might have been turned to salvation by that religious tract of mine during all these years during which I was branded as a blasphemer!

Let me give one illustration as to the things that get through. I was once asked by a leading American magazine to write an article on the subject of the censorship. I replied that it was quite impossible for me to describe the most scandalous of the plays passed by the censorship and performed under the Lord Chamberlain's license in a magazine intended for family reading.

They said they were interested in this question, and they went so far as to count the words in my article and to give me a pledge that every single word would be published. But when it came to the point they had to cut it drastically in spite of their solemn pledge,[1] and I did not wonder at it. It really was not fit for publication, and yet all that stuff had been licensed by the Lord Chamberlain, and if you had been the Lord Chamberlain you would have licensed it.

The political situation is a quaint one. Every one of the plays that come along to the provinces has been licensed by the Lord Chamberlain; and the Lord Chamberlain is the chief officer of the King's household. Well, if you prosecute a play that has been licensed in that way, it appears to me you are committing an act verging on high treason.

You go into court to prosecute a play on the ground that it is blasphemous, obscene, or seditious, and the manager immediately protests that the Lord Chamberlain has licensed it from St James's Palace, and certified that it is fit and proper for presentation. And he has had two guineas for doing it and you have had nothing for your opinion. What are you to do under these circumstances? Your conduct cannot be challenged in Parliament, because any member of Parliament can move the reduction of the Police vote by £100 in order to draw attention to the conduct of a Chief Constable. Not so the Lord Chamberlain. His salary does not come up in the House of Commons; he is part of the King's household. Years and years ago it was asked how are we to get rid of the censorship of the Lord Chamberlain, and I said, "You will have to abolish the Monarchy first."

My advice to you is to resist any attempt to put on you the duty of the Lord Chamberlain. For my own part, I do not want to abolish the Lord Chamberlain only to expose myself to the attacks of the common informer—to the secretary of the vigilance society which looks after public morals. I should be in a much worse case than I was before. I should be at the mercy, too, of every Chief Constable. Now, the Chief Constable would

[1] "The Censorship of the Stage in England," *North American Review*, CLXIX (August 1899), 251-62; reprinted in E. J. West (ed.), *Shaw on Theatre* (New York: Hill & Wang, 1958). For the full story concerning the unauthorised bowdlerisation, see George Leveson Gower, *Mixed Grill* (London: Frederick Muller, 1947), 90-1.

have nothing to fear from me. I am only an author. But he would be up against big money in this matter. A play often represents a very large investment of money. There is not only the production of the play in London, but the carefully-planned tour round the country. If a Chief Constable suddenly butts in in the middle of a tour, and throws the touring company idle for a week or a fortnight, he is knocking big business on the head to that extent; and immediately he has the whole power of the big business men against him.

That is an antagonism which no prudent Chief Constable will lightly take on. You would have all the managers up against you, because they are strenuous supporters of the Lord Chamberlain. For the two guineas which they give him they receive what is practically an insurance policy against being prosecuted for the production of the play. If you prosecute, you are breaking that bargain.

I call attention especially to this point because some of you might imagine that, because the managers support the Lord Chamberlain so strongly, they would also support you strongly. Not a bit of it. The reason for which they support the Lord Chamberlain will make them oppose you furiously.

Is the theatre, then, to be left unregulated? That is a thing which virtually cannot be done. There are still theatres in this country which are little more than disorderly houses. You may have a theatre where tickets of admission are given away wholesale in order to induce people to visit them. When they get there the attraction is the drinking bar and a promenade full of prostitutes, and the money is made out of them in that way. Of course, numbers of theatrical managers, especially in London, will be horrified at this statement. Such things do not go on while they are there, but what goes on at other times may make it necessary for the police to keep an eye on the theatre, and to make it possible for them to get it closed.

I suggest that the proper way to deal with the theatre question is to have the theatre licensed by the local authority from year to year. In London, the establishment of this control by the London County Council over the London music halls made a most beneficent transformation. From being places to which respectable people did not go, they have been turned into variety theatres in which you find the most distinguished audience. Sometimes half the House of Lords is there with its wives and daughters; and all that change has been made by municipal control.

People will say, "Is the London County Council, or the Birmingham Corporation, for instance, going to read all the plays?" There is nothing of that kind proposed. If the theatres were licensed, the police in the first place would have access to them and would have the power to oppose the renewal of the license. They could bring forward what evidence they liked as regards the way the place was conducted, and they could call attention to the character of the entertainment.

I do not suggest that local authorities should be empowered to refuse licenses for other than judicial reasons. Justices must not refuse to renew licenses of public houses because they individually may happen to think that there should be no public houses in the world. In the same way, I should not allow a Puritan member of a local authority to oppose the renewal of a license merely because he thought that the theatre was the gate to Hell and that there should be no such things as theatres. The judicial reason is a perfectly well understood and established feature of licensing practice.

Unless a theatre was really badly conducted, and was an undesirable and disreputable place, you could never get a majority of our large councils or city corporations to vote for the closing of the house. But the power to close it would keep the managers in good order for all practical purposes.

Then there is the question of the prosecution of a play. That should not be done locally, but by the Public Prosecutor. No common informer should have the power to institute a prosecution. Chief Constables should not have the power to do it. It would be very undesirable and troublesome to themselves. It is one of the things of which you have a right to say, "This is not a proper function for us. If a play is improper for one town, it is improper for all towns; and it should be prosecuted by a central authority representing the whole country."

To sum up, I advise you to press for the licensing of theatres by local authorities as a substitute for the censorship. I have taken up an unconscionable amount of time, but I thought it better to do the thing thoroughly while I was about it.

THE NEED FOR EXPERT OPINION
IN SEXUAL REFORM

(Address delivered before the third International Congress of the World League for Sexual Reform, held in the Wigmore Hall, 13 September 1929. *Sexual Reform Congress*, ed. Norman Haire, London, 1930. An unauthorized verbatim report, at variance with the official text as approved by Shaw, appeared in *Time and Tide*, 20 *September* 1929)

I am sorry I cannot read you a paper. I am constitutionally incapable of doing such a thing. I must improvize as best I can; and for the sake of others whom you have to hear as well as myself I will try to be concise, though I am not usually so on the platform.

I am not going tonight to beg the question of what sexual reform means. Everybody is a sexual reformer: that is, everybody who has any ideas on the subject at all. The Pope, for instance, is a prominent sexual reformer; and the Austrian Nudists are sexual reformers. If you had a general congress of all the sexual reformers, not merely the members of one particular Society, but all the people who are demanding sexual reform: Nudists and Catholics, birth controlers and self-controlers, homosexualists and hetero-sexualists, monogamists, polygamists, and celibates, there would be some curious cross-party divisions. The Pope would find himself on nine points out of ten warmly in sympathy with Dr Marie Stopes. And it is quite possible that the most fanatical Nudists and the most fanatical homosexualists might have in common the strongest objection to polygamy and divorce. All of them would probably disagree on such questions as the age of consent.

My point tonight is that, no matter what people's views are on sexual reform, it is desirable that they should take expert opinion as to the practicability and probable social effect of the particular measures they are advocating. I shall not discuss the measures for or against. I simply put before you the general proposition, that instead of following the usual human practice of inventing your science according to what you happen to desire yourself, and inventing your facts in the same accommodating way, you should make some attempt to find out from people who have practical experience, who are experts in the matter, what they think would happen if the particular measures you are advocating were carried into effect.

There are two effects to be considered in any definite measure of sexual reform. There is the psychological effect, and there is the political effect. Now, it is on the psychological side that I wish to speak tonight, because I am speaking as an expert. [*Laughter.*] I do not in the least know why that remark of mine has elicited laughter; but as a matter of fact I am an expert in sex appeal. What I mean is that I am a playwright. I am connected with the theatre. The theatre is continually occupied with sex appeal. It has to deal in sex appeal exactly as a costermonger has to deal in turnips; and a costermonger's opinion on turnips is worth having. He is an expert. In the same way the opinion of playwrights and other theatre people is worth having because they know how the thing is done through having to do it as part of their daily work.

One very important function of the theatre in society is to educate the audience in matters of sex. Besides the people who take that duty seriously there are those who only exploit sex appeal commercially. But no matter, they all have to know how to do it, because if their sex appeal fails, they lose money; and you can hardly call any man a real expert unless he loses money if his practice happens to be wrong.

And yet when sex appeal has to be discussed scientifically nobody ever calls in the playwright, and he himself does not come forward without an invitation. But the priest always rushes in and demands to be accepted as an authority on sex. Well, if he went behind the scenes of a theatre and made such a claim, we should say: "Mind your own business. This evidently is the one subject about which you as a celibate can know nothing. If you attempt to meddle with it you will make literally an unholy mess of it!"

However, there is always a certain tendency to go to the man who knows nothing about it, because we are always a little afraid that if we consult a genuine expert his opinion will go against us.

The Pope represents the priest in this matter. The Pope is the Chief Priest of Europe, and he speaks very strongly on the subject of sex appeal. I, of course, should never dream of appealing in that matter to the Chief Priest of Europe, but if there were such a person as the Chief Prostitute of Europe I should call her in immediately. I should say: "Here, clearly, is a person who deals professionally in sex appeal, and will lose her livelihood if her method is wrong. She can speak to us with authority."

Unfortunately, or fortunately, just as you choose to look at it, there is no such person as the Chief Prostitute of Europe to balance the Chief Priest, which is perhaps the reason that the priest's opinion gets heard whilst the prostitute's opinion is not heard. Therefore it is that I proffer myself as being the next best authority to the prostitute, that is to say, the playwright.

I find myself up against two sets of amateurs. One set seeks to minimize sex appeal by a maximum of clothing. The other seeks to maximize sex appeal by a minimum of clothing. I come in as an expert and tell them that they are both hopelessly and completely wrong. If you want sex appeal raised to the utmost point, there is only one way of doing it, and that is by clothes. In hot climates the purpose of clothing must have been sex appeal and not protection from the inclemency of the weather, because in such places the weather tempts people to take off their clothes instead of to put them on.

Let me give you an actual example. Some years ago I was at a place in Germany called Kissingen, where people go to take mud baths and drink unpleasant radioactive waters. I did not take mud baths; but I went one evening to one of those beer-garden places where they have variety entertainments. One of the performers had two accomplishments which are usually incompatible. She was a singer and also an acrobat. That is a rare combination, because an acrobat is very highly trained muscularly, with the curious result that he or she seldom has any voice at all.

Consequently I was interested in this lady at Kissingen, because I had never seen an acrobat combine a vocal exhibition with a gymnastic one. Her interest for us here tonight lies in her dress. She first went through her performance on the horizontal bar and for that she wore skin tights from head to foot. Except for the artificial color of the webbing she was exactly as if she had no clothes on at all; and this was accepted without question as right and inevitable, because it suited the work she was doing, and was natural. Then she retired for a moment before coming out again to sing a mildly naughty little song. And how did she dress for that? She felt that the costume in which she had revolved on the horizontal bar somehow or other would be an impossible one to sing a naughty song in. So she put a little skirt on, and, of course, immediately became indecent. She knew it, and had put on the skirt for that purpose. She felt that in some way that little skirt had sex appeal in it, and therefore she could sing her naughty little song.

I wish the Pope had been there. It would have been a very instructive lesson for him—just the sort of lesson that a priest needs.

I remember the nineteenth century. People who remember it are now becoming scarce. But I remember it well, as I was at an impressionable age then. Being a born artist I have always been specially impressionable by sex. My first impressions were derived from the Victorian women. The Victorian woman was a masterpiece of sex appeal. She was sex appeal from the top of her head to the sole of her feet. She was clothed, of course, from head to foot: all clothes! Everything about her except her cheeks and her nose was a guilty secret, a thing you had to guess at. All young men and boys then thrilled with the magic and mystery of the invisible world under those clothes. In the Christmas pantomime the call-boy always played the old woman in the harlequinade, and the one unfailing joke was when the old woman, in scrambling over a wall, shewed one leg with its white stocking visible up to the knee. Then the whole house shrieked and rocked and roared with laughter. A modern London audience, which sees a hundred thousand stockings every day, would hardly see the joke.

When you turned from the ridiculous call-boy dressed as a woman to the real lady, the way she was dressed was like the temptation of St Anthony. They did not dress her: they upholstered her. That is the only word. Every contour, all her contours, all four of them, may I say, were voluptuously emphasized. When the lady herself could not emphasize them sufficiently by her own person, artificial aids were introduced. She fitted on her breasts little wire-cages which were called palpitators. She had, of course, the bustle which gave the Hottentot outline. I really think if I could exhibit here one of the ordinary portraits of the fashionable woman of that day, you would be shocked. But if you stopped to think "What is the woman like?" you would see that the idea was to conceal the fact that she was a human being and make her like a very attractive and luxurious sofa. It was done by clothing, and could not have been done by any other means. And every woman knew that. Every actress knew that. Those actresses of the French stage who made a speciality of sex appeal never undressed themselves in public. I do not know how many petticoats they wore; but at any rate, instead of exposing their persons, they just gave you a little glimpse of what looked like a dozen frilled pink petticoats round the ankles, and the effect was tremendous.

The result was that the Victorian age was an exceedingly immoral age: an age in which there arose the reaction which modern psychiatrists call exhibitionism. The upholstered ladies felt that they must do something dreadful: shew their ankles, for instance. Hardly the most desperate or abandoned of them ever dreamed of shewing anything more. Thus you had on the one hand this intense sex appeal produced by clothes, and on the other hand the tendency to defy it or exploit it by making a naughty little revelation of some kind.

Alexandre Dumas *père*, in describing the great French actress Mademoiselle Mars, who used to receive people in her dressing room when she was changing, said that she was a wonderful woman because she could change from head to foot and never let you see more than a thumbnail. That gives you the measure of sex appeal in the nineteenth century. If only they could have combined the complete concealment of a woman with an insistence on her sex, they would have been perfectly happy.

We have been trying to get rid of all that. We have had a significant spread of Nudism, not carried to the extreme that it has reached in Austria, where you have clubs of people who have the extremely wholesome habit of meeting oneanother without anything on at all, for that gets rid of sex appeal altogether, but still enough to keep our grandmothers in a chronic ecstasy of incredulous amazement. You see, we do not want to get rid of sex appeal.

The Nudist points out that, though a single human pair could not be innocently nude together, yet if a hundred other nude persons were present they would no longer feel that they were nude: there would be nothing in it, though a dressed person would feel unbearably awkward. But when you tell the ordinary man that there would be nothing in it, he at once says: "Then dont let us have any of it. I like sex appeal. I prefer to be in an atmosphere of sex appeal."

I shall not deliver judgment as to whether it is desirable to live as I did in the nineteenth century, where life was saturated with sex appeal, or under existing conditions where women have taken a very large step towards nudity, and the correspondingly reduced sex appeal has become far saner and pleasanter. My business is not to say which is the more desirable phenomenon. I simply want to point out to the public and to the sex-reformers how the difference is produced. The Pope wants to bring back the old clothing, not to bring back the old sex appeal, but to do away with it. If [clothing] does come back, it will increase sex appeal and defeat the Pope's good intentions. There is no doubt about that. Some people will tell themselves that quite frankly and rejoice in it. Others will advocate it with graver faces, but will not tell themselves why they advocate it.

The other day I visited a Jesuit church in Trieste, and I have never been more disgusted than I was in that church. Instead of the usual notices that you see in churches in Italy that women will not be admitted unless they are modestly dressed (a thing quite simply stated, and meaning nothing more than that a woman who has short sleeves must carry with her a shawl to wrap over her arms as she comes in), there were half-a-dozen different notices in different parts of the church, all elaborately composed and all suggesting some impropriety or other which would never come into the head of a decent normal person if it were not officially placarded. Every placard pointed out some particular aphrodisiac effect that would be produced on young men if women were not muffled up so that no one could see that they had bodies.

I should like to have met the Pope in that church. I can fancy myself saying: "Look here, your Holiness. I propose that for the moment we try to imagine ourselves soldiers of the old type. Absolutely licentious abandoned men, who fought for anybody who would pay them and became soldiers because they wanted to live licentious lives, and occasionally have the glorious experience of sacking a city, one of the great incidents of the sack of a city being unlimited rapine. Let us honestly and candidly imagine ourselves taking part in such a sack. We are looking about for women to ravish. We come upon two. One is a nun, in a nun's dress. The other is a harlot, with as little dress on as possible, rouged and painted and shameless. I ask your Holiness to tell yourself which of these women you would go for. I have not the slightest doubt which I should go for. We should fight oneanother for the piously-dressed woman."

Now I have come to the end of my time. I point no moral. I have simply given you the expert's practical directions. If you want sex appeal, [wear] clothes. If you want to minimize sex appeal, get rid of as many clothes as possible.

I hope some other speakers will deal with the political effects of sexual reform. I will content myself with a warning. Modern democracy has become associated with ideas of liberty, because it has abolished certain methods of political oppression. And as we all allow ourselves to be actuated far too much by mere association of ideas, we are apt to think that what makes for liberty in one thing will make for liberty in all things.

Make no such mistake about modern democracy and popular government. The more the people at large have to do with government, the more we—now I am talking to the members of this Society—will have to fight for our ideas and perhaps for our lives.

EXPERT OPINION IN SEXUAL REFORM

I will just take one minute to tell you an anecdote which illustrates the situation. A friend of mine, the late Cecil Sharp, collected many peasant songs, especially in Somerset. He began there in the rectory of the Rev. C. L. Marson, another old friend of mine. They are both dead. One day they were walking in the rectory grounds near an enclosed fruit garden. Cecil Sharp heard a man on the other side of the wall singing a song, to what seemed to him to be a beautiful tune. He immediately noted it down, and said to Marson, "Who is that singing?" "He is my gardener," was the reply. Sharp insisted on finding out whether he had any more songs. He went in, full of the enthusiasm of the artist who had discovered something beautiful; and they told the man that they had heard him singing. He instantly threw down his spade, and called God to witness that he was an honest and decent man who had never sung a song in his life, and was not going to be accused of such debauchery and wickedness by any gentleman.

They were amazed, because as members of our cultivated classes they did not understand that to the mass of the people art and beauty are nothing but forms of debauchery. They had the greatest trouble in persuading that gardener that they were both of them just as great blackguards as he was; and then he told them where they would find other songs, and undertook to introduce them to the singers.

Think of the moral of that! That is the sort of thing you have to face. The mass of people, brought up as they have been, have no idea of liberty in this direction. On the contrary, they are the most ferocious opponents of it; and you will have to fight, I will not say for a super-morality, because it will appear to them to be a sub-morality, but for a class morality and even an individual morality. Certain circles of people in different degrees of spiritual development will have to claim moralities of their own in their own circles, and will have to tolerate other circles with different moralities. That is the utmost you can hope for. Do not think your own particular morality can be imposed on the whole nation; and do not dream that such liberality is inherent in Democracy, for that is the greatest mistake you can possibly make.

SAINT JOAN

(B.B.C. radio talk, delivered on the five hundredth anniversary
of the burning of Joan of Arc, 30 May 1931. *The Listener*,
3 *June* 1931)

I have promised to give a chat here tonight about that very
extraordinary young woman who was burnt five hundred years
ago. Now, when I say that I promised to give a chat, I really
mean that. I am playing the game quite strictly with you. I have
not got a manuscript, mostly copied out of the *Encyclopedia
Britannica*, to read solemnly to you giving all the historical
details about Joan of Arc. I am sitting here in London quite
comfortably, and I shall say anything about her that comes into
my head, quite obviously.

You know, of course, that Joan of Arc was a young girl who
was burnt. But I want you to get that out of your head; it is not
really a matter of very great consequence to us now, the particular
way in which she died, and the fact that she was burnt does not
distinguish her at all, and does not explain why we are talking
about her here tonight, although hundreds of thousands of
women have been burnt, just as she was burnt, and yet they are
quite forgotten and nobody talks about them.

It was not that she was young, because after the Bull of Pope
Innocent VIII, which began the burning of witches (and Joan
was burnt because she was a witch), young girls were burnt;
but also young children were burnt; quite beautiful young
children were thrown into the flames. All that you read. She is
only one of a great many people.

There is a parallel case really to Joan's which is very well
known throughout all Christendom, and that is the case of
the Founder of Christianity Himself, and I sometimes have to
remind people that a belief in Christianity does not mean getting
very excited in a sensational way about the very horrible way in
which the Founder of Christianity was executed. I think of all
the hymns in the English Hymnal the one that I dislike the most
is When I survey the wondrous Cross. When people sing that
I always feel inclined to say, "Will you please stop surveying the

wondrous Cross, which is not an emblem of Christianity but an emblem of what the Romans called justice, a very cruel, unchristian, and horrible thing, and I am sorry to say that we still call exactly the same sort of thing justice." Not very long before Jesus Christ was crucified, 60,000 persons were crucified because they had revolted against their conditions as slaves and gladiators, and they all suffered in the same way that Jesus suffered. And, therefore, in talking of people like Joan and of Jesus Christ you must not think of Jesus Christ as the Crucified One, because there were a great many crucified ones, and the two who were crucified with Him were not persons of very respectable character.

What we have to consider then is, simply, what manner of persons these executed people were that we should, five hundred years and nineteen hundred years after their executions, be still talking about them. And I want particularly to insist on this in the case of Joan, because people think it is such a romantic thing to be burnt, and to be a young woman being burnt, that they begin to insist on the young woman being a beautiful young woman and they begin to imagine that she must have had some very touching and charming love-affairs in her life. Now, I am sorry to disappoint those of my hearers who have that particular romantic turn, but it is a perfectly well-established fact that Joan was not beautiful. It is not merely that people have not mentioned whether she was beautiful or not, but it has been placed on record by her military comrades, by the officers with whom she worked in battle and also by the men, who adored her and believed her to be something divine. These officers liked her very much, always remembered her with affection as a comrade, and the men, as I have said, worshiped her; but they all expressly—those of them whose testimony we have still got—explicitly said that the reason, or one of the reasons, why they believed her to be divine was that, although she was a woman, she had none of what our American friends in Hollywood and elsewhere call "sex appeal." She was outside that. They felt towards her as they felt towards the Saints and towards the Blessed Virgin; but all that romantic kind of thing was out of the way, was a thing almost blasphemous. And so you must make up your minds to Joan of Arc as being a person who was not beautiful, who was not romantic, but who, as I said, was a very extraordinary person.

Now, she was burned by a Christian Tribunal. You hear people occasionally discussing whether the French burned her or whether the English burned her and who was to blame in the matter. You need not worry about that. The really significant thing for us today is that she was burnt by a Tribunal which represented Christianity in the world. She was burnt by a Catholic Tribunal, one which at that time really represented the whole Christian feeling of the world. And, furthermore, they gave her a very long, a very careful, and a very conscientious trial; they found her guilty on all the counts of the indictment that was made against her, and she was guilty on every one of those counts according to the ideas of those people, and, I may say, probably according to the ideas of a great many of you ladies and gentlemen whom I am now addressing. She was found guilty of heresy; she was found guilty of witchcraft; she was found guilty of homicidal soldiering, which was a horrible sin for a woman; and she was found guilty of a blasphemous habit of wearing men's attire, which also was considered a very grave and frightful thing for a woman to do. But I may say that the reason it was called blasphemous was that she not only wore men's dress and insisted on wearing it, but she said that she had been ordered to do it by St Margaret and by St Catherine, and that was an appalling blasphemy in those days, and I think it may possibly shock one or two of those whom I am now addressing.

You cannot deny that all these accusations were true accusations. To begin with the heresy. At a time when the whole world was Catholic and when the Reformation had not yet taken place, she was a Protestant; that is to say, she said that God came first with her. He came before the Church; and when she was asked, "Will you not accept the Church's interpretation of God for you?" she said, "No; God must come first." That was heresy. That was about the most shocking thing that could be said to a true Catholic by a true Catholic. And she said this quite naturally. She was not a person who had studied the works of Wycliffe or any of the early Reformers or their precursors. She said that as a mere obvious matter of course. She was so ignorant of the fact that she was a Protestant—she had never heard the word—that she actually proposed to go and lead a Crusade against the Bohemian Protestants, against the followers of John Huss [Jan Hus]—as we call them, Hussites; and she was quite ready to lead a Crusade to fight and suppress those people, not knowing that she herself was uttering precisely the thing for which the Church had quarreled with them. They tried her quite mercifully; they did everything they possibly could when they were trying her to get her to take that back; they implored her to consider what she was saying, but she did not realize herself its gravity; it seemed to her to be the perfectly natural thing. She could not understand that the "men of the Church," as she spoke of them, rather slightingly, although she was such a devout Catholic, as she believed—she could not understand how anybody could propose to come between her and God. In that way she was guilty of heresy, in a manner of speaking the most shocking heresy, the most terrible thing that you could be guilty of in those days, the crime for which people were burnt; and it was that mainly for which she was burnt.

Furthermore, she was guilty of witchcraft in the sense of the Tribunal before which she was standing, because she declared that her inspiration had been conveyed to her by voices and by visions. In particular, there were three saints—St Catherine, St Margaret, and St [sic] Michael—and these, she said, visited her, spoke to her, told her what to do, and she undoubtedly honestly believed that these voices that came to her did come from these saints. Now, the main sin of witchcraft in these days was having intercourse with spirits, and the Church told her that those spirits were evil spirits come to tempt her to damnation. As I have just told you, she said that one of the things that they told her to do was to dress like a man and, furthermore, to take a sword and go and slay men, and to take part in war. In saying that, in claiming it proudly as being her justification, she was condemning herself to execution for the crime of witchcraft. There was no question of trapping her into these admissions. They did not try to trap her. On the contrary, they really did their best, as you will find, if you read the accounts of the trial;

they did all that could be expected of them to make her withdraw them. But she was perfectly steadfast in these statements.

As for the soldiering, that was considered a dreadful thing for a woman to undertake; and I think we who are now speaking to oneanother may say that it is a shocking thing to think of a woman going out to kill, and risking being killed; I happen to think that it is an equally shocking thing for a man to do, and perhaps some of you will agree with me. But there are certain people who have the misfortune to be born with a talent for soldiering, and there is no doubt that Joan was an inveterate soldier. Whenever there was a battle within her reach Joan got into the thick of it. She fought as a company officer; when her men were flinching or faltering she threw herself into battle, she led them into danger, right up to the danger point. When they were storming a fort she was the first officer at the fort wall and made them come after her. Even when her battles had been successful, to such a point that many of the statesmen and soldiers of her time wanted to stop the fighting, she wanted to go on with it, and, as I told you, even when there was no more fighting to be done in France, she was looking forward to having some more fighting in Bohemia, by conducting a Crusade against the Hussites in that country.

I have already spoken to you about the male attire. So that you see on these counts—heresy, witchcraft, homicidal soldiering, male attire—Joan was guilty. If you consider that sort of conduct guilty, she was unquestionably and on her own confession guilty. She was accordingly sentenced to be burnt to death, that being the usual punishment, the alloted punishment, by the custom of the time, and practically by the rules of the Inquisition, because although the Catholic Church and the Inquisition would not kill anybody directly, they nevertheless handed the condemned person over to what they called the secular arm—that is to say, the military or the civil power—knowing perfectly well the result would be that the person would be burnt to death.

On that particular point of the burning, I want to remind you of one thing. Joan chose to be burnt. She could have escaped being burnt. She tried to escape being burnt by recanting. When they told her that she would be burnt if she persisted, she then said, very well, she did not want to be burnt; she was a very sensible kind of woman and she said, "Since you say so, I do not want to be burnt; I will take it all back and I will sign a recantation." She signed a recantation and then it became impossible to burn her. But when she learned that she was not going to be set free, but that she was to be condemned to perpetual imprisonment, she then deliberately withdrew her recantation; she put on her man's dress again, she reaffirmed that her voices, her saints, were saints and not devils, and that she was going to obey their instructions; she relapsed, as they called it, completely into her heresy, and by her own deliberate choice was burnt instead of being perpetually imprisoned. Now, I recommend that to all of you who are listening to me, because in almost all your criminal codes, here in England, in America, in Italy, in France, we are always condemning people for crimes to this very punishment of imprisonment, of long terms of imprisonment, sometimes of solitary imprisonment, and in that we are using a crueler punishment than burning, according to the judgment of this woman who had her open choice between the two. That is something for you to think about. I will not dwell any more on it.

Now let me say a word as to Joan's life and her abilities. She was, unquestionably, an exceptionally and extraordinarily able woman. She was a farmer's daughter, with no special advantages of education. She could not read and she could not write, although she could dictate letters and did. She had, unquestionably, military ability. In her campaign, the campaign by which she brought King Charles to the throne, she knew exactly what to do at the time when the military commanders of her time were muddling, were hesitating, were wasting their forces in all directions. She concentrated them, she knew how to make soldiers fight, which they did not; she made them fight, she made them conquer soldiers by whom they were accustomed to be conquered. She had great political ability. She saw exactly what was needed to strike the imagination of the French people in getting the Dauphin crowned in the cathedral at Rheims, and she fought her way and made him fight his way to that cathedral and that place, and saw that he was consecrated with the holy oil. She knew that that was the way in which you could swing the political feeling in France to his side as being the anointed King. She had tremendous parliamentary ability. Her trial was a very long business, in which she had to discuss, dispute, argue, and debate with very clever persons. And there she was in a very desperate situation, as she very well knew, and she held her own with all of them.

The trial is very curious. It is not so much the trial of judges who are speaking from the height of their position to a culprit. The whole thing became something like a parliamentary argument, of which she very often got the best, or the better. I cannot elaborate that because my time has drawn to an end. I want only to tell you this: that although the burning of Joan was an inexcusable thing, because it was a uselessly cruel thing, the question arises whether she was not a dangerous woman.

That question arises with almost every person of distinguished or extraordinary ability. Let us take an example from our own times. After the late war the late Marshal Foch was asked by somebody, "How would Napoleon have fought this war?" Foch answered, "Oh! he would have fought it magnificently, superbly. But," he said, "what on earth should we have done with him afterwards?" Now, that question arose in Joan's case. I want to bring it close to the present day. It is arising today in the case of a very extraordinary man, a man whose name is Leon Trotsky. Leon Trotsky's military exploits will probably rank with those of the greatest commanders in future history. The history of Trotsky's train—the railway train in which for a couple of years he practically lived while he threw back the whole forces of Europe, at a time when the condition of his country seemed desperate —that was a military exploit which we are too close to appreciate, but there is no doubt whatever as to what history will say about him; it will rank him along with the greatest commanders. But he is just in the position of Napoleon: when the question arose what was to be done with him afterwards, his own country, Russia, banished him. They banished him to a place at first very much like St Helena, which we put Napoleon into because we believed it would kill him, and it did kill him. Trotsky was put in a very unpleasant place. He is now in Turkey, under happier circumstances. But the question arises there. We are all very much afraid of him: we dare not allow him to come to England, not so much because we are afraid of him making war here, but because his own country is so afraid of him that we feel that any hospitality that we extended to him would be almost interpreted as an attack on the Russian Government. You may think of Trotsky as being a sort of male St Joan, in his day, who has not been burnt. You may connect him, again, as I say, with Napoleon. You will have to think it all out for yourself because I have no time here tonight to go into it. I have already exceeded my time.

I will just give you one more thing to think about. If you want to have an example from your own time, if you want to find what women can feel when they suddenly find the whole power of society marshaled against them and they have to fight it, as it were, then read a very interesting book which has just appeared by Miss Sylvia Pankhurst describing what women did in the early part of this century in order to get the parliamentary vote. Miss Sylvia Pankhurst, like so many other women in that movement, was tortured. In fact, except for burning, she suffered actual physical torture which Joan was spared. Other women suffered in that way with her. She describes from her own experience what those women felt, and how they did it. They were none of them exactly like St Joan, but I believe every one of them did regard herself as, in a measure, repeating the experiences of St Joan. St Joan inspired that movement, that curious movement, which I think is within the recollection of most of you. Think of it in that way. If you read Miss Pankhurst, you will understand a great deal more about the psychology of Joan, and her position at the trial, than you will by reading the historical accounts, which are very dry.

I say one thing finally. Joan was killed by the Inquisition. The Inquisition, you think, is dead. The Inquisition is not dead. Whenever you have a form of government which cannot deal with spiritual affairs, sooner or later you will have the Inquisition. In England it was said there was no Inquisition. That was not true. It was called by another name—it was called "Star Chamber"; but you always will have a spiritual tribunal of some kind, and unless it is an organized and recognized thing, with a body of law behind it, it will become a secret thing, and a very terrible thing; it will have all the worst qualities of the Inquisition without that subjection to a body of law which the Inquisition finally had. And when in modern times you fall behindhand with your political institutions, as we are doing, and try to get on with a parliamentary institution which is entirely unfitted to modern needs, you get dictatorships, as you have got in Hungary, and in Italy, and—I need not go through the whole list—as you may have at any moment almost in any country, because, as Signor Mussolini has so well said, there is a vacant throne in almost every country in Europe; and when you get your dictatorship you may take it from me that you will with the greatest certainty get a secret tribunal, dealing with sedition, with political heresy, exactly like the Inquisition.

That is all I can say to you tonight. I have not, I am aware, said the conventional thing, or said the historical thing. Well, you can read that. You will find it told very often in a very dull way. I have only spoken here because the whole value of Joan to us is how you can bring her and her circumstances into contact with our life and our circumstances. Now, the British Broadcasting Corporation is in a state of great impatience because I have already stolen nearly ten minutes. I should have taken twenty minutes; I have taken half-an-hour. Just like me, isnt it? Goodnight.

LENIN

(Extemporaneous speech for simultaneous radio broadcast and motion picture filming, delivered at Moscow, 27 July 1931. *The Left Review, December* 1934)

I myself am like Lenin. I am a revolutionist. I think I was born a revolutionist. Until the year 1917 I had never heard the name of Lenin, and most people in England, where I was then, where I come from, were in the same position. We did not learn very much of Lenin personally after that.

Other speakers have this evening told you about his studies, about his discoveries, about the original ideas that he put forward. But the curious thing is that in those countries where nothing of his personality and appearance was known, he made the same extraordinary impression, personally, that he made in Russia.

Now I cannot explain that to you; I dont know why it was. It may have been some curious magnetism. Science has not yet explained how these things occur. But it nevertheless is true, just as here in Russia. Although he was only one of a body of men, some of whom were of most extraordinary, exceptional, and outstanding intelligence and determination and political ability—men, several of whom in one point or another surpassed Lenin himself, so that he owed a great deal of his work to their co-operation—nevertheless, in that group of extraordinary, distinguished men, he stood out as a unique personality.

I cannot explain that, as I say. I can only tell you the curious thing, that just as he stood out in Russia where a great deal was known about him, he stood out in the same way in England where nothing was known about him.

But you must not think that this, the importance of Lenin, the great importance of Lenin, is a thing of the past because Lenin is dead. We have to look to the future. What significance has he for the future? Well, his significance is this. If the experiment that Lenin made, of which he was the head, which he represents to us —if that experiment in social organization fails, then civilization falls, as so many civilizations have fallen before.

We know from our recent historical researches that there have been many civilizations, that their history has been very like the history of our civilization, and that when they arrived at the point which Western capitalistic civilization has reached, there began a rapid degencracy, followed by complete collapse of the entire system and something very near to a return to savagery by the human race. Over and over again the human race has tried to get round that corner and has always failed.

Now, Lenin organized the method of getting round that corner. If his experiment is pushed through to the end, if the other countries follow his example and follow his teaching, if this great communistic experiment spreads over the whole world, we shall have a new era in history. We shall not have the old collapse and failure, the beginning again, the going through the whole miserable story to the same miserable end. We shall have an era in human history of which we can now have no conception.

And that is what Lenin means to us.

If the future is the future as Lenin foresaw it, then we may all smile and look forward to the future without fear. But if the experiment is overthrown and fails, if the world persists on its capitalistic lines, then I shall have to take a very melancholy farewell of you, my friends.

I shall bid you farewell in any case, because I have already spoken quite enough. . . .

THE ONLY HOPE OF THE WORLD

(Lecture delivered at the Independent Labour Party National Summer School, Digswell Park, 5 August 1931. *The New Leader* (London), 7 *August* 1931)

When I gave my usual undertaking to fill up one of your mornings here I did not know what I should talk about. Afterwards an opportunity arose from my visit to Russia. Now, everybody who can possibly do so should go to Russia. That does not mean that a very large proportion will be able to go, because it is not a specially cheap undertaking. But I have been preaching Socialism all my political life and here at last is a country which has established Socialism, made it the basis of its political system, definitely thrown over private property, and turned its back on Capitalism—a country which has succeeded in conducting industry successfully, and in achieving a political constitution. It is, therefore, almost a duty for people in those Capitalist countries who have been preaching Socialism in the wilderness to go over and find out exactly how the thing is being done and how it came about. It is full of surprises, and when I give you a rough and chatty description of what it is, I do so with a consciousness that, if the Soviet leaders were present here, they would regard me as one of the most monstrous paradoxes, to say nothing of liars, that ever existed.

For instance, the first thing I discovered with great gratification is that the Socialism which has established itself is Fabian

Socialism. [*Laughter.*] You see, you laugh, but I am perfectly serious. What is more, Stalin and Trotsky would laugh, because they regard a Fabian as a harmless person who is not a revolutionary. The Fabians have turned out to be perfectly right, and the system which has established itself is a Fabian system. I didnt say that to them, by the way. That was one of the things which I observed. The other thing which I did say quite freely to his [Stalin's] intense and great amusement is that it is a definitely religious system. Russia is a religious country. They could not imagine that we were serious when we said that the Third International is a Church, distinctly and unmistakably, but it is perfectly true. But I say it is Fabian Socialism, and its inspiration is a religious one all through. And here I am speaking the exact and careful truth.

There is so much to be said that I can only take odd bits and scraps to illustrate. It is amazing the rate at which things have changed. The fact that they are making a success of it is not so enormously creditable to them in comparison to us as it may seem. I dont want to grudge them credit, but you must remember that they are working under conditions which are almost ideal. They are working the machines with oil in their bearings, while we are working our machines with sand in the bearings, and the friction is enormous. That friction does not exist in Russia. Here you have private proprietors and a proletariat which lives by selling its labor. The principle of the whole thing here is that the capitalist's business is to get as much as he can out of the proletariat and to give the people as little as possible in return, and the principle of the proletariat is to get as much as possible, and to give as little as it can.

I remember going through a big electrical factory in Moscow. I was keeping my eyes open for the things I wanted to see, things they never thought of shewing me. (I may say at once that all this rubbish of people who say you will only see what they want to shew you is just rubbish.) I dont want to go to Russia to see what remains of poverty and ignorance from the Capitalist system. I can see that within twenty minutes of my own door in London. I want to see the best that can be done. While I was in this factory a young man, with an air of conscious virtue, was presented to me. He had an Order of some sort pinned to his coat, and he was the young man who had set the pace in that factory in the carrying out of the Five Year Plan. He had done more than any other, and I said to him, "Young man, if you were in England, and you set up about double the pace of your fellow workers, you would not be a popular character, you would be called a 'slogger'—at least, that was the oldfashioned word, I dont know what it may be now—and you would run the risk of a brick being dropped on your head in a dark lane. If you are going on in this way, my friend, you stay in Russia." Certainly there the young man was popular. He led for efficiency. [Shaw went on to remind his listeners that in spite of all the bad times through which we are now passing, the proprietary class at the present time in this country is getting more than it ever did.]

Taking the Five Year Plan in the lump, evidently we want a Five Year Plan here, very badly. They want a Five Year Plan very badly in America.

Why is it they cant have it? They have it quite easily in Russia. "Put your back into it," they say there. "Starve yourself a bit, dont expect any luxuries, work as hard as you can for the next five years." But put that to the workers here, say to them, "Make a splendid effort for the next five years." They would say: "Go short for five years in order that the idle and rich class may become idler and richer than ever? My job as a worker is to get as big wages as I can, but to give as little as I can for it." In Russia it is simple. They know in Russia that what comes out of the Plan they will get.

There are things which perhaps will surprise some of you in Russia. They may seem a little too Fabian for you. In Russia you pay rent for the place you live in. The Russians are not people who are strong on what you might call privacy, and if you want to understand how Russians live you must understand that. They never seem to live less than five in a room and have no particular objection to ten in a room, provided there are beds enough. This may seem a little uncomfortable to some of us. I personally cant sleep if there are other people in the room, but they cant sleep unless there are other people in the room.

I went to the Russian State Bank in Moscow. I wanted to see

the Crown jewels and I wanted to cash a letter of credit, so I first asked about the letter of credit. Oh, you neednt bother about any letters of credit, your cheque will go for any amount! Then I asked about interest. Certainly, eight per cent. So I thought I'll put all my money here, which they suggested was quite all right, but they would not allow me to take it out of the country. But still, I think that some of you may have visions of a land in which money does not produce any interest. In Russia money bears interest and the interest fluctuates, as it does in other countries.

With reference to rent, the difference here is that you pay it to the man who, for all you know, may go and blow it at Monte Carlo. But in Russia it is paid to a local Soviet and employed for public purposes, of which you get the benefit. Nevertheless, you have to pay for your accommodation.

If all the rents of London were paid to the London County Council there would be no rates, and not only would this be very pleasant but there would be a good deal to spend on amusements and amenities. But in London this is Bolshevism, Socialism, Communism, everything frightful and horrible. In other words, people in London are fools and the people of Moscow are sensible people. Which reminds me of a rather interesting point.

It is exceedingly difficult for Russians to believe that we are as stupid as we really are. A great many of the things we do seem to them to be designed. . . . But I said our people are not intelligent. That is the very first thing you have to upset. And I could see that Stalin was incredulous that people could be so foolish as not to see the points in the Communist system. You must remember this. An English statesman believes himself to be morally and intellectually superior and superior in education to the Russian statesman. He is totally deceived in this. Morally, he is really abysmally inferior. As for intellectually, what he has got at Eton and Oxford . . . well, you know the sort of stuff. In Russia they are not only in the enormously morally superior position of Communism, but they are intellectually superior. They begin by reading Marx, and the danger of that is that it produces an intellectual snobbery. When you have read Marx you know so much more that it makes you believe you know everything, and you are rather apt to despise the man you are dealing with.

I said to Litvinoff, "You remember your relations with the late Lord Curzon?" (Lord Curzon had said, "I cant deal with this person; he is a common person. I cant discuss politics with a person of this rank; you might as well expect me to discuss the Government of my country with my footman.") This social snobbery was really very disastrous for the moment. When people complain of Curzon's snobbery, the social snobbery with which he looked down on Litvinoff is as nothing compared with the intellectual snobbery with which Litvinoff regarded Curzon. They look on us as imbeciles, and we cannot realize that we are imbeciles.

Their system is fireproof—hell-fireproof. Nobody could go and see what they are doing, even hardened Conservatives, and wish that the Five Year Plan could fail. The success of the Five Year Plan is the only hope of the world. Our plan is certainly running us to the abyss, and they know it perfectly well. But others, of course, even if they appreciate that we are fools and not schemers, feel that fools can be as dangerous as schemers, and sometimes more so. They know very well that Mr Churchill threw all the British forces into the counter-revolution, and the most I could do was to tell him [Stalin] that this was done without a single vote being taken in the House of Commons. It was done with the stocks remaining from the Great War, and the moment he [Churchill] brought it to the House, he crumpled up. But the Russians know that since that time other Governments have been elected in England. For instance, the Government that was responsible for the Arcos burglary—a burglary which a lot of silly schoolboys acting as brigands would have been ashamed to do.[1] And necessarily, they say, they have to be careful, and I could not exactly tell them that they were in no danger. I could say, so far as the masses of the people are concerned, they dont want war, but they say the masses of the people dont seem able to prevent the Mr Churchills going to war whenever they like.

There are certain contrasts which strike one. In some respects

[1] On 12 May 1927, the London offices of Arcos, Ltd, the headquarters of the Soviet trading corporation, were raided by the police in the belief that evidence of subversive action and secret documents stolen from the War Office would be found there. Nothing was found, but as a result of the raid, all relations between the British and Soviet governments were severed.

the Government is ruthless, in others extraordinarily humane. I remember Lady Astor, who, by the way, is very interested in the treatment of children, and who was converted by the late Margaret McMillan, telling the Russians they didnt know anything about children. In the first place, the children we had seen were remarkably clean, and no child ought to be clean in its playtime. Of course, at mealtimes and bedtimes it is perhaps desirable that they should be cleaned up, but during their playtime no child ought to be clean. And the second thing was that the children had come in because of a shower of rain. A child ought not to know or care whether it is raining or not, and Lady Astor urged them to send some responsible woman to England to study child care under the McMillan system. And they probably will do it, because they jump at everything.

If a man has an idea they jump at it and try it for all it is worth. Everybody who has a new idea has his photograph taken and stuck up. In this country everything that possibly can be done to starve and worry an inventor is done. If he invents a new machine all the men who are working on the old method are down on him. If he invents methods of avoiding breakages all the firms who live by these breakages are down on him. In Russia this friction vanishes.

Let us take some of the more humane aspects. The relations with the police are unlike the relations here, though they are jolly enough in this country. An American I met when traveling began taking photographs in Leningrad. A policeman came up and said, "You cant do this here; I believe it is forbidden." The American said he could do what he liked. The question then arose, was the American breaking the law? An English policeman, in doubt, would have said, "You must come along to the station and there present your case to the Inspector." This policeman said, "I will go and ask at the station; you wait here." He went away and, of course, the American, being on his honor, waited. And the policeman came back and said, "That is all right."

When Lady Astor spoke to Stalin about the children, Stalin turned round with an expression extremely eloquent, and he said, "In England you beat children." And I dont think anything more clearly expresses the enormous difference between England

and Russia. In Russia it is a crime to beat children. And children actually summon their parents in the police court for doing it.

Of course there is no capital punishment. Capital punishment is absolutely abolished, and you can do a murder on very reasonable terms; four years, for instance, is about what they give a murderer. Possibly for a very bad one indeed it might be five. But although there is no capital punishment, there is shooting for political offences. If a man begins to sabotage, if he begins speculating, if he tries to take advantage of the system in any way to enrich himself, then that man disappears. After a few days his relatives are told he might like them to send him some food, and after a few more days he either comes back, or his relatives are informed that he does not require any more food, and a few days more they are definitely informed that he has been shot. On all these points they are entirely ruthless.

The speculator here is the man you admire. You send him to represent you in Parliament, you send him to the House of Peers. Some years ago speculation began, and just as after the war certain misguided people here began to hoard German notes, so they began to hoard currency in Russia, and commerce was almost paralyzed by the fact that money disappeared. It was dealt with very simply. They searched about a thousand people whom they had reason to suspect, and then they shot two of them in every one of the principal centres of population, and almost the next day money flowed back.

Recalling the reports one has seen that the intelligentsia were less well looked after than the proletariat, that their needs were only provided after those of the proletariat, I was interested to meet authors who looked more prosperous than many I have seen here, authors who never even attempted to borrow money from me. And I said to them, "But you are the intelligentsia." They replied, "We are not the intelligentsia, we are the intellectual proletariat."

And the reason why we cant do anything in this country for the public is that we have a parliamentary system which is the pride and wonder of the capitalist world, and which has reached such a pitch of tremendous efficiency that it takes thirty years to do half-an-hour's work, no matter how urgently necessary. In

Russia half-an-hour's work has to be done in half-an-hour, and no mistake about it. There is no Parliament and no nonsense of that sort. There are bodies which do discuss policy, but when a job has to be done it is always by a dictator. That is, someone is made to do it on his own responsibility. If he goes wrong, he crashes. He knows while he is there he must deliver the goods, and if he doesnt, he must make way for somebody who can. No man can turn round, having made a mess of a job, and say, "I am democratically elected and there is nothing to be done about it." There is no danger of Stalin choosing a man who is the eldest son of a duke, or because he met him at dinner last week.

That motive has gone. You cant discover any other motive. They cannot enrich themselves, they cannot keep themselves in their position except by delivering the goods. And, as a result, there is no fear of class selection as we have it here. And that, of course, is a complete reversal of our system. What we call democracy, instead of creating responsibility, absolutely destroys it, and the only people who do anything are those who have the corrupt motive of making themselves rich. And when we get Socialism here, we shall have to introduce that system from beginning to end.

I want to say one word about Lady Astor. She said they could not do without God, and they must come back to religion. There is no need for them to come back to it. They are full of it. The Greek Church and the Russian Church were hopeless Churches. People here are horrified when they hear that one of the great cathedrals has been turned into an anti-theological museum, but I assure you I went through that museum, and I wished I could get Martin Luther back from the dead. Or a group of Christians from Belfast. The whole thing is an attack on priestcraft. The priests took and took, and the people got nothing out of it.

But the point is that the whole institution is necessarily religious. It is not saying to the people, "You will have enough to eat and a shorter working day," but the people who are managing it are filled with a purely spiritual impulse. An ir-religious man is a man looking after himself, looking after his own stomach, seeing that he has a pleasant house to live in, a man who does not feel that his fate is bound up in the fate of the community around him. A man who is religious is a man who is bored with himself and wants to make the world better, who is looking forward to a future better than the past, [who is] working for something greater and larger than himself. That is the essence of religion, to be working for things outside yourself, and it is not sacrifice. You are living far more abundantly because of it.

As for the Third International, I suggested that there must be a final conflict between Church and State in which the State had to get the upper hand, and I suggested that the Third International might yet come into serious conflict with the Soviet system. And I think I noticed an expression on the faces of the people I was speaking to which suggested that a little of that kind of thing was beginning to occur already, that there might come a certain condition in which the Soviet State might become the supreme thing and the Third International have to take second place.

LOOK, YOU BOOB!
A LITTLE TALK ON AMERICA

(Shortwave broadcast to the United States from London, 11 October 1931. An expurgated text was published in Hearst's *New York American*, 12 *October* 1931. The full text, reproduced below, was published as a pamphlet by the Friends of the Soviet Union, London, 15 *December* 1931)

Hello, America! Hello, all my friends in America! Hello, all you dear old boobs who have been telling one another for a month past that I have gone dotty about Russia! Well, if the latest news from your side is true, you can hardly be saying that now. Russia has the laugh on us. She has us fooled, beaten, shamed, shewn up, outpointed, and all but knocked out. We have lectured her from the heights of our moral superiority, and now we are calling on the mountains to hide our blushes in her presence. We have rebuked her ungodliness, and now the sun shines on Russia as on a country with which God is well pleased, whilst His wrath is heavy on us and we dont know where to turn for comfort or approval. We have prided ourselves on our mastery in big business and on its solid foundations in a knowledge of human nature; and now we are bankrupt: your President [Herbert Hoover], who became famous by feeding the starving millions of war-devastated Europe, cannot feed his own people in time of peace; the despairing cries of our financiers here have resounded throughout the world and created a run on the Bank of England and broken it; our budget shews a deficit of 850 million dollars: yours shews a deficit of 4500 millions; our business men cannot find employment for three millions of our workers and yours have had to turn twice as many into the streets; our statesmen on both sides can do nothing but break the heads of starving men or buy them off with doles and appeals to charity; our agriculture is ruined and our industries collapsing under the weight of their own productiveness because we have not found out how to distribute our wealth as well as to produce it. And in the face of all this business incompetence, political helplessness, and financial insolvency, Russia flaunts her budget surplus of 750 millions, her people employed to the last man and woman, her scientific agriculture doubling and trebling her harvests, her roaring and multiplying factories, her efficient rulers, her atmosphere of such hope and security for the poorest as has never before been seen in a civilized country on earth.

Naturally, the contempt of the Russians for us is enormous. "You fools," they are saying to us, "why can you not do as we are doing? You cannot employ nor feed your people: well, send them to us, and if they are worth their salt we will employ and feed them. You cannot even protect your citizens against common theft and murder, or keep your armed gangsters and racketeers from flourishing their pistols in your streets at noonday: well, send them to us and you will have no more trouble with them: people who will not make good as citizens in Russia do not trouble anyone long." And what can we say in reply but "Who would have thought it?" Pretty feeble that, eh? Too true to be pleasant, isnt it?

Well, let me give you a word or two of consolation. After all, some of the most wonderful things the Russians are doing were suggested fifty years ago by Americans, many of whom have been sent to jail for their pains. I am not an American, but I am the next worst thing—an Irishman. When I was a young man I was got hold of by an American named Henry George, who opened my eyes so surprisingly that I felt I must follow up his notions. So I tried a German Jew named Karl Marx, who opened my eyes still wider, leaving it quite plain to me that our capitalist system, though we could foozle along with it for a time at the cost of frightful unhappiness and degrading poverty for nine-tenths of the population, was bound to end in the bankruptcy of civilization. Fourteen years later a Russian named Ulyanov, better known to you as Lenin, followed my example and read Marx.

In 1914 our Imperialists involved us in a war. You tried to keep out of that war, but you were forced in. Thanks to you, that war, instead of doing what the Imperialists meant it to do, abolished three empires, changed Europe from a royal continent to a republican one, and transformed the only European power that was bigger than the United States into a federation of Communist republics. That was not quite what you expected, was it? Your boys were not sent to the slaughter cheering for Karl Marx and echoing his slogan, "Proletarians of all lands, unite." However, that is what happened. This wonderful new power in the world, the Union of Soviet Socialist Republics, or, for short, the U.S.S.R., is what you got for your Liberty Loan and the blood of your young men. It was not what you intended to get, but it seems that it was what God intended you to get. Anyhow, you got it, and now you must make the best of it. I know it is hard, because you and poor old England are in the bankruptcy court, where France has already had to compound with her creditors for ten cents in the dollar, whilst the U.S.S.R., your baby, is soaring on the upgrade. That looks a little, doesnt it, as if the Russians were managing their affairs better than we?

However, you do not bear all the responsibility for establishing Communism in Russia. You share it with me—*me*, now speaking to you, Bernard Shaw. In 1914, as some of you may remember, I declared that if the soldiers on both sides had any commonsense they would come home and attend to their business instead of senselessly slaughtering oneanother because their officers ordered them to.[1] Some of you were very angry with me for taking a

[1] *Common Sense about the War*, supplement to *The New Statesman*, IV (14 November 1914); reprinted in *What I Really Wrote about the War* (London, 1930).

commonsense view of war, which is an affair of glory and patriotism and has nothing to do with commonsense. Well, the British soldiers had no commonsense and went on slaughtering. The French soldiers had no commonsense and kept blazing away. The German and Austrian soldiers were just as foolish. The Italian soldiers joined up, and presently the American soldiers rushed in and were the silliest of the lot.

But in 1917 an astonishing thing happened. The Russian soldiers took my advice. They said, "We have had enough of this," and came straight home. They formed bodies of workmen and soldiers called Soviets; and they raised the cry of "All power to the Soviets." The government of the Tsar, which was as rotten as it was abominably tyrannical, collapsed like a house of cards; but the Soviets could do nothing without leaders and a plan of social reconstruction. That was the opportunity for Lenin and his friends, who had followed my example and educated themselves politically by reading Marx. They had the courage to jump at it. They took command of the Soviets, and established the Union of Soviet Socialist Republics exactly as Washington and Jefferson and Hamilton and Franklin and Tom Paine had established the United States of America 141 years before. If you have any doubt about the similarity of the two cases let me suggest an amusing Sunday game: one of your Sunday papers might hunt up the material for it. Make a collection of the articles in the royalist newspapers and political pamphlets, American as well as British, issued during the last quarter of the eighteenth century. Strike out the dates, the name of the country, and the names of its leaders. The game is for your friends to fill up the blanks. What country is this, you will ask, which has broken every social bond and given itself over to anarchy and infamy at the bidding of a gang of atheists, drunkards, libertines, thieves, and assassins? Your friends will guess wrong. When the right answer is America they will guess Russia. When the right name is Washington they will cry Trotsky. They will declare that the puzzles are too easy to be worth solving: that Jefferson is Lenin, that Franklin is Litvinoff, that Paine is Lunacharski, that Hamilton is Stalin. When you tell them the truth they will probably never speak to you again, but you will have given them

229

a valuable moral lesson, which ought to be the object of all Sunday games.

Today there is a statue of Washington in London; and tomorrow there will no doubt be a statue of Lenin in New York, with the inscription, "Blessed are ye when men shall revile you and say all manner of evil against you." By the way, you might finish the game by looking at the newspaper you yourself are in the habit of reading; and if, as is possible, you find that it is pumping into your household day by day the same scurrilous venom that your grandfather used to have to swallow about the founders of the United States of America, you might write to the editor to hint that you would prefer something a little more up-to-date, and that if he cannot give you some reasonably believable and cleanmouthed news about the most interesting political experiment in the world, you will have to take in a saner paper, or, if you cannot find one, to read the Bible instead.

And now perhaps you would like to know what was my reaction to Russia when I visited it. Americans always want to know my reaction to the latest thing in scareheads. Well, my first impression was that Russia is full of Americans. My second was that every intelligent Russian has been in America and didnt like it because he had no freedom there. This was only an illusion produced by the fact that all the Russians who thought they could speak English really spoke American. But the same can be said of all European countries now. To get to and from Russia I traveled through France, Belgium, Germany, and Poland. In each of these countries I was received with some sort of official welcome. But in every case the official or deputation advancing to receive me was shoved aside by an enthusiastic American, beaming with hospitality, and shouting genially, "Mr Shaw: welcome to France (or Poland or Russia or Germany, as the case might be): I am an American." That is what makes you so popular all over the world: you make yourself at home everywhere; and you always have the first word. It is such a pleasant surprise for me when I think I am giving my hand coldly and formally to a native king, or a president, or a secretary of state, or an archbishop, or a chairman of the local Academy of Literature, to find that I am being embraced by one of dear old Uncle

Jonathan's nephews, who has been only two hours longer in the country than myself. Mind, I am not complaining; I like it. But I dont think the kings and presidents and secretaries and chairmen do; so I just thought I'd mention it. You dont mind, do you?

And now let me give you a few traveling tips in case you should join the American rush to visit Russia and see for yourself whether it is all real. If you are a skilled workman, especially in machine industry, and are of suitable age and good character (they are very particular about character in Russia) you will not have much difficulty: they will be only too glad to have you; proletarians of all lands are welcome if they can pull their weight in the Russian boat. Even if you cannot work, and are only a useless lady or gentleman with lots of money, they will graciously allow you to spend as much of it as you like in Russia, and will make you quite comfortable. Only if you are stingy, and spend less than ten roubles a day, they will make you pay the difference before you leave; so there is no use trying to save on that minimum. They will not treat you with the smallest deference, for these Russians do not stand in awe even of an American lady. In fact, I must break it to you that their feeling towards you will be a mixture of pity for you as a refugee from the horrors of American Capitalism, with a colossal intellectual contempt for your political imbecility in not having established Communism in your own unhappy country. But they will be quite friendly and helpful, just as they would be to a lost and starving monkey; and if you are nice to them they will take you to their bosoms and tell you the stories of their lives on the smallest provocation. They are so free from all your worries and anxieties about your affairs and your children and your rents and rates and taxes that they can afford to be kind to you; and they are so proud of their Communistic institutions that they are only too anxious to shew them to you.

But you must be careful. You must not count on human nature being the same in Russia as in America. My friend General [Charles Gates] Dawes, your ambassador here, was talking to me the other day about human nature: how you cant change it no matter how you change your institutions. Now, before you go to Russia you had better study human nature scientifically. The easiest way to do that is to send to the nearest glazier's for a piece of putty. Putty is exactly like human nature. You cannot change it, no matter what you do. You cannot eat it, nor grow apples in it, nor mend clothes with it. But you can twist it and pat it and model it into any shape you like; and when you have shaped it, it will set so hard that you would suppose that it could never take any other shape on earth. Now, the Russian putty is just like the American putty, except perhaps that the American putty is softer in the head and sets harder. Well, the Soviet Government has shaped the Russian putty very carefully into a shape different from the American, and it has set hard and produced quite a different sort of animal. The noses are much the same, and the chins and ears and eyes not so very different, but the inside doesnt work in the American way. In particular, the conscience is startlingly different, so that the achievements which are an American's pride and glory seem to the Russian to be infamous crimes.

For instance, the first thing that would occur to a real hundred per cent. American in Russia is that with its huge natural wealth it must be a splendid country to make money in. Even without touching the natural resources a good deal might be made by speculating in the difference between the value of the half-dollar rouble in Moscow and the six-cent rouble in Berlin. Wages are low and profits high; so why let all the profit be wasted on the Government when a capable man can organize business for himself, and put the profit in his own pocket? What is the use of wasting good money on the public? As a deceased American financier once said at a public inquiry, "Damn the public!" Men make money by looking after themselves, not by looking after the public.

If you take that line in Russia you will soon get rich. But when this fact comes under the notice of the income tax authorities, they will ask the Gay Pay Oo, the celebrated secret police which acts as an Inquisition, to inquire into your methods. An agent will tap you on the shoulder and conduct you to the offices of that famous force. There you will be invited to explain your commercial proceedings and your views on life in general. You will be allowed to vindicate your American business principles and your belief in individualism and self-help to the full hundred per cent. You will not be reproached, nor bullied, nor argued with, nor inconvenienced in any way. All that will happen to you is that when you have made yourself quite clear, you will suddenly find yourself in the next world, if there be a next world. If not, you will simply have ceased to exist, and your relatives will be politely informed that they need have no anxiety about you, as you are not coming home any more.

Now, do not for a moment think that this is a punishment, or that it has anything to do with the criminal law. All it means is that the Russian putty has been shaped to believe that idiots are better dead. Idiot, as you know, is a Greek word which means a person who can see no farther than himself. Your views will satisfy the Russians that you are an idiot, and in mercy to yourself and society they will just liquidate you, as they call it, without causing you a moment's unpleasantness.

In this they are merely carrying out a proposal made by me many years ago. I urged that every person who owes his life to civilized society, and who has enjoyed since his childhood all its very costly protections and advantages, should appear at reasonable intervals before a properly qualified jury to justify his existence, which should be summarily and painlessly terminated if he fails to justify it, and is either a positive nuisance or more trouble than he is worth. Nothing less will make people really responsible citizens, and a great part of the secret of the success of Russian Communism is that every Russian knows that unless he makes his life a paying proposition for his countrymen he will probably lose it.

I am proud to have been the first to advocate this most necessary reform. A well-kept garden must be weeded. So you must be careful.

To console you, let me assure you that if you lose your temper in Russia you need not fear the sort of savagery with which we treat our criminals. If you happen to kill somebody in an honest and natural way you will not be hanged nor roasted in the electric chair, for capital punishment is abolished in Russia. You will probably get off with four or five years of quite mild restraint. They are very lenient to their criminals.

All this will perhaps feel a little strange at first, but once you get the idea of Communism you will understand the Soviet point of view, and find yourself wondering how it would work in Chicago or Pittsburgh or Detroit. It grows on you amazingly after a day or two.

However, you must not expect a paradise. Russia is too big a place for any government to get rid, in fourteen years, of the frightful mass of poverty, ignorance, and dirt left by the Tsardom. Russia is eight million square miles big, which is more than four millions bigger than the United States. The population is nearly 160 millions, seventeen millions more than you have. I am afraid there is still a good deal of the poverty, ignorance, and dirt we know so well at home. But there is hope everywhere in Russia because these evils are retreating there before the spread of Communism as steadily as they are advancing upon us before the last desperate struggle of our bankrupt Capitalism to stave off its inevitable doom by reducing wages, multiplying tariffs, and rallying all the latent savagery and greed in the world to its support in predatory warfare masquerading as patriotism.

But you will not go to Russia to smell out the evils you can see without leaving your own doorstep. Some of you will go because in the great financial storm that has burst on us your own ship is sinking, and the Russian ship is the only big one that is not rolling heavily and tapping out S.O.S. on its wireless. But most of you will go, I hope, with stout hearts, knowing that what is the matter with us is not natural poverty, but sheer stupid mismanagement and lazy abandonment of public interests to private selfishness and vulgar ambition. You will have heard that the Russians have put a stop to this, and you will want to see how they have done it. For what the Russians can do, you can do. You may think you cant, but you can. At present you are like an old prisoner in the Bastille, sawing the bars of his little window with a watchspring so intently that he does not notice that the door has long been wide open.

Perhaps you will all go on sawing in America until you are dead, but I expect your sons will be wiser than you, and will not let themselves be outrun in the great race of civilization by any Russian that ever set foot to the ground.

And so goodbye until next time, and good luck to you!

IN PRAISE OF GUY FAWKES

(One in a course of lectures, under the auspices of the Fabian
Society, delivered in the Kingsway Hall, 25 November
1932. *The New Clarion*, 3 and 10 *December* 1932; reprinted
in *Where Stands Socialism Today*, London, 1933)

I rise to address you with a reluctance which has been growing
on me for a long time past. For fortyeight years I have been
addressing speeches to the Fabian Society and to other assemblies
in this country. So far as I can make out, those speeches have not
produced any effect whatever. In the course of them I have solved
practically all the pressing questions of our time; but as they go
on being propounded as insoluble just as if I had never existed,
I have come to see at last that one of the most important things
to be done in this country is to make public speaking a criminal
offence.

I do not know why it is that you are assembled here tonight.
I suspect that a great many of you are what I call public-speaking
addicts. Public speaking is a sort of drug which you take to make
you feel that when you have heard somebody talking about an
important subject you have done your duty and disposed of that
subject. I am inclined to think that a still greater proportion of
my audience has not come to hear me at all. I wonder how many
of you believe me to be the Reverend Ira D. Goldhawk, the
worthy pastor of Kingsway Hall. I should not be at all surprised
if quite a large number of you did.

Now, what is Parliament in this country? It is the central
engine of public speaking from which the tradition of public
speaking spreads through the community. I do not know whether
you ever heard anybody ask a question as to the qualifications of
a parliamentary candidate for the work of legislation and governing the country. I never did. But there is one question which you
may sometimes hear asked. Is he a speaker? Is he a good speaker?
If it turns out that he is a good speaker, or is believed by a certain
number of people to be a good speaker, then that is considered
a sufficient qualification. And I think it is. I think that the real
function of Parliament in this country is to prevent anything

being done by endlessly talking about it. Parliament reminds me of a locomotive engine, but a locomotive engine made in a peculiar way. You know a modern locomotive is attached to seventyfive trucks with ten tons of coal in each, and it has to move the lot. In order to do that, there must be an enormous pressure of steam in the cylinders to make the wheels go round with all that weight against them. To prevent that pressure from blowing the boiler to bits there is a hole in the boiler which is closed with a spring strong enough to resist the pressure needed to move the train; but if the pressure goes beyond that the spring lifts and the steam evaporates. This contrivance is called a safety-valve. Now, the only difference between the parliamentary loco-motive and the engineers' locomotive is that the safety valve in the parliamentary locomotive is made so extremely weak that it blows off in hot air before there is the slightest possibility of the train moving at all.

It is interesting to notice the effect of public speaking on audiences. I have been watching audiences now for fifty years, including this Fabian audience, which is believed, for some reason which I have never been able to ascertain, to be a specially intelligent audience. Perhaps it is. But I, having seen it come to this hall year after year, listening to the same sort of thing with-out anything happening, regard the presence of any person in this hall as being a sign of a weak intellect. For instance, take my friend Mr [A. L.] Rowse, who delivered an admirable lecture here a fortnight ago. He interested me specially because it became plain shortly after he began that he is actually a Socialist, and is actually in earnest about it, which is not invariably the case even when the person on the platform is nominally a Socialist—you cannot depend upon anything of the kind nowadays. But Mr Rowse, among other quaint things, is a member of All Souls College, Oxford, which is such an entirely unreasonable and amazing academic institution that when it is described to foreigners they fall down speechless and never smile again. It is not possible for Mr Rowse, sound Socialist as he is, to go and dine at that extra-ordinary place without picking up a few of its habits of speech. Consequently, when we were all following his lecture with the greatest attention, he suddenly, by reflex action, said that the

English workman was the best workman in the world. Immediately there was the beginning of an enthusiastic response to him. He crushed it and went on. But as I sat there, there came into my head suddenly those lines written by the poet Keats in which he condenses the whole of the first chapter of Marx's Das Kapital into a single stanza. You may perhaps remember his poem of Isabella, in which he describes how the workers of the world enriched Isabella's commercial brothers:

> For them the Ceylon diver held his breath,
> And went all naked to the hungry shark

in search of pearls. Simultaneously with that vision there came into my head another of a London policeman plunging in full uniform to the hungry shark and bringing up in his helmet twelve outsize pearls to show the barbarous Cingalese how very much better an Englishman could do their work if he set his mind to it. I do not think Mr Rowse meant exactly that; and yet, upon my honor, if he did not mean it, I do not quite know what he did mean. The next time he dines at All Souls, he might put the point to the Fellows, and see what they can make of it.

Now, suppose Mr Rowse had not been Mr Rowse, but a popular parliamentary orator—say Mr Lloyd George or the Prime Minister [J. Ramsay MacDonald]—what would he have done? He would immediately have made a note in his mind, "That's got em"; and then he would have proceeded to get you. He would have said passionately, "Can you shew me in the world the equal of the English plumber?" He would then have gone on through the whole range of industries, more and more vehemently asserting the superiority of the Englishman in every one of them. With each succeeding challenge the enthusiasm of the audience would have risen to its culmination in thunders of triumphant applause; and everybody would have declared the meeting the most successful the Fabian Society had ever held. That is how the world is ungoverned at present. That is the way to prevent its being governed.

No meaning is attached to these speeches which are received with so much enthusiasm. They are forgotten in five hours, and often contradicted flatly, either by events or by the speaker himself, within five days. And nobody notices the discrepancy. Looking back on my now rather too long career, I can remember instance after instance of the most sensational kind. I can remember the assurances given us in Parliament before the war by the Prime Minister [Herbert Asquith] and the Foreign Secretary [Sir Edward Grey], that we were entirely wrong in suspecting that there was any treaty between France, Russia, England, and Belgium with regard to a contemplated war on Germany. After that, when it turned out that, though there was no formal treaty, not only was there a war with Germany in contemplation, but that our share in it had been carefully arranged by the Liberal Imperialists in the Cabinet, for many years beforehand, nobody seemed conscious of having been humbugged. On the contrary, the tendency to speak of the Liberal Imperialists as typical straightforward English gentlemen, entirely incapable of making a statement that was not strictly true, increased notably as our militant patriotism kindled.

Early in the war we were all registered. I still have my ticket, with its number. The people were numbered like the people in the Bible. There was some uneasy suspicion that this must be a preliminary to Conscription. Accordingly, the Prime Minister hastened to make a speech, in which he assured the nation that not the slightest idea of such a violation of British liberty had ever entered into the minds of the Government, the registration being a mere question of rationing. I forget the exact number of days—I think it was inside a week—which elapsed between that statement and the announcement of Conscription. But nobody noticed any sort of discrepancy between the speech and the announcement. Quite recently Mr Ramsay MacDonald, once our colleague, now the Leader of the Opposition to us, defended the Gold Standard with an eloquence which so touched our hearts that we wiped out the Labor party at his command and gave him such a majority as Gladstone never dreamed of. He told you that as long as you stuck to the Gold Standard, the trade of England was safe, and her position in the world impregnable. The next thing that happened was that the Bank of England broke—at least that is what they would have called it if it had been I who suddenly announced to my creditors that I was only going to pay them 13s. 6d. in the £. But the papers said that all the Bank of England had done was to come off the Gold Standard; and Mr MacDonald, who had just been hailed as the man who, in a dreadful crisis, saved the nation by keeping it on the Gold Standard, was now hailed as the man who saved the nation by knocking it off the Gold Standard. Unbounded prosperity was promised as a result of that. It has not come yet, but Mr MacDonald is as popular as ever.

I have gone all through this rigmarole about public speaking because I want to impress on you the fact that nothing is going to be done as long as you are all satisfied with hearing public men talk about it. This continual talk, talk, talk in Parliament that never comes to anything has provoked reactions in other countries which have made public speaking there a capital crime, and we are within sight of the same reaction here. The art of fooling the public has been cultivated to such perfection that an election nowadays is not an election at all, but a stampede. The stampede of the Zinovieff letter[1] has been improved upon by the stampede of the Gold Standard. Both were eclipsed the other day by the really magnificent stampede of the presidential election in America. Never was such a thing seen on the face of the earth. You saw in the papers the white map and the black map, and how the white suddenly became black. The whole of America was swept in one headlong rush to substitute Mr Roosevelt for Mr Hoover. The substitution will not make the slightest difference to any American. What the people of America thought they were voting for I do not know, but I suppose they were tired of Hoover and thought they would try Roosevelt; and when they are tired of Roosevelt they will try somebody else. On each occasion they will have a vague idea that something is going to happen in consequence; but nothing will happen in consequence except, of course, a noisy escape of hot air through the platform safety valve.

[1] A forgery, published in 1924 in several English newspapers, which purported to be a secret letter written by Grigori Zinovieff, then head of the Russian Comintern, containing instructions for a Communist uprising in England. It proved effective in bringing about, in British elections that year, the defeat of Ramsay MacDonald and the Labour party, and resulted in a strain in British-Russian relations.

All this guff and bugaboo, all this deception, all this stampeding, all this perpetual talk, talk, talk, with the central talk machine blowing off noisily and wasting the national steam, is supposed to be Democracy. What is the effect of it? It keeps Congress and the State Legislatures in countenance in America. It keeps copies of them in countenance in Europe. In this country it keeps Parliament in countenance.

What is the historical function of Parliament in this country? It is to prevent the Government from governing. It has never had any other purpose. If you study the constitutional history of this country, you will see that Parliament has grown up out of the old struggle against tyranny. The Englishman, being a born Anarchist, always calls government tyranny. The result of that generally is that the Government does become a tyranny, because its subjects cannot interfere intelligently with it: they can only riot and get their heads broken. Parliament was not in the first place an English institution: it was introduced into this country by a Frenchman named Simon de Montfort, whose father was concerned with the Parliament of Toulouse in France. Its object was to resist and disable the King: its use—the only use it has ever had—was to ventilate grievances, to give the people it represented an opportunity of complaining of how they were being made uncomfortable. But it never forgot its object of delaying, defeating, and if possible destroying whatever power happened to be governing the country at the time, whether it was the King, the Church, the Barons, or the Cromwellian Majors-General. Bit by bit it broke the feudal Monarchy; it broke the Church; and finally it even broke the country gentlemen. Then, having broken everything that could govern the country, it left us at the mercy of our private commercial capitalists and landowners. Since then we have been governed from outside Parliament, first by our own employers, and of late by the financiers of all nations and races.

Of all madnesses which afflict this country politically, I should think the worst is to expect that this instrument called Parliament, made and developed for the express purpose of checkmating government, and of unrivaled efficiency for that purpose, can possibly be an instrument of Socialism or Fascism, of any modern system which requires a continuous positive governmental activity. Such a government must keep its hand not merely on law and order in the Police sense, but on industry, on foreign trade, on the accumulation and investment of capital, on education, on public health, on religion, on all our most vital interests. And the hand must be a controling and swiftly-acting hand, not a checking, delaying, thwarting, defeating hand, always negative and inhibitive, but a positive and powerful organ of national welfare.

Now you will see why [in the title of this lecture] I simply mentioned Guy Fawkes. Guy Fawkes wanted the Government to do something, and saw that the first thing to enable the Government to do anything was to blow up Parliament. I think it is very much to be regretted on the whole that he failed, because, ever since he failed, the whole history of Parliament has been a triumphant vindication of his grasp of the situation. It has been a continual demonstration that you not only defeat government by entrusting it to Parliament, but in a far more complete way you defeat Democracy; for you cannot defeat government altogether, because, as some degree of it is absolutely necessary to the life of the country, a certain minimum of it must by mere force of circumstances force itself on the country, whether Parliament likes it or not. But as to Democracy, Parliament can defeat that every time and describe the process as carrying out the will of the people.

Now, how are we to get out of this mess? Not only we who are Socialists, but everybody who really has any sort of grasp of what is happening at the present time, and what is inevitably going to happen pretty soon, whether we are Socialists or Conservatives, Fascists or Communists, realizes that the Government of the future has to be a powerful, active, and positive Government. Therefore they all have a common interest in getting rid of Parliament, and they will finally get rid of Parliament because they have a life-or-death pressure of necessity behind them.

When they get rid of Parliament, what are you likely to get in its place? Let us start with the democratic foundation of the new positive Government; because such a Government, if it is to take root, must have some touch with the people. It must have continual opportunities of learning the effect of its measures on the common citizen. A real Government is a sort of national shoemaker. It has to make the political shoe in which the nation is to walk; and it is very necessary that it should have the means of knowing where the shoe pinches; because if it makes the shoe in the air, on theoretical principles, without knowing the actual effect on the bunions and corns of the population, it may end by producing a misfit which, even if it can be forced on for a moment, will be violently kicked off. The more you develop your Government in the direction of Socialism, Fascism, or whatever you like to call your positive State, the more necessary it will be for the Government to keep touch with the people. In the experiments which have been made in Italy with its new Corporate State and in Russia with its new Communist State we see, to begin with, the people electing representatives. Now, there are certain conditions which must attend the election of representatives if the representatives are to be really representative. In the first place, the candidate must be known to the electors. That is obviously the first requisite. He must also belong to the same class as the electors. And he must have no interest in being elected except the satisfaction of his own taste and faculty for doing public work. He must, of course, be paid for his work like other people, but beyond this his work must be its own reward.

As you know, that mysterious force in Nature that we call Providence produces a certain percentage of persons born with a taste for public work, just as it produces a percentage of poets and composers of music. Call such persons, for want of a better term, Fabians. The born Fabian is a person who, instead of going to the pictures, or playing golf, or doing all the usual things that non-Fabians do in their spare hours, attends meetings and reads Karl Marx, or Bernard Shaw, or Sir Oswald Mosley— a very interesting man to read just now: one of the few people, who is writing and thinking about real things, and not about figments and phrases. You will hear something more of Sir Oswald Mosley before you are through with him. I know you dislike him, because he looks like a man who has some physical courage and is going to do something; and that is a terrible thing. You instinctively hate him, because you do not know where he will land you; and he evidently means to uproot some of you. Instead of talking round and round political subjects and obscuring them with bunk verbiage without ever touching them, and without understanding them, all the time assuming states of things which ceased to exist from twenty to six hundred and fifty years ago, he keeps hard down on the actual facts of the situation. When you pose him with the American question, "What's the Big Idea?" he replies at once, "Fascism"; for he sees that Fascism is a Big Idea, and that it is the only visible practical alternative to Communism—if it really is an alternative and not a halfway house.[1] The moment things begin seriously to break up and something has to be done, quite a number of men like Mosley will come to the front who are at present ridiculed as Impossibles. Let me remind you that Mussolini began as a man with about twentyfive votes. It did not take him very many years to become the Dictator of Italy. I do not say that Sir Oswald Mosley is going to become the Dictator of this country, though more improbable things have happened: for instance, Mr Ramsay MacDonald became Prime Minister, which was very much more improbable when Ramsay was Sir Oswald's present age.

However, I must return to my theme. You will see that the conditions I have laid down for securing really representative representatives are all violated by our present system of election. What happens is that somebody sets up in my district as a candidate to represent me in Parliament. I do not know him. None of my neighbors know him. We have never seen him. We can only judge of his personal appearance by an election address photograph which is thirty years old. We read the address, which he probably has not written, his election agent having compiled it from the current political phrases of the day, which do not mean anything. He evidently has plenty of money, which means that he is either a used-up tradesman in retirement or a parasitic landowner. He is socially ambitious: otherwise why should he want to get into the House of Commons? In short, he is either worn-out and untrained or hostile to my interests. Yet my only choice

[1] For evidence, however, that Shaw essentially was not sympathetic to the political views and activities of Mosley, see Bernard Shaw, "I am not a Fascist, but . . .," *Sunday Referee*, London, 21 July 1935, and Richard Nickson, "GBS: Mosleyite?" *The Shavian*, London, September 1960.

is between him and some other person equally ineligible. Also, in the case of the great majority of us, he does not belong to our class. If his son proposed to marry our daughter, he would cut him off with a shilling.

What you need to represent you is somebody whom you know and whose interests and class are the same as yours. If you want to know, for instance, why Mosley—if I may mention him again—declares for an occupational franchise, and why in Russia the franchise is practically occupational, it is because only in that way can you get groups of electors who actually know the candidates. If the candidate is a person of shifty character, somebody in his trade is sure to get up and say: "Look here: where is the five shillings you borrowed from me a fortnight ago?" "Why did you take my wife off to Brighton from Friday to Tuesday without saying anything to me about it?" "Have you ever gone to bed sober since you were sixteen?" "Can you tell me offhand the infant death-rate in my street and what are you going to do about it?" His fellow tradesmen would not only know all these things, but they would have a sort of guarantee, in the fact that the candidate was not going to get anything out of his election but a lot of hard public work of a kind which most people, unless they are naturally specialized for it, would hate, that he is one of those queer Fabian sort of people with a genuine natural turn for public affairs.

In that way you can conceive the new State getting a basic representative democratic Congress to keep it in touch with its subjects. This Congress would have sufficient local knowledge to elect the local chiefs of industry throughout the country. These local chiefs can elect provincial chiefs who can elect national chiefs. These national chiefs—you may call them if you like a Cabinet—in their turn have to elect the national thinkers; for a nation needs two Cabinets: an administrative Cabinet and a thinking Cabinet. Of course, this would be an unheard-of idea in the British Empire. The notion that anybody connected with politics need ever have time to think, or capacity to think if he had the time, or any intention of thinking or sense of its necessity, is something so staggering that I really feel that most of you are shaking your heads and saying: "Look here, Shaw: you are going too far this time. This is beyond anything. The country will never stand this." Nevertheless, a thinking Cabinet is one of the political organs that has to be evolved if we are going to get out of our present mess.

So, you see, it is possible to have a Government which is in touch with the common people and must satisfy them—that is, a Democratic State—without the mock-democratic folly of pretending that the intellectual and technical work of Government can be dictated, or its ministers directly chosen, by mobs of voters. The State will be a hierarchy, like the Corporate State of Italy and the Communist State of Russia; but Heaven knows what we shall call the new State here, when we build it up. Probably we will call it the Conservative State, or the Nationalist State, or the British Imperial State, or perhaps the King Georgian State: why not? it would not commit you to anything. It can claim to be a democratic system because it is a voting system, with votes for everybody—that is, for the mass of nobodies—at the base, and votes for somebody all the way up. But the voters will not enjoy their present unlimited opportunities of making fools of themselves by electing sentimentally popular generals, actors, and orators to do work for which they are unfitted.

The basic Congress will consist of representatives with some turn for politics and taste for history, some public spirit and some relevant knowledge, simply because the work will not attract any other sort of candidate. They will be to that extent self-elected; and self-election, provided you eliminate all corrupt inducements, is the best sort of election, for the willing worker is the best worker. For the higher grades the most efficient persons will come to the top by sheer gravitation: the command will force itself on them even if they are platonically reluctant to assume it. They will be the only ones able to deliver the goods. There will be, of course, a sifting out, as even the most capable people may break down. Also you must bear in mind that you never quite know what a man is until you have given him power. Revolutionists always seem to have noble characters because they never have power, but when the Revolution becomes the Government a wholesale removal of its heroes may be the first step towards stable conditions.

And there is another thing that you must remember. When a man gets absolute power, he goes more or less mad. Sometimes, like Nero or Paul the First of Russia, he becomes a horrible homicidal maniac, and has to be slaughtered by his courtiers. A Washington or a Lenin will come through with credit. An Elizabeth or a Catherine will keep her wits about her to the end. The two Napoleons could not keep their crowns, but they died fairly sane. The capacity for leadership carries with it a sense of reality that saves its possessor from being too much deluded by it; and the hereditaries are brought up to exercise their personal power conventionally and leave the rest to their ministers. A democratic leader is always a beggar on horseback, and the only real security against abuse of his powers is to establish in his mind a certainty that if he does not prove himself a capable rider he will be thrown off ignominiously. Our notion is to set the horse to govern with a curb in its mouth and a whole House of Commons on its back to pull at the reins as hard as they can, all shrieking for Liberty and protesting against dictatorship. In a really going concern every ruler, from the humblest foreman or boatswain to the most distinguished chief of staff, must be a dictator. The persons known to the public may be parliamentary dummies, but there is a dictator somewhere if anything real is being done. The pretense that there are no dictators increases their power by concealing it. The choice is not between dictators and no dictators, but between avowed and therefore responsible dictators and hidden irresponsible ones. Mussolini is the most responsible ruler in Europe because he gives his orders with his own voice and not through an imaginary megaphone called "The Voice of the Italian People." Mr MacDonald's voice is a National Voice. When he says one thing on Tuesday and the contrary on Friday, dont blame him: it is only the nation changing its mind.

In such a system as I have sketched for you, the ruling hierarchy culminates in a Cabinet of Thinkers. The leading spirit in that Cabinet will be as nearly a head dictator as you can very well get. I repeat, you need not be alarmed at the name. You have never had anything else than dictators governing you although you did not call them so, and most of them were routineers who could not dictate. The system is not, as people imagine when they talk of Stalin in Russia, of one dictator at the top. It is a hierarchy of dictators all through. There is no opposition, no obstruction, no talking out of Bills. The dictators do their job with their counsellors about them as best they can; and they are really responsible because there is no reason for leaving them there or putting them there except that they do the work better than the next best. The moment they fail to do it they go; for there is nothing to keep them there. They have no power to hold on and nobody wants them to hold on, because the moment they cease to do their work well they become nuisances.

Up to this point the political structure I have sketched is just as necessary for Fascism or for Communism as it is for that doubtless extremely superior British version of it which we will produce in course of time. We can walk hand in hand with Stalin and Mussolini up to this point, because the Government of the future, whatever else it may be, will have to be a positive governing government and not an organization of Anarchism flying the flag of Liberty. And all positive and stable governments must have the same contact with the governed at the base and organ of pure constructive thought at the apex.

Now, that being so, where will the division come? That question drags in the apparently irrelevant and personal subject of my age. You notice that I am an old man, exhibiting very distinct symptoms of second childhood. I go back like a child to the ancient simplicities, the old Fabian simplicities. In the early Fabian days there were certain things that we hammered continually into the public mind. One of them was that the existing system is in essence nothing but a gigantic robbery of the poor. What is the matter with society is that the legal owners of the country and its capital are getting for nothing whatsoever an enormous share of the wealth produced from day to day in this country. You are all probably shrinking and saying, "Now Shaw is getting ungentlemanly." But in the '80s and '90s we were shouting this all over the place; and it was by insisting on it in season and out of season that we counted for something in politics. Since we ceased mentioning it and took to glorifying the Labor party, which means trusting to Parliament, we have ceased to count, and we shall never count again until we go back to the old shout. Why did we not raise it at the last general election? Mr Ramsay MacDonald would have raised it loudly enough if he had been in Socialism instead of being in Parliament. The question at issue was how to balance the Budget. That was the great thing. Now, in the old Fabian days the duty of the Labor party, if it was a Socialist party, would have been clear. There was, as a matter of fact, no ambiguity whatever about it. The process of balancing the Budget or of forming a Budget in England was simply this: how much money can we get out of the people? At the present time balancing the Budget means collecting 850 millions a year. A Capitalist Chancellor of the Exchequer has to ask himself: "Where can I get the money? There is the rent of the Crown lands; there is the interest on the Suez Canal shares; but they do not amount to a row of beans. There is indirect taxation: customs and excise and stamps and motor licenses and entertainment duty. There is inflation, always popular with debtors but quite the reverse with creditors. But these will not suffice: there is a shortage which I fear I must extort from the propertied class by income tax, surtax, and death duties; and they will never consent to pay unless I can convince them that I have screwed the last farthing from the people by indirect taxation first, and that the balance is the inevitable ransom of their possessions."

The attitude of a Socialist Chancellor is clearly just the contrary. Mr MacDonald's line at the last election, as it would have been if he had been the old Fabian he once was, was plain. He was ostensibly a Socialist Prime Minister without a Socialist majority. Logically he should have said: "Now that we have come to the balancing of the Budget I must resign. You gentlemen of the Capitalist majority will have to take this Budget in hand yourselves. I know perfectly well that you will do everything you can to get the money without coming down on the owners of property. You will put every farthing you can on wages and as little as you can on unearned incomes. My business is to put the boot on the other leg, and rub into the public that while you are pretending that the Empire must perish if the seventeen and ninepence a week to the unemployed is not cut down to fifteen shillings you are subsidizing the idleness of the rich to the tune of four hundred millions a year ripe for taxation."

Mr Ramsay MacDonald quite forgot that figure. He had got out of his old Fabian habits. Nobody else mentioned it. Is it a hidden figure? Is it a recondite matter that has been kept so secret that the ordinary citizen cannot be expected to know it? Nothing of the sort. It is in Whitaker's Almanack. The mischief of throwing away money like this is that its recipients take out of our proletariat an enormous mass of workers who might be producing positive wealth and wasting their labor on pressing idle gentlemen's trousers, cleaning idle ladies' shoes, and doing all the other things that idle people want done by their retinues of servants and tradesmen. Huge industries are built up to produce elaborate and expensive nothings for them: things that nobody wants, but which they purchase to present to oneanother. Incidentally we have learnt in their service to produce real conveniences and comforts which everyone will enjoy some day; but after all deductions for these, our waste of capital and demoralization of labor in supplying the unreal or mischievous wants of the parasitic rich is so great that a nation which tolerates it loses all excuse for making a poor mouth about trifles of twenty or thirty millions and cutting the seventeen and ninepence of the involuntarily unemployed poor down to fifteen shillings.

Here are the old Fabian simplicities that I want to go back to. What is the Fabian Society for if not to rub them into the consciences of our grossly humbugged taxpayers. The other day I happened to have occasion for the services of a West End professional man. It was rather a curious business, because I paid him three guineas for the service, though by taking a tuppeny bus and spending another twenty minutes on the job I could have got it performed for five shillings. I cannot tell you why I paid the three guineas instead of the five shillings, for I knew that his landlord and not he would get the extra two pound eighteen; but, as a matter of fact, I did. He said to me: "I have to work all day pretty hard from ten in the morning. Do you know that I calculate that not until half-past four in the afternoon do I begin to make money for myself." All the rest of the time he is working practically for the idle, useless, and unhappy ladies and gentlemen who draw that four hundred millions a year out of his and other people's labor for nothing. Why do we stand it? One would suppose that every professional man in the West End must be a raging Communist; yet if I mention that sort of thing I am told that is old hat, that I am a back number, that harping on ground rents is Fabianism, and that Fabianism is dead and done for. Well, I am sorry to be out of fashion; but you will have to go back to that sort of Fabianism, or, let me tell you, you will not get out of your present mess.

Let me deal with the question of why it has ever been possible to induce intelligent men to acquiesce in the levy of this enormous tribute on industry. I have not told you the whole of it. Incomes derived from business amount to more than a thousand millions in addition to the four hundred millions. Some of this business income—I cannot disentangle it—I cannot tell you how much— is a reasonable remuneration for work, but a good deal of it is made up of salaries, profits, and commissions big enough to bear additional taxation without any such personal privation as must follow a cut of a few shillings in weekly wages.

Why do you leave all this mass of rent, interest, and profit in private hands, and treat it as so sacred that we must all tighten our belts sooner than touch it? The only reason that pretends to be an economic reason is this. To develop the resources of the country requires a constant supply of fresh capital to start new industries. With the march of science you not only have to start new industries but to provide entirely new machinery for old industries. How are you going to provide for the accumulation of that capital? The accepted commercial answer is that you must throw an immense mass of wealth into the hands of a small class of people. You must throw so much of it into their hands that they cannot consume it. After stuffing themselves with every luxury that can be imagined on the face of the earth they still have millions which save themselves because they cannot be spent. That is the argument for having an enormously rich class amongst you. Well, what have we Fabians to say to that? We have to say several things. In the first place, it is ridiculous waste to overfeed a handful of idle people and their millions of hangers-on before you can save money when no money need pass through their

250

hands at all. No sane nation which could accumulate its capital in any other way would choose that way. Well, what on earth is to prevent us from accumulating our capital in another way? Why not take its sources out of the hands of these gentlemen and accumulate it ourselves? They would then have to work for their living, but we should be all the richer and they all the happier. After all, though we let them plunder us so monstrously we plunder them back again by income tax, super-tax, and death duties, only to waste the booty on unemployment benefit instead of organizing employment.

Besides, what guarantee have you that these people will invest their savings for the good of the nation? As a rule they try to send it wherever labor is cheapest. Before the war they were steadily sending two hundred millions of English capital abroad to anywhere on the face of the earth except England. Here we are with our cities rotted out with slums and with the most urgent need for capital to do away with those slums and to improve the condition of our people, to give them better food, better clothing, better housing, and better education, for bringing our obsolete machinery up-to-date, organizing agriculture collectively, and introducing all the new scientific methods. We need capital for those things; but if there is a penny more in the way of dividend to be got by our capitalist class by sending money to the Argentine or to anywhere else they send it there. Consider the danger of living on foreign investments. The income from them is created in foreign countries by foreign labor. It is then sent here and spent here. Suppose the foreign nations go bankrupt! Already not one of them can pay twenty shillings in the pound. We ourselves can pay only thirteen shillings or less. Suppose they take to Communism or Fascism or something of that kind, and stop paying tribute! We should be starved out, and serve us right. A great deal of the starvation we are complaining of at the present time exists because we have become much too much dependent on supplies from abroad and not enough on supplies from home. So you see, the one defence you can set up for the conspiracy of silence about unearned income is nothing but a silly excuse for shirking the great enterprize of Socialism. It is not true that wages must be cut, unemployment benefit must be cut, education must be cut, public enterprize must be starved, and stopped in order that more hundreds of millions can be added to those which are being wasted at present on the idleness, extravagance, and corruption of labor which are ruining us.

That is what I call the old Fabian simplicity which in my second childhood I go back to. I used to insist that the Government had no right to take a penny from the private capitalist until it was ready to use it productively. At that time income tax was twopence in the pound. I little thought that I should live to pay half my income to a nominally Socialist Chancellor of the Exchequer every January only to see it helplessly and foolishly wasted in doles.

An intelligent Government would not let a single farthing go out of this country until we were quite saturated with capital, which is very far from being the case. Just consider the scaring and glaring fact that there are 100,000 people in London living in one-room tenements, some of them underground, at the present moment. Every human being, in my opinion, ought at least to have, as one of the first necessities of a properly equipped home, a private room always to himself or herself. I do not mean one room for everybody in the house except the husband and wife, and one room for them. I mean two rooms for them. I suppose I shall be denounced for a dastardly attack on the family, but I feel as a husband that I must have a room that I can lock my wife out of, and she has exactly the same view with regard to a room that she can lock me out of. Well, until you have the population properly housed to that extent we have no excuse for sending capital out of the country, and we need a positive Government to stop it and not a Cabinet of talkers and Laisser-fairists.

I am not forgetting what is called the importance of foreign trade. The important thing is to get rid of as much of it as possible as soon as possible. I want to point out to you, as one of the childish simplicities which I go back to, that trade is in itself an evil. I am quite aware that our private capitalist system has brought us into such a state of lunacy that all the City articles in the newspapers, all the speeches, all the assumptions made in the debates and underlying our legislation are that the more trade the country has the better. Also they insist that the balance of trade must be in our favor or we are lost. King Charles the Second would have agreed with that. But he would not have believed his ears if he had been told that what they meant by a balance of trade in our favor is that we are sending more goods out of the country than we are getting in. He would have said, "You mean just the opposite, dont you?" But they really do mean it, though all the time they go on with their foreign investments, which must finally produce a continual stream of imports without any exports to balance them at all. To me it seems simply insanity, but I am an old man and my brain is failing; but I venture to suggest that a country which exports more than it imports is bleeding to death, and a country which imports more than it exports is being pauperized. No private trader cares which effect is being produced if he can make a profit on the particular private transaction which happens to come his way. That is why foreign trade should be taken out of private hands.

And now, what about all this tariff business? A tariff is simply a method of disguised or indirect taxation, like currency inflation and the rest of our fiscal dodges. Let us, however, leave out that part of the tariff business which is for revenue purposes and let us go on to the question of keeping out the foreigner's goods and protecting native industries. I attach great importance to that. I believe that the present movement throughout the world to make every State self-supporting is not merely a healthy movement but an absolutely necessary movement. The old Cobdenite notion that every country produces the goods it consumes at a loss and produces what foreigners consume at a profit is not only, as Carlyle called it, heartbreaking nonsense, but is no longer even the partial matter of fact it was in Cobden's time. In his time England could manufacture better than other nations, and it paid our capitalists to go in for their trade and let agriculture go to the dogs. Today all nations produce with the same machinery, and we are badly behindhand in harnessing the powers of Nature to that machinery. We are still only talking about our unused tidal water power whilst the Italians have not only covered their mountains with flumes, but bored through the earth to the central fires and are driving their machines by artificial volcanos. I doubt that there is a single member of the Cabinet who is aware of this staggering advance, which will be copied in the volcanic countries where earthquakes are six a penny. They still bleat about revivals of irrecoverably lost trades, and pity the Italians for not being governed by them instead of by Mussolini.

Let us look at the question of national self-support from the militarist point of view. Nowadays wars are won, not by fighting, but by blockade. The military experts know perfectly well that all those tremendous old-style infantry offensives which were launched on the western front between 1914 and 1918, at an appalling cost in slaughter and mutilation, were pure waste. The old style was to throw masses of infantry soldiers on other masses of them and let them fight it out with the bayonet. Our commanders, always doing what was done the last time, threw the masses on to barbed wire and machine-guns, and had them blown and torn to pieces. No doubt it was very heroic, meaning very bloody. The Germans were wonderful in their fighting. They won any amount of victories. So did we. But not one of our offensives and not one of the German offensives ever reached its objective. They were shot down by machinery on the wires before they got there. The whole affair was one of blockade and nothing else. I used to say that the war would last thirty years because I could not be persuaded that the Central Empires could not live on their own natural resources. I was wrong. Thanks to the capitalist system they did not know how to support themselves, and had to surrender when their foreign trade was cut off. That is why people who have any power of observation are beginning to feel that one of the first necessities of the present dangerous time is for a nation to become self-supporting, and are clamoring for tariffs. But tariffs will not do the trick. Taxing foreign trade is no use: you must prohibit it. Tariffs do not keep foreign goods out: they only raise the price of native goods without regard to their quality. What we need is a Government which, with regard to those industries that we are determined shall grow up and be developed in our country so as to make ourselves self-supporting, will decree absolute prohibition of foreign trade by private speculators. What the Government should do in such cases, as it seems to me, is to prohibit private foreign trade absolutely, and then if the native industry cannot produce a sufficient supply, itself buy the necessary supplementary foreign supply and put it on the market at a fixed price. In that way it can give all the protection that is necessary to the native industry whilst taking care that the native industry keeps itself up-to-date and is not trying to get trade by being lazy and behindhand under the shelter of a tariff.

I must now deal with something that was said the other day in Parliament by my friend George Lansbury. It was very like what Mr Rowse said here the other night about the English workman being the best in the world, only that George Lansbury's remark was a Marxist echo and not an echo from All Souls. He said in effect that all our social questions are now international questions, implying that we cannot do anything until everybody else in the world does it simultaneously. Well, that is not very cheerful. If you will not do anything until everybody else does it (although I know that is English morality in a nutshell), you will never get anything done at all. I wish I had my friend George here just to ask him in a friendly way why on the face of the earth we cannot carry out enormous instalments of Socialism without caring one snap of our fingers whether they are simultaneously carried out in Paris, in Berlin, in Budapest, in Madagascar, and in Jerusalem. Take the case of that professional man whom I was with the other day. When he told me he was working up to half-past four for other people, I told him that I myself always have, before I can touch a penny of the money that I earn—not that I really earn it all: a lot of actors and other people of that kind earn most of it for me—to pay about £500 a year to support somebody who does nothing for me in return but give me his gracious permission to live in London. Why should I pay him for permission to live in London? I am an ornament to London. London owes at least half its present celebrity to the fact that I live in it. Take the redistribution of income which is so urgently necessary as between the citizens of London at large and the ground landlords headed by the Duke of Bedford, the Duke of Portland, the Duke of Westminster, and Lord Howard de Walden; may I ask what person in Berlin, or in Paris, or in Jerusalem, or in Madagascar can do anything to prevent this country effecting such a redistribution? Absolutely nobody.

Take the cognate question of the redistribution of leisure. Millions of our people, some living on the dole and some on property, do not work at all, whilst other people are working fourteen hours a day. I assure you that quite a number of people are working fourteen hours a day. Can anything be more ridiculous? one man unemployed and the other man working fourteen hours a day! Surely the sensible thing is to take the unemployed man and let him do seven hours of the work of the fourteen hours man, and then see whether you cannot split it up a little bit further. About four hours work a day all round, accompanied by a sensible redistribution of income, would make us all much healthier and happier than we are at present.

What influence from abroad can prevent us from doing that, if we like? What state would Russia be in if Stalin had waited for us to give him a lead? Suppose Mussolini had waited for us, where would Italy be? I suggest the time has come for us to give a lead now.

The truth is that the redistribution of income, the redistribution of leisure, the municipalization and nationalization of land, the national control of industry, the accumulation of capital by the State, the regulation of foreign trade to make this country more and more self-supporting are things that we can do every single bit of without troubling our heads for one moment whether the rest of the world is going to be sensible enough to follow our example. You applaud, but faintly and depressingly. If this audience had two-penn'orth of political sense, it would have jumped up madly to cheer me, and request me to become the dictator of this country. You mistrust the old Fabian simplicities, the things which are really at the back of any movement worth counting in this country, and are the only considerations which will really change the minds of the people, which is what we want to do. All these things you have forgotten. You have gone slack about them: you have lost faith in the possibility of their being done. Well, unless you regain that faith, they will not be done; because after all, until you manage to produce the atmosphere which will make even parliamentary politicians feel that you want things to go in a certain direction, they will stick in their old ruts on the road to ruin.

In conclusion, I must point out that to effect these changes there must be a genuine transfer of political power in this country. All through our agitation of the last fifty years we have been continually beaten by the fact that we cannot get hold of the children. Every fresh generation of children has been brought up in the old habits of thought which act as impregnable defences for our system, which I have called the system of robbery of the poor, this enormous brigandage of privately-owned land and capital. I must not start at this time of the evening on the Disarmament question; yet I will say that I do not care twopence about the Disarmament talky-talky at Geneva. The Disarmament question that concerns me is who is going to have control of the machine-guns in this country. The other day at the Marble Arch you had your heads broken in the old way by the sticks of the police. But Geneva has just set the example of substituting machine-guns for sticks on such occasions. I should simply be spitting in the face of history if I pretended to believe that the propertied classes in this country will give up their property without fighting for it if they control the machine-guns. They have a great deal of money; and as long as you leave them with money they will be able to pay men to fight for them. If you pay an Englishman to kill another Englishman and have the law at his back, he will do it in the most cheerful manner. Under our Capitalist class system every Englishman dislikes every other Englishman so much that it is hardly necessary to pay him to kill: you have to make severe laws to prevent him from killing.

You must make up your minds that this question may not be settled in a pacifist manner. Once or twice Sir Stafford Cripps, and also Mr Rowse, said that the catastrophe might be deferred. I do not want the catastrophe to be deferred. I am impatient for the catastrophe. I should be jolly glad if the catastrophe occurred tomorrow. But being an average coward, as most unblooded citizens are—especially people in my profession—I would rather that the catastrophe were settled without violence. But I am afraid our property system will not be settled without violence unless you make up your minds that, if it is defended by violence, it will be overthrown by violence. That is very depressing, but there is no use shirking it. You have to look final issues in the face. There comes a time in all human society when there is a certain constitution of society which a number of people are determined to maintain and a number of other people are determined to overthrow. Both have the conviction that the whole future of the world and civilization depends (a) on its being maintained, (b) on its being overthrown. The only way in which it can finally be settled, it seems to me, is by one party killing the other to the extent that may be necessary to convince the rest that they will be killed if they do not surrender. I do not think there is any use in burking that sort of fact by cherishing the old Liberal illusion that fundamental reforms can be effected by votes in Parliament. For thirty years the Irish question was left to Parliament, where it was carried at last by votes. Instantly the officers in the army mutinied, and the real settlement was by blood and fire. There is only one way of avoiding a repetition of the Irish experience here, and that is to get at the children and raise a new generation educated as Socialists. That would give you a Socialist movement in the country overwhelming enough to put out of countenance the propertied resistance. Without that the thing will be done by the forcible determination of a resolute minority, as it has been done in Italy and Russia. But make up your mind the thing has to be done one way or another: we cannot go on as we are much longer. I am past military age; but, still, I may be gassed or have my house burnt over me. The old are no longer exempt from the risks they thrust on the young; so I speak with a due sense of responsibility.

Well, ladies and gentlemen, take my advice and do not try to defer the catastrophe. Do everything you can to bring it about, but do your best to let it be done in as gentlemanly a manner as possible.

UNIVERSITIES AND EDUCATION

(Verbatim report of "the main parts in full" of an address to the students of the University of Hongkong, delivered 12 February 1933. *The New York Times*, 26 *March* 1933)

I have a very strong opinion that every university on the face of the earth ought to be leveled to the ground and its foundations sowed with salt.

I am never tired of pointing out that only very recently civilization was almost destroyed by a tremendous war. We do not as yet know whether civilization has not been entirely destroyed by that war, but it does not matter, because one of the things that the war proved was that there was very little civilization at all.

That war was made by people with university educations. There are really two dangerous classes in the world. There are the half-educated, who have destroyed one-half of civilization, and there are the wholly educated, who have nearly completely destroyed the world.

You ought very carefully to study the works of Professor Flinders Petrie. When I was young, which was an incalculable number of years ago, nobody knew anything about old civilizations. We knew a little about Greece and Rome. Rome somehow had collapsed into the Dark Ages, but until Professor Flinders Petrie began to dig up old civilizations, we had no idea of how many civilizations exactly like our own had collapsed. They almost all collapsed through education.

I think the reason of that was that, in order to keep civilization together, you really require people of more or less original minds. Now, the university turns out people with artificial minds. You come here and they turn out your mind and substitute an artificial mind. And, accordingly, I foresee the complete collapse of our civilization, and we in turn will go back to what will be called the Dark Ages.

Of course, what you are going to do I dont know. You may say, "Shall I leave the university?" or "Shall I go into the street?"

Well, I dont know. There is something to be got from the university. You get a training in communal life which is advantageous, and [which] I should recommend to a son of mine, if I had a son. I should send him to a university and say to him: "Be very careful about letting them put an artificial mind in you. As regards the books they want you to read, dont read them."

A school textbook is, by definition, an unreadable book. The fact that I am an entirely uneducated man is due to the fact that I never could read schoolbooks of any kind. The time I was supposed to devote to reading schoolbooks I [spent in] reading real books—books written by people who could really write, which is never the case with the authors of textbooks.

Be careful, as I say, to read the real books and just do enough of your textbooks to prevent your being ignominiously kicked out of the university. Read the good books, the real books, and steep yourselves in all the revolutionary books. Go up to your neck in communism and everything of the kind. If you dont begin to be a revolutionist at the age of twenty, then at fifty you will be a most impossible old fossil. If you are a red revolutionary at the age of twenty, you have some chance of being up-to-date when you are forty!

I can only say to all of you: Go ahead in the direction I have indicated. Always argue with your teacher. If possible, if you have a professor of history who gives you his views on history, what you have got to say is, "Now, look here, we have heard your views, but what we are going to do is to find another professor of history who disagrees with you." (You will find that very easily.) "Now let us hear you two argue it out."

Always learn things controversially. You will find there is a continual plot to teach you one side of a thing dogmatically. A great many young men come to the university who are entirely incapable of profiting, and yet you have to give them degrees; consequently you teach them something by which they can answer questions.

If you taught them that there are two sides to a question, they would be hopelessly confused. To pass an examination never ascertain the truth of any question that is asked. Go to your teacher and ask, "What is the answer I am expected to make to that question?" . . .

In my young days I was a critic. I used to criticize the pictures and the theatres for a weekly paper. When I went into a picture gallery—say, into an exhibition at the Royal Academy—I realized that I could only write one article about it. At most I could only write two, and there were about two to three thousand pictures. What I had to do was to go rapidly through them and to select the twelve or fifteen pictures which were above the "unmentionable" line.

That is what you have to do. When your professors and tutors put some facts before you all occasionally, you have got to say: "Nothing doing; that is not worth remembering." Like a rag-picker going over the dust-heaps of history, you have to evaluate what you find, keep the sound things, and forget the rest as completely as possible. Then you will go about like an educated man; you will go about with a few things worth remembering. The man who keeps everything not worth remembering often attains the highest university degree. The only thing you can do with such a man is to bury him.

FILM CENSORSHIP

(B.B.C. radio talk, delivered 20 January 1935. *The Listener*, 30 *January* 1935)

The Prime Minister is quite right in hinting that, though everyone desires morally wholesome theatres and picture-houses, censorships are the very devil. Mr [Ramsay] MacDonald did not use these blunt words, but you may take it from me that they represent his meaning precisely. The Archbishop [of Canterbury] speaks of undesirable films. There are no undesirable films. No film studio in the world would spend fifty thousand pounds in making a film unless it was a very desirable film indeed. Possibly not desirable by an archbishop, but certainly desirable by that very large section of the human race who are not arch-bishops. Still, as archbishops are very like other respectable gentlemen except that they wear gaiters instead of trousers, any film corporation which devoted itself to displeasing archbishops would soon be bankrupt. In short, nobody wants to produce undesirable films.

Therefore, let us stop talking about desirable and undesirable, and consider whether we can weed out from the great mass of desirable films those which are detrimental to public morals. The censorship method, which is that of handing the job over to some frail and erring mortal man, and making him omnipotent on the assumption that his official status will make him infallible and omniscient, is so silly that it has produced the existing agitation, and yet some of the agitators are actually clamoring for more of it. Others are obsessed with sex appeal. Now, sex appeal is a perfectly legitimate element in all the fine arts that deal directly with humanity. To educate and refine it is one of the most sacred functions of the theatre. Its treatment under the censorship is often vulgar; yet I believe that, on balance, the good that has been done by the films in associating sex appeal with beauty and cleanliness, with poetry and music, is incalculable. It is in quite other directions that the pictures are often mischievous; and if a new public inquiry is set on foot people who consider sex as sinful in itself must be excluded from it like other lunatics, and its business be to ascertain whether, on the whole, going to the films makes worse or better citizens of us.

As to the remedy, the most successful one so far has been the licensing of places of public entertainment from year to year by representative local authorities, accessible to complaints from individuals or deputations, and with powers to withdraw licenses from ill-conducted houses for what are called judicial reasons by a majority vote. The subject is difficult, delicate, and complicated; but so far the licensing has proved the most effective expedient for keeping decent order pending the time when theatres and picture-houses will be public institutions under the control of a Ministry of Education and the Fine Arts.

This is my considered opinion, and I am an old hand and know what I am talking about. Sleep on it before you join the outcry.

FREEDOM

(One of a series of B.B.C. radio talks, delivered 18 June 1935. *The Listener*, 26 June 1935. Reprinted in *Freedom*, London, 1936)

What is a perfectly free person? Evidently a person who can do what he likes, when he likes, and where he likes, or do nothing at all if he prefers it. Well, there is no such person, and there never can be any such person. Whether we like it or not, we must all sleep for one third of our lifetime—wash and dress and undress—we must spend a couple of hours eating and drinking —we must spend nearly as much in getting about from place to place. For half the day we are slaves to necessities which we cannot shirk, whether we are monarchs with a thousand slaves or humble laborers with no servants but their wives. And the wives must undertake the additional heavy slavery of child-bearing, if the world is still to be peopled.

These natural jobs cannot be shirked. But they involve other jobs which can. As we must eat we must first provide food; as we must sleep, we must have beds, and bedding in houses with fireplaces and coals; as we must walk through the streets, we must have clothes to cover our nakedness. Now, food and houses and clothes can be produced by human labor. But when they are produced they can be stolen. If you like honey you can let the bees produce it by their labor, and then steal it from them. If you are too lazy to get about from place to place on your own legs you can make a slave of a horse. And what you do to a horse or a bee, you can also do to a man or a woman or a child, if you can get the upper hand of them by force or fraud or trickery of any sort, or even by teaching them that it is their religious duty to sacrifice their freedom to yours.

So beware! If you allow any person, or class of persons, to get the upper hand of you, he will shift all that part of his slavery to Nature that can be shifted on to your shoulders; and you will find yourself working from eight to fourteen hours a day when, if you had only yourself and your family to provide for, you could do it quite comfortably in half the time or less. The object of all honest governments should be to prevent your being imposed on in this way. But the object of most actual governments, I regret to say, is exactly the opposite. They enforce your slavery and call it freedom. But they also regulate your slavery, keeping the greed of your masters within certain bounds. When chattel slavery of the negro sort costs more than wage slavery, they abolish chattel slavery and make you free to choose between one employment or one master and another, and this they call a glorious triumph for freedom, though for you it is merely the key of the street. When you complain, they promise that in future you shall govern the country for yourself. They redeem this promise by giving you a vote, and having a general election every five years or so.

At the election two of their rich friends ask for your vote, and you are free to choose which of them you will vote for to spite the other—a choice which leaves you no freer than you were before, as it does not reduce your hours of labor by a single minute. But the newspapers assure you that your vote has decided the election, and that this constitutes you a free citizen in a democratic country. The amazing thing about it is that you are fool enough to believe them.

Now mark another big difference between the natural slavery of man to Nature and the unnatural slavery of man to man. Nature is kind to her slaves. If she forces you to eat and drink, she makes eating and drinking so pleasant that when we can afford it we eat and drink too much. We must sleep or go mad: but then sleep is so pleasant that we have great difficulty in getting up in the morning. And firesides and families seem so pleasant to the young that they get married and join building societies to realize their dreams. Thus, instead of resenting our natural wants as slavery, we take the greatest pleasure in their satisfaction. We write sentimental songs in praise of them. A tramp can earn his supper by singing Home, Sweet Home.

The slavery of man to man is the very opposite of this. It is hateful to the body and to the spirit. Our poets do not praise it: they proclaim that no man is good enough to be another man's master. The latest of the great Jewish prophets, a gentleman named Marx, spent his life in proving that there is no extremity

of selfish cruelty at which the slavery of man to man will stop
if it be not stopped by law. You can see for yourself that it
produces a state of continual civil war—called the class war—
between the slaves and their masters, organized as Trade Unions
on one side and Employers' Federations on the other. Saint
Thomas More, who has just been canonized, held that we shall
never have a peaceful and stable society until this struggle is
ended by the abolition of slavery altogether, and the compulsion
of everyone to do his share of the world's work with his own
hands and brains, and not to attempt to put it on anyone else.

Naturally the master class, through its parliaments and schools
and newspapers, makes the most desperate efforts to prevent us
from realizing our slavery. From our earliest years we are taught
that our country is the land of the free, and that our freedom was
won for us by our forefathers when they made King John sign
Magna Charta—when they defeated the Spanish Armada—when
they cut off King Charles's head—when they made King William
accept the Bill of Rights—when they issued and made good the
American Declaration of Independence—when they won the
battles of Waterloo and Trafalgar on the playing-fields of Eton
—and when, only the other day, they quite unintentionally
changed the German, Austrian, Russian, and Ottoman empires
into republics.

When we grumble, we are told that all our miseries are our
own doing because we have the vote. When we say "What good
is the vote?" we are told that we have the Factory Acts, and the
Wages Boards, and free education, and the New Deal, and the
dole; and what more could any reasonable man ask for? We are
reminded that the rich are taxed a quarter—a third—or even a
half and more of their incomes; but the poor are never reminded
that they have to pay that much of their wages as rent in addition
to having to work twice as long every day as they would need if
they were free.

Whenever famous writers protest against this imposture—
say Voltaire and Rousseau and Tom Paine in the eighteenth
century, or Cobbett and Shelley, Karl Marx and Lassalle in the
nineteenth, or Lenin and Trotsky in the twentieth—you are
taught that they are atheists and libertines, murderers and

scoundrels; and often it is made a criminal offence to buy or sell their books. If their disciples make a revolution, England immediately makes war on them and lends money to the other Powers to join her in forcing the revolutionists to restore the slave order. When this combination was successful at Waterloo, the victory was advertized as another triumph for British freedom; and the British wage-slaves, instead of going into mourning like Lord Byron, believed it all and cheered enthusiastically. When the revolution wins, as it did in Russia in 1922, the fighting stops; but the abuse, the calumnies, the lies continue until the revolutionized State grows into a first-rate military Power. Then our diplomatists, after having for years denounced the revolutionary leaders as the most abominable villains and tyrants, have to do a right turn and invite them to dinner.

Now, though this prodigious mass of humbug is meant to delude the enslaved masses only, it ends in deluding the master class much more completely. A gentleman whose mind has been formed at a preparatory school for the sons of gentlemen, followed by a public school and university course, is much more thoroughly taken in by the falsified history and dishonest political economy and the snobbery taught in these places than any worker can possibly be, because the gentleman's education teaches him that he is a very fine fellow, superior to the common run of men whose duty it is to brush his clothes, carry his parcels, and earn his income for him; and as he thoroughly agrees with this view of himself, he honestly believes that the system which has placed him in such an agreeable situation and done such justice to his merits is the best of all possible systems, and that he should shed his blood, and yours, to the last drop in its defence. But the great mass of our rack-rented, underpaid, treated-as-inferiors, cast-off-on-the-dole workers cannot feel so sure about it as the gentleman. The facts are too harshly against it. In hard times, such as we are now passing through, their disgust and despair sometimes lead them to kick over the traces, upset everything, and have to be rescued from mere gangsterism by some Napoleonic genius who has a fancy for being an emperor, and who has the courage and brains and energy to jump at the chance. But the slaves who give three cheers for the emperor might just as well have made a cross on a British or American ballot paper as far as their freedom is concerned.

So far I have mentioned nothing but plain natural and historical facts. I draw no conclusions, for that would lead me into controversy, and controversy would not be fair when you cannot answer me back. I am never controversial over the wireless. I do not even ask you to draw your own conclusions, for you might draw some very dangerous ones, unless you have the right sort of head for it. Always remember that though nobody likes to be called a slave, it does not follow that slavery is a bad thing. Great men, like Aristotle, have held that law and order and government would be impossible unless the persons the people have to obey are beautifully dressed and decorated, robed and uniformed, speaking with a special accent, traveling in first-class carriages or the most expensive cars, or on the best-groomed and best-bred horses, and never cleaning their own boots, nor doing anything for themselves that can possibly be done by ringing a bell and ordering some common person to do it. And this means, of course, that they must be made very rich without any obligation other than to produce an impression of almost godlike superiority on the minds of common people. In short, it is contended, you must make men ignorant idolaters before they will become obedient workers and law-abiding citizens.

To prove this, we are reminded that, although nine out of ten voters are common workers, it is with the greatest difficulty that a few of them can be persuaded to vote for the members of their own class. When women were enfranchised and given the right to sit in Parliament, the first use they made of their votes was to defeat all the women candidates who stood for the freedom of the workers and had given them years of devoted and distinguished service. They elected only one woman—a titled lady of great wealth and exceptionally fascinating personality.

Now this, it is said, is human nature, and you cannot change human nature. On the other hand, it is maintained that human nature is the easiest thing in the world to change if you catch it young enough, and that the idolatry of the slave class and the arrogance of the master class are themselves entirely artificial products of education and of a propaganda that plays upon our infants long before they have left their cradles. An opposite mentality could, it is argued, be produced by a contrary education and propaganda. You can turn the point over in your mind for yourself; do not let me prejudice you one way or the other.

The practical question at the bottom of it all is how the income of the whole country can best be distributed from day to day. If the earth is cultivated agriculturally in vast farms with motor ploughs and chemical fertilizers, and industrially in huge electrified factories full of machinery that a girl can handle, the product may be so great that an equal distribution of it would provide enough to give the unskilled laborers as much as the managers and the men of the scientific staff. But do not forget, when you hear tales of modern machinery enabling one girl to produce as much as a thousand men could produce in the reign of good Queen Anne, that this marvelous increase includes things like needles and steel pins and matches, which we can neither eat nor drink nor wear. Very young children will eat needles and matches eagerly—but the diet is not a nourishing one. And though we can now cultivate the sky as well as the earth, by drawing nitrogen from it to increase and improve the quality of our grass and, consequently, of our cattle and milk and butter and eggs, Nature may have tricks up her sleeve to check us if the chemists exploit her too greedily.

And now to sum up. Wipe out from your dreams of freedom the hope of being able to do as you please all the time. For at least twelve hours of your day Nature orders you to do certain things, and will kill you if you dont do them. This leaves twelve hours for working; and here again Nature will kill you unless you either earn your living or get somebody else to earn it for you. If you live in a civilized country your freedom is restricted by the laws of the land enforced by the police, who oblige you to do this, and not to do that, and to pay rates and taxes. If you do not obey these laws the courts will imprison you, and, if you go too far, kill you. If the laws are reasonable and are impartially administered you have no reason to complain, because they increase your freedom by protecting you against assault, highway robbery, and disorder generally.

But as society is constituted at present, there is another far more intimate compulsion on you: that of your landlord and that of your employer. Your landlord may refuse to let you live on his estate if you go to chapel instead of to church, or if you vote for anyone but his nominee, or if you practise osteopathy, or if you open a shop. Your employer may dictate the cut, color, and condition of your clothes, as well as your hours of work. He can turn you into the street at any moment to join the melancholy band of lost spirits called the Unemployed. In short, his power over you is far greater than that of any political dictator could possibly be. Your only remedy at present is the Trade Union weapon of the strike, which is only the old Oriental device of starving on your enemy's doorstep until he does you justice. Now, as the police in this country will not allow you to starve on your employer's doorstep, you must starve on your own—if you have one. The extreme form of the strike—the general strike of all workers at the same moment—is also the extreme form of human folly, as, if completely carried out, it would extinguish the human race in a week. And the workers would be the first to perish. The general strike is Trade Unionism gone mad. Sane Trade Unionism would never sanction more than one big strike at a time, with all the other trades working overtime to support it.

Now let us put the case in figures. If you have to work for twelve hours a day you have four hours a day to do what you like with, subject to the laws of the land, and your possession of money enough to buy an interesting book or pay for a seat at the pictures, or, on a half-holiday, at a football match, or whatever your fancy may be. But even here Nature will interfere a good deal, for, if your eight hours' work has been of a hard physical kind, and when you get home you want to spend your four hours in reading my books to improve your mind, you will find yourself fast asleep in half a minute, and your mind will remain in its present benighted condition.

I take it, then, that nine out of ten of us desire more freedom, and that this is why we listen to wireless talks about it. As long as we go on as we are—content with a vote and a dole—the only advice we can give oneanother is that of Shakespear's Iago: "Put money in thy purse." But as we get very little money into our purses on pay-day, and all the rest of the week other people are taking money out of it, Iago's advice is not very practical. We must change our politics before we can get what we want; and meanwhile we must stop gassing about freedom, because the people of England in the lump dont know what freedom is, never having had any. Always call freedom by its old English name of leisure, and keep clamoring for more leisure and more money to enjoy it in return for an honest share of work. And let us stop singing Rule, Britannia! until we make it true. Until we do, let us never vote for a parliamentary candidate who talks about our freedom and our love of liberty, for, whatever political name he may give himself, he is sure to be at bottom an Anarchist who wants to live on our labor without being taken up by the police for it as he deserves.

And now suppose we at last win a lot more leisure and a lot more money than we are accustomed to. What are we going to do with them? I was taught in my childhood that Satan will find mischief still for idle hands to do. I have seen men come into a fortune and lose their happiness, their health, and finally their lives by it as certainly as if they had taken daily doses of rat poison instead of champagne and cigars. It is not at all easy to know what to do with leisure unless we have been brought up to it.

I will therefore leave you with a conundrum to think over. If you had your choice, would you work for eight hours a day and retire with a full pension at fortyfive, or would you rather work four hours a day and keep on working until you are seventy? Now, dont send the answer to me, please: talk it over with your wife.

BRITAIN AND THE SOVIETS

(Speech delivered before the Congress of Peace and Friendship with the U.S.S.R., London, 7 December 1935. *Britain and the Soviets*, London, 1936)

One of the things I have to do this morning is to set an example of brevity. I have prepared nothing to say, and all that occurs to me at the moment as remarkable is that we should be here in this hall, and our hosts should be the Society of Friends. The Society of Friends believes in Providence: that is, in some power which takes all the vain contrivances of man and Congress and Parliament, and overrules them for its own ends. That is, if I may say so, a very Marxist belief [*laughter*], though the Marxists call it historical necessity or something of that kind. . . . It doesnt matter: it is the same thing. May I point out to our hosts how very remarkably their belief has been confirmed by what has occurred between England and Russia ever since 1917. Since that time we, with extraordinary foolishness, have done everything we possibly could to destroy the new experiment and the new Government in Russia. Our press has been full of the most absurd vilifications of the Soviet Government. Even a newspaper like The Times, instead of having a properly accredited correspondent in Moscow as it has in every other capital of the world, takes any rubbish it can get from White Russian correspondents in Riga and publishes it as authentic political news.

Also we have refused to trade with Russia. We have refused to invest our money there. If we had an atom of sense we would have done the reverse. When first there was the question of a loan to Russia, I can remember standing on an election platform and explaining that even if, as all the newspapers assured us, a loan to Russia would never be repaid or acknowledged, it would still be far more economical for us to make a loan to Russia, and with that loan practically to make machinery for Russia, than to keep our own workmen on the dole doing nothing. The result was that my candidate was defeated. [*Laughter.*]

But what a fortunate thing that was for Russia. If we had been sensible enough to seize our opportunity, and made a rush to put our spare capital in Russia, by this time Russia would have belonged to English capitalists and not to the Russians themselves.

Again, when the civil war broke out in Russia, and when every good-for-nothing in Europe joined the White Army, Mr Winston Churchill gave the White Army £100,000,000. He was wise enough not to take a direct vote of the House of Commons on that: it went down as part of the expenses of the European War. Mr Winston Churchill, believing that revolutionary Russia was the common enemy of mankind, handed over that

£100,000,000, and probably would have handed over a little more if we hadnt, some of us, started a movement—the "Hands Off Russia" movement. [*Applause.*]

But Providence was too much for Mr Churchill. He meant that money to be the destruction of the Soviet Government. You see, the Soviet Government had no equipment—just a few young men with Browning pistols—and they had all Europe against them. And they now had the £100,000,000 against them. What was the result? It was with that £100,000,000 that the Soviet Government practically destroyed all its adversaries, and cleared the White Armies out of Russia. [*Applause.*]

Because what did the £100,000,000 mean? It meant equipment, rifles, khaki uniforms, boots. When the Russian troops made that magnificent rally, the Red soldiers were wearing British boots, British khaki uniforms, and using British rifles. Mr Winston Churchill proposed, but Providence disposed. All that we sent out to the White Army was extremely useful to the Red Army, which presently got hold of it. Talk of the finger of Providence! Can our hosts here cite a plainer proof of it?

Our Chairman [Lord Listowel] has alluded to a new loan. I am not convinced that Russia cannot do without a loan very much better now than when I made that electioneering speech about Russia. Russia at its present rate of development will accumulate capital very rapidly. There is no doubt about that. And what I am afraid of is that Russia will invest that capital in this country, with the result that the British Isles will belong to the Russians [*laughter*], and *they* may shorten *their* working day whilst we lengthen ours in order to pay them interest. Of course, they will not introduce Capitalism in their own country between themselves; but there is no reason why they should not take advantage of Capitalism in other countries in order, in that perfectly peaceful and legitimate Capitalistic way, to get the rest of the world under Russian control. We know only too well that it does not matter who the government is, but it does matter who the shareholders and directors are.

We must face it. Things are going Russia's way, and there is every evidence that things are not going our old way. Even the strongest Conservative cannot possibly be satisfied with the general trend of events in the stage Capitalism has reached in this country. Apparently, Providence is getting sick of Capitalism. I myself wonder very much that it did not get sick of it before. If it knew as much as we know about it, it would have got sick a hundred years ago.

Not only is Providence getting sick of Capitalism, but Capitalism is getting sick of itself. Communism is certainly not getting sick of itself. The Russians are bursting with Communism. They are not going to turn their attention to another system. They are not clamoring for this, that, and the other old makeshift to keep them afloat. All they ask for Communism is more of it.

I agree with the Chairman as to the importance of Russia in the cause of peace. But there is one way of looking at it which is not generally mentioned (because in this country nothing of importance is ever mentioned; in fact, there is usually a general struggle not to say anything about it). Instead of having one League of Nations and a badly constituted one at that—if they had only made that League of Nations in the first place in the way I told them to make it,[1] there would not have been all this trouble [*laughter*]—what you have is one League of Nations between two other Leagues of Nations. Russia is not a nation in our sense of the word: it is a League of Nations, and a very important League of Nations. The United States of America, on the other side, is a League of Nations: not a single State but a whole group of States. There are these two great balancing forces and we must not forget that, unless Russia and America are at the back of Geneva, Geneva will count for nothing in diplomacy.

TRUTH BY RADIO

(Special talk filmed for the motion picture, "B.B.C., the Voice of Britain." Amended for publication in *World Film News*, *July* 1936)

I have to speak to everybody, and I never could do that until this wonderful invention of the radio and the microphone

---

[1] *The League of Nations*, Fabian Tract No. 226 (1929); reprinted in *What I Really Wrote about the War* (London 1930).

enabled me to do it. I know very well that my friend Mr [H. G.] Wells has told us that when you buy a wireless set you never use it after the first two days, and that here I am, talking to absolute vacancy under the impression that I am talking to millions. But I do not believe that. I always believe and feel that I really am talking to millions.

The politicians have not yet found out the microphone. They still imagine that they are addressing political meetings, and they do not understand that the microphone is a terrible tell-tale and a ruthless detective. If you speak insincerely on the platform to a political meeting, especially at election time, the more insincere you are the more they cheer you and the more they are delighted. But if you try that on the microphone, it gives you away instantly. The sober citizen at his fireside hears nothing but a senseless ranting by a speaker whose pretended earnestness is the result of the extra pint of champagne which has loosened his tongue and fuddled away his conscience and commonsense.

If there is anything wrong with you, remember that the microphone will make the worst of it. If you nerve yourself to face it by taking, say, half a glass of whisky, the microphone will convince all the listeners that you are shockingly drunk. I can tell by listening what the speaker has had for dinner.

The microphone tells you other things as well: for instance, where you were born. It brings out and exaggerates your native accent mercilessly. Tones in your voice that the naked ear cannot hear become audible through the microphone, betraying thoughts and feelings that you think you are concealing from every living listener. The preacher who is a hypocrite is unmasked as completely as the Cabinet Minister who is a bunk merchant. When this becomes known, it will raise the moral level of public life. It will raise the character of public speaking. It will even raise the character of our existing platform politicians, who will broadcast, not as spellbinders, but as repentant humbugs. Speeches made through the microphone to millions of listeners will take on a necessary sincerity hitherto unknown. If the speakers are insincere or pretentious for a moment, they will be found out and despised. And it is not very pleasant to be found out. I will go on so far as to say that, when all parliamentary orators have to use the microphone, most of the governments at present in power will vanish into private life with badly damaged reputations.

I do not think this side of the microphone has ever been pointed out before. It is curious: it puts you into the confessional box. It makes you a perfectly different man. When I go away from the microphone and begin to speak to my friends, I tell them all sorts of things that I do not believe, because I think it will please them. But at the microphone I know that those of you who have good ears will catch me out every time that I attempt to gammon you. Moral: never listen to great statesmen or great churchmen except through your wireless set.

SCHOOL

(B.B.C. radio talk to Sixth-Form students, delivered 11 June 1937. *The Listener*, 23 *June* 1937)

Hallo, Sixth Forms! I have been asked to speak to you because I have become celebrated through my eminence in the profession of Eschylus, Sophocles, Euripides, and Shakespear. Eschylus wrote in school Greek, and Shakespear is "English Literature," which is a school subject. In French schools I am English Literature. Consequently, all the sixth forms in France shudder when they hear my name. However, do not be alarmed: I am not going to talk to you about English literature. To me there is nothing in writing a play: anyone can write one if he has the necessary natural turn for it; and if he hasnt he cant: that is all there is to it.

However, I have another trick for imposing on the young. I am old: over eighty, in fact. Also I have a white beard; and these two facts are somehow associated in people's minds with wisdom. That is a mistake. If a person is a born fool, the folly will get worse, not better, by a long life's practice. Having lived four times as long as you gives me only one advantage over you. I have carried small boys and girls in my arms, and seen them grow into sixth-form scholars, then into young men and women in the flower of youth and beauty, then into brides and bridegrooms who think oneanother much better and lovelier than they really are, then into middleaged paterfamiliases and anxious mothers with elderly spreads, and finally I have attended their cremations.

Now you may not think much of this; but just consider. Some of your schoolfellows may surprise you by getting hanged. Others, of whom you may have the lowest opinion, will turn out to be geniuses, and become the great men of your time. Therefore, always be nice to young people. Some little beast who is no good at games and whose head you may possibly have clouted for indulging a sarcastic wit and a sharp tongue at your expense may grow into a tremendous swell, like Rudyard Kipling. You never can tell.

It is no use reading about such things or being told about them by your father. You must have known the people personally, as I have. That is what makes a difference between your outlook on the world and mine. When I was as young as you the world seemed to me to be unchangeable, and a year seemed a long time. Now the years fly past before I have time to look round. I am an old man before I have quite got out of the habit of thinking of myself as a boy. You have fifty years before you, and therefore must think carefully about your future and about your conduct. I have no future and need not care what I say or do.

You all think, dont you, that you are nearly grown up. I thought so when I was your age; and now, after eightyone years of that expectation, I have not grown up yet. The same thing will happen to you. You will escape from school only to discover that the world is a bigger school, and that you are back again in the first form. Before you can work your way up into the sixth form again you will be as old as I am.

The hardest part of schooling is, fortunately, the early part when you are a very small kid and have to be turned into a walking ready reckoner. You have to know up to twelve times twelve, and how many shillings there are in any number of pence up to 144 without looking at a book. And you must understand a printed page just as you understand people talking to you. That is a stupendous feat of sheer learning: much the most difficult I have ever achieved; yet I have not the faintest recollection of being put through it, though I remember the governess who did it. I cannot remember any time at which a printed page was unintelligible to me, nor at which I did not know without counting that fiftysix pence make four and eightpence. This seems so magical to me now that I sometimes regret that she did not teach me the whole table of logarithms and the binomial theorem and all the other mathematical short cuts and ready reckonings as well. Perhaps she would have if she had known them herself. It is strange that if you learn anything when you are young you remember it forever. Now that I am old I forget everything in a few seconds, and everybody five minutes after they have been introduced to me. That is a great happiness, as I dont want to be bothered with new things and new people; but I still cannot get on without remembering what my governess taught me. So cram in all you can while you are young.

But I am rambling. Let us get back to your escape from your school or your university into the great school of the world; and remember that you will not be chased and brought back. You will just be chucked out neck and crop and the door slammed behind you.

What makes school life irksome until you get used to it, and easy when you do get used to it, is that it is a routine. You have to get up at a fixed hour, wash and dress, take your meals, and do your work all at fixed hours. Now the worst of a routine is that, though it is supposed to suit everybody, it really suits nobody. Sixth-form scholars are like other people: they are all different. Each of you is what is called an individual case, needing individual attention. But you cannot have it at school. Nobody has time enough nor money enough to provide each of you with a separate teacher and a special routine carefully fitted to your individual personality, like your clothes and your boots.

I can remember a time when English people going to live in Germany were astonished to find that German boots were not divided into rights and lefts: a boot was a boot and it did not matter which foot you put it on, your foot had to make the best of it. You may think that funny; but let me ask how many of you have your socks knitted as rights and lefts? I have had mine knitted that way for the last fifty years. Some knitters of socks actually refuse my order and say that it cant be done. Just think of that! We are able to make machines that can fly round the world and instruments that can talk round the world, yet we think we cannot knit socks as rights and lefts, and I am considered a queer sort of fellow because I want it done and insist that it can be done. Well, school routines are like the socks and the old German boots: they are neither rights nor lefts, and consequently they dont fit any human being properly. But we have to manage with them somehow.

And when we escape from school into the big adult world, we have to choose between a lot of routines: the college routine, the military routine, the naval routine, the court routine, the civil service routine, the legal routine, the clerical routine, the theatrical routine, or the parliamentary routine, which is the worst of the lot. To get properly stuck into one of these grooves you have to pass examinations; and this you must set about very clearheadedly or you will fail. You must not let yourself get interested in the subjects or be overwhelmed by the impossibility of anyone mastering them all even at the age of five hundred, much less twenty. The scholar who knows everything is like the little child who is perfectly obedient and perfectly truthful: it doesnt exist and never will. Therefore you must go to a crammer. Now, what is a crammer? A crammer is a person whose whole life is devoted to doing something you have not time to do for yourself: that is, to study all the old examination papers and find out what are the questions that are actually asked, and what are the answers expected by the examiners and officially recognized as correct. You must be very careful not to suppose that these answers are always the true answers. Your examiners will be elderly gentlemen, and their knowledge is sure to be more or less out-of-date. Therefore begin by telling yourself this story.

Imagine yourself a young student early in the fifteenth century being examined as to your knowledge of the movements of the sun and moon, the planets and stars. Imagine also that your father happens to know Copernicus, and that you have learnt from his conversation that the planets go round not in circles but in ellipses. Imagine that you have met the painter Leonardo da Vinci, and been allowed to peep at his funny notebook, and, by holding it up to a mirror, read the words "the earth is a moon of the sun." Imagine that on being examined you gave the answers of Copernicus and Leonardo, believing them to be the true answers. Instead of passing at the head of the successful list you would have been burnt alive for heresy. Therefore you would have taken good care to say that the stars and the sun move in perfect circles, because the circle is a perfect figure and therefore answers to the perfection of the Creator. You would have said that the motion of the sun round the earth was proved by the fact that Joshua saw it move in Gibeon and stopped it. All your answers would be wrong, but you would pass and be patted on the head as a young marvel of Aristotelian science.

Now, passing examinations today is just what it was in the days of Copernicus. If you at twenty years of age go up to be examined by an elderly gentleman of fifty, you must find out what people were taught thirty years ago and stuff him with that, and not with what you are taught today.

But, you will say, how are you possibly to find out what questions are to be asked and what answers are expected? Well, you cannot; but a good crammer can. He cannot get a peep at the papers beforehand, but he can study the old examination papers until he knows all the questions that the examiners have to keep asking over and over again; for, after all, their number is not infinite. If only you will swot hard enough to learn them all you will pass with flying colors. Of course, you will not be able to learn them all, but your chances will be good in proportion to the number you can learn.

The danger of being plucked for giving up-to-date answers to elderly examiners is greatest in the technical professions. If you want to get into the navy, or practise medicine, you must get specially trained for some months in practices that are quite out of date. If you dont you will be turned down by admirals dreaming of the Nelson touch, and surgical baronets brought up on the infallibility of Jenner and Lister and Pasteur. But this does not apply to all examinations. Take the classics, for instance. Homer's Greek and Virgil's Latin, being dead languages, do not change as naval and medical practice changes. Suppose you want to be a clergyman. The Greek of the New Testament does not change. The creeds do not change. The Thirtynine Articles do not change, though they ought to, for some of them are terribly out of date. You can cram yourself with these subjects and save your money for lessons in elocution.

In any case you may take it as a safe rule that if you happen to have any original ideas about examination subjects you must not air them in your examination papers. You may very possibly know better than your examiners, but do not let them find out that you think so.

Once you are safely through your examinations you will begin life in earnest. You will then discover that your education has been very defective. You will find yourself uninstructed as to eating and drinking and sleeping and breathing. Your notions of keeping yourself fit will consist mostly of physical exercises which will shorten your life by twenty years or so. You may accept me as an educated man because I have earned my living for sixty years by work which only an educated man, and even a highly educated one, could do. Yet the subjects that educated me were never taught in my schools. As far as I know, my schoolmasters were utterly and barbarously ignorant of them. School was to me a sentence of penal servitude. You see, I was born with what people call an artistic temperament. I could read all the masterpieces of English poets, playwrights, historians, and scientific pioneers, but I could not read schoolbooks, because they are written by people who do not know how to write. To me a person who knew nothing of all the great musicians from Palestrina to Edward Elgar, or of the great painters from Giotto to Burne-Jones, was a savage and an ignoramus even if he were hung all over with gold medals for school classics. As to mathematics, to be imprisoned in an ugly room and set to do sums in algebra without ever having had the meaning of mathematics explained to me, or its relation to science, was enough to make me hate mathematics all the rest of my life, as so many literary men do. So do not expect too much from your school achievements. You may win the Ireland scholarship and then find that none of the great business houses will employ a university don on any terms.

As to your general conduct and prospects, all I have time to say is that if you do as everyone does and think as everyone thinks you will get on very well with your neighbors, but you will suffer from all their illnesses and stupidities. If you think and act otherwise you must suffer their dislike and persecution. I was taught when I was young that if people would only love oneanother, all would be well with the world. This seemed simple and very nice; but I found when I tried to put it in practice not only that other people were seldom lovable, but that I was not very lovable myself. I also found that to love anyone is to take a liberty with them which is quite unbearable unless they happen to return your affection, which you have no right to expect. What you have to learn if you are to be a good citizen of the world is that, though you will certainly dislike many of your neighbors, and differ from some of them so strongly that you could not possibly live in the same house with them, that does not give you the smallest right to injure them or even to be personally uncivil to them. You must not attempt to do good to those who hate you: for they do not need your officious services, and would refuse to be under any obligation to you. Your difficulty will be how to behave to those whom you dislike, and cannot help disliking for no reason whatever, simply because you were born with an antipathy to that sort of person. You must just keep out of their way as much as you can; and when you cannot, deal as honestly and civilly with them as with your best friend. Just think what the world would be like if everyone who disliked you were to punch your head.

The oddest thing about it is that you will find yourself making friends with people whose opinions are the very opposite to your own, whilst you cannot bear the sight of others who share all your beliefs. You may love your dog and find your nearest relatives detestable. So dont waste your time arguing whether you *ought* to love all your neighbors. You cant help yourself, and neither can they.

You may find yourself completely dissatisfied with all your fellow creatures as they exist at present and with all their laws and institutions. Then there is nothing to be done but to set to work to find out exactly what is wrong with them, and how to set them right. That is perhaps the best fun of all; but perhaps I think so only because I am a little in that line myself. I could tell you a lot more about this, but time is up, and I am warned that I must stop. I hope you are sorry.

THIS DANGER OF WAR

(B.B.C. shortwave broadcast to the Empire from London, 2 November 1937. *The Listener*, 10 *November* 1937; *Vital Speeches of the Day*, 15 *November* 1937)

What about this danger of war which is making us all shake in our shoes at present? I am like yourself; I have an intense objection to having my house demolished by a bomb from an aeroplane and myself killed in a horribly painful way by mustard gas. I have visions of streets heaped with mangled corpses, in which children wander crying for their parents, and babies gasp and strangle in the clutches of dead mothers. That is what war means nowadays. It is what is happening in Spain and in China whilst I speak to you, and it may happen to us tomorrow. And the worst of it is that it does not matter two straws to Nature, the mother of us all, how dreadfully we misbehave ourselves in this way or in what hideous agonies we die. Nature can produce children enough to make good any extremity of slaughter of which we are capable. London may be destroyed, Paris, Rome, Berlin, Vienna, Constantinople may be laid in smoking ruins, and the last shrieks of their women and children may give way to the silence of death. No matter. Nature will replace the dead. She is doing so every day. The new men will replace the old cities, and perhaps come to the same miserable end. To Nature the life of an empire is no more than the life of a swarm of bees, and a thousand years are of less account than half an hour to you and me. Now, the moral of that is that we must not depend on any sort of Divine Providence to put a stop to war. Providence says: "Kill oneanother, my children. Kill oneanother to your hearts' content. There are plenty more where you came from." Consequently, if we want the war to stop we must all become conscientious objectors.

I dislike war not only for its dangers and inconveniences, but because of the loss of so many young men, any of whom may be a Newton or an Einstein, a Beethoven, a Michael Angelo, a Shakespear, or even a Shaw. Or he may be what is of much more immediate importance, a good baker or a good weaver or builder. If you think of a pair of combatants as a heroic British Saint [*sic*] Michael bringing the wrath of God upon a German Lucifer, then you may exult in the victory of Saint Michael if he kills Lucifer or burn to avenge him if his dastardly adversary mows him down with a machine gun before he can get to grips with him. In that way you can get intense emotional experience from war. But suppose you think of the two as they probably are, say two good carpenters, taken away from their proper work to kill oneanother. That is how I see it. And the result is that whichever of them is killed the loss is as great to Europe and to me.

In 1914 I was as sorry for the young Germans who lay slain and mutilated in No Man's Land as for the British lads who lay beside them, so I got no emotional satisfaction out of the war. It was to me a sheer waste of life. I am not forgetting the gratification that war gives to the instinct of pugnacity and admiration of courage that are so strong in women. In the old days when people lived in forests like gorillas or in caves like bears, a woman's life and that of her children depended on the courage and killing capacity of her mate. To this day in Abyssinia a Danakil woman will not marry a man until he proves that he has at least four homicides to his credit. In England on the outbreak of war civilized young women rush about handing white feathers to all young men who are not in uniform. This, like other survivals from savagery, is quite natural, but our women must remember that courage and pugnacity are not much use against machine guns and poison gas.

The pacifist movement against war takes as its charter the ancient document called the Sermon on the Mount, which is almost as often quoted as the speech which Abraham Lincoln is supposed to have delivered on the battlefield of Gettysburg. The sermon is a very moving exhortation, and it gives you one first-rate tip, which is to do good to those who despitefully use you and persecute you. I, who am a much hated man, have been doing that all my life, and I can assure you that there is no better fun, whereas revenge and resentment make life miserable and the avenger hateful. But such a command as "Love one another," as I see it, is a stupid refusal to accept the facts of human nature. Why, are we lovable animals? Do you love the rate collector? Do you love Mr Lloyd George, and, if you do, do you love Mr Winston Churchill? Have you an all-embracing affection for Messrs Mussolini, Hitler, Franco, Atatürk, and the Mikado? I do not like all these gentlemen, and even if I did how could I offer myself to them as a delightfully lovable person? I find I cannot like myself without so many reservations that I look forward to my death, which cannot now be far off, as a good riddance. If you tell me to be perfect as my Father in heaven is perfect, I can only say that I wish I could. That would be more polite than telling you to go to the Zoo and advise the monkeys to become men and the cockatoos to become birds of paradise. The lesson we have to learn is that our dislike for certain persons, or even for the whole human race, does not give us any right to injure our fellow creatures, however odious they may be.

As I see it, the social rule must be "Live and let live," and people who break this rule persistently must be liquidated. The pacifists and non-resisters must draw a line accordingly. When I was a young man in the latter half of the nineteenth century war did not greatly concern me personally because I lived on an island far away from the battlefield, and because the fighting was done by soldiers who had taken up that trade in preference to any other open to them. Now that aeroplanes bring battle to my housetop, and governments take me from my proper work and force me to be a soldier whether I like it or not, I can no longer regard war as something that does not concern me personally. You may say that I am too old to be a soldier. If nations had any sense they would begin a war by sending their oldest men into the trenches. They would not risk the lives of their young men except in the last extremity. In 1914 it was a dreadful thing to see regiments of lads singing Tipperary on their way to the slaughter-house, but the spectacle of regiments of octogenarians hobbling to the front waving their walking sticks and piping up to the tune of "We'll never come back no more, boys, we'll never come back no more," wouldnt you cheer that enthusiastically? I should. But let me not forget that I should be one of them.

It has become a commonplace to say that another great war would destroy civilization. Well, that will depend on what sort of war it will be. If it is to be like the 1914 war, a war of nations, it will certainly not make an end of civilization. It may conceivably knock the British Empire to bits and leave England as primitive as she was when Julius Cæsar landed in Kent. Perhaps we shall be happier then, for we are still savages at heart, and wear our thin uniform of civilization very awkwardly. But, anyhow, there will be two refuges left for civilization. No national attack can seriously hurt the two great federated republics of North America and Soviet Russia. They are too big. The distances are too great. But what could destroy them is civil war —wars like the wars of religion in the seventeenth century—and this is exactly the sort of war that is threatening us today. It has already begun in Spain, where all the big capitalist powers are taking a hand to support General Franco through an intervention committee which they think it more decent to call a Non-Intervention Committee. This is only a skirmish in the class war, the war between the two religions of capitalism and communism, which is at bottom a war between labor and land owning. We could escape that war by putting our house in order as Russia has done, without any of the fighting and killing and waste and damage that the Russians went through. But we dont seem to want to. I have shewn exactly how it can be done, and in fact how it must be done, but nobody takes any notice. Foolish people in easy circumstances flatter themselves that there is no such thing as the class war in the British Empire, where we are all far too respectable and too well protected by our Parliamentary system to have any vulgar unpleasantness of that sort. They deceive themselves. We are up to the neck in class war. What is it that is wrong with our present way of doing things? It is not that we cannot produce enough goods; our machines turn out as much work in an hour as ten thousand hand workers used to. But it is not enough for a country to produce goods. It must distribute them as well, and this is where our system breaks down hopelessly. Everybody ought to be living quite comfortably by working four or five hours a day with two Sundays in the week. Yet millions of laborers die in the workhouse or on the dole after sixty years of hard toil so that a few babies may have hundreds of thousands a year before they are born. As I see it, this is not a thing to be argued about or to take sides about. It is stupid and wicked on the face of it, and it will smash us and our civilization if we do not resolutely reform it. Yet we do nothing but keep up a perpetual ballyhoo about Bolshevism, Fascism, Communism, Liberty, Dictators, Democracy, and all the rest of it. The very first lesson of the new history dug up for us by Professor Flinders Petrie during my lifetime is that no civilization, however splendid, illustrious, and like our own, can stand up against the social resentments and class conflicts which follow a silly misdistribution of wealth, labor, and leisure. And it is the one history lesson that is never taught in our schools, thus confirming the saying of the German philosopher Hegel: "We learn from history that men never learn anything from history." Think it over.

THE UNAVOIDABLE SUBJECT

(Written for a B.B.C. broadcast in June 1940, but "cancelled" by the British Ministry of Information. "The B.B.C. was inclined to demur," Shaw informed Beatrice Webb, but the sudden entrance of Italy into the war on 10th June, extending the war "from a scrap between the Reich and the Allies to the European scale, made my stuff childish." Published in Anthony Weymouth's *Journal of the War Years* (*1939–1945*) *and One Year Later*, 1948)

The other day a young man from Scotland told me that he was going to be a conscientious objector. I asked him why. He replied, "Because this is a silly war." I quite agreed with him. All wars are silly wars nowadays between civilized peoples. I pointed out, however, that this will not stop the onset of Mr Hitler's tanks, nor turn his bombs into picnic baskets. I took it that my conscientious friend did not desire a triumphant victory for us. Not he; he thought that such a victory would go to our heads and we should abuse it. But did he desire a triumphant victory for Mr Hitler? Certainly not; for that would be still worse, because the English would only come into the streets and maffick for a fortnight and then forget all about it; but the Germans would make a philosophy of it and try to follow it up by a conquest of Europe. We agreed that our business is to reduce Mr Hitler and his philosophy to absurdity. So I asked, is there any other way of doing this now except putting up such a devil of a fight that Germany will at last say to Mr Hitler, What hast thou done with my legions? and turn on him as the French turned on Napoleon.

The young Caledonian was open to reason. He immediately borrowed £2 from me, and joined up. If he had been an Englishman he would have quoted the Scriptures to me or said he did not hold with Churchill and that lot. I should not have argued with him. I should have taken a hint from my friend [J. B.] Priestley and just reminded him that the Germans have sunk the Gracie Fields. That would have sent him to the front like a thunderbolt. I have not forgotten the sinking of the Lusitania.

We always lose the first round of our fights through our habit of first declaring war and then preparing for it. And then we find that our troops are short of shells as they were in 1914, and short of planes and tanks as they are just now. We waste precious time squabbling about whose fault it is, and declaring that all the members of the Government whom we happen to dislike should be shot. We must stop that. The nation which is always preparing for war is like a hypochondriac who is always making his will: a dismal occupation which prevents him from doing anything else.

Mr Hitler did wonders for his country by his National Socialism, and then threw it all away to prepare for war by turning his workers into soldiers and his factories into munition works when they might have been making themselves happy and comfortable as sensible welfare workers. Heaven defend us from Governments who can think of nothing but the next war and do nothing but prepare for it! So again I say, stop squabbling about it. We are guilty of our unpreparedness; and quite right we were too. It was worth it.

But we must not give ourselves moral airs as a peace-loving people because we have been deliberately careless. Mr Hitler did not begin this war; we did. It is silly to revile him as a treacherous wolf pouncing on a nation of innocent lambs. We are not innocent lambs; we are the most formidable of all the great European Powers, claiming command of the sea, which is nothing more or less than the power to blockade and starve to death any of our rivals. Having that terrible power we are under the most sacred obligation to use it to defend, not ourselves alone, but common humanity.

When Mr Hitler reconquered Poland, and had half his conquest immediately taken from him by Russia, there was peace for the moment, because Europe was terrified by his victory. The nations trembled and said, What will he do now? Who will be the next victim? Which of us dare bell this wild cat? Thereupon we, the British Commonwealth, on our own single responsibility deliberately punched Mr Hitler on the nose and told him in the plainest terms that his notions of humanity are not compatible with ours, and that we are going to abolish his rule by shot and shell, bayonet and blockade; and what had he to say to that? What could he do but take off his coat and come on? As to what he had to say he was explicit enough. He assured us that our view of the Hitleristic German Reich was exactly his view of the Imperialist British Empire; and that though *he* would be fighting with a rope round his neck, he would give us ten shots and shells for our one, and sink, burn, and destroy until he had done unto us what he had already done to Poland. And so we are at it hammer and tongs; and as it was we who asked for it, it is up to us to make good. I have no patience with the journalists and the tub thumpers who are breaking our spirits by snivelling about our being the victims of a foul and treacherous aggression. We are the challengers and the champion fighters for humanity.

The British people, the real British people, feel this instinctively. But they are puzzled by the intellectuals and the politicians and journalists. They want to know exactly why we hit Mr Hitler on the nose, when he had his hands in his pockets—and in some of his neighbors' pockets as well. And they are told officially what fine fellows we are, and that we are sure to win because God is on our side, and that a trumpery scrap in which three British warships drove one German one [the Graf Spee] into the River Plate was a greater victory than Jutland or Trafalgar or Lepanto. That is not good enough. God has rebuked it in Belgium promptly and sharply. The people still ask, What exactly is the Big Idea that we must risk our lives for?

Until our people get a clear answer they will not know where we stand against the German legions and the Fifth Column.

What makes it so puzzling is that nine-tenths of what Mr Hitler says is true. Nine-tenths of what Sir Oswald Mosley says is true. Quite often nine-tenths of what our parliamentary favorites say to please us is emotional brag, bunk, and nonsense. If we start hotheadedly contradicting everything Mr Hitler and Sir Oswald say, we shall presently find ourselves contradicting ourselves very ridiculously, and getting the worst of the argument. We must sift out the tenth point for which we are fighting, and nail the enemy to that.

Let us come down to brass tacks. What am I, a superannuated non-combatant, encouraging young men to fight against? It is not German national socialism: I was a National Socialist before Mr Hitler was born. I hope we shall emulate and surpass his great achievement in that direction. I have no prejudices against him personally; much that he has written and spoken echoes what I myself have written and spoken. He has adopted even my diet. I am interested in him as one of the curiosities of political history; and I fully appreciate his physical and moral courage, his diplomatic sagacity, and his triumphant rescue of his country from the yoke the Allies imposed on it in 1918. I am quite aware of the fact that his mind is a twentieth-century mind, and that our governing class is mentally in the reign of Edward the Third, six centuries out of date. In short, I can pay him a dozen compliments which I could not honestly pay to any of our present rulers.

My quarrel with him is a very plain one. I happen to be what he calls a Nordic. In stature, in color, in length of head, I am the perfect blond beast whom Mr Hitler classes as the salt of the earth, divinely destined to rule over all lesser breeds. Trace me back as far as you can; and you will not find a Jew in my ancestry.

Well, I have a friend who is a Jew. His name is Albert Einstein; and he is a far greater human prodigy than Mr Hitler and myself rolled into one. The nobility of his character has made his genius an unmixed benefit to his fellow creatures. Yet Adolf Hitler would compel me, the Nordic Bernard Shaw, to insult Albert Einstein; to claim moral superiority to him and unlimited power over him; to rob him, drive him out of his house, exile him, be punished if I allow a relative of mine to marry a relative of his; and finally to kill him as part of a general duty to exterminate his race. Adolf has actually done these things to Albert, bar the killing, as he carelessly exiled him first and thus made the killing impossible. Since then he has extended the list of reprobates from Semites to Celts and from Poles to Slavs; in short, to all who are not what he calls Nordics and Nazis. If he conquers these islands he will certainly add my countrymen, the Irish, to the list, as several authorities have maintained that the Irish are the lost tribes of Israel.

Now, this is not the sort of thing that sane men can afford to argue with. It is on the face of it pernicious nonsense; and the moment any ruler starts imposing it on his nation or any other nation by physical force there is nothing for it but for the sane men to muster their own physical forces and go for him. We ought to have declared war on Germany the moment Mr Hitler's police stole Einstein's violin. When the work of a police force consists not of *suppressing* robbery with violence but actually *committing* it, that force becomes a recruiting ground for the most infernal blackguards, of whom every country has its natural-born share. Unless such agents are disciplined and controled, their heads are turned by the authority they possess as a State police; and they resort to physical torture as the easiest way to do their work and amuse themselves at the same time. How is that discipline and control to be maintained? Not by an autocrat, because, as Napoleon said when he heard about Nelson and Trafalgar, an autocrat cannot be everywhere. When his police get out of hand and give his prisons and concentration camps a bad name, he has to back them up because he cannot do without them, and thus he becomes their slave instead of their master.

And this reminds me that we must stop talking nonsense about dictators. Practically the whole business of a modern civilized country is run by dictators and people who obey their orders. We call them bosses; but their powers are greater than those of any political dictator. To prevent them abusing those powers we have Factory Acts which have made short work of our employers' liberty to sacrifice the nation's interests to their own. It is true that we cannot get on without dictators in every street; but we can impose on them a discipline and a code of social obligations that remind them continually that their authority is given to them for the benefit of the commonwealth and not for their private gain. Well, one of our aims in this war is to impose a stiff international Factory Act on Mr Hitler, one that will deal not with wages and hours of labor, but with the nature of the work done, for peace or war.

When I say that we must stop talking nonsense about the war what I mean is that we must be careful not to go on throwing words about that we do not understand. Could anything be more ridiculous than people who were terrified the other day when Sir William Beveridge very properly used the word "Socialist" to describe our war organization? They flooded the B.B.C. with letters asking whether all their property was going to be taken away from them. Whilst they were writing, the Government in two hours and twenty minutes placed the country under the most absolute Military Communism. Everything we possess— our properties, our liberties, our lives—now belong to our country and not to ourselves. To say a word against Socialism or Communism is now treason. Without them we should soon have no property or liberty at all, and would be lucky if we were alive. Therefore I beg you, if you must talk, to confine yourself to what the lawyers call vulgar abuse, which will relieve your feelings and hurt nobody. I hope you are too much of a gentle-man (or a lady) to call the Germans swine; but if you want to blow off steam by calling Mr Hitler a bloodstained monster do so by all means: it wont hurt him, nor need you worry if it does. But be careful; if you call Stalin a bloodstained monster you must be shot as the most dangerous of Fifth Columnists; for the friendship of Russia is vitally important to us just now. Russia and America may soon have the fate of the world in their hands;

that is why I am always so civil to Russia.

Remember that the really dangerous Fifth Column consists of the people who believe that Fascism is a better system of government than ours, and that what we call our democracy is a sham. They are not altogether wrong; but the remedy is for us to adopt all the good points of Fascism or Communism or any other Ism, not to allow Mr Hitler and his Chosen Race to impose it on us by his demoralized police. We are fighting him, not for his virtues, but for his persecutions and dominations, which have no logical connection whatever with Fascism and which I hope we will not put up with from Mr Hitler or anyone else. He is as sure that God is on his side as Lord Halifax is that God is on ours. If so, then we shall have to fight God as well as Mr Hitler. But as most of us believe that God made both Mr Hitler and Lord Halifax, we must reasonably believe that God will see fair. And the rest is up to us.

" GOODBYE, GOODBYE "

(Recorded and filmed for television by the B.B.C. at Ayot St Lawrence on 26 July 1946, Shaw's ninetieth birthday. Edited from an unpublished transcript of the verbatim text)

Hallo! now where did you all come from and what did you come to see? An old man who was once a famous playwright and talked about everything on earth and wrote about it? Well, here is what is left of him—not much to look at, is it? However, it is pleasant to find that I have so many friends. It is almost the only thing that a man of letters, a writer, playwright, artist—it is almost the only thing that he has left. The war taxation has left me very little more than that although you all think I am a very rich man. Still, I have nothing to complain of and when I look round too (Ah! I see some Americans there)—Oh! I daresay there are a few foreigners. I have friends everywhere, and one man—a very famous man in his way—used to say that I had friends everywhere—that I hadnt an enemy in the world and that none of my friends liked me. Now, what do you think of that? But I think they liked me just a little more than they used to, which shews that I am getting old and feeble and nobody is afraid of me any longer.

Now, you musnt think that because I am very old I am very wise; age doesnt bring wisdom but it brings experience that young people cant have. Even the stupidest person when he's ninety has seen things that none of you can have seen. I have seen politicians, artists, writers, all sorts of people, and I carried them in my arms to bed when they were small children. I have seen them grow up young and handsome, and get married. I have seen those same people middle-aged people, and I have seen them elderly persons and then theyve died. Well, most of you have not [had] that experience. I myself have experienced obscurity and failure and Ive got now success and celebrity. I daresay a great many of you think that is a very fine thing, but you are mistaken.

Now, I have never had time—been far too busy, hardworked all my life—to bother about my being a great man, but now that I am no longer a great man but only an old dotard, I can look on at the "great man" business. I assure you, all the fun of that business is yours—it is the people who celebrate me who have the fun; I have all the hard work and I have all the applications for interviews or to go to dinners, and I am half dead from the experience.

So, particularly the young people who are beginning life— dont go in for being great people. To begin with, the people who think they are going to be great and, as young people inform you that they are going to be great, very seldom come to anything.

When I was young I didnt want to be a great writer at all; I wanted when I was a small boy to be a pirate and so on, then I wanted to be an operatic singer, then I wanted above all to be a great painter. I wanted to be a great musician. The one thing I never wanted was to be a writer and the reason was that I was a born writer. The thing was as natural to me as the taste of water in my mouth—it has no taste because it is always there. At least, it is always in *my* mouth because I am a teetotaler. However, do not imagine that being a teetotaler will make you great—it wont. I have known some people and they have become great people, and very distinguished great people too, and their principal diet was whisky and big cigars, so I am not trying to shove myself down your throat in any way.

However, I am beginning to talk, as old men do. Before I go —now I dont want the young people to listen to this—let me give a word of advice to the parents. If your son or your daughter —if they inform you—the son that he wants to be a great artist or a great musician—I was going to say a great politician but there may be something in that—he may try that if he likes—but if he wants to be a great artist and so on, do your utmost to prevent it; dont let him. If you tell him that his business in life [is] to be prosperous and well spoken of and all that, let him be a shopkeeper or a stockbroker, and if your daughter tells you that she wants to be a very great actress and thinks that she is the only person in the world who can play my Saint Joan, try to prevent her. Tell her to marry the shopkeeper or the stockbroker. Thats the way for them to be prosperous and happy, and instead of being great people to have the great fun of celebrating great people, admiring them, reading their books and looking at their pictures and listening to their music and all that. Not writing at all and composing—it's jolly hard work and more kicks than ha'pence in the pursuit of it.

If you knew all I have had to put up with in my life you would say, "Heaven defend me from living *that* man's life." However, I dont complain—it doesnt matter if one dies poor, which I am not going to do by the way, as long as your life is happy, and the way to have a happy life is to be too busy doing what you like all the time, having no time left to you to consider whether you are happy or not and— Oh! look here—I am getting talking—I must stop.

Well, it is very pleasant to have seen you all here and to think that you are my audience and all that because I am a born actor myself; I like an audience, I am like a child in that respect.

Well, goodbye, goodbye, goodbye, goodbye—all of you.

INDEX

INDEX

INDEX

Kautsky, Karl Johann (1854–1938), 141, 142

Kean, Charles (1811–68), 16

Keats, John (1795–1821), 237

Kemal Atatürk (1881–1938), 284

Kipling, Rudyard (1865–1936), 37, 174, 276

LABOUR LEADER, 23, 93

LABOUR WORLD, x

Lang, Most Rev. & Rt. Hon. Cosmo Gordon [Archbishop of Canterbury] (1864–1945), 261

Lansbury, George (1859–1940), 255

Lassalle, Ferdinand (1825–64), 265

Laurence, Dan H. (b.1920), 164n.

Lazarus [New Testament personage], 76-8

LEAGUE OF NATIONS, 273n.

Lecky, James, x

Lee, George John Vandeleur (c.1831–1886), 162-3

Leech, John (1817–64), 173

LEFT REVIEW, 216

Lemaître, Jules (1853–1914), 12, 17

Lenin, Nikolai [Vladimir Ilich Ulyanov] (1870–1924), 114, 142-3, 216-218, 228, 229, 230, 246, 265

Leveson Gower, Sir George (1858–1951), 197n.

Liberal and Social Union, 1

LIBERTY, 1

Lincoln, Abraham (1809–65), 156, 283

LISTENER, THE, 208, 261, 263, 275, 282

Lister, Joseph (1827–1912), 279

Listowel, 5th Earl of [William Francis Hare] (b.1906), 272

Litvinoff, Maxim (1876–1951), 222, 229

Lloyd George, David (1863–1945), 157, 165, 237, 284

London, Bishop of, see Temple (1885–1896), Creighton (1897–1901)

London, Jack (1876–1916), 176n.

London Anti-Vivisection Society, 31, 36

London Pavilion Theatre, 178

Louis XIV [France] (1638–1715), 104

Lunacharski, Anatoli Vasilievich (1875–1933), 229

Lusitania, 287

Luther, Martin (1483–1546), 107, 143, 225

Lytton, Victor Alexander, Earl of (1876–1947), 36

Macaire, Robert [character in L'Auberge des Adrets], 17

McCormick, "Boy," 165

McCulloch, John Ramsay (1789–1864), 7

MacDonald, James Ramsay (1866–1937), 237, 238-9, 243, 246, 248-9, 261

McMillan, Margaret (1860–1931), 223

Magdalen College, xiii-xiv

MAJOR BARBARA, xiv, 40-1

Mallaby-Deeley, Sir Harry (1863–1937), 160

Malthus, Thomas Robert (1766–1834), 5, 134, 135

MAN AND SUPERMAN, 40

Marcus Aurelius, 100

Margaret, St, 210, 211

Mars, Mlle [Anne Boutet] (1779–1847), 204

Marson, Rev. Charles Latimer (1858–1914), 207

Marx, Karl (1818–83), 75, 117-18, 132, 134-8, 221, 228, 229, 237, 242, 255, 264, 265, 271

Mascarille [character in Les Précieuses Ridicules], 15

Masefield, John (b.1878), 39

Medico-Legal Society, 49

Merlino, Dr, 23

Michael, St [sic], 211, 283

Michael Angelo Buonarroti (1475–1564), 283

Mikado, see Hirohito

Mill, John Stuart (1806–73), xiv, 7, 131, 135

INDEX